Through My WINDOW

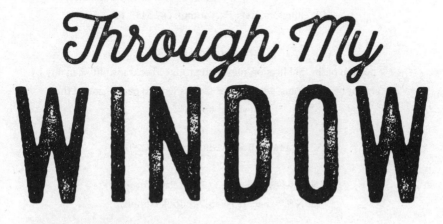

Through My WINDOW

ARIANA Godoy

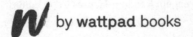

by wattpad books

wattpad books **W**

Published in Canada by Wattpad Books, a division of Wattpad Corp.
36 Wellington Street E., Toronto, ON M5E 1C7

www.wattpad.com

First Wattpad Books edition: January 2022

ISBN 978-1-99025-933-3 (Trade Paper original)
ISBN 978-1-99025-948-7 (eBook edition)

Library and Archives Canada Cataloguing in Publication information is
available upon request.

Printed and bound in Canada
3 5 7 9 10 8 6 4

Cover design by Penguin Random House Grupo Editorial / Manuel Esclapez
Images © Koki Jovanovic / © Stocksy

For my readers all over the world who never stopped believing in me, even when I did.

ONE
The Wi-Fi Password

- RAQUEL -

It all started with the Wi-Fi password.

I know, it sounds simple and unimportant, but nowadays your Wi-Fi password is more valuable than almost any other thing you own. The internet alone is addictive enough; add wireless technology, and you have a permanent way to feed that addiction under the roof of your house. I know people who would much rather stay inside than give up their Wi-Fi connection.

To back up the importance of Wi-Fi, I want to share a story about my neighbors: the Hidalgos. The only neighbors we don't interact with. But I need to go back even further to when my mother immigrated to the United States from Mexico while she was pregnant with me. She's struggled since arriving in this small North Carolina town. Growing up, I witnessed her victories and her defeats, her efforts and her perseverance. She's an amazing woman who commands everyone's respect. And in fact, she hasn't had trouble socializing with our neighbors, but the Hidalgos are the one exception. Why? Well, they're wealthy and rather obnoxious.

The family consists of Sofia Hidalgo, her husband Juan, and their three children: Artemis, Ares, and Apolo. Their parents clearly had an obsession with Greek mythology. I can't imagine how the poor kids are doing in school. I can't be the only one who has noticed their peculiar names. You may be wondering: How do I know so much about them if we don't even talk to each other?

The reason has a first and last name: Ares Hidalgo.

I sigh, and imaginary hearts float around me.

Even though Ares doesn't go to my school—he goes to a fancy private school instead—I've spent a lot of time checking him out. Let's just say I've had an immense, years-long crush on him. It began the first time I saw him playing with a soccer ball in his backyard when I was just eight years old. I was shocked because he was the first member of his family that I saw back there.

Naturally, my crush has diminished a bit over the years because I've never actually talked to him. We haven't even shared a simple glance. I don't think he's ever noticed my presence, not even when I stare at him like an idiot.

However, the little contact I've previously had with my neighbors is about to change, as it turns out that Wi-Fi is not only capable of connecting our devices, but it's also able to bridge different worlds.

>> <<

Imagine Dragons plays throughout my small room as I sing and take off my shoes. I just got home from my summer job, and I'm exhausted. Since I'm eighteen, I'm supposed to be full of energy, but my mother says she has a lot more energy than I do, and she's right. I stretch out, yawning, and my husky, Rocky, mimics me, stretching out his paws. People say dogs become more like their owners, and it's true that Rocky is my doggy incarnation. I swear he sometimes even mimics my facial expressions.

My eyes land on the posters with positive messages hanging all around my room. My dream is to be a psychologist and help people. I'm really hoping to get a scholarship because I know that college isn't something I'll be able to easily afford.

I walk to my window, intending to watch the sunset. It's my favorite time of day. I love watching as the sun disappears across the horizon and makes way for the arrival of the beautiful moon. It's as if they have a secret ritual between them, a pact where they promised never to meet, but to share the majestic sky. My room is on the second floor, so I have a wonderful view.

However, when I open my curtains, it's not the sunset that surprises me but the person sitting in my neighbors' backyard: Apolo Hidalgo. It's been a long time since I saw a member of that family out there.

Apolo is the youngest of the three brothers. He's sixteen and from what I hear he's a nice kid, although I can't say the same for his older brothers. No doubt the beauty gene runs in their family, since all three brothers are incredibly attractive. Even their father is good-looking. Apolo has a face that exudes innocence, light brown hair, and amber-colored eyes just like his father's.

Leaning on the windowsill, I gaze directly at him. He has a laptop and seems to be typing something in a hurry.

Where are your manners, Raquel? my mother's voice sounds in my mind, scolding me.

Should I say hi?

Of course, he's your future brother-in-law, I answer myself.

Taking a chance, I clear my throat and put on my best smile.

"Good afternoon, neighbor!" I shout, waving my hand in the air. Apolo looks up and his little face stretches in surprise.

"Oh!" He jumps up, and his laptop abruptly drops to the ground. "Shit!" he mumbles, picking it up and checking it.

"Is it okay?" I ask, noticing his laptop is an expensive brand.

Apolo breathes a sigh of relief. "Yeah, it's fine."

"I'm Raquel, I'm your neigh—"

"I know who you are," he interrupts. He smiles kindly at me. "We're lifelong neighbors."

Oh, I guess Apolo has noticed me.

"Sure," I mutter, knowing my cheeks are flushed.

"I have to go." He picks up his chair. "Hey, thanks for sharing your Wi-Fi password, by the way. We're going to be without internet for a few days while they install a new service. It's really nice of you to share."

I freeze. "Share my internet? What are you talking about?"

"You're sharing your Wi-Fi with us, that's why I'm here in the yard. The signal doesn't reach the house."

"What?" But I didn't give you the password . . ." Confusion barely lets me speak.

Apolo frowns. "Ares told me that you gave him the password."

My heart flutters in my chest when I hear that name. "I've never even exchanged a word with your brother."

Believe me, I would remember in great detail if I had!

Apolo seems to realize that something's off, and his cheeks turn red. "I'm sorry, Ares told me that you gave him the password. That's why I'm here. I'm sorry, really."

"Relax, it's not your fault."

"But if you didn't give him the password, then how does he have it? I just connected to your internet."

"I don't know."

"It won't happen again. I apologize, again." With his head down, he disappears back toward his house.

I stare at the place where Apolo had been sitting. What was that all about? How does Ares have my Wi-Fi password? Ares is not only the most handsome of the three brothers, but he's also the coldest, and probably the least likely to ask for a favor. This is turning into a mystery. I can even imagine the title: *The Wi-Fi Password Mystery*. I shake my head at the idea.

I close the window and lean against it, biting my lip. My password is embarrassing, and somehow Apolo now knows it. How did Ares get it?

"Raquel! Dinner is ready!" my mom calls from downstairs.

"I'm coming, Mom!"

I glance back at the Hidalgos' house before heading downstairs. This is not over. I'll find out how Ares got my password. It'll be like my own crime scene investigation. Who knows? Maybe I'll even buy some sunglasses to look like a professional detective.

"Raquel!"

"I'm coming!"

A smirk slips across my lips.

Project Wi-Fi Password: activated.

TWO
The Obnoxious Neighbor

I hate being disturbed when I sleep.

It's one of the few things I can't stand. Normally, I'm a quiet, peaceful person, but if you wake me up, you'll see my darker side. So, when I'm awakened by an unfamiliar tune, I can't help but grunt in annoyance. I toss and turn in my bed, covering my head with my pillow, but the damage is done, and I can't fall asleep again. Irritated, I toss the pillow aside and sit up, muttering profanities. Where the hell is that sound coming from?

I groan. It's midnight. Who could be making noise at this hour? It's not even the weekend. I stumble like a zombie to my open window, and the cool breeze sneaking through the curtains gives me goose bumps. I'm used to sleeping with the window open because I've never had a problem with noises during the night, until now. I recognize the song: "Rayando El Sol" by Maná. Tilting my head to the side, I part the curtains to find out where it's coming from.

There's someone sitting on the small chair in the Hidalgos' yard.

But it's not Apolo this time.

My heart bursts when I realize it's none other than Ares.

Ares is the best-looking guy I've ever seen in my entire life, and believe me, I've seen quite a few. He's tall and athletic, with muscular legs and *an ass to die for*. His face is perfectly proportioned, with high cheekbones and a gorgeous nose. His lips are full and look wet all the time. His upper lip forms an arch like the top of a drawn heart and his lower lip is accompanied by an almost imperceptible piercing. His eyes take my breath away every time I see them. They're deep blue with a flash of stunning green. His hair is jet black, contrasting nicely with his creamy white skin, and falls carelessly over his forehead and ears. He has a tattoo on his left arm of a curvy dragon that looks professionally done. Everything about Ares screams mystery and danger, which should keep me away from him, but instead draws me in with a force that takes me aback.

Under the floodlight, I can see that he's wearing shorts, a pair of Converse, and a black T-shirt that matches his hair. I gawk at him as he types something on his laptop, nibbling on his lower lip. *Sexy*!

But then it happens. Ares's head snaps up, and he sees me. Those beautiful blue eyes meet mine, and my world stops. He and I have never made direct eye contact. Without meaning to, I blush immediately, but I can't look away.

Ares arches an eyebrow, and his gaze is as cold as ice. "Do you need something?"

His voice lacks any emotion. I swallow, struggling to find my voice. His look paralyzes me. How can someone so young be so intimidating?

"I . . . Hi," I almost stutter. He doesn't say anything, just stares at me, making me more nervous. I grip the edge of my windowsill. "I-I—your music woke me up."

I'm talking to Ares.

God, don't faint, Raquel. Breathe.

"You have a good ear. Your room is quite far."

That's it? He's not going to apologize for waking me up? He returns his attention to the laptop and continues typing on it. I twist my lips in irritation. After a few minutes, he notices that I haven't moved, and he looks back at me, lips pursed.

"Do you need something?" he repeats with an air of annoyance.

That gives me the courage to speak. "Actually, yes. I wanted to talk to you."

He makes a gesture for me to continue.

I frown. "Are you using my Wi-Fi?"

"Yes." He didn't even hesitate to answer.

"Without my permission?"

"Yes."

God, his audacity is infuriating. "You shouldn't do that."

"I know." He shrugs, showing me how little he cares.

"How do you have my password?"

"I have good computer skills."

"You mean you obtained it in some fraudulent way."

"I hacked into your computer."

"And you can say that so calmly?"

"Honesty is one of my best qualities."

"You're an . . ." He waits for my insult, but his sharp gaze affects my mind, and I can't think of anything creative, so I go for the traditional: "You're an idiot."

His lips curve upward in a small smile. "What an insult! I thought you'd be more creative after discovering your password."

My cheeks heat up, and I can only imagine how red I must be. He knows my password. My frustrating childhood crush knows my ridiculous Wi-Fi password. I'm doomed.

"No one was supposed to know about it." I lower my head. Ares closes his laptop and focuses on me, amused.

"I know a lot of things about you that I shouldn't know, Raquel." Hearing him say my name sends butterflies to my stomach. I try to stay cool.

"Oh yeah? Like what?"

"Like those websites you visit when everyone else is asleep."

My mouth opens in surprise, but I quickly close it. Oh my God, he's seen my browsing history? I'm so embarrassed. I've visited several porn sites out of curiosity. Just curiosity. "I don't know what you're talking about."

"Yes, you do." Ares smiles.

I don't like where this conversation is going. "Anyway, that's not the point, stop using my Wi-Fi and stop making noise."

Ares stands up from the small chair. "Or what?"

"Or . . . I'll tell on you."

Ares bursts out laughing. His laugh is hoarse and sexy. "Are you going to tell your mom?" he asks in a mocking tone.

"Yes, or yours." I feel safe standing at my window, but I don't think I'd be so brave if we were facing each other in the yard.

He leans back in his chair. "I'll keep using your Wi-Fi, and you won't do anything about it."

"Really?"

The challenge in his eyes is overwhelming. I know mine must be the same.

"There's nothing you can do. If you tell my mother, I'll deny it, and she'll believe me. If you tell yours, I'll show her the pages you visit when no one is watching you," he says.

"Are you blackmailing me?"

He strokes his jaw as if he's considering my question. "I wouldn't call it blackmail, but rather coming to an agreement. I get what I want, and you get my silence in return."

"Your silence about information you got by hacking me. That's not fair."

Ares shrugs his shoulders. "Haven't you heard that life isn't fair?"

I grit my teeth. *Jerk.*

"If you have nothing more to say, I was doing something important." He sits up and opens his laptop.

I stare at him like a fool, not knowing if it's because he's that much of a jerk or because the feelings I had for him as a child haven't completely gone away. Either way, I have to get back inside; the cold breeze isn't pleasant. I close the window and defeatedly crawl back between my warm sheets.

My iPhone vibrates on the bedside table. Who could be texting me at this hour? I open the message and gasp in surprise.

Unknown Number: Good night, Witch.

Sincerely yours,

Ares.

I groan in frustration. Who is he calling a witch? And how the hell does he have my number? Apparently, things with Ares are nowhere near over, but he's sorely mistaken if he thinks I'll sit by and do nothing.

You messed with the wrong neighbor!

THREE
The Soccer Practice

"You what?" Daniela, my childhood best friend, almost spits her soda in my face.

We're hanging out in the most popular café in town, hiding away from the summer heat. God bless the AC. We love it here. The calm music and dimly lit surroundings create a soft, comfortable energy, and it's become our favorite spot to hang.

"Yes, I did exactly what I said," I sigh, playing with the straw of my orange juice.

Daniela grins broadly as if she's won the lottery. Her black hair falls to the sides of her face, framing it perfectly. She has that kind of hair where even if you don't comb it, it still looks good. I'm so envious! But it's the good kind of envy, of course.

Daniela has been by my side for as long as I can remember. Our friendship started in kindergarten when she stuck a pencil in my ear. Yes, it was an unconventional way to start a lifelong friendship, but that's us: unconventional and crazy. Somehow, we adjusted to each other in a perfect, synchronized way. If that's not true friendship, then I don't know what is.

Dani keeps that goofy grin on her face.

"Why are you so discouraged? We're talking about Ares . . . your crush since you were seven, or something."

"I told you how he treated me."

"But he treated *you*, Raquel. He talked to you; he noticed your presence in this world. That's a start! It's much better than just looking at him from afar like a creepy stalker."

"I don't stalk him!"

Dani rolls her eyes. "Really? Are you going to try to deny it? *To me*? I've seen you stalk him from the shadows."

"Of course not, it's pure coincidence that I see him in the distance when I walk around town."

"Walking through town or hiding behind a bush?" she teases.

"Anyway," I change the subject. "You're supposed to help me, I need to find a way to stop him from using my Wi-Fi. I don't want him to get away with it."

"Why don't you change the password?"

"So he can just hack my computer again? No, thank you."

Dani takes out her makeup and looks in the mirror to adjust her hair. "I really don't know what to say, girl. What if we ask Andres for help?"

"Are you kidding? And for the last time, Dani, it's André, no *S*."

"Whatever." She takes out her lipstick and starts to apply a bright red color to her lips. "He's good at computer stuff, right?"

"Do you really have to do that here?" I ask, even though she does it all the time. "And yes, I guess so; he helped Francis with his computer project."

"There you go." Dani puts her makeup away and stands up. "See how I always find solutions for you?" I open my mouth to speak, but she continues. "In fact, do you know what my advice is?"

"Get over it?"

"Yes. You're wasting your time, really."

"He's just so . . ." I sigh. "Perfect."

Dani ignores my last statement. "I have to go to the bathroom; I'll be right back."

She turns and walks away, earning a few stares from the guys that she passes. Dani is tall and has a great curvy body. I can honestly say that my best friend is one of the hottest girls at my school.

I take a sip from my straw, finishing the last of my OJ. It's hot as hell outside, but I rejoice in it. I don't want summer to end because that means classes will begin and, to be honest, the idea of entering my senior year of high school scares me a little.

Thoughts of Ares invade my mind again, and I remember his voice as well as his arrogant smile from the night before. I know he doesn't have the best personality in the world. As I've watched him, I've come to realize how cold and meticulous he is. He barely smiles and doesn't usually talk much, preferring curt answers and gestures. It's like he's a robot, incapable of feeling. Part of me is hoping that I'm wrong and he's actually a sweet person on the inside or something.

I scroll through Instagram until I see a post from Dani's brother, Dean. He goes to the same school as Ares and plays on his soccer team. He posted a picture of the guys at practice on a public field near my neighborhood. It's a chance to see Ares from a distance.

After settling the bill, I lean against the wall in front of the bathroom to wait for Dani, running my fingers through my long, light brown hair to check for tangles. I shuffle my feet impatiently until my best friend deigns to come out.

Dani raises an eyebrow. "You already paid? I thought we would have dinner here."

"Soccer practice."

"You're going to abandon me here to go see a bunch of beautiful, attractive, possibly shirtless guys?" she jokes.

"Do you want to go?"

"No, stalking guys from a distance isn't my thing. I'm more into action and you know it." She winks.

"Stop rubbing your experience in my face." I pretend to sound hurt.

"Stop being a virgin." She sticks her tongue out at me.

"Maybe I'm not anymore." I also stick out my tongue.

"Yeah, sure, stop saving your virginity for that crush of yours."

"Dani! I'm not saving anything for him."

She averts her gaze. "Of course, of course, go away. God forbid you miss the chance to see him shirtless because of me."

"He never takes his shirt off," I mutter.

Dani laughs. "He's making you go crazy, naughty girl."

"Dani!"

"I'll shut up. Go, I have things to do anyway, don't worry."

With my cheeks on fire, I leave the café, and head toward the field.

Once I arrive, I buy a pineapple milk shake—my favorite—and slip on my dark glasses. I flip the top of my hoodie over my head to cover my hair and sit in the stands out front to enjoy the view. Other than me, there are four girls sitting there—they are probably the players' girlfriends or just their friends. I'm pretty sure I've seen one of them kissing one of the guys before. It's so hot, I'm roasting inside this hoodie. It was a poor choice of camouflage on my part.

The boys are spread out across the field doing routine stretches. Although this is the soccer team from an elite private school, they have to practice here during the summer while some kind of yearly maintenance is performed on their own field, or at least that's what Dean told Dani. Ares jogs around the field, wearing black shorts and a green T-shirt with the number five on his back. His black hair flips in the wind as he jogs. I watch him like a fool and forget all about our interaction last night.

He's so handsome!

Clouds swallow the bright sun as practice ends, thunder rumbles, and, without warning, it begins to rain. Cold raindrops fall on me and I curse to myself, pulling the top of my hood tighter over my head. I run down the stands and quickly pass the parking lot. The guys are about to leave, and therefore the risk of Ares seeing me is high. In my rush to get out of there I crash right into someone.

"Ow!" I touch my nose, looking up.

It's one of the guys on the team, a tall, dark-haired, tanned guy who looks like he's straight out of a TV series. "Are you okay?"

I push past him, trying to get away as quickly as possible. And then it happens, I hear the voice of my enduring, frustrated love.

"What are you doing standing here in the rain?" Ares asks the boy behind me.

"I bumped into a weird girl. She was wearing sunglasses and a hoodie in this heat."

"You're the weird one," I murmur and try to hear Ares's reply through the rain, but I've already walked too far away. That was close.

I urge my legs to move faster, sighing in relief when I see the exit. I turn right to continue home. The rain is heavy, but I don't see a place where I can take cover, not even a bus stop. I hear voices and instinctively duck into an alley. With my back against the wall, I dare to peek down the street. Ares is standing there, chatting with some guys from the team. They all have umbrellas, of course.

I should have checked the weather forecast!

"Are you sure you don't want to come with us?" the tanned guy I crashed into earlier asks insistently.

"No, I have things to do at home," Ares says.

His friends walk away, and Ares just stands there in the rain, as if waiting for something. I narrow my eyes. What is he waiting for? Ares starts to move and, to my surprise, he doesn't go in the direction of his house but instead turns the opposite way. Did he lie to his friends? My curiosity encourages me to make a bad decision.

I follow him.

It's getting darker and darker, and we're moving away from the downtown area into a neighborhood of lonelier streets. This is a bad idea. What am I doing? I've never followed him before, but I'm interested to know why he lied to his friends. Although, honestly, that's not my problem.

Ares doesn't slow down and it's as if he knows exactly where he's going. I pass a small wooden bridge, and a cool night breeze brushes over me as dark clouds swallow what sunlight is left. I hug myself and moisten my lips. Where is he going in the dark?

I can no longer see the road, only a dirt path that takes us into the forest. My confusion is growing. I know that there's nothing here but trees and darkness. Ares jumps over a small fence to the place I least expected to see—the town cemetery.

What the hell? I didn't even know you could get to the town cemetery by going this way. And what's he doing here? Oh no. My imagination is running wild again.

He's a vampire, and he comes here to reflect on whether or not to kill his next victim. Or worse, he knows I'm following him and brought me here to suck my blood dry.

No, no, no, no, I can't die a virgin.

Hesitantly, I hop over the small fence too. I can't believe I'm following him into the cemetery. To say that this place is spooky is an understatement. The clouds that are still covering the sky paired with an occasional flash of lightning make me feel like I'm in a horror movie.

Being the fool that I am, I continue to follow my crush as he weaves through the graves. I consider that maybe he's going to visit someone, but there haven't been any deaths in Ares's family that I can remember. Believe me, in a small town you hear about everything, and everyone knows everyone.

Ares walks faster, and I struggle to catch up with him, all while keeping a safe distance. We enter an area of mausoleums, which resemble small houses for those who are no longer with us. Ares turns a corner, and I hurry to follow him, but when I round the corner, he's gone.

Shit.

Staying calm, I cross the little path between mausoleums, but I don't see him anywhere. I swallow thickly, my heart beating like crazy in my chest. A flash of lightning followed by a rumble of thunder startles me. This was a really bad idea. What was I doing following him to the cemetery? I turn around. I need to get out of here before one of these souls decides to come after me.

This is what I get for being curious, I deserve it. Another flare of lightning, another crash of thunder, and my poor heart is on the verge of collapse. I'm passing in front of a crypt when I hear strange noises.

Shit, shit, shit.

I'm not going to stick around to find out who or what it is. I hurry, almost running, and of course, because I'm clumsy when I'm scared, I trip over a tree root and fall to my hands and knees. I sit on the back of my thighs, shaking my hands when I feel it. Something, or someone, is behind me. A shadow falls over the path in front of me, a shapeless silhouette.

I scream so loud that my throat burns. I get up fast and turn to start praying in defense and then I see him.

Ares.

FOUR
The Cemetery

Ares stands in front of me, his black jacket partially covering the green T-shirt I saw him wearing at practice, an umbrella over his head, and his free hand in the pocket of his black shorts. He looks like what he is: a rich, athletic young man.

He appears calm, as if he hasn't just scared me so badly that I almost fainted. It's the first time I've been this close to him. I underestimated his height, which is very intimidating, and his cold gaze only makes me more nervous. A faint sheen of sweat dampens the back of my neck, and I squeeze my hands at my sides. It's surreal to face him after watching him from a distance for so long. I'm not ready even though I've pictured this moment a thousand times, but in none of those imaginary scenarios were we in a cemetery, nor was I sweaty and wet from the rain.

"You scared me," I say, clutching at my chest.

He doesn't speak but just stands there, silently watching me.

Seconds go by that feel like years before a smirk unfolds on his full lips.

"You deserve it," he replies.

"Why?"

"You know why." He turns his back on me and walks back toward the mausoleums.

"Wait!"

Ares comes to a clearing and sits on a small headstone, putting his umbrella aside. I stand there watching him like an idiot, unsure of what to do with myself. He takes a lighter and a box of cigarettes out of his pocket and starts smoking. His eyes are on the cemetery sprawling around us, but he seems absorbed in his thoughts, smoke curling out from his mouth.

I know he has this habit so I'm not surprised, but it's a long walk just to sit there and smoke. Although it makes sense. His parents wouldn't approve of their star-athlete son puffing away on cancer sticks.

"Are you going to stand there all night?"

How can someone so young have such a cold voice? I take a seat on a headstone in front of him, keeping my distance. My mouth dries and I can feel my heart in my throat. I wasn't ready to interact with him. He looks at me as he exhales the smoke from his cigarette again, and I swallow hard. I don't know what I'm doing, but there's no way I'm going back down that dark path by myself.

"I'm just waiting for you so I don't have to go back alone," I explain. The lights from the small orange lamps in the cemetery illuminate him.

"What are you doing here, Raquel?" Hearing him say my name causes a strange oscillating sensation in my stomach.

"I came to visit a relative."

Liar, liar.

Ares raises an eyebrow. "Oh yeah? Who?"

"My . . . He's a distant relative."

Ares tosses his cigarette on the ground and steps on it to put it out. "Of course, and you decided to come to visit this relative alone? At night? And in the rain?"

"Yes, I didn't realize it was already so late."

Ares leans forward, placing his elbows on his knees, staring at me. "Liar."

"Excuse me?"

"We both know you're lying."

I fiddle with my hands on my lap. "Of course not."

He stands up and I feel helpless sitting, so I stand up too. We're finally facing each other, and my breathing becomes rapid and inconsistent.

"Why are you following me?"

I wet my lips. "I don't know what you're talking about."

Ares approaches me, and I back away until my back hits a mausoleum behind me. He presses his hand against the wall next to my head, making me jump a little. "I don't have time for your stupid games. Answer me."

My breathing is a mess. "I really don't know what you're talking about, I just came to visit my . . . someone who . . ."

"Liar."

He is too close for my poor heart's health. "It's a free town; I can walk wherever I want."

Ares takes my chin in his hand and forces me to lift my head and look up at him. His touch feels warm on my cold skin, and I stop breathing. His wet hair sticks to his beautiful, pale, perfect face, and his lips glisten. I've only ever seen him from afar. Having him this close is too much for me.

"You think I don't know about your little childish obsession with me?" he asks.

Embarrassment sets my cheeks on fire, and I try to lower my eyes, but he gently holds my chin in place.

"Let me go," I demand, removing his hand. However, he stays in front of me, not backing away, and the intensity of his presence disarms me.

"You're not going anywhere until you answer me," he says, sounding determined.

"I don't know what you're talking about," I repeat, trying to ignore the heat that emanates from his body and warms mine even more.

"Let's refresh your memory, shall we?" he asks. I don't like where he's going with this at all.

"You've been watching me for a long time, Raquel."

I swallow.

"Your desktop background is a picture of me that you stole from my Facebook, and your Wi-Fi password includes my name."

His words make my stomach bottom out. I knew there was a possibility that Ares knew about my crush. After all, he'd hacked my computer. But he knows *everything*. To say I feel mortified is an understatement. This is another level of shame.

He looks so victorious, as if he's in complete control of the situation. There's mockery and superiority in his expression. He enjoys cornering and humiliating me like this. He's waiting for me to deny it, to put my head down, and let him laugh at my embarrassment.

And that thought snaps me out of my self-conscious state. A defiant side of me surfaces when I feel cornered; it's like a defense mechanism. Mom says I got it from my father. Now it comes out and this becomes a challenge, almost a game, and I will not lose. I won't give Ares the satisfaction. I'm tired of hiding behind jokes and sarcastic comments. I feel the need to prove to this handsome guy that he's wrong about me, that everything he thinks he knows is pure lies, and that I'm not easily intimidated. I've had enough with hiding in the shadows. I've had enough with not telling anyone what I think and feel for fear of being rejected and cast aside. So, I raise my gaze and look directly into those infinite blue eyes.

"Yes, I have a crush on you."

I underestimated how startled he would be. His cockiness disappears, replaced by pure confusion. He takes a step back, looking stunned.

I give him a half-sided smile, crossing my arms over my chest. "Why are you so surprised, pretty boy?"

He doesn't say anything. Ladies and gentlemen, I, Raquel Mendoza, have left my lifelong crush speechless.

Ares recovers, running his hand along his jaw as if taking everything in. "I wasn't expecting that, I must admit."

"I know." I can't get rid of the stupid grin caused by the feeling of being in control of the situation.

"And may I know why you have a crush on me?" he asks, tilting his head to the side.

"Isn't that obvious?" I say, amused. "Because I like you."

Ares's eyes threaten to pop out of his face. "Since when are you so . . . forward?"

Since you cornered me and had every intention of embarrassing me, I think, running my hand through my damp hair. "Since always."

Ares chuckles under his breath. "I thought you were just another quiet, introverted girl playing innocent, but, apparently, I'm wrong. You're a bit interesting."

"A bit?" I snort. "I'm the most interesting girl you've ever met in your life."

"And, from what I can see, you also have decent self-esteem."

"That's right."

Ares approaches me again, but this time I don't step back. "And what does this interesting girl want from me?"

"Can't you figure it out? I thought you had the highest IQ in the county."

Ares laughs openly, the sound echoing around the surrounding mausoleums. "It's amazing how much you know about me, and yes, of course I can figure it out. I just want you to say it."

"I think I've talked enough. It's your turn to guess what I want."

Ares leans in until our faces are merely inches apart. Having him so close still affects me, and I swallow thickly. "Do you want to see my room?"

The suggestion in his voice doesn't go unnoticed, so I push him away and shake my head. "No, thank you."

Ares frowns. "What do you want then?"

"Something very simple," I tell him casually. "I want you to fall in love with me."

For the second time in the evening, Ares laughs. I don't know what he finds so funny because I'm not joking, but I'm not complaining because the sound of his laughter is wonderful. When he stops laughing, he gives me a bemused look.

"You're crazy. Why would I fall in love with you? You're not even my type."

"We'll see about that." I wink at him. "And maybe I'm crazy, but my determination is impressive."

"I can see that." He turns around and goes back to the headstone where he was sitting before.

Trying to defuse the tension between us, I speak. "Why did you come here?"

"It's quiet, and people usually don't come here."

"Do you like being alone?"

Ares shoots me a look, putting another cigarette between those red lips I'd like to taste. "I do."

I realize how limited my knowledge about Ares really is, despite having had a crush on him for so long.

"Why are you still here?" His question hurts me a little. Does he want me to leave?

"I'm afraid to go back alone, I told you."

Ares releases the smoke in his mouth and touches a space next to him before speaking.

"Come, sit next to me. Don't be afraid of me. According to this bizarre situation I should be the scared one, little stalker."

I swallow, but I obey like a puppet. I sit next to him, and he continues to smoke. We remain silent for a while and my thoughts wander. I can't believe I said all those things to him. I shiver a little. Even though it's dark, I can see clearly. The moon has already made its way out from the black clouds, illuminating the cemetery. It's not the most romantic view in the world, but being next to Ares makes it tolerable.

I glance at his profile, and his eyes are on the horizon. God, he's so handsome. As if sensing my gaze, Ares turns to me.

"What?"

"Nothing." I look away.

"You like to read."

"Yes. How do you know?"

"Your computer had a lot of information. It's like an electronic diary."

"You still haven't apologized for hacking my computer."

"I won't."

"You violated federal law by doing that, you know that, don't you?"

"And you violated, like, three by stalking me, you know that, too, don't you?"

"Good point."

My phone rings, and I answer it quickly. It's Dani.

"Why aren't you answering your phone?" she demands. "This is, like, my third attempt. Your mother couldn't reach you, so she just called me and asked what time you'll get home. She thinks you're still with me."

"Tell her I'm on my way."

"Where the hell are you? I know soccer practice ended a long time ago."

"I'm . . ." I glance at Ares, and he gives me a mischievous smile. "At the bakery, I'm craving a donut." An extremely attractive donut.

"A donut? But you hate them!"

I bite my lip. "Just tell my mom I'm on my way." I hang up before she can ask me another question.

Ares keeps that smile on his lips, and I can't help but wonder what it would feel like to kiss him. "You just lied. Am I your dark secret?"

"No, it's just that explaining over the phone would have been complicated." Before he asks more questions about why I didn't tell Dani the truth, I continue. "Could you . . . walk with me? At least as far as the street, from there I can go on alone."

"Yes, but that comes at a price." He gets up.

"A price?"

"Yes." He takes his umbrella and points it at me, forcing me to step back to keep the tip of it from touching my chest. "Let me kiss you wherever I want."

My cheeks burn. "That's . . . that's a high price, don't you think?"

"Are you afraid? Or was being straightforward and brave just an act?"

I narrow my eyes. "No, it just seems like an excessively high price to me."

He shrugs. "Then enjoy your walk in the dark alone."

He turns to sit down again, but I can see him look at me out of the corner of his eye. I know it's to make sure I don't leave alone, even if I don't give him the kiss, but who am I kidding? I want that kiss too; every part of me is on fire just imagining it.

"Wait," I say, keeping true to my new extroverted attitude. "Okay."

Ares turns to me again. "Really?"

"Yes!" My heart is going to collapse at any moment. "C-can we go now?"

Ares draws in his bottom lip seductively. "I need my incentive to start walking."

"I said I would pay the price."

His face is only inches away from mine. "Do I have your word?"

"Yes."

"Let's see if that's true."

"What?" A gasp escapes my lips as he leans down and buries his face into my neck, his hair brushing my cheek. "Ares, what are you . . . ?" My voice fails me, everything fails me.

His hot breath caresses my skin, awakening my senses and, instinctively, I move closer to him.

"Raquel," he says my name in my ear, sending delicious shivers all over my body.

I can't believe this is happening. I have Ares pressed against me, his warm breath on my neck, and his hand on my waist. *Am I dreaming?*

"You're not dreaming."

Oh shit! I said it out loud.

I feel flustered; however, the moment Ares's lips meet the skin of my neck, I forget everything. He leaves wet kisses along my skin, up until he reaches my earlobe, which he lightly sucks. My legs get weak, and if it weren't for Ares holding me firmly in place, I would be on the ground by now. What is he doing to me?

While I stand there trembling, little spasms of pleasure cross my body and make my breath hitch. A pressure blooms in my lower belly, and I can't believe how much havoc he's causing just by kissing my neck. His breathing quickens, and I realize I'm not the only one affected by this. When he finishes his attack on my neck, he proceeds to kiss the side of my face, moving across my cheek, until he presses his lips to the corner of mine. I open my mouth in anticipation, waiting for contact, waiting for his kiss, but it never comes.

Ares breaks away and gives me a smirk. "Let's go."

I gasp. *Are you going to leave me like this?* I want to ask him, but I stop myself before the plea leaves my lips. Ares picks up his umbrella and starts walking, apparently unaffected by what just happened. Regaining control of my body, I reluctantly follow him.

I know tonight was just the beginning of something. I don't know if I can handle it, but I'm going to at least try.

FIVE
The Best Friend

The walk back isn't as uncomfortable as I expected, but I'm nervous and my hands are shaking. Part of me still can't believe I'm walking next to Ares. I stay a step behind him so I don't have to be opposite that cute face of his. However, my curious eyes travel down his defined arms and legs. Playing soccer suits him. He has an athletic body that makes him look strong. I continue to gawk at him until he catches me, and I look away.

Ares glances over his shoulder at me with a mischievous, knowing grin that takes my breath away. Why does he have to be so fucking attractive?

Grumbling, I focus on the street to one side of us. Ares plays on his phone the rest of the way. As we reach my front door, the atmosphere gets a little awkward. He stops next to me and runs his hand through his hair. "You've arrived at your cave, Witch."

"Stop calling me that."

"Comb your hair more often, and I will."

Low blow.

I immediately run my fingers through my tangled hair, trying to unknot it. "It's the weather's fault."

Ares just smiles. "Whatever you say." He pauses. "Witch."

"Very funny."

Ares checks his phone, as if checking the time. "Get in before your mom comes out and drags you in."

"My mom wouldn't do that, she knows what kind of daughter she raised," I say arrogantly. "She trusts me."

And as if hearing me, my mother's voice calls from inside the house. "Raquel? Is that you?"

"Shit!" I panic. "Oh . . . that was fun, good night, bye." I turn around to walk to the door.

"Didn't you just say that your mother knows who she raised?"

"Raquel?" my mother calls again.

I turn to him again.

"Shhhh!" I gesture with both hands for him to leave. "Go away! Shoo!"

Ares laughs showing those perfect teeth. He has a beautiful smile, I could stare at him all night, but my mother is about to come out and make a fuss. Ares gives me the "Okay" sign with his fingers.

"All right, I'm off, Stalker Witch."

"Wow, a special nickname now?" Sarcasm drips from my tone.

He shrugs. "I'm very creative, I know."

"So am I, Greek God." As soon as my so-called nickname for him leaves my lips, I regret it. *Greek God? Are you serious, Raquel?*

"I like that nickname."

Of course, you like it, arrogant—

"Raquel!" My mom's voice is louder now.

I turn my back to him again and this time he says nothing. I hear his footsteps fading further into the distance as I open my front door. I walk in and put my back against the door as a stupid grin comes over my face. I had a good time with Ares. I still can't believe it.

"Raquel Margarita Mendoza Álvarez!"

You know you're in trouble when your mom uses your full name.

"Hi, my beautiful mom," I say with the cutest look I can conjure up.

My mother, Rosa Maria Álvarez, is a hard-working, dedicated woman. She's a respected nurse at the local hospital. She's the best person I know, but as a mother she can be strict. Although she doesn't spend much time at home because of her job, when she is at home, she likes to take control and maintain order.

"Don't *mom* me," she warns, holding up her pointer finger. "It's ten o'clock at night, can you tell me where you were?"

"I thought we agreed that I could arrive at eleven o'clock at the latest during the summer."

"Only on weekends," she reminds me. "As long as you let me know where you are, and who you're with."

"I stopped by the bakery, and I was eating a donut and—"

"The bakery closes at nine o'clock."

I clear my throat. "You didn't let me finish. I stayed outside the bakery eating the donut."

"Do you expect me to believe that?"

I put my hands on my hips. "That's what happened, Mom. You know me, what else could I be doing?"

Letting a boy kiss my neck in the cemetery.

My mom narrows her eyes. "You better not be lying to me, Raquel."

"I would never dare, my sweet mother." I give her a hug and kiss the side of her face.

"Your dinner is in the microwave."

"You are the best."

"And go upstairs and give that dog of yours some love, he's done nothing but crawl around the house depressed."

"Aww! He misses me!"

"Or he's hungry."

Both are very possible.

After devouring my food, I go up to my room, and Rocky comes running out to greet me. He almost knocks me down. He's getting bigger every day.

"Hello, beautiful, cutie, fluffy doggy." I rub his head gently. "Who's the cutest doggy in the world?" Rocky licks my hand. "That's right, you are."

My phone chirps in my jacket pocket and, closing my bedroom door with my foot, I check the message. It's from Joshua, my other best friend. I haven't seen him in days because I've been spending so much time with Dani.

> **Joshua BFF:** Are you awake?
>
> **Me**: Yes, what's up?

A second later, my phone lights up with a call from him.

"Hi, Rochi," he says as soon as I answer. He has always affectionately called me Rochi.

"Hi, Yoshi." And I, of course, call him after the dinosaur from *Mario Kart*. He reminds me of Joshua, and he's cute. They're not the most mature nicknames in the world, but in my defense, we picked them when we were children.

"First of all, the crazy girl is not with you, right?"

"No, Dani must be at home."

"Finally. You've completely abandoned me for her. I'm already forgetting your face."

"It's been four days, Yoshi."

"That's a long time. Anyway, how about tomorrow we binge-watch *The Walking Dead*?"

"Only if you swear to me that you haven't seen the new episodes without me."

"You have my word."

I walk around my room distractedly. "It's a deal then."

"Your place or mine?"

I look at the calendar on the wall. "Mine. Mom has a double shift tomorrow, and my TV is bigger."

"All right. See you tomorrow, Rochi."

"See you tomorrow."

I smile at the phone as I hang up and remember the times when I thought I had a crush on Joshua. He's the only guy I've interacted with and shared so much with. But I would never dare put our friendship at risk when I wasn't sure how I felt. Joshua is nothing like Ares. He's shy and cute in his own way. He wears glasses and a hat that he never wants to take off.

Unconsciously, I walk over to the window. Will Ares be out there on the patio stealing my Wi-Fi? My heart skips a beat just imagining him sitting there with his laptop and that stupid, arrogant smile that looks so good on him. But when I open my curtains, all I see is the empty chair with a few drops of water on it from the rain this past evening.

I look at Ares's house and at his window. The light is on, but I don't see him. I sigh in disappointment. I'm about to give up when he appears in my field of vision and grabs the hem of his shirt to take it off over his head. I blush instantly at the sight of his naked torso.

That flat, defined abdomen . . .

Those strong arms . . .

Those tattoos . . .

That V in his lower abdomen . . .

It's hot in here suddenly.

I drop my gaze, cheeks coloring, but I can't help but take one last look at him. To my surprise, Ares is standing in front of the window, looking directly at me.

Shit!

I drop to the ground and crawl away from the window. Rocky tilts his head to the side in confusion.

"Don't judge me," I tell him seriously.

My phone rings again, scaring me. I pray to God it's not Ares making fun of what just happened. I open the message nervously.

> **Ares <3**: Do you like what you see?
>
> **Me**: Nah, I was just looking at the moon.
>
> **Ares <3**: There is no moon. It's cloudy.
>
> **Me**: I just wanted to make sure I didn't have neighbors stealing my Wi-Fi.
>
> **Ares <3**: Your signal doesn't reach here.
>
> **Me**: Just making sure.

A long time goes by and I don't think he'll say anymore, so I take a shower and put on my pajamas. I come out of the bathroom, drying my hair with my towel, and I see a new message on my phone.

> **Ares <3**: Why don't you come over here and make sure in person?

The message is from five minutes ago and takes me by surprise. He wants me to come to his house? At this hour? Is he . . . Is he inviting me to . . .

The towel falls out of my hands.

No.

I'm a virgin, but I'm not stupid, I know how to read between the lines.

I get another message that makes me jump.

Ares <3: It's fun to scare you. Good night, Stalker Witch.

Was it a joke?

I don't think so. Ares Hidalgo just invited me to his room to do who knows what in a subtle way, but he still did it. And what confuses me the most is the fact that I hesitated instead of running over there. Apparently, I'm all talk and no action, as Dani would say.

Silly, silly, Raquel.

SIX
The Advice

"He can't die!" I scream at the TV screen. "This is what I hate about *The Walking Dead*! That fear that one of my favorite characters could die at any moment."

Yoshi eats Doritos next to me. "The episode is about to end, and we won't know who dies."

I snatch the bag of Doritos out of his hands. "Shut up. If that happens, I swear I'll never watch this show again."

Yoshi rolls his eyes and adjusts his glasses. "You've been saying that since the first season."

"I'm weak, okay?"

We're both sitting on the floor, our backs against the bed behind us. It's warm, so I'm wearing shorts and a white tank top without a bra. I'm comfortable around Yoshi and I know he's comfortable around me too. Rocky is sleeping peacefully by the window.

My room is a decent size, with a queen-size bed and posters of my favorite inspirational quotes all over the purple walls. I have a few small Christmas lights attached to the top of the walls that look beautiful at night. In front of the bed is the TV, on one side of it is the window, and the door to my bathroom is on the other side.

We are completely focused on the TV when the episode ends and the credits roll.

"I hate you, producers and screenwriters of *The Walking Dead*! I hate you!"

"I told you," Yoshi taunts like a smart-ass. I smack the back of his head. "Ow! Don't take it out on me."

"How can they do this to us? How can it end like this? Who's going to die?"

Yoshi rubs my back soothingly. "It's okay, it's over." He hands me a glass of cold Pepsi. "Here, drink."

"I'm going to die."

"Relax, it's just a TV series."

Totally depressed, I turn off the TV and sit down in front of Yoshi. He looks restless, and I know it's not because of the series. His little honey eyes have a spark in them that I haven't seen before. He gives me a nervous smile.

"Is something wrong?" I ask.

"Yes."

The atmosphere feels heavy for some strange reason. I don't know what he has to tell me, but it makes me uneasy to see him hesitate so much. What's wrong?

Yoshi licks his lower lip before speaking. He removes his hat, freeing his messy hair. "I need your advice on something."

"I'm listening."

"What would you do if you liked one of your friends?"

"You make it sound like I have so many friends." I smile, but

Yoshi doesn't. His expression becomes even more strained.

"I'm serious, Raquel."

"Okay, okay, excuse me, Mr. Seriousness." I hold my chin as if in deep thought. "I would tell them."

"Wouldn't you be afraid of losing the friendship?"

And then my little brain clicks, and I realize what Yoshi is telling me. Is that . . . that friend he likes—me? Yoshi doesn't really have any other female friends, just me and a few acquaintances. My heart rises in my throat as my sweet, lifelong best friend watches me intently, waiting for my advice.

"Are you sure about what you feel?" I ask, playing with my fingers.

"Yes, I'm very sure, I like her a lot."

My throat gets dry. "When did you realize you liked her?"

"I think I've always known it. I've been a coward, but I can't hide it anymore," he says.

He looks down and sighs, and when he looks at me again, his eyes have a glint in them, so full of emotions. "I'm dying to kiss her."

"Oh yeah?"

Yoshi moves a little closer. "Yes, her lips are pure temptation; it's driving me crazy."

"She must have very nice lips then."

"The most beautiful I've ever seen in my life, they have me spellbound."

Spellbound . . .

Spell . . .

Witch . . .

Ares . . .

No! No! Don't think about Ares! Not now!

Inevitably, those sea-blue eyes come to my mind, that cocky smile, those soft lips suckling my neck.

Oh no! I hate you, brain!

My best friend since childhood is about to confess his love to me, and I'm thinking about my arrogant, Greek godlike idiot neighbor.

"Raquel?"

Yoshi's voice brings me back to reality. He looks disconcerted, and it's no surprise. I chose the worst moment to disconnect mentally. But it also helped to clear my mind a bit. Seeing Yoshi so vulnerable in front of me made me realize that I can't handle a confession. Not now.

"I need to use the bathroom." I rush out of the room before he can say anything.

I walk into the bathroom and lean against the door. I shake my hair out in frustration. I'm a fucking coward and stupid too. I didn't even bring my phone into the bathroom to ask Dani for support. Who goes into the bathroom without their phone these days? No one, just me. I grunt and massage my face, thinking.

"Raquel?" I hear Yoshi's call on the other side of the door. "I have to go. I'll talk to you later."

"No!" I open the door as fast as I can, but I only catch a glimpse of his back disappearing out the door of my room. Throwing myself on my bed, I let myself be consumed by laziness. I don't want to think anymore; I just want to rest my mind. I close my eyes and quickly fall into dreamland.

Rocky's barking wakes me up abruptly. The barks are continuous and loud—what I call his "serious barks"—and he only gets this worked up when there is someone he doesn't know in the house. I get out of bed so fast that I get dizzy and crash against the side of the wall. "Ow!"

Rocky is barking in the direction of the window, as if sensing something out there. It's already dark outside, and the night breeze moves my curtains gently. There's nothing at the window, so I calm down.

"Rocky, there's nothing there."

But he just keeps barking. Maybe there's a cat outside, and his dog senses are tingling? Rocky doesn't stop, so I walk to the window to soothe him. When I peek out, I yell so loudly that Rocky jumps up beside me.

Ares.

On a ladder.

Climbing up to my window.

"What the hell are you doing?" Is the only thing that comes out of my lips as I see him standing there in the middle of a wooden ladder. He looks as cute as ever in his jeans and purple T-shirt, but the craziness of this situation keeps me from drooling.

"It's called climbing, you should try it."

"I'm not in the mood for your sarcasm," I say.

"I need to reboot your router. The signal is down, and it's the only way to recover it."

"And you decided to sneak into my room without permission, climbing into my window like that? Do you know what people who do that are called? Burglars."

"I tried to reach you, but you didn't answer the phone."

"That doesn't give you the right to come into my room like this."

"Can you cut the drama? I just need to come in for a second."

"Drama? Drama? I'll teach you drama." I grab both ends of the ladder stuck to my window and shake them as hard as I can.

Ares holds onto the rungs tightly and gives me a death stare. "Do that again, Raquel, and you'll see what happens."

"I'm not afraid of you."

"Then do it."

"Don't challenge me," I warn.

"Really? Are you going to drop me?"

"It's not worth it."

I watch as Ares finishes climbing, and he's level with me, his face inches away from mine. Rocky goes crazy, barking as soon as he sees the intruder, but I'm too busy gawking to call him off.

"Could you control that fleabag?"

"Rocky hasn't had fleas this month, show more respect."

"I don't have all night."

I sigh in frustration. "Rocky, sit down." My dog obeys me. "Quiet."

I step back to let Ares into my room. Once inside, his height makes my room feel small. His eyes look me up and down from head to toe, lingering on my breasts, and that's when I remember I don't have a bra on.

"I need to go to the bathroom," I say quickly.

For the second time tonight, I try to use the bathroom as an escape strategy, but I forget one small detail. Ares is not Yoshi. Ares won't let me flee so easily. His hand grabs my arm, preventing me from moving.

"There's no way you're leaving me alone with that dog."

"Rocky won't do anything to you."

"I'm not taking any chances." He holds me by my shoulders, forcing me to walk to my computer. He pushes me until I sit in the chair and then kneels down to restart my router.

"Why do you feel like the owner of my internet connection?" I ask, but he just shrugs. "I could report you for entering my house like this, you know that, don't you?"

"I know. But I also know you won't do it."

"How can you be so sure?"

"Stalkers do not usually report those they stalk. It's usually the other way around."

"This." I point to the window, and then to him. "Would also be considered stalking."

"It's not the same thing."

"Why not?"

"Because you like me." He pauses. "But I don't like you."

Ouch! Right in my heart!

I want to argue with him, but his words are like alcohol in a fresh wound. He keeps working on the router, and I stay quiet.

Because you like me, but I don't like you.

He said it so casually, so honestly. If he doesn't feel anything, then why did he kiss my neck that day in the cemetery?

Ignore his words, Raquel, don't let him get to you.

Ares looks up at me. "What? Did I hurt your feelings?"

"Please! Of course not," I lie. "Just hurry up with that so I can get back to sleep."

He doesn't say anything, and I watch him work. Having him this close still feels so unreal. I can see every detail of his face. His smooth skin is without even a trace of acne. Life is so unfair sometimes. Ares has it all: health, money, skills, intelligence, and beauty.

"Done." He shakes the dust off his hands with a disgusted look on his face. "You should clean your room once in a while."

I let out a sarcastic laugh. "Oh, excuse me, Your Royal Highness, for forcing you to step into my unworthy room."

"Cleanliness has nothing to do with money, lazy."

"Don't play that card! I don't have time to clean. Between my summer job, sleeping, eating, stalking you—" I cover my mouth as the words slip out.

Why did I say that?

Ares smiles from ear to ear, a sharp glint of derision in his eyes. "Stalking me is time-consuming, huh?"

"Nope, no, that's not what I meant."

Still on his knees, Ares crawls toward me, and I shudder in my chair. He stares at me and he gets so close that I have to spread my legs to let him pass. His face is only inches from mine.

"What are you doing?"

He doesn't answer, he just puts his hands on the arms of the chair, on either side of my waist. I can feel the heat radiating from his defined body. We are too close. The intensity he emanates doesn't allow me to breathe properly. My eyes fall to his full lips, and that piercing I can see so well now.

His gaze moves down from my face to my breasts and my exposed legs, and then back up to my face, a mischievous smile crossing those luscious lips. The air becomes heavy and hot around us.

Ares takes my hands in his and places them on top of the arms of the chair, moving them out of his way. His eyes never leave mine as he lowers his head until it's between my knees.

"Ares, what are you . . . ?"

His lips touch my knee with a simple kiss, leaving me breathless. "Do you want me to stop?"

His eyes search mine, and I shake my head. "No."

The way the muscles in his arms and shoulders contract as he leaves wet kisses on the tops of my thighs is so fucking sexy. His tattoo just adds fire to this volcano he's awakening inside me. His soft lips kiss, lick, and suck at the sensitive skin of my inner thighs. My body trembles, and little shivers of pleasure run through me, setting my senses on fire and clouding my mind. His black hair tickles as it brushes against my exposed skin.

Ares looks up as he bites into my skin, causing a small moan to escape my lips. My breathing is erratic, and my poor heart is beating like crazy. He continues his onslaught, moving up and down my thighs, his lips attacking, devouring. My hips move on their own, begging for more, wanting his lips in a place a little higher.

My eyes close by themselves.

"Ares," I moan his name, and I can feel his lips stretch into a smile against my skin, but I don't care.

"Do you want me?" His lips brush against the spot between my legs, right over the fabric of my shorts and I feel like I'm going to die of a heart attack. I can only nod. "I want you to say it," he demands.

"I want you."

He stops, and I open my eyes to find his face so close to my own that I can feel his heavy breath on my lips. His eyes are locked on mine.

"You're going to be mine, Raquel."

And then, just as suddenly as he came into my room, he leaves.

SEVEN
The Club

"Welcome to Dream Burgers. What would you like?" I ask with the Bluetooth device pressed to my ear.

"I'd like two Big Dreamy burgers and a cappuccino," a woman's voice says in response.

I select the order on the computer in front of me. "Anything else?"

"No, nothing else."

"Okay, your order will be seven dollars and twenty-five cents. You can pay at the window. Thank you."

A car appears next to the drive-thru window, and the woman who ordered hands me her card to pay. After finishing the transaction, I politely say good-bye and pray that no more cars show up, although it's true that I'd rather serve people here than face them at the counter inside the restaurant. I adjust my cap with the *DB* for Dream Burgers on it and sigh. I'm exhausted. There's still an hour before my shift is over, but I'm ready to jump out the window. The sensor alerts me that there's a new car in the drive-thru, and I curse to myself.

Stop coming in for food, people!

"Welcome to Dream Burgers. What would you like?"

I hear a high-pitched giggle, and then someone clearing their throat. "I would like to order a Raquel to go."

"Pass to the next window, ma'am," I say, grinning like a fool.

In a matter of seconds, Dani is idling by my window. Her hair is perfect as always, and she's wearing cute sunglasses.

"I can't believe you're spending the rest of the summer here."

"I need the job, and you know it. What are you doing here?"

"I've come to kidnap you."

"I've got another hour before I can leave."

Dani grins like a Cheshire cat. "What part of kidnapping don't you understand? The part where it's involuntary? You have no right to say no."

"I can't leave."

"Yes, you can, stubborn."

I'm about to open my mouth to protest when I feel someone behind me. I turn to see Gabriel, a coworker who wasn't on the schedule today. His reddish hair escapes from his cap as he gapes at Dani.

My attention returns to my best friend. "What's going on?"

"Gabriel will cover your remaining hour."

My eyes flick between Gabriel and Dani. "Why would he do that?"

"We do things for our friends," Dani says with a shrug. "Don't we, Gabo?"

He looks at her as if stunned. "Yes."

"Great." Dani's gaze falls on me again. "Get your things, and I'll wait for you in the parking lot. We have to go now."

"But . . ." I protest feebly to no avail. A few minutes later, I jump into Dani's car, clutching my small backpack. I can't believe it. She busted me out.

"I'm supercool. I know," she says.

"Gabriel? Really? I thought redheads weren't your type."

"Ed Sheeran changed my mind."

"What did you do?"

"I promised to accept an invitation to go out."

"You can't go through life using your looks to get your way."

"Of course I can."

I snort. "Where are we going?"

"Insomnia, of course."

My eyes widen in surprise. Insomnia is the most popular club in town, and Dani's favorite place to go on Friday nights. I've never been there because you have to be twenty-one to get in. And I'm only eighteen, which Dani seems to have completely forgotten.

"I don't know if you forgot but I'm eighteen. And, you don't really expect me to go smelling like French fries and looking like this, do you?"

"One, I'm eighteen too. Two, you'll change at my house."

"So you can lend me one of those dresses where you can see right down to my soul? I'll pass."

Dani bursts out laughing. "You are so dramatic. It's not a crime to show your knees, Raquel."

"For your information, in some parts of the world it is."

"We are not in *some parts of the world*."

"Green," I tell her when I see the traffic light turn green. Dani is easily distracted while driving.

"Relax, we only have two weeks of summer left, and you've done nothing but work."

"Fine, but I won't spend a penny."

"That's not a problem."

"Of course, I forgot your ability to get what you want."

Dani puts her sunglasses on top of her head and winks at me. "Oh yes. Now." She parks one house away from hers. "Time to get beautiful."

Once we get to her house, I watch her walk past the front door and go to her bedroom window. "Dani?"

"Oh, I forgot to tell you that my parents don't know about my nights out, so we have to sneak in and out."

This girl is incredible.

>> <<

What feels like an eternity later but was actually only an hour, we arrive at Insomnia, and somehow we're able to get in despite being underage. Dani lent me a tight, black dress that fits my body perfectly. Even though she's more voluptuous than I am, the dress is molded to my silhouette, as if it had been mine to begin with. It doesn't go all the way to my knees, landing about midthigh, but I feel like I can move around and still stay covered.

The first thing I notice is that not everyone else can get in. The admission line is really long, and there are a lot of people that the doormen send away. Now that I'm inside, I understand why. This is not just any club. It's chic and modern and very upscale. There are colored lights and moving effects all around us. The dance floor is wide and full of couples. The place is vibrating with music—I'm vibrating with it—and it's impossible to hear anything else. How are people supposed to communicate in places like this? As if Dani hears my thoughts, she comes closer to me.

"I'm going to get us something to drink!" she shouts in my ear and then disappears.

Shaking my head, I take my time to inspect my surroundings. There are lots of pretty, well-dressed girls here. I was expecting something like this because Dani doesn't go just anywhere. Her family has money, sure, not in an exaggerated way like Ares's family, but they live well. So it's only natural that the places Dani frequents are classy and impressive. There are some very handsome guys here too.

However, they're nothing like my Ares.

My Ares?

I've already appropriated him without his consent.

Scanning the place, I notice that there's a second floor with tables overlooking the dance floor, and it's at that moment that my eyes meet the pair of deep blue eyes that haunt my days and nights.

Ares.

My unrequited love is sitting there, looking beautiful as usual. He's wearing black pants, black shoes, and a gray shirt with the sleeves rolled up to his elbows. He's playing with the piercing in his lip, and his black hair is in that perfect messy style that only looks good on him. Unconsciously, I move toward him, like metal toward a magnet. His eyes have me trapped, and I'm under his spell. It's not until I meet the security guard in front of the staircase that leads to my prince charming that I wake up from my trance.

"This is a VIP area, Miss," the guard says to me firmly. Ares smirks down at me from on high, all mighty and arrogant.

I look away from Ares and shake my head to clear it. "Oh, I-I, he . . . I thought we could all go up there."

"No, access reserved." The guard makes a gesture for me to go away.

Of course, the self-important Ares is in the VIP area, I think. *He's too special to mix with the sweat and pheromones of the common people dancing down here.*

Reluctantly, I go back the way I came and meet Dani on the way.

"I thought I wouldn't find you!" she screams in my ear and hands me a fluorescent pink drink.

"What is this?"

"It's called Orgasm! You have to try it!"

A drink called Orgasm. . . .

Even a drink has had more sex than me.

Slowly, I inspect the small glass from all sides. I sniff it and the smell is so strong. My nose becomes irritated, and I sneeze. Dani downs hers in one gulp, leaving me stunned. She encourages me to drink and for some reason my eyes travel to that little VIP area. Ares raises a glass with what looks like whiskey in it, as if making a toast with me and then takes a sip.

Are you challenging me, Greek God?

In one gulp, I drain the glass, and the bittersweet liquid slides down my throat, setting everything in its path on fire.

This definitely doesn't feel like an orgasm!

When I cough, Dani pats me on the back. We head to the bar, where Dani hands me two more drinks. I dumbly think it's one for me and one for her, but no, they're both for me. Five drinks later, Dani takes me to the dance floor, and I have too much alcohol in my system to care.

"Let's dance!" she encourages as we make our way through the mass of people.

It feels good to be so spontaneous and not to feel embarrassed. Oh, the advantages of alcohol. Everything around me is colorful and the music reverberates throughout my body as I dance and dance and dance. Out of curiosity, I glance up at the stupid royalty sitting in the VIP section. He's staring at me like a hawk watching from the heights for its prey.

Can't he stop looking at me? Or does he like what he sees?

Don't be delusional, Raquel, he clearly told you he doesn't like you.

Then why is he looking at me?

I feel the urge to show off to him.

I'll give you something to look at, Greek God.

I begin to dance slowly, moving my hips to the rhythm of the music. Running my hands through my long hair and then down the sides of my breasts, my waist, my hips, I reach the end of my dress and play with the hem, lifting it a little. Even from this distance, I can see Ares's eyes darken, and he brings his glass to his lips. Those lips that licked my neck and thighs, leaving me wanting more. Ares has teased me twice, and it's about time he gets what he deserves.

I'll prove to him that I don't forget anything, and that even a Greek god can have a taste of his own medicine.

Seductive Raquel mode: activated.

EIGHT
The Candle Room

With so much alcohol in my veins, it's very hard to focus on being sensual.

I have to try anyway. I need to get revenge on Ares. He's played with me twice already, and he can't go through life inciting innocent souls like mine and leaving them wanting.

Innocent souls . . .

I really am drunk. My stalker soul is not innocent, not with the things I do in the dark of my room when no one sees me. I blush as I remember all of the times that I've touched myself, thinking about Ares. In my defense, Ares was the first male presence I had access to when I hit puberty. It's his fault for being in my field of vision when my hormones were raging.

I turn my back to him to give him a good view of my body. It's not a spectacular body, but I have a good figure and a decent ass. Sweat rolls down my forehead, the sides of my face, and the neckline of my dress. I'm immediately thirsty, and I find myself licking my dry lips more often.

I don't know how much time has passed, but when I turn again to look at Ares, he's gone. My heart races even faster as I look around for him.

Did he come downstairs and come after me? What was I supposed to do in that case?

I haven't worked out my seduction plan to that extent.

Stupid, Raquel, always getting into games you don't know how to play.

But this isn't going to stop here. Determined, I walk back to the staircase where the guard is.

"VIP area," he says, giving me a tired look.

"I know," I answer reluctantly, "but a friend of mine is up there, and he told me to come up."

"Do you expect me to believe that?"

"It's the truth. He's going to be angry if he knows you have me waiting here." I lift my chin in defiance.

"If your friend wants you up there, he should come and get you, don't you think? That's the way the rules are."

"Just a second," I beg him, but he doesn't listen. I try to pass by him on the side, and he stops me, grabbing my wrist. "Let me go."

I struggle to get free, but he just tightens his grip on me.

"She said to let her go." A sweet voice fills my ears from behind, and I turn to look over my shoulder to see Apolo Hidalgo standing behind me with his jaw set.

"This is none of your business," the guard says rudely.

Apolo's expression is kind but assertive. "A lawsuit for assault is pretty serious; I doubt you can come out of one unscathed."

The guard snorts in derision. "If you're trying to scare me, you're just making a fool of yourself, brat."

Doesn't he know who he's talking to? Apolo may look like a child, but he's a member of one of the most powerful families in the state.

Apolo lets out a laugh. "Brat?"

The guard maintains his stance, and I try to free myself, but he tightens his grip again. "Yes, brat. Why don't you go away and stop meddling where you're not wanted?"

"Apolo, it's okay," I say, looking over my shoulder. "I tried to go up even though he told me not to." I turn toward the guard. "Could you let me go?"

The guard's expression turns guilty, and he finally releases me. "I'm sorry."

We walk away from the guard and Apolo lifts my arm and inspects it. It's red but not bruised.

"Are you all right?" he asks.

"Yes, thank you."

"If he hadn't apologized, I would have fired him."

"Fired him? You own this bar?"

"No." Apolo shakes his head. "It belongs to my brother."

I stare at him with wide eyes. "This belongs to Ares?"

Apolo shakes his head again. "Ares with a bar? No, Mom would die. It belongs to Artemis."

Oh, the big brother.

"Don't worry. I'll text Artemis. He'll deal with it when he gets here later."

Part of me feels sad for the guard, but then I remember how rude he was. He doesn't say anything when we pass by him this time. Our little argument sobered me up a bit, but I still have a long way to go before I'm fully alert. I realize just how drunk I am when it's difficult for me to climb the short staircase to the VIP area. A lump rises in my throat at the prospect of meeting Ares.

It's beautiful up here, with glass tables and plush armchairs. Waiters are serving the wealthy groups spread out across the lounge. At the far end, I see crimson curtains blocking what lies beyond.

Apolo guides me to one of the armchairs in front of an empty table. "Sit down, what would you like to drink?"

I search my brain, trying to remember what I was drinking with Dani, but she has already given me so many different drinks that I don't even remember most of them. I only remember one by its peculiar name: Orgasm. But there is no way in this life or the next that I will ever say that word to Apolo.

"What do you recommend?"

"I don't drink, but my brothers love whiskey," Apolo says kindly.

"A glass of whiskey, then."

He orders it from a waiter and then sits down next to me. I clasp my hands in my lap, nervous.

"I'm very sorry about the guard," Apolo apologizes, looking at me with those pure eyes of his. "Sometimes they hire just anyone."

"It's okay, I shouldn't have tried to go upstairs either."

"I'll tell Artemis to give you a pass so that way when you come, you can go upstairs whenever you want."

"Thank you, but you don't have to do that."

"Hey, we're neighbors, and, while we may not be best friends, I remember the times we played and talked through the fence together."

"I didn't think you would remember that. You were so little."

"Of course I remember. I remember everything about you."

The way he says it makes something in my stomach tighten with tension. Apolo notices the expression on my face. "I don't mean to sound weird or anything, I just have a good memory."

"Don't worry," I say. "You're not weird."

I'm the last person who's qualified to judge you regarding matters of stalking, anyway, I think.

The bartender brings the whiskey and I take a sip, struggling to swallow it. It tastes awful. As I take another sip, my attention is drawn back toward the crimson curtains. "What's in there?"

Apolo scratches his head but before he can answer me, his phone rings. He makes an apologetic face as he gets up to answer the call and walks away. I look down at the dance floor and see Dani dancing and laughing with a guy. I'm not surprised. She has such a charming, bubbly personality. My eyes dart back to the curtains, my curiosity getting the best of me as always. What lies beyond them?

Apolo is still on his call, so I stand up and head toward the mysterious place. The first thing that envelops me when I cross the curtains is darkness. It's hard for my eyes to adjust to it, since the only light is from small candles scattered around the area and nothing else.

I see couples kissing and groping each other on the sofas positioned around the room. Some of them look like they're having sex with clothes on. I pass so many curtains that are all the same color that I no longer know where the exit is, and I'm terrified to open the wrong curtain and interrupt couples doing God knows what. I decide to head toward a soft light coming through what looks like a clear glass door in the distance, in hopes that it's an exit. But I'm met by an unexpected sight on the other side.

Ares is sitting in a chair with his head tipped back and his eyes closed. Carefully, I step out and join him on the balcony. The fresh night air hits me, and it's like I just walked out of a spell. The candle room seems to have that effect, engulfing you in a dreamlike vibe. Now, I'm back in the real world, facing a dark night and a Greek god.

Ares looks so beautiful with his eyes closed. He seems almost innocent. His long legs are stretched out in front of him, and one hand

holds his glass of whiskey, while the other is subtly giving his noticeable hard-on a gentle squeeze. Eventually he removes his hand, looking
frustrated. He's obviously trying to calm his little friend down by getting
some fresh air, but it doesn't seem to be working.

A smile of victory crosses my lips.

*So you aren't immune to my attempts at seduction. I've got you,
Greek God.*

I clear my throat, and Ares's eyes shoot open, lifting his head up
to look at me. I can't get this stupid victorious grin off my face, and he
seems to notice. "Why am I not surprised to see you here?"

"Getting some fresh air?" I give a little laugh.

Ares runs his hand over his jaw. "Do you think I'm like this
because of you?"

I cross my arms over my chest. "I know you are."

"How are you so sure? Maybe I've been making out with a beautiful girl, and she left me like this."

His response doesn't affect my smile. "I'm sure because of the
way you looked at me back in there. And the way you're looking at
me right now."

Ares stands up, and my courage falters a little. "And *how* exactly
am I looking at you?"

"As if you were a second away from losing control and kissing
me."

Ares laughs with that husky laugh that I find so sensual. "You're
delirious, maybe it's the alcohol."

"Do you think so?" I push him backward, and he falls into the
chair.

Those deep eyes don't leave mine as I move closer, and with both
legs on either side of his, I sit on him. Immediately, I feel how hard he
is against me, and I bite my lower lip. Ares's face is inches away from

mine, and having him so close makes my poor heart beat like crazy. He smiles, showing off his perfect teeth.

"What are you doing, Witch?"

I don't answer him and bury my face in his neck instead. He smells delicious, a combination of expensive cologne mixed with his natural scent. My breathing accelerates as I leave a trail of wet kisses all over his neck. I make him put his glass of whiskey on the floor and guide his hands to my ass and leave them there. Ares sighs, and I continue my attack on his neck. His hands squeeze my body, and I feel him get even harder against me. I start to move against him gently, tempting him, torturing him.

A slight moan escapes his lips. I smile against his skin and move my mouth until I reach his ear. "Ares," I moan his name in his ear and he presses me tighter against him.

I pull away from his neck so I can look into his eyes. The dark desire I find in them disarms me. His nose touches mine, and our accelerated breaths mingle.

"Do you want me?" I ask, moistening my lips.

"Yes, I want you, Witch."

I lean in to kiss him, and as our lips are about to meet, I turn my head to the side, and stand up quickly.

"Karma is a bitch, Greek God."

Feeling like the queen of the universe, I walk away from him and back into the club.

NINE
The Plan

"Are you all right?" Apolo asks as soon as I appear at his side again. "You're all red."

I try hard to fake a slight smile as I sit down. "I'm fine. I'm just a little hot."

Apolo's eyebrows furrow, almost touching. "You saw something unpleasant, didn't you?"

No, actually, I just left your brother with an erection the size of the Eiffel Tower.

Apolo takes my silence as a yes and shakes his head. "I've told Artemis that the candle room isn't a good idea, but he won't listen to me. Why would he listen to me, anyway? I'm just the kid in the family." I notice a certain bitterness in his sweet voice when he says it.

"You're not a child," I say.

"To them I am."

"Them?"

"Ares and Artemis." He sighs and takes a sip of his soda. "Even to my parents, they don't take me into account when making decisions at all."

"That can be a good thing, Apolo. You have no responsibilities. This is a stage of life that, according to my aunts, you have to enjoy. There will be time to worry about those things when you're an adult."

"Enjoy? My life is boring. I have no friends, at least not real ones, and in my own family I'm a nobody."

"Wow, you sound very sad for such a young man."

He plays with the metal rim of his soda. "My grandfather says I'm an old man in a child's body."

Ah, Grandpa Hidalgo. The last I heard, he'd been placed in a nursing home. The family made that decision after discussions among his four children, including Apolo's dad. From the sadness in Apolo's eyes, I could tell that this was one of the many decisions where they didn't take his feelings into account.

That innocent, beautiful face shouldn't look that sad, so I stand up and offer him my hand. "Do you want to have fun?"

Apolo offers me a skeptical look. "Raquel, I don't think that . . ."

The alcohol still circulating in my veins motivates me even more. "Get up, Lolo, it's time to have some fun."

Apolo laughs, and his laugh reminds me so much of his brother's, except that Ares's laugh doesn't sound innocent, just sexy.

"Lolo?"

"Yes, that's you now, forget about Apolo, the good, boring boy. Now you're Lolo, a boy who came to have fun tonight."

Apolo stands up and follows me apprehensively. "Where are we going?"

I ignore him and lead him down the staircase back to the dance floor. I'm surprised I don't fall in these heels. I look around and once again find Dani dancing with someone, but it's a girl this time.

Okay, Dani, you seem to be having a great night.

I head straight to the bar and order four glasses of vodka and four more of lemonade. The bartender pours them in front of us.

"Are you ready?"

Apolo smiles from ear to ear. "I'm ready."

Before I can say anything, Apolo downs one drink after another. Leaving the four small glasses empty, he turns to me, and I watch in horror as he holds onto the bar while his body tries to handle so much alcohol at once. "Oh shit, I feel so strange."

"You're crazy! Those were for me! The lemonade was for you!"

Apolo covers his mouth with his hand, grinning. "Oops!" He takes my hand and leads me to the dance floor.

"Apolo, wait!"

Okay, things are starting to get ugly. My original plan was to toast with Apolo—with him drinking lemonade—take him dancing, introduce him to a girl who he could talk to, and then let him go with a smile back on that sweet face. Needless to say, my plan has gone a little bit to shit. Anything that starts with excessive alcohol ends badly. I give a cry for help to Dani, and within no time, the three of us are in a taxi on the way to my house. Apolo is so drunk that we know we couldn't abandon him at the club or take him to his house, where his family would probably give him the scolding of the century.

Let me tell you something: dealing with a drunk person is hard but transporting them is even harder. I think Dani and I are going to get two hernias from carrying Apolo up to the second level of my house. Why didn't we leave him downstairs? Because that's where my mother's room is, and there's no way in the world I'm going to let Apolo sober up there. If he vomits in my mother's room, my days in this world will come to an end.

We throw him on my bed, and he collapses like a rag doll.

"Are you sure you'll be all right?" Dani asks.

"Yeah. My mom's on duty at the hospital, and she won't be back until tomorrow," I answer. "You've helped me enough. I don't want to cause you problems with your parents. Go on."

"If you need anything, call me, okay?"

"Calm down and go, the taxi is waiting."

Dani gives me a hug. "As soon as he sobers up, send him home."

"I will."

Apolo is lying on his back on my bed, mumbling things I don't understand. His shirt is open and his hair is a mess. He still looks cute and innocent despite the alcohol in his veins and some vomit on his pants.

"Oh, Rocky. What have I done?"

Rocky just licks my leg in response. I take off Apolo's shoes and hesitate as I look at his pants. Should I take them off? They have vomit on them. Decidedly, I take off his pants and his shirt, which also has vomit on it. I leave him in his boxers and tuck him in with my sheet.

A loud ringing makes me jump. That's not my ringtone. I follow the sound and grab Apolo's pants off the floor, pulling out his phone, and my eyes widen when I see the screen.

Incoming call: *Ares bro*

I mute it and let it ring until the call drops, and then I see how many messages and missed calls Apolo has from Ares and Artemis. Oh shit. I hadn't thought about how his siblings and parents would react if he disappeared from the club and didn't get home safely.

Ares calls again, and I hang up. I can't answer him. He'd recognize my voice. I can send him a text message, but what do I tell him?

Apolo: Hey, bro, I'll sleep at a friend's house.

I hit send. That's it; that should calm him down.

Ares's answer comes quickly.

Ares bro: Answer the damn phone, now.

Okay, Ares has not calmed down. He calls back. I watch in alarm as his name taunts me from Apolo's cell phone screen. It feels like years pass, but Ares finally stops calling. A sigh of relief escapes my lips, and I sit on the edge of my bed, where Apolo is still sleeping deeply. At least he hasn't vomited again. His cell phone screen lights up, catching my attention. I check it to see if Ares is calling again, but it's just a notification from a cell phone app called Find my iPhone.

Find my iPhone!

It's an app used to locate any Apple devices that are registered to an account. If Ares uses the app on his Mac, he can get the exact location of the phone I'm holding. Panicking, I throw the phone on the bed.

He found me!

I know he found me. Why does Ares know so much about technology, why?

He's going to kill me. Ares is coming for me, and not even a miracle can save me.

TEN
The Discussion

Don't panic, Raquel!

Don't panic!

"Argh!" I groan in panic, pacing back and forth in my room.

Rocky follows me faithfully, perceiving my anxiety. I glance at Apolo, who is beyond dreamland. I bite my nails. Ares is definitely very angry, and he's coming for me.

I hate you, technology! You've caused me so much trouble lately.

"Okay, calm down, Raquel. Breathe. One thing at a time," I say to myself, tousling my hair. "If he comes, don't open the door and that's it, nothing happens."

I sit on the edge of the bed, taking a deep breath. Apolo's hand is dangling off the bed. Rocky sniffs at it and growls, baring his teeth. Apolo's a stranger to him.

"Rocky, no, come on." I lead him out of the room and close the door. The last thing I want is Rocky biting Apolo while he sleeps.

That would just complicate things even more.

I don't know how much time passes, but I yawn. I check my phone and Apolo's, but there are no new notifications, not even a call. Could it be that Ares has calmed down? The clock on my nightstand shows me the time: 2:43 a.m. The night has flown by.

I walk into my bathroom and my reflection in the mirror is like a slap in the face. *Wow, I look awful.* My eyes are red and my brown hair is a mess, with locks pointing in every direction. My eyeliner is smudged under my eyes, and I could easily go out on the street and scare people. At which point did I go from looking great to awful?

It's called alcohol, my dear.

I tie my hair into a messy bun and wash my face to remove my makeup. Barefoot, I leave the bathroom and head to my bed. I sit on the opposite side of the bed from Apolo, hesitating, but sleepiness wins the battle. My first night out has been too chaotic, and I'm exhausted. It's a miracle I'm not already asleep and hitting REM. I sigh and rub my face. My eyes are slowly closing, and the breeze coming through the window gives me chills. My eyes shoot wide open again when I remember the time Ares climbed up to enter my room through the window.

"Shit!"

I run to the window, but halfway there I stop abruptly. A silhouette is clearly visible through the curtains. I don't have time to think before Ares jumps into my room, pulling the curtains out of his way.

¡Oh, mierda!

As Dani would say in her attempts at Spanish.

Ares Hidalgo is in my room. Again. His height making my room feel small, again. He's still wearing that gray shirt with the rolled-up sleeves that fits him so well. He looks at me with such coldness that I swear it gives me more chills than the breeze. He is annoyed.

He is very, very annoyed. His features look tense. His lips are pressed tight, and his hands are bunched into fists. His entire body language indicates that I need to handle this carefully if I don't want to end up as Greek god food.

"Where is he?" he shouts, surprising me.

"Ares, let me explain what happened."

Ares pushes me aside and walks toward my bed. "You don't have to explain anything to me." His eyes travel to his brother's soiled clothing on the floor and then back to Apolo's prone form. "Did you get him drunk?" he asks, apparently changing his mind.

"It was an accident."

"You left me and went to get my little brother drunk?"

"It was . . ."

"An accident? How can you be so irresponsible?" he snaps and shakes his brother, but Apolo just mumbles something about wanting his mom and hides his head under the pillow. "Just look at him!" Ares straightens up and glares at me. "Did you do it on purpose? Did you want to ruin my night so badly?"

He approaches me, and I stand my ground. I'm not going to let him intimidate me. "Listen to me, Ares, it was an accident. I ordered shots for me, and your brother thought they were for him. Since he's not used to it, he got drunk on basically nothing."

"Do you expect me to believe that?"

"Whether you believe me or not, I don't care, I'm telling you the truth."

"The little girl has character," he says in a mocking tone.

"I'm not a little girl, and unless you're going to apologize for yelling at me and coming into my room like that, I don't want to talk to you. Go away."

"Apologize?"

"Yes."

Ares sighs but says nothing, so I speak again. "Your brother isn't going to come back to life any time soon, so I suggest you let him sleep, and then come and get him in the morning."

"Let him sleep with you? Over my dead body."

"You sound like a jealous boyfriend."

"You wish."

He approaches me, and I watch him cautiously. "What are you doing?"

Ares takes my hand and brings it to his face, pressing his soft lips against my skin. "Apologizing." He kisses the inside of my hand, his eyes fixed on mine. "I'm sorry, Raquel."

I want to scream at him and tell him that an apology is not enough, but that gentle gesture, and the honesty in his eyes when he says it, disarms me. My anger melts away and that tingling in my stomach that I always feel when I'm around Ares returns.

I pull my hand from his. "You're crazy, you know that?"

Ares shrugs his shoulders. "No, I only know how to admit my mistakes."

I walk away from him because my stupid mind is having a flashback to when I left him hot and bothered in the bar. *Don't think about that now!* I pretend to check on Apolo and fix the sheet covering him. Ares moves to the other side of the bed, and I watch him take off his shoes.

"What the hell are you doing?"

He says nothing, finishes with his shoes, and starts unbuttoning his shirt.

"Ares!"

"You don't expect me to leave him in this state, do you?" He makes puppy eyes at me that take my breath away. "Besides, it wouldn't be appropriate . . . if you slept with a man alone."

"And it's appropriate for me to sleep with two?"

Ares ignores my question and takes off his shirt.

Holy Mother, Blessed Virgin of Abdominals!

The blood rushes to my cheeks and I turn as red as a tomato. Ares has another tattoo on his lower abdomen and on the left side of his chest. His fingers touch the button of his pants.

"No! If you take off your pants, you sleep on the floor."

Ares gives me a crooked smile. "Are you afraid of not being able to control yourself?"

"Of course not."

"So?"

"Just leave them on."

He raises his hands in obedience. "As you say. Come, time for bed, Witch."

I struggle not to look at him. Ares is shirtless in my room. This is too much for me. He lies down in the middle of my bed and leaves enough room for me near the edge. I'm thankful that I have a big bed and Apolo is curled up in the corner, otherwise there's no way we could all fit. Nervously, I lie down on my back next to Ares, who watches me with amusement. I stare up at the ceiling without moving a muscle. I can feel his body heat against my arm. I'm going to die of sexual tension. I take my pillow and put it between the two of us for a sense of protection.

Ares laughs. "A pillow? Really?"

I close my eyes. "Good night, Ares."

A few seconds pass before the pillow is pulled away. The next thing I feel is Ares's arm pulling me toward him until my back is flat against his chest. I can feel him completely pressed against me. All of him. Ares presses me even tighter against him, and his hot breath brushes against my ear.

"Good night? I don't think so. The night is just beginning, Witch. And you owe me one."

Virgin of Abdominals, protect me!

ELEVEN
The Sexy Greek God

I'm going to have a heart attack.

I can feel my poor heart beating desperately in my chest, and I'm sure Ares feels it too. He's still pressed against me, and the heat emanating from his body warms my back. His hand is on my hip, and my nerves make my muscles tense and my breathing quicken.

You owe me one . . .

Ares's words echo in my head.

His breath caresses the side of my neck, giving me goose bumps. Slowly, Ares's hand moves up over my dress until he reaches my ribs. I stop breathing as his hand stops just below my left breast and remains there.

"Your heart is going to burst," he whispers in my ear.

I lick my lips. "It must be the alcohol."

Ares's lips brush my ear. "No, it's not."

He begins to leave wet kisses on my neck, moving up to lick

my earlobe. I feel my legs weaken at the sensation of his lips on that sensitive part of my body. "Did you enjoy it?"

His question confuses me. "What?"

"Leaving me horny?"

I gasp at his raw words. As if to emphasize his point, his hand moves down from my chest to my hip and presses me even closer to him. That's when I feel how hard he is. I know I should pull away from him, but his tongue licks, his lips suck, and his teeth bite into the skin of my neck, driving me crazy.

Don't fall into his game, Raquel.

"I know you just want revenge," I whisper, thinking that maybe this will make him give up.

"Revenge?" He smiles into my skin and his hand moves up to my breasts once more, but this time he massages them shamelessly. I shiver in his arms. It's the first time a boy has touched me like that.

"I know that's what you want," I say, biting my lip to hold back a moan.

"That's not what I want."

"So, what do you want?"

His hand leaves my breasts, and his fingers trace a line down my stomach. I jump when his hand touches between my legs. "This is what I want."

Okay, that's very clear.

Ares takes the edge of my dress and slides it up painfully slowly. My heart has already suffered through two heart attacks and survived. I have no idea why I'm letting him touch me like this again. Or maybe I do, because I've always been drawn to him in an inexplicable way. Ever since I saw him playing soccer in his backyard when we were kids, his stoic expression and cold eyes caught my attention. He was just a kid and there was already something mysterious about him that made me want to know more, made me want to find a way to make him smile and abandon that bitter expression. To this day, I still want to see more of him. I want all of him.

A slight murmur of denial leaves my lips as Ares slips his hand under my dress, his fingers moving up and down over my underwear. His slow torture continues as I unconsciously begin to move my hips back toward him, wanting all of him pressed against me. Ares growls softly, and it's the sexiest sound I've ever heard in my life.

"Raquel, I can feel how wet you are through your panties."

The way he says my name makes the pressure in my belly grow. I'm nibbling on my lower lip so hard to keep myself from moaning that I'm afraid I'll bleed. His torture continues, slow, up and down, circles . . . I need more. I want more.

"Ares . . ."

"Yes?" His voice is no longer that robotic, cold voice I'm used to. It's guttural and his breathing is inconsistent. "Do you want me to touch you there?"

"Yes," I answer shyly.

Obediently, Ares moves my panties aside, and, the moment his fingers touch my skin, I shudder, arching my back.

"Oh God, Raquel," he moans in my ear. "You're so wet, so ready for me."

His fingers work magic, making my eyes roll back. Where the fuck did he learn to do that? My breathing is chaotic; my heart doesn't even have a normal rhythm anymore; my body is overloaded with delicious, addictive sensations. I can't and won't stop. My hips move even more against him, making him harder.

"Keep moving like that, keep teasing me, and I'll spread those pretty legs and fuck you so hard I'll have to cover your mouth to silence your moans."

His words are like fire to my burning body. His fingers are still moving in me, his mouth still on my neck, his body pressed against mine.

"I can't take it anymore." My self-control is gone; it vanished the moment he slipped his hands inside my underwear. I am so close to an orgasm and he seems to know it because he speeds up the movement of his fingers. Up, down, I can feel it coming, my body trembles in anticipation.

"Ares! Oh God!" I am only sensations, delicious sensations.

"Do you like it?"

"Yes!" I moan uncontrollably, approaching an orgasm. "Oh God, I'm yours!"

"All mine?"

"Yes! All yours!"

My whole body explodes into tingling sensations that run through every part of me, electrifying me, making me moan so loudly that Ares uses his free hand to cover my mouth. This is nothing like the ones I've achieved by touching myself. This orgasm disarms and shakes me.

Ares releases my mouth and takes his hand out of my panties. He moves away from me a little and the next thing I hear is the sound of plastic ripping. *A condom*? And then the sound of his pants zipper. I panic and turn my body around to face him. But not even a hundred years of life would have prepared me to see him like this: half-naked on my bed, blushing, his beautiful blue eyes staring back at me with lust. My searching eyes travel down his abs to that forbidden zone I've already felt so much but haven't seen and, wow, I confirm that Ares is completely perfect as I watch him put on the condom.

I swallow thickly, frowning.

"What's wrong?" he asks, pulling me to him.

Well, I'm a virgin and I panicked because I felt your big friend against me, I think, and I'm immediately thankful I didn't say that out loud.

"Mmm, I . . . I don't want . . ." I swallow and feel my throat dry up. Where the hell did all my saliva go?

You lost it when you were moaning like crazy in Ares's arms, my mind answers me.

Ares raises an eyebrow. "You don't want me to fuck you?"

How direct. "I . . ."

"Raquel, we both know how wet and ready you are for me."

"I'm sorry."

Ares wraps his hand around himself, stroking. "Leaving me like this is beyond cruelty, Raquel."

Should I return the favor? Is that what he's implying? And why does that turn me on so much? Is it the idea of touching him? Feeling him? I've never touched a boy in my life, though.

I act on instinct and nervously bring my hand toward him. Ares watches me like a predator, playing with the piercing in his red, provocative lips. Having him so close and naked after I let him give me the best orgasm of my life gives me some confidence; the intimacy barrier has already been crossed between us.

The moment my hand makes contact with his hardness, Ares closes his eyes and sinks his teeth into his lower lip, ripping any doubts out of my head. Seeing him shudder like that, tensing his stomach muscles as I move my hand, is the sexiest thing I've ever seen in my life.

"Shit . . ." he mumbles, putting his hand on mine and speeding up the movement. "You know what I'm imagining, Raquel?"

I move my legs together, the rubbing between them making me want to feel his fingers there again. "No, what?"

He opens his eyes, and I can see they are filled with desire. "How good it must feel to be inside you. I imagine you under me with your legs around my hips, making you mine as you scream my name."

Oh my goodness, I never thought words could turn me on so much.

He removes his hand and I continue the fast rhythm he showed me. He massages my breasts wildly and after a few seconds, he closes his eyes, muttering profanities. His abdomen contracts as do the muscles in his arms and then Ares lets out a grunt mixed with a moan and comes in my hand.

We are both breathing rapidly, our chests rising and falling together.

"I need to go to the bathroom," I say, hiding my hand.

I run for my life and lock myself in the bathroom. I wash my hands and look at my reflection in the mirror. "What in the world just happened?" I ask myself in a whisper.

Part of me can't believe it. Ares and I just gave each other some pretty good orgasms right next to his sleeping brother. I'm thankful my bed is large enough that there was considerable distance between us and Apolo while it was all happening. *Poor Apolo!*

I point to my reflection in the mirror. "Who are you, and what did you do with my innocent self?"

Perhaps there never was an innocent self.

Regaining my composure and my missing morals, I decide to go out and face the Greek god.

TWELVE
The Conversation

I realize that the Greek God nickname fits Ares perfectly, especially after seeing him naked.

I saw Ares naked. I touched him. I saw him come. Am I dreaming? Maybe I got too drunk and it's one of those crazy, vivid, drunken dreams.

As I walk out of the bathroom, I mentally thank Ares for getting dressed, but I find it strange that he has put everything on. His shirt, his pants, his shoes. Is he leaving? My heart twists a little when he doesn't even turn to look at me. He's too busy typing on his phone, sitting in my desk chair.

"Who are you texting at this hour?"

"That's not your problem, Raquel."

And there I stand, feeling superuncomfortable. What should I do? Or say? After a few seconds, Ares lifts his eyes from his phone and glances at me. I swallow, fiddling with my hands in front of me.

Really, Raquel? After you've done all that with him, you're this nervous?

My conscience is an idiot.

"I'm leaving." Ares stands up, sticking his phone into the back pocket of his pants. My heart sinks in my chest. "When Apolo wakes up, tell him to jump the fence and enter through the back door, I'll leave it open for him."

"I thought it wasn't *appropriate* to sleep with a man alone," I joke, but Ares doesn't smile.

"It's not, but it's your room, your life. It has nothing to do with me."

Okay, this guy is moody. He arrived annoyed, then he was tender, then sexual, and now he's back to being cold.

"Is something wrong?"

Ares walks to the window. "No."

Oh no, you won't leave. You won't leave here with that attitude without explaining what's wrong with you. You won't leave me with a feeling of having been used that is eating away at my heart.

I catch up to him and stand in front of him, blocking the window. "What's wrong with you now, Ares?"

"There's nothing wrong with me."

"Yes, something is wrong with you. Your sudden mood swings are giving me a headache."

"And your drama is bothering me. That's why I'm leaving."

"Drama?"

He points between us. "This drama."

"I hadn't even said anything to you until I saw that you were about to leave."

"Why can't I leave?"

"You said you would sleep here."

Ares sighs. "I changed my mind. It happens. Didn't you know *that*?"

"You're being an idiot. Didn't you know that?"

"That's the very reason I'm leaving. I don't understand why women assume that we owe them something just because we've had a little sexual fun. I don't owe you anything. I don't have to stay. I don't have to do anything for you."

Ouch!

Ares continues. "Look, Raquel, I like to be honest with the girls I get involved with."

Whatever he's going to say, I know I'm not going to like it.

"You and I are having fun, but I'm not looking for a relationship. I'm not looking to cuddle after fooling around a little. That's not me. I need to be clear with you about that because I don't want to hurt you. If you want to have fun with me with no strings attached, fine. And if that's not what you want, if what you want is a boyfriend, romance, Prince Charming, then tell me to stay away, and I will."

Thick tears run down my cheeks, and it's like I've stepped out of a sweet dream and entered a painful reality. I moisten my lips to speak. "I understand."

Ares's expression crumples with sadness, but, before he says anything, I wipe away my tears and open my mouth again.

"Then stay away from me."

The surprise on his face is all too obvious. I know that wasn't what he expected. But my mother taught me to never attempt to change someone. I know that no amount of sex, no matter how good, is enough to change someone if that person is unwilling to try.

Do I like him? I really do. I would dare to say that I'm falling in love with him. But I saw my mother put up with—and forgive—my father's infidelities over and over again. I saw that she forgot how much she was worth, and that no matter how much she endured, cried, and suffered, my father never changed. He finally left with a woman much younger than her. After living through all that, I promised myself I wouldn't be the same, I wouldn't let myself be trampled over and mistreated for love, I wouldn't let myself be completely carried away by my emotions. The pain of a broken heart passes, but the knowledge that you let someone make you forget your worth and walk all over you stays with you forever.

So I look Ares straight in the eye, not caring that I still have dried tears on my cheeks. "Stay away from me. And don't worry, I'm not interested in watching you anymore, so you can put your mind at rest."

He doesn't come out of his daze. "You never cease to amaze me, you are so . . . unpredictable."

"And you're such an idiot. Do you think that going around banging girls and then dumping them will bring you happiness? Do you think this 'I just want to have fun and nothing serious' nonsense is going to get you anywhere? You know, Ares, I thought you were a different person. I get why they say, 'never judge a book by its cover.' You have a beautiful cover, but your content is empty, and you're not a book I'm interested in reading, so get out of my room and don't come back."

"Wow, you really want the whole romance story, don't you?"

"Yes, and there's nothing wrong with that. At least I know what I want."

Ares tenses his jaw. "Fine, as you wish."

I step aside and he starts to climb out the window. "And Ares?"

He turns to me, with his hands on the ladder, and his body already outside on the rungs.

"I hope you've got the internet working at your place, because

I am going to change my Wi-Fi password. I can't see any point in it being *AresAndMeForever* now."

A hint of pain crosses his features, but I chalk it up to my imagination, and he just nods and disappears down the ladder.

I let out a long sigh as I watch the boy of my dreams walk away.

>> <<

I feel horrible.

Both physically and emotionally, which is a very bad combination for a single human being. My head hurts, and my body and my stomach are not quite stabilized after drinking. I haven't slept at all, and it's already morning.

And Apolo?

He's good, thank you, sleeping like a vampire on a sunny day.

My cup of coffee warms my hands. I'm sitting on the floor in front of the bed with a blanket around me. I hope the coffee does something for my soul. I feel like a zombie, and I'm pretty sure I look like one too. From my position, I can see the top of the ladder on the windowsill. I still can't believe I convinced Mom to let me keep it after she saw it. I told her I was practicing some new trendy Instagram exercise, and she believed me. Maybe I should get rid of it now. I sigh.

I feel like shit.

The physical discomfort is nothing compared to the feeling of disappointment that pierces my soul. I feel used, rejected, and unappreciated. It's amazing what Ares can do to me with just a few words. Even though I know I did the right thing by kicking him out of my life, it doesn't reduce the disappointment and dejection in my heart.

As unexpectedly as he appeared in my life, he's gone.

The sun is peeking through my window, and I remember Ares

disappearing through it as if it happened minutes ago, not hours. I can't help but analyze every moment over and over again. My poor brain, guided by my heart, tries to look for gestures, expressions, any hidden words that give me hope that he wasn't just playing with me, that he didn't just use me, that he's not an idiot.

During the time I've observed him, I've realized that his personality isn't the greatest, but I didn't expect him to have such a narrow perception of romance. He doesn't want a relationship, and he thinks women are something to be used and discarded. I know that if I didn't have such strong views about valuing myself as a woman, I would have fallen into his net. I would have given myself to him completely simply because I like him. I like everything about him. I have never in my life felt so attracted to someone. The things Ares makes me feel just by looking at me are overwhelming.

So I don't blame the girls who have gone through with it and tried to change him. I would try, too, if I hadn't experienced first-hand what my mother went through. That memory has always given me strength.

I sigh again, taking a sip of my coffee. I am so tired of being alone.

I want to have love, experience, fun. I want so many things. But I also want someone who respects me, who yearns to be with me, who *wants* to be with me. I don't want to be anyone's toy, no matter how much I might like him.

I lay my head against the edge of the bed and put my coffee cup to the side to watch the ceiling fan spin. It moves so slowly, blowing cool air over my face.

Without realizing it, I fall asleep.

>> <<

A few hours later, Apolo finally wakes up, and leaves with his head down, mumbling a thousand apologies. I've come to realize how much Apolo fears and respects Ares, but most of all how tender and kind Apolo is. I like him a lot, and I hope that this situation, although bizarre, is the beginning of our friendship.

As I watch Apolo climb down the ladder outside my window, I can't help but remember the moment that Ares left. His eyes had been fixed on me, as if waiting for me to change my mind and tell him to come back.

Ah! Get out of my head, Greek God.

I need to go back to sleep. I cover myself with my blanket and try to do just that.

THIRTEEN
The Incident

I consider myself a hard worker.

I help my mom, and I buy things for myself that she can't give me. It's not because she doesn't want to, but simply because her nursing salary is barely enough to pay our rent, utilities, her car, and the necessities. We're a team.

Today, however, I don't want to go to work. I've thought of a hundred excuses, but the truth is that I need the money. Classes start on Monday, so these are my last days to work double shifts. When school starts, I'll only be able to work during the evenings and weekends.

It's been almost a week since I saw Ares. To be honest, I didn't expect to miss him. How could I? We only saw each other a few times. But I think I miss stalking him too. It was a weird hobby that gave me an adrenaline rush and now it's gone. I sigh, gather my things, and stuff them into my backpack. To say I've had a bad day is putting it mildly. I've been distracted and yawning constantly. My boss has already called me out three times, and we had to give a customer free fries because I mixed up his order.

I take off my Dream Burgers cap and put it in my locker. I consider changing my shirt, but I don't even bother. I'm too lazy to walk to the bathroom, so I'll do it when I get home.

"Bad day, huh?" Gabriel's voice makes me jump, and I hit my shoulder with the locker door.

"Jesus! You scared me."

"Sorry." Gabriel takes off his cap, letting his reddish hair escape and allowing me to see his face better. He has that kind of soft face that would make you fall at his feet if he were to make eyes at you. "So, I'm curious. Any reason as to why you gave a milk shake to someone who ordered an ice cream?"

"Oh, you saw that?"

"Everyone saw it. You were like on another planet." He opens his locker and takes out his things.

"It's so embarrassing."

"Relax, it's happened to me too." He gives me a meaningful look.

I look at him sadly. "Dani?"

"Yeah." He stares into his locker, deep in thought. "She and I are from different worlds. I'm just the pretty boy who works at Dream Burgers to her, nothing more."

"I'm sorry."

"Relax. I knew it wouldn't work, but I didn't expect to care about her so quickly."

Oh, believe me, I know about that. "I don't know what to tell you, Gabo."

"Tell me your story."

"My story?"

84

"Why are you so distracted today?"

I close my locker and put on my backpack. "I-I cut a person out of my life a little while ago, he . . ." I remember Ares's cold words. "He wasn't what I expected."

"Disappointment, huh? That hurts."

"A lot." I sling my backpack over my shoulder. "I have to go. Good night, Gabe."

"Good evening, Raquel Milk shake."

"Really?"

"It will be days before I forget about it."

I gave him the finger, and he acts surprised. "Bye, silly."

Walking home has never been as depressing as it is today. The sound of cars passing on the avenue is like white noise, and the orange glow of the street lamps illuminates the route precariously. It seems as if my surroundings have molded to my mood. It's almost midnight, but I'm not worried because crime is low in this area and my house isn't that far away.

However, due to laziness, I make a very bad decision.

I take a shortcut.

To get to my neighborhood faster, I decide to cross under a bridge to shorten the path. It's dark and lonely under there, and I don't take into account the men who rely on that darkness to get high or sell illegal substances. My feet freeze when I see three men under the bridge. With the darkness serving as camouflage, I don't see them until I'm almost in front of them.

"Do you want something, pretty girl?" one of them asks. His voice is deep, and he coughs a little.

My heart speeds up, and my hands sweat. "No, I don't. . . . No."

"Did you get lost?"

"I … I took the w-wrong way," I stutter, and one of them laughs.

"If you want to come through here, you have to give us something."

I shake my head. "No, I'm going the other way."

I'm about to turn and leave when my phone rings, breaking the silence. Frantically, I take it out of my pocket, silence the call, and put it away again, but it's too late.

"Oh, that phone looks nice, don't you think, John?"

"Yeah, that would be a good birthday present for my daughter."

I try to run, but one of them grabs my arm, dragging me into the darkness under the bridge. I scream as loud as I can, but he covers my mouth and holds me by the hair, keeping me still.

"Shh! Easy, pretty girl. We're not going to do anything to you, just give us the phone."

Tears fill my eyes. The man smells of alcohol and other chemicals I don't recognize.

"The phone. Now," demands another one of them, but I can't move. Fear has me paralyzed. I want to move my hand and take out my phone, but I can't.

The third man emerges from the shadows. He has a cigarette clamped between his teeth and a scar on his face. "It's in her pocket, hold her."

No, don't touch me!

I scream, but the sound is muted by the hands of the man holding me. The one with the scar approaches me and puts his hand in the pocket of my pants, licking his lips. I want to vomit.

Please help me.

He pulls out my phone and examines it. "Nice, and it looks as good as new, it'll be a good gift for your daughter." He passes it to the other man, but his disturbing eyes never leave my face. "You're very pretty."

"Shall we let her go? We already have the phone," asks the one holding me.

"Yeah, John, that's enough."

John looks at me and his eyes lower to my body.

No, please don't.

The one holding me lets me go, but John grabs me and pulls me backward toward him, covering my mouth again. I can't breathe properly, and I can't move.

Help!

"John, she's probably my daughter's age."

"Shut up, assholes!" His shout echoes in my ear. "Get out of here."

"But . . ."

"Get out of here!"

The two men exchange glances, and I plead with them with my eyes, but they leave.

No. God, please don't.

John drags me under the bridge, and I start kicking and fighting desperately. He grabs me by the hair and turns me toward him. "Cooperate, I don't want to hurt you more than necessary. But if you scream, it's going to go real bad for you, pretty girl."

As soon as he releases my mouth, I scream. "Help me! Please—"

He hits me. I didn't even see him raise his hand. I only feel the strong impact on my right cheek. I've never been hit before; I've never felt such strong, sudden pain. It throws me off balance and sends me to the ground. Everything spins, and my right ear throbs. I can taste blood in my mouth.

"Is anyone there?" I hear a voice from the bridge above, and it sounds like God. "What's going on?"

John panics and runs away, and I crawl to sit up. "Help! Down here!" My voice sounds weak. The whole right side of my face throbs.

"Oh God!" It's a man's voice. In a few seconds that feel like an eternity, he appears in front of me. "Oh my God, are you okay?"

I can't talk, I have a lump in my throat. I just want to go home. I just want to be safe. He kneels in front of me.

"God, are you all right?"

I manage to nod my head.

"Should I call the police? Can you walk?"

With his help, I get up, and we move away from that hellish darkness.

Mom . . .

House.

Safe.

That's all my brain can think of when the man lends me his phone. With trembling fingers, I dial the only number I know: my mother's. But she doesn't answer, and my heart sinks in my chest. Tears blur my vision.

"Do you want me to call the police?

No, I don't want cops, I don't want questions. I just want to go home where I'm safe and where no one can hurt me. But I don't have the courage to walk alone, not again, and I don't want to ask this stranger to walk with me. And then I remember that my mother's phone number was the only one I knew until recently. Until Ares started texting me.

At this point I don't care what he and I have agreed, I just need someone to take me home. This call is my only salvation, and if Ares doesn't answer, I don't know what I'll do.

On the third ring, I hear his voice.

"Hello?"

The lump in my throat makes it almost impossible for me to say anything. "Hello, Ares."

"Who is it?"

"It's . . . Raquel." My voice breaks. I have tears falling from my eyes. "I . . ."

"Raquel? Are you okay? Are you crying?"

"No, well, yes . . . I . . ."

"For God's sake, Raquel, tell me what's wrong."

I can't talk, I can only cry. For some strange reason hearing his voice has made me burst into tears. The guy takes the phone from me.

"Hi, I'm the phone's owner. The girl was attacked under a bridge." There's a pause. "We're at the park on Fourth Avenue, in front of the construction building. Okay, all right." He hangs up.

I'm just a sea of tears. The man touches my shoulder.

"He'll be here in a few minutes. Calm down, breathe."

The minutes fly by. Like I said, my neighborhood isn't far, but I didn't expect to see Ares running toward us. He's wearing gray pajama pants and a T-shirt of the same color, and his hair is a mess. His beautiful eyes meet mine, and the concern on his face disarms me. I stand up to walk toward him. Ares doesn't say anything but quickly embraces me, smelling of soap, and in this moment of safety, of reassurance, I am safe. He leans back and holds my face.

"Are you okay?" I nod faintly and his finger brushes against my busted lip. "What the hell happened?"

"I don't want to talk. I just want to go home."

Ares doesn't push me to say more. He looks at the man to one side of us. "I'll take care of it; you can go. Thank you very much."

"You're welcome. Take care of yourselves."

We're left alone, and Ares lets go of me, turns around, and leans forward to offer me his back.

I look at him strangely. "What are you doing?"

He gives me a smile over his shoulder. "Taking you home."

Carefully, I climb onto his back and he carries me easily, as if I weighed nothing. I rest my head on one of his shoulders. My face is still throbbing with pain, and tears flood my eyes as I think about what just happened, but I feel safe.

In the arms of the idiot who broke my heart, I feel safe.

The silence between us isn't uncomfortable, it's just silence. The sky is clear, the streets are quieter now, and the orange streetlights are still there as if nothing has happened.

We arrive at my house, and Ares puts me down. My mom is at work, so he comes in with me. I go up to my room while he looks for ice in the kitchen. Rocky greets me enthusiastically, and I manage to rub his head a little before sending him to sit in the corner of the room. I take off my backpack and sit on my bed.

Ares appears with a plastic bag full of ice and sits down next to me. "This will help." He presses the bag against my face, and I let out a groan of pain.

"I'm sorry," I say quietly.

Ares frowns. "Why?"

"For calling you, I know that . . ."

"No," he interrupts me. "Don't even think about it. Never hesitate to call me if you're in trouble, ever, understood?"

"Understood."

"Now lie down, you need to rest, tomorrow will be another day." I obey him and lie down, holding the ice pack against my cheek. He covers me with blankets and I just watch him. I've forgotten how cute he is.

I missed you.

I think about it, but I don't say it. Ares seems to be getting ready to leave, and the panic of being alone overcomes me. I sit up. "Ares . . ."

Those blue eyes look at me, waiting, and I don't know how to ask him to stay. How can I ask him to stay when a week ago I asked him to leave and never come back? But I don't want to be alone. I can't be alone tonight. He seems to read my mind.

"Do you want me to stay?"

"You don't have to if you don't want to, I'll be fine, I—"

He doesn't let me finish, throwing himself on the opposite side of the bed. Before I can speak, he puts an arm around my waist and pulls me close to him, hugging me from behind affectionately.

"You're safe, Raquel," he murmurs. "Sleep. I won't leave you alone."

I put the ice pack on the bedside table and close my eyes. "Do you promise?"

"Yes. I won't leave. Not this time."

Sleepiness comes over me, and I fall between that state of consciousness and unconsciousness. "I missed you, Greek God."

I feel a kiss on the back of my head and then a quiet whisper.

"Me too, Witch, me too."

FOURTEEN
The Gentleman

Rocky's habit of licking my hand when he wants food wakes me up. The sunlight is streaming through my window, warming the room. My eyes burn, and my face hurts, and it takes me a few seconds to remember everything that happened last night.

Ares . . .

With a jump, I sit up and look at the other side of my bed. My heart sinks when I see that it's empty. But what did I expect? That I'd wake up to him cuddling with me? I'm so naive.

Slowly, I walk to the bathroom to brush my teeth. When I look in the mirror, I let out a squeal. "Holy mother of bruises!"

My face looks horrible. The whole right side is swollen and there's a bruise going up from the middle of my cheek to my right eye. The corner of my mouth has a small cut on it. I had no idea that man hit me so hard. As I inspect my face, I notice bruises on my wrists and arms—I guess from when those other guys grabbed me.

A shiver runs through me as I remember what happened. After taking a shower and brushing my teeth, I leave the bathroom in my underwear, toweling my hair.

"Pokémon panties?"

I scream at the sight of Ares sitting on my bed. There's a bag of take-out food and two coffees on the nightstand. I cover myself with the towel.

"I thought you left."

He smiles. "I just went for breakfast. How are you feeling?"

"I'm fine, and thank you, that's very kind of you."

And kindness is not your thing, I think.

"Get dressed and have something to eat. Unless you want to do it this way? Without clothes. I wouldn't complain."

I gave him a murderous look. "Very funny, I'll be right back."

After getting dressed, I start on breakfast, trying to ignore the beautiful creature in front of me so I can eat.

Ares takes a sip of his coffee. "I have to say it. I won't be able to live in peace if I don't say it."

"What?"

"Pokémon? Really? I didn't even know Pokémon underwear existed."

"It's my underwear; no one is supposed to see it."

"I've seen it." His eyes catch mine. "I've touched it too."

I almost choke on my breakfast. "Ares . . ."

"What?" He looks at me playfully. "Oh, you're remembering that, aren't you?"

"Of course not."

"Then why are you blushing?"

"It's hot."

He smiles mischievously but says nothing. I finish eating and take a sip of coffee, keeping my eyes anywhere but on him, even though I can feel his gaze on me. It's making me nervous and hyper-aware of how I'm dressed, and every detail about me that he can see and disapprove of, like my wet, tousled hair.

Ares sighs. "What happened last night?"

I look up, and I feel like I can tell him everything. Why do I trust him after he broke my heart? I'll never understand.

I run a hand through my hair. "I decided to take a shortcut."

Ares gives me a disapproving look.

"What? I was tired, and I thought nothing would happen."

"The shorter, darker roads are not somewhere you should be at that time of the night."

"Now I know. Well, I walked under the bridge, and three men were there."

Do you want something, pretty girl?

I clench my hands in my lap. "They took my phone from me, and one of them . . ."

It's going to go real bad for you, pretty girl. The man's words haunt me.

Ares puts his hand on mine. "You're safe now."

I take a deep breath. "Two went away and left me with the third one. He dragged me into the dark and told me not to scream, but I did and so he hit me. The man who called you heard me, and then the other guy ran away."

"Did he do anything to you?" Ares's eyes have a flash of anger that surprises me. "Did he touch you?"

I shake my head. "No, thank God."

"It's okay." He squeezes my hand, and his palms are soft. "You'll be fine." He smiles at me, and for the first time it's not a smug or mischievous smile. It's a genuine smile, one that he hasn't shown me before.

Ares Hidalgo looks so honestly grateful that I'm okay that I feel the stupid urge to kiss him.

It's at this moment that I realize that he and I have never kissed even though we've done intimate things together. *Why have you never kissed me?* I want to ask him, but I don't have the courage, not now. Besides, what would I gain by asking him that? Especially if being with him is out of the equation.

He has been sweet and kind. He behaved like a gentleman, but that doesn't mean that his way of seeing things has changed, nor mine. Ares strokes the back of my hand with his thumb, tracing circles, and I feel the need to thank him. "Thank you, really. You didn't have to do all this. Thank you very much, Ares."

"I'm at your service, always, Witch."

Always . . .

That makes my stomach flutter and my heart beat faster. He reaches over and takes my chin.

"What are you doing?"

He assesses the bruised side of my face. "I don't think you need to take anything, but if you're in pain, you could take an analgesic. You should be fine."

"Are you a doctor now?"

Ares gives a small laugh. "Not yet."

"Not yet?"

"I want to study medicine when I finish high school."

That surprises me. "Really?"

"Why so surprised?"

"I thought you'd study business or law like your father and brother."

"To work for my father's company?"

"I never imagined you as a doctor."

You would be a beautiful doctor, though.

"That's what everyone thinks." He grimaces. "I'm sure my parents and Artemis think the same thing."

"They don't know that you want to study medicine?"

"No, you're the first person I've told."

"Why? Why me?" The question leaves my mouth before I can stop it.

Ares looks away. "I don't know."

I bite my tongue so as not to ask him any more questions.

He stands up. "I should go, I promised Apolo I would take him to the animal shelter."

"To the animal shelter?"

"You ask a lot of questions, Raquel." He doesn't say it in a bad way. "Apolo fosters puppies when Mom is in a good mood and lets him. If it were up to him, we would be overrun with dozens of dogs."

Ah, that explains the different doggies I sometimes see in the backyard.

"Apolo is a really sweet boy."

Ares becomes serious. "Yes, he is."

"Could you give him my regards?"

"Do you miss sleeping with him?"

And here we go, mischievous Ares is back.

"Ares, I'm going to forget you said that because you've been good so far."

Go away, before you ruin the moment, Greek God.

Ares starts to say something but stops. He finally says, "Well, I hope you feel better soon. If you need anything, let me know."

"I'll be fine."

I don't have a phone to let you know.

I want to say it, but I don't want to sound needy. Maybe he's just saying that to be nice and he doesn't really expect me to "let him know" about anything.

Before I can say answer, Ares climbs out my window.

>> <<

Dani doesn't blink, doesn't move, doesn't speak.

I'm not even sure if she's breathing until she starts asking me what happened and if I'm okay, saying that I need to file a report, and reproaching me when I tell her no. She says the same thing that my mom said when I told her: that if I don't, those men could attack another girl.

I don't want anyone else to go through what I went through.

So, with Dani and my mom's support, I decide to go to the police station. I make sure to mention the bridge in hopes that they will be there again, and that the police will find them before they find other victims. Afterward, Mom drops us off at Dani's house because she's on duty at the hospital and doesn't want to leave me home alone tonight.

In the comfort of Dani's room, I tell her everything that happened with Ares. It takes her a few minutes to take it all in. For her, I jumped from stalking Ares from the shadows to fighting with him over Wi-Fi to suddenly doing things with him. I blush as I remember what we've done. We are sitting on her bed, cross-legged in our pajamas, with a bowl of popcorn between us.

"Breathe, Dani."

She takes a breath, letting out a big breath of air, and adjusts her black hair behind her ears. "I must admit that I'm impressed."

"Impressed?"

"Yes, you put him in his place when it was required. You're brave. I'm really proud of you."

"It's no big deal."

"Of course it is. I never thought you'd have anything to do with him, let alone put him in his place. Bravo!" She raises her hand and gives me five.

I give her five insecurely. "It wasn't easy, Dani. You know how much I like him."

"I know it wasn't easy. That's why I'm congratulating you, silly."

I grab a fistful of popcorn. "Sometimes I can't believe I ever had anything with him. He's always been so out of my league." I pop as much popcorn as I can into my mouth.

"I can't believe it either," she jokes. "Who knew? Life is unpredictable." Dani eats her popcorn more slowly.

"Although I think he's still out of my league. He's not interested in me for anything serious; he just wants to have fun. I don't even know if he likes me."

Dani clicks her tongue. "He must like you. He's physically attracted to you, yes, but no one gets involved with someone they don't like, that wouldn't make sense."

"But he told me, with his stupid, beautiful face: 'Because you like me, but I don't like you,'" I repeat bitterly, trying to imitate his voice.

"If he didn't like you, he wouldn't have tried anything with you. Nothing."

"Stop, Dani."

"Stop what?"

"Don't say things like that, you'll make me get my hopes up about him again."

Dani puts two fingers together and slides them across her mouth like a zipper. "Well, I'll shut up, then."

I throw popcorn at her. "Don't be angry."

She makes signs with her hands as if she can't speak.

"Are you serious, Dani?" I throw a piece of popcorn at her, and she catches it and eats it, but she still doesn't reply. "Dani . . . *Dani*, talk to me."

She puts her arms across her chest. "I'm just telling you the truth and that bothers you. Ares is hot. He's got money. He's smart, and he can have any girl at his feet. And, even so, you're telling me that he would be with someone he doesn't even like? So, maybe he doesn't want anything serious, but he *does* like you, Raquel."

"Okay!"

Dani puts her hair over her shoulder with a smug grin. "Now let's go to sleep. The last thing we want is to be tired on the first day of school. It's our last year, we have to make an impact."

"We're always the same. We live in a small town, Dani."

"You love to take the fun out of life." Dani gets up and puts the popcorn bowl on the floor.

We settle into the bed and get under the covers. Turning off the lamp on the bedside table, we both sigh. After a brief silence, Ares's beautiful, genuine smile invades my mind.

"Stop thinking about him, Raquel," Dani says knowingly.

"No one has ever made me feel this way."

"I know."

"And it hurts. It hurts that he doesn't want to take me seriously. It makes me feel like I'm not good enough."

"But you are. Don't let him make you doubt that. You were right to push him away, Raquel. It would have been much more painful later on."

I take a lock of my hair and start playing with it. Dani rolls over, and we lie there, facing each other. "Dani, I like him a lot."

"You don't have to say it, I know you."

"The way I feel about him makes me want to cling to any shred of hope."

"Don't complicate your life by thinking so much. If he doesn't know how to value you, someone else will come along who will."

"Do you really think so? It sounds so impossible to find some-one like Ares."

"Maybe not someone like him, but someone who makes you feel like he does."

I doubt it so much. "Well, it's time to sleep."

"Good night, shorty."

She has always called me that because she's taller than me.

"Good night, crazy girl."

FIFTEEN
The Gift

My first day as a senior in high school begins with bright sunshine and fresh breezes. I rub my eyes as I shuffle inside the building, and I realize it's going to be hard getting used to waking up early every day again. I already miss summer vacation, and it's only day one.

I make my way through the sea of students in the main hallway and run into Apolo, who is standing next to a locker. "Apolo! What are you doing here?"

"Hey, Raquel." He smiles at me. "I go here now."

"You've changed schools? Has Ares too?"

He shakes his head. "No, he'd never leave that school. He loves his soccer team too much."

I try not to let my disappointment show.

"Oh. Well that's great you're here. I—"

A scream echoes down the hallway, interrupting us.

"Raquel, queen of my heart!"

I turn to see Carlos, my long-standing admirer, and I smile in spite of myself. It all started the day I defended him from some boys who were bullying him in the fourth grade. Since then, he has sworn eternal love to me almost every day. I only see him as a friend, and even though I've made that clear to him, he doesn't seem to understand.

"Hi, Carlos." I wave. I still like him. Even if he's a little crazy, he's fun.

"My beautiful princess." He takes my hand and kisses it dramatically. "This has been the longest and most agonizing summer for me."

Apolo looks at us with a what-the-fuck-is-going-on face but says nothing.

Carlos turns to him. "And who are you?"

"This is Apolo. He's new," I answer, freeing my hand. "Apolo, this is Carlos, he is . . ."

"Her future husband and father of her four children," Carlos says quickly.

I hit the back of his head. "I told you to stop saying things like that! People sometimes believe it."

"Haven't you heard that if you tell a lie enough times it becomes true?"

Apolo chuckles. "Wow, you have a very dedicated admirer."

We share a laugh before heading off to our classes.

>> <<

The first day of school ends as quickly as it began. I can't believe I'm already in my senior year. Going to college is something that terrifies me but at the same time excites me so much. I rush home to feed Rocky, who won't eat, and then I take my clothes off and throw them in the laundry. My old habits make me want to go and look out my window, because this is the time when Ares comes home from school. I used to watch him walking around his room.

No more, Raquel.

I look at my bed and notice a small white box on it. When I reach over and pick it up, a note falls out. My eyes widen as I see that it's the box for the newest iPhone. I quickly check the note.

So you don't walk around without a phone. Take it as consolation for everything you had to go through that night.

Don't even think about giving it back to me.

Ares

I laugh so loudly that Rocky looks at me quizzically. "Are you crazy, Greek God?" I ask aloud. "You're completely crazy!"

There's no way I can accept this cell phone; it's too expensive. Money is definitely not an issue for Ares, but how the hell did he get into my room with Rocky here? I look at the dog, remembering that he didn't want to eat when I came in, and I realize his belly is fat and full.

"Oh no. Rocky. Traitor!"

Rocky puts his head down as if admitting his guilt.

I have to give this phone back, so I put on some jeans and a T-shirt and head out. I go around the block so I can get to the Hidalgos' front door, because there's no way I'm going in from the back. I don't want to be mistaken for a burglar and get shot or whatever.

In front of the house, my courage dwindles. It's a three-story house with Victorian windows and a garden with a fountain at the entrance. It's as intimidating as him. Regaining my nerve, I ring the doorbell.

A pretty girl with red hair opens the door. If it weren't for her uniform, I would have thought she was part of the family. "Good evening, can I help you?"

"Hey. Is Ares here?"

"Yes, who's asking?"

"Raquel."

"All right, Raquel, for security reasons I can't let you in until he tells me. Will you wait for me for a second while I look for him?"

"Of course."

She closes the door, and I play with the box in my hands. I don't think it was a good idea to come here. If Ares tells her he doesn't want to see me, she'll probably slam the door in my face.

A few minutes later, the girl reappears. "You can go in now. He's waiting for you in the playroom."

Playroom?

Ares's house is stupidly luxurious inside, and I'm not at all surprised. She leads me through the living room into a long hallway and stops. "It's the third door on the right."

"Thank you."

I don't know why I'm suddenly so nervous. I'm going to see Ares. I feel like it's been so long, but it's really only been a few days.

Just give him back the phone, Raquel. Walk in, give him the phone, and walk out. Simple. Easy.

I knock on the door and hear him shout, "Come in!"

I open the door and peek inside. It's an ordinary playroom with a pool table, a huge TV with different consoles underneath it, and plush furniture. Ares is sitting on a couch in front of the TV with a controller for what looks like a PlayStation 4 in his hands, playing something with a lot of shooting. He's shirtless with only his school uniform pants on. His hair is messy from the headphones he's wearing, and he's biting his lip as he plays.

Why the hell do you have to be so hot, Ares? I've forgotten why I'm here. I clear my throat, uncomfortable.

"Guys, I'll be right back," Ares says into the microphone connected to his headset. "I know, I know, I have a guest." He exits the game and takes off his headphones. His eyes meet mine. "Let me guess. You came to return the phone?"

He stands up, which makes me feel small, as usual. Why does he have to be shirtless? That's not how you greet a visitor.

I find my voice. "Yes. I appreciate the gesture, but it's too much."

"It's a gift, and it's rude to refuse a gift."

"It's not my birthday or Christmas, so there's no reason for a gift." I hold out the box to him.

"Do you only receive gifts on your birthday and Christmas?"

Yes, and sometimes not even on those dates.

"Just take it."

Ares just looks at me, and it makes me want to run away. "Raquel, you had a horrible experience that night and lost something you worked hard to get."

"How do you know that?"

"I'm not an idiot. I'm guessing that with your mother's salary and the bills she has to pay, she could never have bought the phone you had. I know you bought it yourself with your money, with your hard work. I'm sorry I couldn't stop them from taking it away from you, but I can give you another one. Let me give it to you. Don't be proud."

"You are so . . . difficult to understand."

"So I've been told."

"No, I'm serious. You tell me you don't want anything to do with me, but then you go and do nice things like this. What are you playing at, Ares?"

"I'm not playing games. I'm just being nice."

"Why? Why are you being nice to me?"

"I don't know."

"You never know anything."

"And you always want to know everything." His blue eyes stare intensely at me as he approaches.

"I'm beginning to think you like to confuse me."

Ares gives me that smirk that suits him so well. "You confuse yourself. I've always been clear with you."

"Yes, very clear, Mr. Kindness."

"What's wrong with being kind?"

"That doesn't help me forget you."

Ares shrugs his shoulders. "That's not my problem."

A wave of rage runs through me. "And here comes the moody Ares."

Ares furrows his brows. "What did you call me?"

"Moody. Your mood swings are too constant."

"As creative as ever." Sarcasm flows through his tone. "It's not my fault that you like to give meaning to everything."

"Everything's always my fault, isn't it?"

"God, why are you so dramatic?"

The rage continues to grow inside me. "If I'm such a bother to you, then why don't you leave me alone?"

Ares raises his voice. "You called me! You looked for me!"

"Because I didn't know another number!" A flash of what looks like disappointment crosses his face, but I'm too upset to care. "Do you think I would have called you if I'd had a choice?"

He clenches his fists at his sides, and, before he can say anything, I throw the phone box at him. He catches it in midair.

"Just take your stupid phone and leave me alone."

Ares throws the box on the cabinet and takes long strides toward me. "You are so ungrateful! Your mother didn't teach you any manners."

I push his bare chest. "And you're an idiot!"

Ares takes my arm. "You're crazy!"

I slap his arm to free myself. "Unstable!" I turn my back and lunge at the doorknob, but he grabs my arm again, making me face him. "Let me go! Let me go!"

His soft lips press close to mine.

And there, in his playroom, Ares Hidalgo kisses me.

SIXTEEN
The Kiss

I would like to say that I didn't kiss him back, or that I pushed him away and ran from him. But the moment his soft lips touch mine, I lose all sense of time, place, space. I lose all rationality.

I kiss him back instantly. His kiss is not gentle or romantic; it is demanding, passionate, and possessive. He kisses me as if he wants to devour me, and it feels incredible. He takes my face in his hands, deepening the kiss. Our lips move in sync, his tongue tempting and brushing. Our breaths quicken, and I feel like I could pass out at any moment from the intensity of this kiss.

I melt in his arms.

I never thought anyone could make me feel this way. My whole body is electrified, blood rushing quickly through my veins. Ares presses my body against his, stealing a small moan from me that gets caught in his mouth. His lips move aggressively against mine, his tongue invading my mouth, sending shivers of pleasure throughout my body.

Ares lifts me up, and I immediately wrap my legs around his waist. I gasp as I feel how hard he is against me. He doesn't stop kissing me for a single second as he carries me over to the couch.

He slowly lays me down and climbs on top of me. I run my hands over his defined chest and down his abdomen, feeling every muscle. He's so fucking sexy. He slips his hand under my shirt to touch my breasts and a moan of appreciation escapes me. I'm too turned on to think of anything. I just want to feel him, all of him, against me.

Ares moves away, kneeling between my legs, and unbuttons my pants with impressive agility. Seeing him like this in front of me—his blue eyes shining with desire, undressing me—takes my breath away. I feel surprisingly comfortable with him as he removes my pants, tossing them aside, and returns his mouth to mine.

He runs his hands down my bare legs and moans. "You're driving me crazy."

I bite his lower lip in response. I want him like I've never wanted anyone before in my life. My rational side goes on vacation and hormones take over. Desperately, I grab the button of his pants to take them off. He stands up and lets his pants fall to the floor along with his underwear.

God, he's naked and his body is perfect. Every muscle, every tattoo . . . everything about him is perfect. His lips are swollen from kissing, and I imagine mine must be the same. He hovers over me again, kissing me leisurely, wet kisses full of passion and desire that bring me to the edge. His hand travels inside my panties, and he moans again into my mouth. It's the most exciting sound in the world.

"I love how wet you are for me."

I can feel how hard he is against my thigh and I'm dying to feel him somewhere else. His fingers find that nerve-filled spot and caress it in circles. I arch my back, panting.

"Oh God, Ares! Please." I want him, that's all my mind can think of. I need more.

As if reading my mind, Ares lifts my shirt, freeing my breasts, attacking them with his tongue, massaging them with his free hand. This is too much.

Wanting more, I take him in my hand, and, for a second, it scares me how big he is, but my desire overwhelms my fear. "Ares, please." I don't even know what I'm asking for.

Ares raises himself just an inch from me, his eyes piercing mine, his fingers still moving inside my panties. "Do you want me to fuck you?" I can only nod, and he licks my lower lip. "Do you want to feel me inside you? Say it."

I bite my lower lip as his fingers drive me insane. "Yes . . . please . . . I want to feel you inside me."

He leans back and reaches for something in his pants, and I watch him pull out a condom and roll it on.

Oh God, I'm really going to do this. I'm going to lose my virginity to Ares Hidalgo.

In seconds, he's on top of me, in between my legs, and a wave of fear sweeps through me, but he kisses me passionately, taking it away, and making me forget everything. He positions himself and leans back from me, looking into my eyes.

"Are you sure?"

I lick my lips nervously. "Yes."

Ares kisses me and I close my eyes, losing myself in his soft, rich lips. But then I feel him slowly penetrate me. I moan in pain and tears fill my eyes. "Ares, it hurts."

He leaves short kisses all over my face. "I know. It's okay; it'll pass."

He sinks into me a little further and I arch my back. I feel something inside me break and then he fills me completely. Tears roll down the sides of my face.

"Kiss me," he says.

He's inside me, but he doesn't move. His kisses are wet, passionate, while his hands touch my breasts gently, distracting me, bringing excitement back to my aching body.

He doesn't hurry to move, he only focuses on exciting me even more, tempting, kissing, biting my lips, my neck, my breasts. The pain is still there, but it's lessening and only the burning discomfort of something that has broken remains. I need more, I need something, and I need him to move. I am so ready for him to move.

"Ares," I gasp.

As if he knows what I want, he starts to move slowly. The friction burns a little, but I'm so wet that it starts to feel delicious. Oh God, the sensation overcomes me, I've never felt so good in my entire life.

Suddenly I want him to go faster, deeper. I put my hands around his neck and kiss him with everything I have, moaning and feeling him perfectly hard inside me. "Ares! Oh God, Ares, faster."

Ares smiles at my lips. "You want it faster, huh? Do you like it?"

He thrusts into me deeply before he starts moving faster.

"Oh my God!"

"Raquel," he murmurs in my ear as I cling to his back. "Do you like feeling me like this, all inside you?"

"Yes!" I can feel the orgasm coming and I moan so loudly that Ares kisses me to silence it. Suddenly, my body explodes, wave after wave of pleasure invading every part of me.

Ares moans with me and his movements become clumsy and even faster. He comes and falls on top of me. Our quickened breathing echoes throughout the room. Our heartbeats can be clearly felt through our glued chests. As the last traces of orgasm leave me, clarity returns.

Oh my God! I just had sex with Ares. I just lost my virginity.

Ares uses his hands to hoist himself up and gives me a short kiss, pulling out of me. It burns a little, but it's nothing I can't handle. I see traces of blood on the condom, and I look away, sitting up. He takes the condom and throws it in the trash and then puts on his pants and hands me my clothes. He sits on the arm of the couch and just looks at me without speaking. He doesn't talk to me, doesn't say nice things to me, doesn't even hug me . . . nothing. It's like he's impatient for me to leave.

The silence is too uncomfortable, so I get dressed as quickly as I can. I stand up and wince.

"Are you okay?"

I nod my head. Ares's eyes land on the couch behind me and I follow his gaze. There's a small but noticeable bloodstain. Ares seems to pick up on my embarrassment.

"Don't worry, I'll have it washed."

I twist my hands in front of me. "I-I should go."

He doesn't object; he doesn't say "don't go" or "why are you leaving?" He doesn't say anything at all, so I start walking toward the door. My heart is in my throat, and I feel like crying, but I won't let the tears form in my eyes. I grab the doorknob, and he suddenly speaks.

"Wait!"

Hope kindles in me, but it shatters right away when I see him walking toward me with the phone box in his hand.

"Please accept it."

And that gesture makes me feel even worse, like he's paying me back for what just happened. Unruly tears fill my eyes, and I can't speak. I open the door and hurry out.

"Raquel! Hey! Don't go like that! Raquel!" I hear him shouting behind me.

Before I know it, I'm running to the exit. I bump into the red-headed girl again, but I ignore her and continue on my way.

Out on the street, tears run down my cheeks. I know I'm responsible for what just happened. He didn't make me do it, but that doesn't make me feel any better.

I always thought that my first time would be magical, a special moment, that the guy I was with would value and appreciate it, that he would at least have feelings for me. The sex was wonderful and increased my feelings for Ares, but this meant nothing to him. It was just sex.

And he warned me, he told me clearly what he wanted, but I was stupid and gave him what was most precious to me. I keep running until my lungs burn. When I get home, I throw myself on my bed and cry inconsolably.

SEVENTEEN
The Message

"Nutella?"

"No."

"Strawberries with cream?"

I shake my head. "No."

"Ice cream?"

"No."

"I know, how about all of them? Ice cream, strawberries, and Nutella?"

I just shake my head again, and Yoshi adjusts his glasses.

"I give up."

We're alone in an empty classroom. The last class just ended, and Yoshi is trying to cheer me up. It's Friday, and I've spent the week dragging myself around school. I haven't had the courage to tell anyone what happened, not even Dani. I'm so disappointed in myself. I don't think I'm capable of talking about it yet.

"Come on, Rochi. Whatever happened, don't let it bring you down. Fight," he advises me, caressing my cheek.

"I don't want to."

"Let's go get some ice cream. Give it a try, okay?" His pretty eyes plead with me from behind his glasses, and I can't say no to him. He's right. I can't do anything to turn back time.

Yoshi extends his hand to me. "Shall we go?"

I smile at him and take his hand. "Let's go."

We buy ice cream and sit in the town square. It's a beautiful day. Even though it's after four o'clock, the sun is still shining as if it were noon.

"Remember when we used to come here every afternoon after elementary school?" Yoshi asks.

I smile at the memory. "Yeah, we became friends with the lady who sold candy."

"And she gave us free ones."

I laugh, remembering our cheeks filled with sweets. Yoshi laughs with me.

"That's the way I like it. You look prettier smiling."

I raise an eyebrow. "Are you admitting that I'm pretty?"

"More or less, maybe with a few drinks in me I would try to win you over."

"Only with a few drinks? Nah!"

"What about Dani? I haven't seen her at school," he says as he eats a spoonful of ice cream.

"That's because she's missed two days. She's helping her mother with a project at the agency."

Dani's mom runs a very prestigious modeling agency. She's a total badass. She started her own business when Dani was a kid, and it has only grown since. Now her modeling agency is one of the most important in the state. Dani's dad on the other hand is more of a relaxed and go-with-the-flow type. He's a college professor in the art department at a nearby community college. I feel like Dani got a good combination of both her parents' personalities. She's fierce like her mom, but also empathetic and relaxed like her father.

Yoshi shakes his head. "It's the first week of school, and she's already missing classes, typical Dani."

"It's good that she's smart and can catch up superfast."

"Yeah."

Licking my ice cream, I notice Yoshi staring at me as if waiting for something.

"Rochi, you know you can trust me?" he asks, and I know where this is going. "You don't have to deal with things alone."

I exhale sadly. "I know, it's just . . . I'm so disappointed in myself, and I don't want to disappoint anyone else."

"You could never disappoint me."

"Don't be so sure."

His eyes look at me expectantly. "Trust me. Maybe talking about it will help you feel a little better."

There's no easy way to say it, so I just say it, straight out. "I lost my virginity."

"*What*?" Yoshi almost spits his ice cream in my face. "You're kidding, right?"

I tighten my lips. "No."

"How? When? With who? Shit, Raquel!" Indecipherable expressions cross his face. He gets up and throws his ice cream aside. "Shit!"

People are starting to stare, so I get up and try to calm him down. "Yoshi, it's okay."

"With who?" His face is red, the veins visible in his neck and forehead. "You don't even have a boyfriend. Tell me who it was!"

"Keep your voice down!"

Yoshi grabs his head and turns his back on me to kick a trash can. Okay, that wasn't the reaction I was expecting.

"Yoshi, you're overreacting. Calm down."

He runs a hand over his face and turns to me. "Tell me who he is, so I can beat the hell out of him."

"This is not the time to act like the jealous, overprotective big brother."

He laughs sarcastically. "Big brother? You think this is the reaction of a *big brother*? You're so fucking blind."

"What the hell is wrong with you?"

He looks at me and a thousand things seem to be going through his mind. "You're blind," he says in a whisper. "I need to get some air. I'll see you around."

And he's gone, just like that, leaving me speechless. Melted ice cream rolls down the waffle cone in my hand and drips to the ground. What the fuck just happened?

Tired and confused, I head home.

>> <<

It's Saturday, and it's my turn to clean.

Grumbling, I refer to the to-do list my mother gave me. I've almost done everything, only my room is left, so I turn on my computer and play music to motivate me to tidy up. I open my Facebook and leave it open because, now that I don't have a phone, it's become my only means of communication.

I'm listening to "The Heart Wants What It Wants" by Selena Gomez while I tidy up my mess. I pick up the air conditioner control and use it as a microphone to sing the words. Rocky turns his head to the side, and I kneel in front of him, singing to him.

"You're crazy!" my mother shouts from the door. "That's why it takes you so long to clean up! You have the poor dog traumatized."

"You always ruin my inspiration," I mutter, getting up. "Rocky is delighted with my voice."

"Hurry up and get your dirty clothes and bring them to me, I'm going to do the laundry today," she orders, before leaving.

Pouting, I look at Rocky. "She still doesn't recognize my talent."

"Raquel!" Mom yells at me from the stairs.

"I'm coming!"

After I bring her my clothes and finish with my room, I sit down in front of the computer. I go to my Facebook messages, and I'm surprised to find a message from Dani and one from Ares. He and I aren't friends on Facebook, but I know he can still message me. My stupid heart races and my stomach fills with butterflies. I can't believe he still has that effect on me despite what happened.

I open his message, nervous.

Ares: Witch.

Really? Who says hello like that? Just him. Curious to know what he has to say, I answer curtly.

Me: What?

He takes a while, and I get more and more anxious.

Ares: Stop by my house when you can.

So he can use me again? No, thank you, I want to write back, but I don't want to give him the pleasure of knowing how bad he made me feel.

Me: You're crazy. Why would I do that?

Ares: You left something here.

Me: I told you I don't want the phone.

Ares sends a photo.

When I open it, it's a picture of his hand holding the silver chain my mom gave me when I was nine years old. It has a pendant with my name on it. Instinctively, my hand goes up to my neck to confirm that I don't have it. I have never taken it off. How did I not realize that I didn't have it? Maybe I was too busy with my postdeflowering spite.

The thought of seeing Ares fills me with both rage and excitement. That jerk has spread his instability to me. Regaining a bit of my dignity, I type a reply.

Me: You can send it to school with Apolo on Monday.

Ares: Are you afraid to see me?

Me: I don't want to see you.

Ares: Liar.

Me: Think what you want.

Ares: Why are you angry?

Me: And you dare to ask. Just send it with Apolo and leave me alone.

Ares: I don't understand your anger, we both know how much you liked it. I remember your moans clearly.

I blush and look away. I feel stupid because he can't see me.

Me: Ares, I don't want to talk to you.

Ares: You're going to be mine again, Witch.

A sinful shiver runs through me. *No, no, Raquel, don't fall.* I don't answer him and leave him on seen. He writes again.

Ares: If you want your chain, come and get it. I'm not going to send it via anyone. I'll wait for you here, bye.

I growl in frustration. If Mom finds out I lost that necklace, she'll kill me. After showering and putting on a casual floral print summer dress, I go to rescue my chain. I have my strategy laid out so I won't fall for his games. I won't even go into his house. I'll wait for him to bring the chain outside.

Project Chain Rescue Without Losing My Dignity Along the Way: activated.

EIGHTEEN
The Party

I can't believe I'm back at the Hidalgos', and it hasn't even been a week. In my defense, if Mom finds out that I don't have the chain, she'll be so upset with me that she will force me to watch all the nighttime soap operas with her. Pure torture, I know.

Taking a deep breath, I ring the doorbell. The red-haired girl opens the door, looking a little agitated.

"Good afternoon," she says, adjusting the skirt of her uniform.

"Is Ares here?"

"Yes, of course." She steps aside and gestures for me to follow. "The party is in the back by the pool, come in."

Party?

She guides me through the hallway until we reach the pool, which is inside the house. I can see steam rising off the blue water—it must be heated—and the pool lights make the water glow in a cool way. There are more lights and torches all around the room, giving it a tropical, beachy vibe. I guess this is what you get to enjoy when you're rich.

As soon as I set foot in there, everyone's eyes turn to me, and I feel superuncomfortable. I look around for Ares. He's in the pool with a girl on his shoulders facing another couple in the same position. They're having a water fight. I can't help feeling jealous of the girl with Ares. She's very pretty and has a dazzling smile. Ares turns to see what everyone is looking at, and our eyes meet. He doesn't look surprised. He looks pleased.

He looks so good all wet. *No, focus, Raquel.* Ares continues his game as if nothing happened. I stand there awkwardly until Apolo walks up to greet me.

"Welcome," he says with a smile. "These are all Ares's classmates, but I know them too." He takes me over to a group of three boys, and I recognize one of them as the guy I bumped into when I was spying on Ares at soccer practice.

"Raquel, this is Marco, Gregory, and Luis," Apolo introduces them, pointing at each boy respectively.

"Ha! Pay me!" says Luis, the blond one. "I told you someone from Apolo's new school would come."

Gregory grunts. "Oh, I can't believe it." He takes a few bills out of his pocket and passes them to Luis.

Marco, the dark-haired boy from practice, says nothing, just glancing at me by way of greeting.

Apolo grimaces. "Your bets suck. I'll be right back, Raquel, make yourself comfortable."

Gregory points at me with his finger. "I would welcome you, but you just made me lose money."

"Don't be a sore loser," Luis says to Gregory while giving me a smile. "Welcome, Raquel, have a seat."

I can't deny that they're very attractive. I would never have imagined sitting with guys like them in my life. But they don't seem to be too obnoxious so far. My eyes wander to the pool as the girl on Ares's shoulders falls into the water, pulling Ares down with her. They emerge from the water, smiling at each other, and she gives him a quick kiss on the cheek.

Ouch!

I can almost hear my heart breaking.

And, for once, I find myself at a crossroads.

I have always said that life is about choices, good and bad, and I've made both. In front of me, I have two:

1. Turn around and walk away with my head down.

2. Stay, get my necklace back, and maybe have a good time with Ares's friends. Show him that I'm okay and that I don't care about him.

And if he can act like nothing has happened, then so can I. I need to regain my dignity; I need to do something to stop feeling like a lovesick girl. So I swallow my heart and, with a big smile, sit down next to Marco, the one who hasn't spoken so far.

"Do you want a beer?" Luis asks me, and I nod, thanking him when he passes it to me.

Gregory raises his bottle. "Let's drink to the fact that the only friend Apolo has made at school is pretty."

Luis raises his. "Yeah, I have to say I am impressed."

Blushing, I clink my bottle with theirs. The two boys look at Marco, but he doesn't move an inch. Luis looks away.

"Let's drink without him. He's grumpy like Ares. No wonder they're best friends," says Gregory.

We toast and continue drinking. When Marco stands up, he's

almost as tall as Ares, and he's shirtless. My eyes have no shame and travel down his chest to his abdomen. The Virgin of Abdominals has been very generous to these guys. My eyes follow his movements as he dives into the pool.

"He's hot, isn't he?" Luis asks playfully.

Fun and daring Raquel surfaces. "Yeah, he's pretty hot."

"Oh, I like her." Gregory gives me five. "She's honest."

I raise my beer to them with a smirk. We talk a bit, and I realize that they're not the pretentious guys I thought they might be, nor do they think they're superior to anyone else. They're very polite. Luis is a fun guy who makes something crazy out of everything and makes you laugh, while Gregory is more into telling interesting stories.

And for a moment, while talking with them, I completely forget about Ares. They make me realize that there are more men in the world and it's possible to get over him. Yes, there could be a guy out there for me who is cuter than he is, with a better heart. I don't have to get stuck with that stupid, sexy Greek god.

I don't even bother to look around to see where he is or what he's doing. Someone puts on a song that I really like, and I get up from my chair, dancing. Luis and Gregory follow my lead, dancing and throwing their hands in the air on the spot. Gregory slips and almost falls, and we crack up. We laugh so hard that everyone looks at us. I notice that people are staring, but I don't pay attention to them. I have to admit that the alcohol is having an effect. I feel freer and more confident when we sit down again.

"Confession time, Raquel," Luis starts in, amused.

Marco returns to the table, his wet hair dripping on his face and lap, and takes a long sip of his beer.

Luis ignores him and continues. "Do you have a boyfriend?"

A chuckle leaves my lips. "Nope."

Gregory wiggles his eyebrows. "Would you like to have one?"

"Ohhhh." Luis snorts. "Apparently you have an admirer."

"Flirting so soon, Gregory?" I tease.

Marco clears his throat and we all look at him. When he speaks, his expression is serious. "Don't waste your time. She's with Ares."

My jaw drops. *What?*

Gregory pouts. "Ugh! It's so unfair."

Offended, I look Marco straight in the eye. "I'm not with any-one. I have nothing to do with him."

"Of course," he replies, sarcasm evident in his tone.

"What is your problem? Why do you hate me if you don't even know me?"

"I don't have a problem with you, I'm just warning the guys."

"You have nothing to warn them about. There is nothing between Ares and me."

Luis intervenes. "The girl said so, Marco, and I believe her."

Gregory raises his beer to me. "Why don't you prove it?"

Frowning, I ask, "How?"

Gregory holds his chin, thinking. "Dance for me."

Marco laughs victoriously. "She never will."

I open my mouth to protest, and my eyes go to the pool. Ares is still in the water with the girl hanging on his back, laughing. I've been here for over an hour and he hasn't even come out to greet me. And he's got that girl attached to him.

The boys follow my gaze, and Luis groans in defeat. "It can't be. She turned to look at him. Marco is right."

I stand up, determined to prove them wrong. "No, he's not."

I take a few steps toward Gregory, and he looks at me with excitement. "Will you dance for me?"

But his expression falls when I pass by him. In front of Marco, my confidence wavers, but his gaze is full of it. It's as if he's telling me that he's sure I'm not capable of this. I ignore the protests of my embarrassed conscience and begin to move my hips in front of him. He leans back to get more comfortable, accepting the challenge.

Imagine you're dancing in front of the mirror, Raquel.

I let the music flow through me and run my hands down my body, pausing for a moment on my breasts and then going down the curve of my waist. Marco's eyes follow my movements. I remember how much power I held over Ares when I danced for him, and that gives me more strength.

I run my hands back up over my breasts as I sway to the music. Marco takes a sip of his beer without taking his eyes off me. I turn my back to him and sit on his lap, moving against him, feeling his wet body soaking the back of my dress. The friction feels so good. Pressing myself against him, I can feel how hard he is. That was fast. I lean back, almost lying on top of him to murmur in his ear.

"If I had a thing for him, I wouldn't turn his best friend on, would I?"

I get up and can feel my heart beating rapidly inside my chest. Saying the three boys are speechless is an understatement. Their faces are priceless. I'm about to turn to face Marco when Ares appears, walking toward me, looking extremely angry. It's like that night he came into my room looking for Apolo, but this time it's for very different reasons.

He stops right in front of me. "Can I talk to you for a second?"

I'm questioning whether to say no, but I don't want to make a scene in front of all these people, so I follow him into the playroom. I close the door behind me, and he pounces on me instantly, taking my face in his hands, pressing his lips to mine. My heart melts at the warm sensation of his lips, but I won't make the same mistake twice. I push him away with all the strength I have.

"Don't even think about it!"

Ares looks upset. His red face reminds me of Yoshi's reaction when I told him I had lost my virginity. *Is he jealous?*

"What the hell do you think you're doing, Raquel?"

"Whatever I'm doing is none of your damn business."

"Are you trying to make me jealous? Is that what you're playing at?" He approaches me again, and I step back.

"The world doesn't revolve around you." I shrug my shoulders. "I was just having fun."

"With my best friend?" He takes my chin between his fingers, his eyes piercing mine. "Five days after what happened in this room?"

Inevitably, I blush. "So? You were having fun with that girl in the pool."

He presses his hand on the wall next to my head. "Is that what this is about? If I do it, you do it?"

"No, and I don't even know why we're having this conversation. I don't owe you explanations. I don't owe you anything."

Ares runs his thumb across my lower lip. "Is that what you think? It's not clear to you, huh?" He slams his other hand against the wall, trapping me between his arms. "You're mine. Only mine."

His words ignite hope in me again, but I push it away. "I am not yours."

He presses me against the wall with his body, his gaze never leaving mine. "Yes, you are. The only one you can dance for in that way is me, only me. Got it?"

I shake my head defiantly.

"Why are you so stubborn? You know very well that the only one you want inside you is me, no one else."

Fighting my hormones, I push him again. I won't show him how much he affects me. He's hurt me enough.

"I'm not yours," I say with determination. "And I won't ever be, I don't like idiots like you."

Lies, lies.

Ares gives me that smirk that annoys me so much. "Oh yeah? That's not what you said that day in this exact room, remember?"

I can't believe he's bringing that up like this. I feel the need to hurt him. "The truth is, I don't remember it very well. It wasn't that good."

Ares takes a step back, the haughtiness on his face replaced by a pained expression. "Liar."

"Think what you want," I say with all the contempt I can muster. "I only came to get my necklace. Otherwise, believe me, I wouldn't be here. Give me my necklace so I can leave."

Ares stares at me with an intensity that leaves me defenseless. I don't know how I gather the strength not to throw myself into his arms. He looks so handsome: his naked torso, all wet, and his black hair stuck to the sides of his face.

He looks like a fallen angel—beautiful but capable of doing so much damage.

Ares turns around, and I struggle not to look at his ass. He reaches for something on one of the tables behind the couch and walks back to me with the necklace in his hands. "Just answer one question, and I'll give it to you."

"Whatever. Let's just get it over with."

He runs his hand through his wet hair. "Why are you so angry with me? You knew what I wanted, I never lied to you. I never tricked you to get it. So why the anger?"

I look down with my heart in my mouth. "Because I . . ." I laugh out of nervousness. "I was expecting more, I thought that . . ."

"That, if we had sex, I would like you and take you seriously?"

His blunt words hurt, but they're true, so I just give him a rueful smile. "Yeah, I'm an idiot, I know."

Ares doesn't seem surprised by my confession. "Raquel, I . . ."

"What's going on?" the redheaded girl asks as she enters the room, surprising both of us.

It's going to be a long night.

NINETEEN
The Girl

My dignity is grateful that his maid showed up and spared me this painful conversation, but my heart is dying to know what Ares was going to say before she interrupted him.

Was he going to break my heart again? Or was he going to say something else?

"Nothing is happening, Claudia," Ares answers her sharply. He hands me my necklace before leaving the room.

I smile at her as I follow him out. I shiver and blame it on my dress, because it's a little wet. Ares is leaning against the wall in the living room, his arms folded across his chest. His eyes meet mine, and I struggle to figure out his cold expression without any success. My gaze falls on Apolo, who is sitting on the couch, using his phone.

I'm about to go sit beside him when the girl who was with Ares in the pool comes out of the kitchen, carrying what looks like a sandwich. Her wet hair looks dark and her eyes are black as night. She has a delicate, pretty face, and her body is well proportioned. She's wearing a see-through beach dress with her bathing suit underneath, and she walks with confidence. She's hot, and she knows it.

Her eyes turn to Ares when she speaks. "I made you one. Chicken and ham."

"Thank you. I'm starving, and it'll take a while for the barbecue to be ready." Ares smiles at her, and just when I think my heart can't break any more, it does. They look so comfortable with each other.

The girl turns toward me and her eyebrows knit together. "Oh, hi, I didn't see you there."

Apolo introduces us. "Samy, this is Raquel, our neighbor."

Samy offers me her hand, and I take it. "Nice to meet you, Raquel."

"Likewise," I say.

She smiles. "Ready for the pool?"

"No, actually, I was just leaving."

"No, stay! I'm dying to know more about the girl who's been a neighbor to these fools all her life." She grabs me and drapes her arm over my shoulder, giving me a half hug. "I can't believe I never met you until now."

Everyone is waiting for me to respond. I can't stay here, not again. But Apolo waits anxiously for my answer, and he looks vulnerable, so I decide to stay for him.

"All right, just a little while longer."

We go back to the pool, and my eyes travel over to where Ares's friends are sitting. Ares moves next to me to whisper in my ear. "Stay away from him."

I know he's referring to Marco. "I don't have to do what you say."

"Pool time!" Samy shouts, taking off her dress. She dives into the water, splashing us all, and I take a step back. Apolo follows her lead and takes off his shirt, diving in after her.

Samy emerges from the water. "Come on, Ares! What are you waiting for?"

I stare at him like a fool, at those lips that have kissed me so deliciously, that abdomen that I touched while he was taking my innocence, that back that I clung to while feeling him inside me. *For God's sake, Raquel!* The blood flows to my face. I feel my cheeks burn and I look away.

"You're red." Ares laughs. "What are you thinking?"

"Nothing," I say quickly.

I can hear the arrogance in his voice. "Or were you remembering something?"

"Raquel!" Gregory calls to me from the table, beckoning me over.

"I'm coming!"

I only manage to take a step before Ares grabs my arm. "I told you to stay away from him."

"And I told you that I don't have to do what you say."

"I warned you."

Before I can process what he just said, Ares pulls me toward the pool with him.

"No, no, Ares! No!" I struggle wildly to get away from his grip, but he is much stronger than me. "Please! No, Ares, no!"

But it's too late. A piercing scream leaves my mouth as Ares dives in, taking me down with him. For a few seasons we're completely submerged in the water, my dress sticking to my body. Bubbles come out of my mouth as I struggle to surface. I gasp for air as I emerge from the water and instinctively wrap my arms around Ares's neck, holding onto him tightly. He holds me by the waist. Our bodies are pressed together, and our faces are only inches apart, with those deep blue eyes gazing into mine.

"Attacking me so fast?"

Despite his arrogant question, I don't let him go. My hair sticks to both sides of my face. "Swimming is not my thing."

He raises an eyebrow in surprise. "Don't you know how to swim?"

"Yes, but not very well," I admit embarrassedly. We are so close, and his lips look so inviting. "Take me to the shallow end of the pool."

"And waste the opportunity to have you pressed against me?" He smiles, showing those perfect, straight teeth of his. "No, I think I'll enjoy it a little more."

"You're a pervert."

"I'm the pervert?"

"Yes." His body emanates warmth, and his skin is so soft.

"Who's the one with the *Fifty Shades of Grey* trilogy on her computer?" My eyes widen in shock. Ares's hands are steady on my waist. "I'm not judging you, I'm just saying you're not as innocent as you like to appear, Witch."

"Reading doesn't make me a pervert."

"Are you saying that reading those sex scenes didn't turn you on?" I look away. "I . . ."

His hands go down to the outside of my thighs and he lifts my legs, encouraging me to wrap them around his waist.

"I'm sure more than once you wished someone would take you that way, hard and fast."

For God's sake, I need to get away from Ares urgently. My breathing becomes rapid and inconsistent, the water moves in small waves around us. "You're crazy."

He uses his now-free hands to remove the wet hair from my face. "And you're beautiful."

My world stops. I don't breathe. I don't move. I just lose myself in the infinity of his eyes.

"Ares! Raquel!" Samy calls from the shallow end of the pool. "It's time to play."

Ares clears his throat and starts to move over there. When we reach the shallow end, I break away from him. Before I can get close to Samy and Apolo, Ares leans over to say something in my ear. "I can be your Christian Grey anytime you want, you perverted little witch."

I freeze, and he moves toward the group as if nothing happened.

That crazy Greek god!

TWENTY
The Game

"Raquel! Raquel! Raquel!"

I never thought that the first bet I would ever make in my life would involve alcohol. Apolo, Samy, and Gregory are around me at the edge of the pool, offering me a shot of tequila. And I hesitate. The truth is that I feel a little dizzy. I've lost count of how much I've consumed so far, and that's not good. Especially since I'm in the pool.

Resigned to my fate, I take the small glass and drink it. The tequila runs down my throat, setting everything on fire on its way to my stomach. I grimace. Apolo gives me a high five. He's already had a few shots. Apparently, when he's home, his brothers are more permissive about him and alcohol.

"I'm surprised," Samy admits, smiling.

I'd like to say that she's a bad person who hits on Ares every chance she gets, who throws shade at me, or says things to make me feel like someone who doesn't belong here, but I can't. Samy has only been nice to me. Even though it's obvious that she likes Ares, I don't feel any anger toward her. Samy hasn't done anything to me.

Gregory takes his drink and coughs, taking a deep breath. "Each time feels easier and easier. It doesn't even burn my throat anymore."

"That's because you're already drunk," I say, patting him on the back.

I look at the deep end of the pool and see the stupid Greek god talking to Marco and Luis. They look very serious. Embarrassment comes over me when I remember how I danced. Are they talking about me? *Oh God!*

I splash my face and the warm water feels good against my cold skin. Small waves form as we swim and they move and crash against the back of my arms.

"We should play a game." Gregory offers, shaking his hair, spraying us all with droplets.

Apolo considers for a moment. "Something like hide-and-seek?"

Samy laughs. "No, something more fun! Like truth or dare, or never have I ever."

I frown in confusion. "Never have I ever?"

"Yeah. I'll explain the rules," she pauses, going into full explanation mode. "For example, I start and say, 'Never have I ever been drunk.' Then anyone who has been drunk before has to drink."

"What if you haven't?"

"You don't drink. It's fun because you'll learn what others have or haven't done when you see them drinking or not. The suspense is great."

"Okay, okay," says Gregory. "But do we need more people or not?"

It's just us, and Ares's group over on the other side of the pool. The others left a little while ago. I have no idea what time it is.

Gregory calls out, and the three boys swim toward us. We get out of the pool and my dress sticks to my body as I put it back on, but I've had so much to drink that I don't care anymore. We sit on the wet floor in a circle. Apolo and Gregory sit on either side of me, Samy sits next to Apolo, then Marco, Ares, and Luis fill the circle. Ares is across from me. The bottle of tequila is in the middle of the circle. Samy explains the rules again to the newcomers. We all listen to her attentively, especially Marco.

"You know, if you've done it, you have to take a drink from your glass." Samy takes some glasses and fills them full of tequila. "Take a drink if you've done it, but if you haven't, then don't drink."

Ares lets out a derisive laugh. "What kind of game is this?"

Samy gives him a dirty look. "I've already explained the rules, so just play. Any brave ones?" No one. Samy sighs. "Cowards, I'll begin," she says, taking her glass. "Never have I ever snuck out of the house."

She drinks and everyone else drinks, too, but not me. They look at me in surprise.

"What?" I say in defense. "I'm a good girl."

Apolo gives me a look. "Even I, who is younger than you, have snuck out."

Gregory pats my head. "Aw! You are a well-behaved little angel."

Ares doesn't pay attention to me; he's too busy lighting a cigarette. The smoke is coming out of his mouth while he waits for Marco to take his turn.

"Never have I ever broken someone's heart."

"Ohhh!" Luis exclaims, amused. "I think we'll all drink."

My eyes fall on Ares, and I watch sadly as he brings his glass to his lips and drinks. I know he has broken many hearts, but somehow, I feel that he's thinking of me as he drinks. Again, everyone drinks but me.

Luis grunts. "Really, Raquel? You've never broken a heart?"

Samy groans in annoyance. "At this rate we'll all end up drunk while Raquel is still sober."

"I'm being honest. I swear."

Ares fixes his eyes on me and his perfect lips form into an arrogant smile. "Don't worry, it's my turn. I'll make her drink."

Gregory gives him a high-five. "Come on, let's see, surprise us."

Ares picks up his glass and raises it to me. "Never have I ever stalked anyone."

Low blow.

Everyone looks at me, waiting for my reaction. I clench my hands at my sides and bite my bottom lip. Feeling like the odd one out in the group, I raise my glass and take a drink. Everyone watches me in silence. Angrily, my eyes meet Ares's and I see him smile. But then he does something that brings me up short. He drinks, surprising us all.

Apolo shakes his head. "We have two stalkers here. I can't believe it."

Luis pats Ares on the back. "I never thought you would be one to stalk someone. I always thought you would be the one being stalked."

Ares doesn't take his eyes off mine. "It started that way, but life takes many turns."

Samy clears her throat. "Okay, okay, next."

Luis lifts the glass. "Let's make this interesting, never have I ever given someone an orgasm with oral sex."

Heat invades my cheeks, and I know everyone is going to drink, except for me and maybe Apolo. Luis, Gregory, Marco, and a very embarrassed Samy take a drink. Agonizingly, I watch Ares.

But he doesn't drink. *Has he . . . ?*

Gregory seems to be saying out loud what we're all thinking.

"I can't believe it! Ares Hidalgo! Haven't you ever made a girl come with oral sex?"

Luis shakes his head. "You're lying."

Ares finishes his cigarette, putting it out on the ground beside him. "I've never done it." He says it so naturally, so calmly. We all look at each other.

Apolo can't control his curiosity. "Why not?"

Ares shrugs his shoulders. "I think it's something intimate and very personal."

Gregory intervenes. "And we all know that Ares is not interested in an intimate, personal relationship."

Samy lowers her head, playing with her fingers on her lap. *Did she . . . and he . . . ?* As far as I know, they're just friends. But Samy's reaction reminds me of my own. Did something happen between them? I glance at Marco, and his expression hardens, giving me such an intense look that I have to look away. *Awkward.*

It's Apolo's turn. "Let's all drink, never have I ever been drunk."

I give him a knowing smile. "Cheers!" Our glasses clink.

It's my turn, and I have no idea what to say. Everyone is waiting for me, impatient. "Never have I ever kissed anyone in this circle."

Marco raises an eyebrow, and Ares lets out a sarcastic laugh. Very carefully, I watch as Ares and Samy drink. Sadly, I drink too. So Samy has kissed Ares. The confirmation makes my heart sink. Watching Samy, I feel at a disadvantage. She really is very pretty and nice. No doubt, Ares would choose her and not me. I know I would choose her.

Gregory grimaces. "Ohh."

After three rounds of the game, we are all too drunk to play decently. We decide to jump into the shallow end of the pool. I splash water on my face and head. I'm dizzy, but I know if I stop drinking now, I can make it home.

Samy hugs me from behind. "Raquel!"

I let go of her embrace and turn around. "Samy!"

"I think we've had too much to drink," she says, and I nod. "You're very nice!"

"You too."

"I need to ask you something."

"Okay."

"When we were playing, you drank when you asked about kissing someone in the group." She pauses. "I know it's obvious, but did you kiss Ares?"

Okay, drunk or not, I'm not ready for that question.

Samy gives me a sad smile. "That silence says it all. Do you . . . do you have something with him?"

"Samy . . ."

"No, no, I'm sorry, don't answer that. I'm being intrusive."

I'm feeling uncomfortable, but at the same time, I identify with her so much. "You . . . and he . . ."

She shakes her head. "I'm just a cliché, you know, the girl who falls in love with her best friend."

"If you two have something, I would never stand in the way."

I'm being honest, I would never interfere in anyone's relationship. I may have very little dignity left, but would I be the other woman? Never.

Samy takes my hand. "He and I have nothing, so stop looking guilty."

"I'm sorry. I don't even know what I'm apologizing for."

"Ares is . . . difficult, you know, he's been through a lot." She takes a drink from her glass. "Somehow, I thought I'd be the girl who would change him. After all, I'm the only one he's ever let in, the one he's told so many things to, and revealed parts of himself he hasn't let anyone else see. But the fact that he trusts me doesn't mean he's in love with me. I understood that too late."

I can hear the pain in her voice. She's definitely not a bad person—she's just a girl who fell in love with a guy who didn't feel the same way, like me.

"I think we have something in common. A broken heart."

"He likes you, Raquel, a lot, and he probably doesn't know how to handle it because it's never happened to him before."

"I don't think so. He's made it very clear that he's not interested in me," I say.

"Ares is really complex, just like Artemis. They're boys being raised by absent parents who have always prioritized business and money over them. Tonight is a good example. Here we are having a party in their house, and they're nowhere to be found. His dad is probably on a business trip, and his mom? Having fun with other high-profile ladies in town somewhere. His parents have always made it clear to them that having feelings is a weakness. It's giving another person power over you."

"And why is Apolo different?"

"When Apolo was born, Grandpa Hidalgo moved here for a while. He was the one who raised Apolo with a lot of love and patience. He tried to instill that in the two older boys, but they were already grown up and living through things they shouldn't have been living at that age."

"Like what?"

"That's not my story to tell, sorry."

"You've told me a lot. How do you know all this?"

"I grew up with them. My mom is close friends with their mother, and she would always drop me off here when she had things to do."

"Samy! The driver is here. Let's go!" the boys shout. Gregory, Luis, and Marco are drying off beside the pool, staggering back and forth.

"I'm coming!" Samy gives me a short hug, breaks away, and smiles at me. "You're a good person, so don't think I'm mad at you or anything because of Ares, okay?" She jumps out of the pool, and I'm left in the warm water. The lights are off, but the torches around the pool are burning softly in the darkness.

I smile back. "Okay."

I watch them leave. Apolo walks behind them, mumbling something about seeing them out. I realize it's time for me to leave too. My eyes scan the pool, and I freeze when I see Ares at the other end, his arms outstretched on the edge of the pool, facing me. We're alone. And from the way he's looking at me, I know he plans to take advantage of that.

Have you ever tried to run in the water? It's freaking hard. Since when did the edge of the pool get so far away from me? Nervously, I glance back to see where Ares is, and he's gone.

Shit! He's coming from underwater! I'm being hunted!

I reach the edge and grip it tightly to lift myself out of the pool, but I'm only halfway there when strong hands grab my hips, pulling me down roughly. Ares presses me against the pool wall. I feel his hot breath brushing the back of my neck. "Are you trying to escape, Witch?"

I swallow, trying to free myself. "It's late, I have to go. I . . ."

Ares sucks on my earlobe while his hands squeeze my hips gently. "You what?"

I make the huge mistake of turning in his arms, my hormones screeching at the sight in front of me. The Greek god all wet, his soaked hair sticking to the sides of his face, his creamy skin looking flawless, and those infinite blue eyes reminding me of the sky at dawn. His lips look so kissable.

I try to think of all the damage he has done to me with his words, with his actions, but it's so hard to focus with him this close. Ares caresses the side of my face. The action puzzles me. It doesn't seem like something he would do.

"Stay with me tonight."

That surprises me, but my absent dignity finally appears and takes over. "I'm not going to be that girl you use whenever you want, Ares."

"I don't expect you to be." He sounds honest, and he seems so different, like he's tired of being an arrogant jerk.

"Then don't ask me to stay."

He gets closer, his thumb still stroking my cheek. "Just stay, we don't have to do anything, I'm not going to touch you if you don't want me to, just . . ." He sighs. "Stay with me, please."

The vulnerability in his expression disarms me. My heart and my dignity are at war.

What can I do?

TWENTY-ONE
The Game II

My reflection in the mirror gives me a disapproving look, as if judging me. I sigh.

What am I doing? Why did I decide to stay? I shouldn't be here.

But how could I say no? He asked me with those puppy eyes, a clear plea on his face. No one can judge me, not even my reflection. Having the guy you're crazy for, all wet and sexy, begging you to stay with him, is too much. The alcohol clouding my brain isn't helping either. Besides, my mom's not home, so I won't get into trouble.

I shake out my wet hair and dry it with a towel. I've already showered, abandoning my wet dress for a shirt that Ares loaned me. In his bathroom. I can't believe I'm here in the bathroom attached to his room. I feel like I'm invading his privacy. It's spotless. The white ceramic shines. I'm afraid to touch anything and ruin the tidiness.

Looking at myself in the mirror, I tug at the bottom of Ares's shirt, trying to cover myself as much as possible. Underneath I'm wearing a pair of his boxers. They're very loose, but it was either wear these or stay wet and freeze. For an instant I wonder if I can stay here, in the bathroom, but I know I can't.

Ares didn't say much after we left the pool. He let me use his bathroom, saying he would use the one down the hall. For some strange reason I know he's already back, waiting for me in his room.

You can do it, Raquel. He promised not to touch you. If you don't want him to . . .

That's the problem, I do want him to. I want to kiss him again, to feel him against me again, and I know I shouldn't. Why does knowing we shouldn't do something always make us want to do it more? Why did I say yes? Now I'm in the lion's den. Determined to get on with it, I open the bathroom door and step out.

The room is illuminated by a single small lamp. It's large and surprisingly tidy. Ares is sitting on the bed, shirtless, with his back against the headboard and a bottle of tequila in his hand. His eyes meet mine, and he smiles at me. "You look good in my shirt."

Don't smile like that! Can't you see you're melting my heart?

I smile back at him and stand there in the semidarkness, not knowing what to do.

"Are you going to stand there all night? Come." He points to a spot next to him. I hesitate, and he notices. "Are you afraid of me?"

"Of course not."

"Of course, of course, come here."

I obey him by sitting on the edge of the bed, putting as much distance as I can between us. He raises an eyebrow but says nothing.

"How about we keep playing?" He lifts the bottle, turning his body toward me.

"The pool game?" He just nods. "It's late, don't you think?"

"Are you afraid to play with me?"

"I told you, I'm not afraid of you."

"Then why are you about to fall out of the bed? You don't have to sit so far away, I made a promise, didn't I?"

Yes, you said you wouldn't touch me if I didn't want you to. The problem is that I do want you to.

"Just a precaution."

"If you say so." He sits cross-legged, and I do the same. We face each other with the bottle between us.

"You start."

I think for a while and decide on something simple. "Never have I ever slept with someone of the opposite sex in the same bed without doing anything." And I drink.

I watch him hesitate, but finally he drinks. He clears his throat. "Never have I ever been interested in my crush's best friend." He doesn't drink.

I look at him in surprise. Is he indirectly asking if I like Marco? Marco is very attractive, but I wouldn't say I'm interested, so I don't drink. His relief is evident on his face.

"Never have I ever had feelings for my best friend," I say and watch sadly as he takes a drink. Does he have feelings for Samy? It hurts me and for some reason I want him to be hurt, too, so I drink as well.

He looks surprised, and runs his hands through his messy, damp hair. "I think I want you to drink." He sounds victorious. "Never have I ever fallen in love one-sidedly."

Ouch! That burns.

That characteristic smirk of his appears, and I try to calm my stupid heart. Silently, I drink.

I raise my gaze to him and there's an edge to my voice. "Never have I ever faked an orgasm during sex."

His mouth opens, and he watches me drink. His ego is hurt. I can see it in the anger in his eyes. I know I'm lying, but I don't care about anything anymore. Ares takes the bottle, thinking for a moment, and I'm prepared for him to destroy me. I know after what I said, he'll only try to hurt me even more.

He looks at me. "Never have I ever lied when I said I don't like someone."

I frown. *Did he . . . ?*

Ares plays with the piercing in his lower lip and drinks.

I'm petrified, looking at him—is he telling me that he does like me, and that he lied when he said he didn't? Or am I overthinking things? Or has the tequila taken effect and made me even more drunk? He smiles at me and puts the bottle in between us. I take it, and I don't know what to say.

"You look surprised." He puts his hands behind him, leaning back, letting me see those abs and his tattoo. I can clearly see the one on his lower abdomen, which is something tribal and small, and very delicate-looking.

"No, it's just that . . ." I pause, playing with the bottle. "I'm thinking about my turn," I lie.

"Let's see, surprise me." He leans forward again and moves closer to me, and now only the bottle separates our bodies.

"I think I've had enough," I say nervously. I excuse myself, handing him the bottle. "It's late, we should sleep."

"Leave me the last turn, okay?"

"Okay."

Ares looks me straight in the eye as he says, "Never have I ever wanted to kiss someone as much as I do now."

The air leaves my lungs as he drinks. His eyes are fixed on my mouth, and he hands me the bottle. I don't hesitate as I take a swig.

In the blink of an eye, Ares is on top of me. His mouth finds mine and throws my fears out the window. His kiss is not tender; it's rough, passionate, and I love it. His soft lips lick, suck. I can't help but moan into his mouth and his tongue enters mine, tempting, provoking me. He tastes like tequila and strawberry gum. I grab his hair, kissing him with everything I have. I've missed him so much, and it's only been a week. He could easily become my addiction.

Ares spreads my legs to get between them and let me feel him all over me. His hand goes up under the long shirt I'm wearing, caressing the back of my thighs. His fingers curl around the waistband of the boxers and he pulls them down. He moves away from my lips for a moment so he can remove them completely.

I take the opportunity to look at his beautiful face in front of mine and caress it. He closes his eyes and I raise a little on my elbows to kiss his neck slowly. I hear him sigh. His skin is so soft and smells like fancy soap.

Ares stands up and my skin feels cold from the lack of contact. He takes my hand and pulls me until I am upright in front of him. His hands grab the hem of my shirt, and he pulls it off over my head. His eyes scan every part of me, making me blush and shiver with excitement.

Ares grabs my waist and kisses me again. Feeling his naked torso against my breasts makes me let out a small moan. He pushes me onto the bed until I fall on my back, and he climbs on top of me still kissing and touching me. His restless lips leave mine and move down my neck. His tongue, as nimble as ever, licks deliciously, sending streams of desire throughout my body.

Then he goes down to attack my breasts, leaving me breathless. This is too much, I close my eyes, biting my lips. To my surprise, Ares keeps going down my stomach, and that puts me on alert.

"Ares, what are you doing?" I ask as he spreads my legs, and I tense up.

He looks up at me. "Do you trust me?"

Tell him no! You don't trust him, do you? Like a fool in love, I nod. "Yes."

He smiles on my skin and keeps going down. I stare up at the ceiling nervously. The moment his tongue makes contact with the spot in the middle of my legs, I arch my back, with a loud moan leaving my lips.

"Oh God!" I clutch the sheets. New sensations invade me, drowning me in pleasure.

Nothing has ever felt so good, so perfect, especially because it's with him. Ares is claiming all my first experiences, and I like that. It makes me feel like we have a unique connection. Ares gets more aggressive with his tongue, moving it up and down and then in circles until I feel like I can't take any more. I cover my mouth with my hand to quiet my moans.

Ares stretches out his hand to grab my wrist and pull my hand away. "No, let me hear you moan. Only I can make you lose control like this."

I shudder, and he continues his torture until I feel like my body is going to explode. "Ares!"

His voice is deep and sexy. "Yes, like that, moan for me, beautiful."

The orgasm that sweeps me is unprecedented. I arch my back, my hands go to his hair to push him away from there, as everything becomes very sensitive. My legs tremble, my breathing is ragged and quick. Ares stands up in front of me, licking his lips, and it's the sexiest thing I've ever seen in my life.

I can see him so clearly, his chest and defined abdomen. His eyes shining with desire. He pulls down his shorts along with his boxers, dropping them to the floor, and lets me stare at him completely naked in front of me. He is so perfect. I want to feel him, all of him.

He takes something off his nightstand, and I watch him put the condom on. I can't wait to feel him inside me again.

He grabs my ankles and pulls me to the edge of the bed. His hand takes my chin. "Do you want me?" I nod. "Turn around."

I obey, and he grabs my hips and lifts me up until I'm on my hands and knees. The anticipation almost kills me as he rubs himself against me but doesn't penetrate me.

"Ares, please."

"Please what?"

He has made me so naughty.

"Please, I want you inside me."

I feel him grab me by my hair and a scream leaves my lips as he penetrates me all at once. It burns and hurts a little, but nothing like the first time. He doesn't move, as if he's waiting for me to get used to it.

"Are you okay?"

"Yes."

He begins to move slowly, and it still burns, but the friction begins to feel amazing.

A few minutes later, I no longer feel anything but pleasure. Ares lets go of my hair and grips my hips to thrust into me even deeper, faster. The sound of skin against skin echoes throughout the room, mixing with our moans. It isn't long before we both collapse on the bed, side by side. Our quickened breathing makes our chests rise and fall rapidly. Ares reaches over to the nightstand and grabs the tequila bottle.

"Never have I ever made a girl come with oral sex." And he takes a drink.

I can't help but smile. "You are crazy, Ares Hidalgo."

His eyes meet mine. "You're driving me crazy, Witch."

He wraps us in his sheets and caresses my cheek tenderly. Suddenly, sleepiness overwhelms me. I blink to try to stay awake, but I fall asleep, naked in the bed of the boy I stalked from the shadows until a few weeks ago.

Life really is unpredictable.

TWENTY-TWO
The Awakening

- ARES -

The first thing I feel when I wake up is something warm next to me. The touch of skin against my arm takes me by surprise, and then I turn and see her.

Her eyes are closed, her long eyelashes rest on her cheekbones, and she is breathing slowly through her nose. She looks so delicate and fragile. A lump forms in my throat, making it difficult for me to breathe. I jump up from the bed, moving away from her, almost hyperventilating.

I need to get out of here.

I need to get away from her.

What the hell was I thinking?

Grabbing my clothes from the floor, I quickly put on my boxers and shorts. I leave my room, careful not to wake her up. I don't want to face her; I can't face her expectations of me and break her heart again. I can't make her cry and watch her walk away from me, not again.

Then get back in there.

The voice of my conscience reproaches me, but I can't do that either. I'm not what she expects, or what she needs. I can't play at having a relationship with someone when I don't believe in that shit, because sooner or later I'll end up hurting her and ruining a nice girl who doesn't deserve it.

If I know I can't give her what she wants, why do I keep luring her to me? Why can't I let her go? Because I'm a selfish fucker, that's why, because just imagining her with someone else makes my blood boil. I can't be with her, but I won't let her be with anyone else either.

I head down the stairs, running, and grab the keys to the car.

Run, like the selfish coward you are.

I'm about to grab the doorknob when I hear someone clearing their throat. I turn to see Artemis sitting on the couch wearing sports clothes. He must have just come in from his morning workout.

"Where are you going looking like that?"

And that's when I realize that I'm only wearing shorts, and I don't even have shoes on.

"Nowhere," I say quickly.

"Running away?"

"No, I'm still just a little tired."

Artemis gives me an incredulous look but says nothing. I grab my sneakers from the guest closet in the hallway and pull a sweatshirt on. Claudia appears to ask me what she should tell Raquel.

"Tell her I had to go out and I won't be back until late," I whisper to her, holding the keys in my hand. "Tell her to go home."

I turn my back on them and leave the house. I get into the

car, but I don't turn it on. I just rest my forehead on the steering wheel. I don't know how much time passes, but when I look up, I see her.

Raquel.

She's walking out of the house. Her dress is wrinkled and still a little wet from the night before and her hair is in a messy bun. My heart drops to the floor. She shudders, wiping her tear-streaked cheeks. She's crying.

Ah, God, what are you doing, Ares?

My eyes go down to her feet and I notice that she's barefoot. She probably couldn't find her sandals and didn't want to stay to look for them. I can't take my eyes off her as she slowly walks away from the house.

I almost go get her, but when my hand falls on the car door handle, I freeze. What am I going to say to her? How am I going to justify myself? I know that if I chase her, I will only hurt her more.

I sit there, not moving, not saying anything. I don't know how long it takes before I finally get out of the car. My eyes scan the road, but it's empty. I wish I had said something to her, but I don't even know what I feel or how to word it. I'm not used to any of this.

A black car pulls up next to me. The rear window rolls down and the scent of expensive perfume hits my nose.

"What are you doing out here, honey?" my mother asks as a false smile forms on my lips.

"I just went for a run."

"As athletic as ever. Come into the house, I've missed you."

"Of course you missed us."

She decides to ignore my sarcasm. "Let's go."

She rolls up the window, and the car continues into the drive-way. With my heart clenched, I take one last look at the street and return to the house.

It's for the best, I keep repeating over and over inside my head.

I have to greet my parents, the beings who made me the way I am, the ones who are to blame for the fact that I can't tell the girl I just lost how I feel about her, and that it's the first time I've felt this way.

Ah! Shit! I let out a long sigh and walk into the house.

- RAQUEL -

I keep replaying the moment when I woke up and looked for him, thinking he had gone for breakfast. I was about to go downstairs when I heard him talking to Claudia.

Tell her I had to go out and I won't be back until late, he said with what sounded like annoyance in his voice. *Tell her to go home.*

I grimace, feeling the burning pavement under my bare feet, but that pain is no comparison to the one I feel inside.

I was such an idiot.

I can't stop crying, I can't stop the tears, and it just makes me feel even more pathetic. I thought this time would be different, and I really believed it. How could I have been so stupid? He would say anything to get inside my pants; that's all he wanted. How could I let him do this to me again and again?

I think back to his genuine smile, how we talked and laughed yesterday in his bed playing that stupid game, and what we did afterward. I trusted him. And he took that trust and shattered it along with my heart. He didn't even have the decency to tell me face to face. I wasn't important enough. He just sent his maid to get rid of me.

Ares can hurt me like no one else, but it's my fault for giving him that power over me. Ares knows I'm crazy about him and uses that to take advantage of me like the jerk he is. All this time I haven't really wanted him out of my life. I've given him chances, believing in his earnest eyes, and hoping that there is something good behind his facade. But no more.

As I get closer to the house, I thank God it's Sunday, and I don't have to go to school feeling like shit. I'm surprised to see Dani in the driveway ringing the doorbell. She's wearing a loose summer dress, with her long black hair tied up in a ponytail and sunglasses on her face. She looks impatient. I know she hates the heat. I try to call out to her, but I can't. The words stick in my throat, and I want to cry again. My lips tremble as she turns and sees me.

She takes off her glasses, and her face tightens in concern. She hurries over to me and grabs me by the shoulders. "What happened? Are you okay?"

I just manage to nod.

"God, let's go inside."

In my room, I don't bother to hold back my tears, not anymore. I sit on the floor against the wall and cry. Dani sits next to me, saying nothing, just sitting there, and that's all I need. I don't need words of encouragement, I just need her to be there, next to me.

I need to let it all out. I need to get this pain out of my chest, and I feel that by crying I can externalize it so that it never hurts like this again. There is something therapeutic in crying with all my heart. There is a certain peace that comes afterward.

Dani slips her arm behind me and grabs me so that I rest my head on her shoulder. "Let it out. That's it. I'm here."

I cry until I have no more tears, and my nose is so stuffed up that it's hard to breathe. The peace settles over me. Dani kisses my head.

"Do you want to talk about it?"

I push myself away from her and straighten up, pressing my

back against the wall. I wipe away my tears and blow my nose. I tell her everything.

Dani's face turns red with rage. "Fucking jerk! Argh!"

I don't say anything.

She blows an unruly strand of hair out of her face. "I want to punch him in his stupid face. Can I? Just one punch and I'll run. He won't even notice."

"Dani . . ."

"I learned a superpunch in my self-defense class, I know it will hurt, and there's always the typical punch in the balls. Oh yeah, I think I prefer that one."

Her crazy anger steals a sad smile from me. "I appreciate the effort, but . . ."

"Or I can tell Dean. They're on the soccer team together. I'll tell him to give him a kick that looks accidental."

"Dani, you can't send your brother to beat him up. Dean is very passive."

"But also excessively overprotective, I only have to tell him that Ares did something to you and *boom*! Ares gets what he deserves."

"I don't like violence, and you know it."

"Fine!" she snorts. "I'll get some ice cream, and you find the most romantic movie you can get online."

"I don't think—"

"Silence! Let's deal with this anger as it should be. Today you will cry and shout insults at the movie screen and talk about how unfair life is because those things don't happen to us." She puts her hands on her hips. "We'll have a sleepover, and tomorrow you'll wake up a new person, leaving everything behind."

I try to smile. "I don't think I can do that overnight."

"At least give it a try, and then we'll go party with some guys.

You'll get distracted and realize that idiot isn't the only guy on this planet. Are we clear?"

"Yes, ma'am."

"I didn't hear you."

"Yes, ma'am!"

"Okay, now look for that movie, I'll be right back."

I watch her leave and smile like a fool, grateful to have her by my side, otherwise I would be falling apart. I think what upsets me the most is that, even knowing what my mother had to go through with my father, I still fell for that idiot. Just another girl, blinded by love. I'm disappointed in myself.

I turn on my computer and open the browser to search for a movie. My Facebook automatically opens while I type into the address bar. I hear a new message ring and my heart crumples in my chest when I see the name and message.

Ares Hidalgo: Sorry.

A sad smile crosses my lips. I leave it on seen and simply continue my search. It rings again and I open his next message:

Ares Hidalgo: I am truly sorry.

I click his name and block him so that he can't send me any more messages.

Good-bye, Greek God.

TWENTY-THREE
The Soccer Game

Soccer: the most popular sport in the world and one of my favorites. I don't know when I developed a passion for watching the games. Maybe it started the day I saw Ares playing in his backyard, or maybe it was when Dani's mom took us to see Dean play in his first game. In any case, I enjoy it, and I didn't hesitate when Dani asked if I wanted to go with her, Carlos, and Yoshi to another of Dean's games to support him. With all my being, I try to forget that Ares is also on the team, and that means I'll see him for the first time since that terrible morning.

I won't deny that it's been a difficult few days, especially at night when I close my eyes. I can't help replaying everything over and over again, as if trying to find the moment or the reason why everything ended up like this. There were even times when I took some of the blame. He warned me. He was very clear about what he wanted, but I still gave myself to him not only once but twice. I've found myself staring at the window sometimes, not daring to look out and peek at his house. It's painful to remember him climbing up the ladder, his smirk, his eyes, all of him there with me in my room.

I shake my head to clear these thoughts. I came here to have fun and enjoy my favorite sport with my friends. Although, if I'm being honest, I know that my racing heartbeat and sweaty hands are not due to the game.

Why does it make me so nervous to know I'm going to see him?

I try to reassure myself that he'll be far away, and he won't even see me or notice me among the people in the stands. I try to calm down as we walk into the field and look for a place to sit. Dani had trouble finding a spot in the parking lot and, as I predicted, the place is full. We see a space in the second row of seats with a good view of the field, so we hurry over. Apolo joins us—he's been hanging out with us at school lately.

Dani sits down first, then Apolo, Carlos, Yoshi, and me. I don't like to be so far away from Dani, but I don't want Yoshi to think that I don't want to sit next to him. There's only a bit of daylight left, the sun is almost gone, and the sky turns gray as it welcomes the darkness of the night. The big field lights turn on, illuminating the freshly mowed grass.

My eyes dance around the players, stretching and practicing with a soccer ball. Our team's uniform is black with red stripes and red numbers, while the other team's is all white.

Number five. Where are you, Greek God?

As if he wanted to answer me, Ares appears, walking with his characteristic confidence. My heart flutters in my chest as if to chase after him. His uniform shorts are perfectly tailored to his defined legs and his shirt fits tightly, exposing his muscular arms. He's wearing some sort of superthin red elastic headband to keep his black hair away from his forehead. And on his left arm he's wearing the captain's armband.

My God, why do you make it so hard for me? Why do you get hotter every day? I'm confused enough as it is.

Ares greets another player, who I can only see from behind, but he seems very familiar. They talk, and Ares's expression grows serious, as if he's deciding something important. The unknown player turns slightly—it's Marco. How did I forget that he also plays on this team?

I make a face remembering the dance I did for Marco. *God, how embarrassing.* But, well, Marco doesn't look bad at all in that uniform. My eyes go down to his ass, and oh—nice.

Raquel, for God's sake!

I mentally slap myself. Having sex has definitely unleashed my wild side. Ares laughs and shakes his head at something Marco says, and I stop breathing. He looks so cute when he laughs.

"Raquel?" Yoshi brings me back to reality.

"Yes?" I look at him, and Yoshi's eyes are narrowed.

"Enjoying the view?"

I let out a chuckle. "A little bit."

"I asked you if you wanted soda, I'll get some."

"No, I'm fine."

Carlos pokes his head out from behind Yoshi's back. "Are you sure you don't want anything, my princess?"

"I'm fine."

Apolo and Dani appear to be having a conversation down the bench. Well, Dani is talking, and Apolo is just sitting there nodding, red as a tomato. Carlos and Yoshi go down the stairs to get sodas as the announcer's voice comes over the speakers.

"Good evening! Welcome to the opening game of this year's municipal soccer championship. Give a warm welcome to the guest team, the Greenwich Tigers!"

The opposing team's fans are howling, yelling, and partying, while we just boo.

The announcer continues. "Now let's give a round of applause in support of our home team, the Panthers!"

Everyone is making a scene, screaming and jumping up and down, including me. I take advantage of the guys leaving and slide down to stand next to Apolo. Dani sees me and immediately grabs Apolo by the shoulders to shuffle in between us.

Dani whispers in my ear. "I get why you were going to practice. Everyone is hot. With the exception of my brother, of course, because, gross."

"Where is Dean?"

Dani takes my chin and moves my face in the direction of the goal. "There. You're too focused on your Voldemort to notice my poor brother."

I'm saved from answering by the announcer. "Well, it's almost time for kickoff, ladies and gentlemen. Let's give both teams a round of applause and wish them all the best!"

The crowd screams, raising their hands in the air. On my side, everyone starts shouting, "Panthers, Panthers!" Excitement seeps into my veins and for a second, I enjoy it fully, forgetting that arrogant captain who has my heart in his hands.

You can feel the rivalry between the two teams in the air. Greenwich is the closest town and they always belittle us, claiming we're talentless villagers. We've made them swallow their words over and over. The Panthers have won several regional championships, and we've even gone to state while they haven't made it past the first play-offs.

The teams take the field, each player to his position, and the stands vibrate with excitement. I clap loudly, my eyes falling on Ares again. How can I not look at him when he looks so confident, so excited?

You're an idiot, Raquel, my brain reproaches me. He has hurt me so much, but I can't stop looking at him and sighing like a stupid girl. I wish feelings had an On and Off button. That would make things easier for so many people. Because I know I have feelings for him, I know I'm fooling myself by saying, "I'm falling in love with him," when the truth is that I'm already in love. There's no turning back, even if admitting what I feel doesn't change anything. He doesn't feel the same way, so I have to swallow my feelings and go on with my life as if nothing happened.

Yoshi appears next to me, and Carlos takes the seat next to him. Yoshi offers me his soda. "Are you sure you don't want some? It's Coke, your favorite."

"Just a sip." I drink a little and give it back to him.

Yoshi adjusts his glasses and throws a glance my way as if he wants to say something, but he doesn't. Our eyes meet.

"Raquel, is there something going on between you and that Hidalgo guy?"

"Apolo? Of course not, he's just—"

"I don't mean Apolo, and you know it."

"No, of course not." Why am I lying to him?

Yoshi opens his mouth to protest, but the referee blows the whistle, starting the game. I smile at Yoshi and turn my focus to the match. The beginning of the game is really lively. Carlos whistles with excitement. "Did you see how hard he ran to get that pass? That guy is really good."

Ares is playing well, which doesn't help me. All I want to do is scream like a fangirl every time he gets close to the goal.

Dani hits me with her elbow. "You have good taste. Not only is he cute and smart, he's good at sports."

And he is also very good at sex.

I want to say it, but I just smile. Nearly halfway through the first half, Ares is running with the ball, approaching the goal. Everyone in the stands is standing up, cheering him on. But then the goalie comes out and runs at him, crashing into Ares with a thud. A scream of horror leaves my lips as I see Ares on the ground, writhing in pain, with his face in his hands.

Without thinking, I jump to my feet and almost run to him, but Dani grabs my arm and stops me, reminding me of the situation between us. Marco helps him up, and a couple of the other players half carry him to the edge of the field, near the bleachers. I grow even more alarmed when I see blood coming out of his nose.

The announcer comes over the speakers again. "It looks like there was a big collision between the striker and the goalkeeper. The referee gave a yellow card, but the Panthers are not happy."

The trainer passes Ares a rag and he takes it, wiping away the blood. His blue eyes meet mine, and I can't help but try to ask him, moving my lips in the hope that he understands the question despite the distance between us, "Are you all right?"

He just nods.

I sit back down, relieved. Yoshi rolls his eyes, and Dani gives me a knowing look. I notice that Apolo isn't in his seat.

"He ran the other way when you got up," Dani explains. "I think he's making sure his brother is okay."

"That was a really dirty move," Carlos says.

Yoshi takes a sip of his soda. "I agree."

Apolo returns, and his face is red but not with grief. It's the first time I've seen him so angry.

Dani squeezes his shoulder comfortingly. "He's going to be fine."

Apolo says nothing, just clenches his fists at his sides and sits back, taking a deep breath. I think it's extremely cute that he cares so much about his brother. The game continues, and the tension between the teams is palpable. The Panthers are angry. Ares continues to play, checking his nose from time to time. There's no more blood, but I imagine it still hurts.

Poor thing.

No, poor little nothing, he broke your heart.

Get it together, Raquel.

It's almost the end of the first half when the best play of the match begins. The midfielder makes a long pass to Marco, who, after outwitting two opposing players, passes it to Ares, who runs to receive it at the side of the goal. Everyone climbs to their feet in excitement. Ares kicks the ball diagonally and it goes into the goal from the corner at an impressive angle.

"GOOOOOOOOOOOOOOOOOOOOOOOOOOOOOOAAAL!" the announcer's voice booms.

We all jump and scream like crazy. The place is going to explode.

"In your face, you fucking goalie!" Apolo shouts, surprising us all.

Ares runs with his arms stretched in the air, celebrating the goal. As he approaches the stands, he grabs the edge of his shirt and lifts it up to reveal something written on his stomach.

Witch.

I stop breathing, bringing my hand to my mouth in surprise.

The announcer speaks. "Wow, it looks like the scorer is dedicating his goal to someone. Who is the lucky witch?"

Ares's gaze meets mine, and he smiles at me before being embraced from behind by all of his teammates in celebration. My heart beats wildly and threatens to burst out of my chest.

Ares Hidalgo is going to drive me crazy with his confusing signals.

Correction: he has already driven me crazy.

TWENTY-FOUR
The Confession

When the game ends, I'm still processing the fact that Ares Hidalgo dedicated a goal to me. A thousand thoughts have run through my head in the last ten minutes. Maybe he has a secret girlfriend that he calls Witch—someone who isn't me. But he looked at me and smiled . . . at me.

I'm overthinking.

I shouldn't let him get to me. I shouldn't let one gesture break my resolve to stay away from him. Yes, he might have dedicated a goal to me, but that shouldn't be enough, not after all the damage he's done.

Part of me—most of me—wants to run into his arms, but the rational part, the part that has regained her dignity, doesn't approve, and I decide to listen to her. Though I wonder if my decision is actually due to a different emotion, one that's new to me: fear. Fear of letting him in and getting hurt once more. I can't take it again, so I won't risk it.

"Wow, that was exciting," Dani says, pressing her elbow into my ribs playfully as we walk down the bleachers.

"Yeah," Apolo agrees. "I loved the game. Three–nil. That goalie deserved it after what he did to my brother."

"We have to celebrate!" Carlos tries to take my hand, but Dani, like an expert ninja, slaps him, deflecting him. "Ow!"

"You deserve it," I say, " I don't like being grabbed like that."

"Understood," assures Carlos.

I look at Yoshi, but he's looking weirdly serious.

"Guys, we should go congratulate the players," Apolo suggests.

Apolo's idea doesn't sound too good right now. I don't want to face Ares. It's one thing to be strong enough to stay away, and it's quite another to have that dedication when he's in front of me.

Dani notices my discomfort. "Nope, we'd better go to the celebration party."

"Celebration party?" I ask, confused.

Carlos pats me on the back. "Aren't you up to date with the social events, princess? It's the party the team holds when they win."

Of course, how could I forget the infamous Panthers' parties? I've only been to one because Dean invited us. Unfortunately, on that occasion I was completely invisible to Ares. He was always in a crowd of people.

We walk past the field as we head to the parking lot. I can't help but glance over to where the players are gathered, talking. Ares is there, completely drenched in sweat, his hair sticking to the sides of his face the same way his uniform is sticking to his body. How can he still look sexy when he's all sweaty? I need professional help.

His eyes meet mine, and I freeze. He gives me a mischievous smile and takes the edge of his shirt and pulls it off over his head. A lot of players walk around shirtless, so no one thinks it's strange.

My eyes travel down his torso to where the word *Witch* has already faded. I bite my lip.

I hate my hormones.

Shaking my head, I look away and continue walking. I only manage to take a few steps before I crash into Yoshi. "Ow! I didn't see you!"

"Let's get out of here," he says. Yoshi takes my hand, and I let him even though I just told Carlos off for doing the same thing. He drags me to the parking lot, where everyone else is already waiting for us in Dani's car. Apolo has taken my place in the passenger seat, so I sit in the back in the middle of Yoshi and Carlos. They both smell great. I love it when a guy smells good. Ares smells divine.

Shut up, hormones!

The party house is located east of town, about ten minutes from my house. You can hear the music from outside, bass booming off the walls of the giant two-story building. There are groups scattered around the garden with plastic cups in their hands. I'm surprised to see so many people there already. They sure move fast when there's a party.

As we head to the front door, I try not to cover my ears. Electronic music vibrates throughout the house. The main lights are off, and the only light comes from a few dimly lit colored lamps. The DJ is in the living room. He's a thin guy with long hair and tattooed arms who looks completely focused on what he's doing.

"Let's get some drinks!" Dani grabs my hand so that we don't get separated in the mass of people.

The kitchen is full of teenagers, but somehow Dani manages to get us all a drink. Taking a sip of whatever's in that plastic cup, I can't help but remember the last time I drank at Ares's house, the tequila, his smile, his kisses.

No, no, Raquel.

I am here to distract myself, not to think about him.

As if Dani can read my mind, she yells, "Let's dance!"

We head to the middle of the room and start shimmying to the rhythm of the music with our cups in the air. For a second, I let my mind fly away from any memories. I dance, I drink, I laugh at Carlos's crazy movements, and at Apolo's blushing face when Dani dances next to him. I'm free.

Yoshi takes my arm and turns me toward him. I play along, putting my arms around his neck and dancing with him, and then I make the severe mistake of looking up. Because when Yoshi's eyes meet mine, the intensity in them takes my breath away. I've always thought Yoshi was cute, but something about this moment, maybe the mood or his closeness, fuels something within me.

"Pillow Talk" by Zayn Malik plays in the background and the soft, seductive rhythm makes us move slowly against each other. His hands slide down my waist until they linger on my hips. My lips open and he licks his, wetting them. I want to kiss him.

These sensations take me by surprise. Yoshi presses his fingers into my hips and leans into me until his forehead touches mine. His nose is touching mine. Memories of all the times we've shared come flooding back, all the times he has made me laugh, forget my problems, and how he's always been there for me. He's my best friend. Up until a few years ago, that was all I thought, but then that innocent boy transformed into a cute boy. I've been attracted to him more than once, but I never dared to do anything about it for fear of losing his friendship.

Yoshi sighs, closing his eyes. "Raquel . . ."

I tense up at the seriousness of his tone. Yoshi always calls me Rochi. He only uses my name when he's talking about something very intense or delicate.

With my heart in my throat, I answer. "Yes?"

"I'm dying to kiss you."

My heart skips a beat, and he watches for my reaction. I just nod, giving him my consent. I can almost feel his lips on mine already as I close my eyes.

Ares's face suddenly appears in my mind, making me take a step back. Yoshi looks at me confusedly, and I'm about to say something when a guy with a microphone interrupts us.

"All right, boys and girls! Time to welcome the players."

Everyone shouts, raising their cups. The team walks into the room, all freshly showered and in regular clothes. Ares is with them, wearing a black shirt that suits him. In fact, black is a color that suits him *too* well for my taste.

The guy who I recognize as the team's goalkeeper continues, "First of all, let's welcome the captain, who gave us three beautiful goals today."

"Ares! Ares! Ares!" Everyone joins the cheers, and I lower my head.

"Captain." The goalkeeper slips an arm behind Ares's shoulders. "You played like never before today, but we also know that you dedicated a goal to a girl."

"Yes!" the people around me shout.

"I think we all want to know who the lucky witch is."

A girl from the audience raises her hand. "I'll be your witch anytime, handsome!"

"Will you reveal her identity?"

Ares laughs, shaking his head. "She knows who she is, and that's enough."

"Boo! Tell us! Tell us! Tell us!"

Ares shakes his head again and walks away.

The goalkeeper shrugs his shoulders. "Okay, back to the party. Enjoy!"

Yoshi grabs my hand and drags me through the crowd.

"Hey, Yoshi!" I complain, surprised by his force.

We leave the house, and he takes me to the sidewalk, far enough away from the people in the garden. He lets go of me, and I can see how annoyed he looks. "What's wrong?" I ask.

"Please tell me it wasn't with him."

"What are you talking about?"

"Tell me you didn't lose your virginity to that idiot."

I freeze, not knowing what to say.

"Raquel, tell me! Ah! Shit! Ares Hidalgo? That arrogant asshole who treats women like dirt? What were you thinking?"

"I wasn't thinking! I was ... just ..."

"You what? You what?"

"I got carried away by my feelings!"

"Feelings? Are you in love with him?"

I want to say no, I want to scream no, but the words stay in my throat. Yoshi looks so disappointed that it hurts. It hurts me to see him like this. "Yoshi ... I ..."

"You are. You're in love with him." He puts his hands on his head and lets out a long sigh of exasperation.

I don't know what to say. I've never been so confused in my life, and then Yoshi starts to talk, disconcerting me even more.

"I like you, Raquel. I really like you."

Everything stops, I can only look into those honey-colored eyes flooded with tears.

"I've always liked you, I thought you and I would end up together like some overused romantic cliché." A sad laugh escapes his lips. "I guess it was too perfect to be real."

"Yoshi ..."

"I'm leaving. Tell the others. Enjoy the evening with your idiot."

"Yoshi. Wait."

He doesn't listen to me and starts to walk away. My heart is beating like crazy. I don't want him to leave, but what will I do if he stays? What do I tell him?

But then Yoshi stops a few feet away and turns to me again. I watch him in surprise as he walks toward me quickly. His eyes are full of determination.

"Fuck it all!"

"Yoshi, what—"

He takes my face with both hands and kisses me.

TWENTY-FIVE
The Celebration

Yoshi's kiss takes me by surprise.

Not only because I didn't expect it but also because the moment his lips touch mine, new and pleasant sensations seize my body. His kiss is soft and slow. He tastes of vodka and something sweet that I can't decipher, but I like it. He sucks on my bottom lip, then kisses me again, deepening the kiss a little.

The thinking part of my brain disappears, and my hormones take the wheel. I allow myself to enjoy this kiss. I'm a single girl being kissed by a cute guy, and there's nothing wrong with that. Yoshi grabs my waist, pulling me closer to him, and I wrap my hands around his neck. I never imagined Yoshi could kiss so well. His tongue caresses the corner of my lips, making me shiver.

Someone clears their throat.

And that's when I remember that we are in front of the house, in full view of everyone. I separate from Yoshi, without taking my hands off his neck, and turn my head to look at the person who cleared his throat.

Marco.

My heart stops, because he's not alone. Behind him, a few steps away, is Ares. His hands are in his pants pockets and his eyes are on me.

Oh shit.

His face is an empty, indecipherable mask. Is he angry? Disappointed? Surprised? Or does he just not care? I can't tell from his expression, which gives nothing away.

My hands drop from Yoshi's neck and fall to my sides. What were the odds of Ares leaving the house at this very moment? Marco gives me an amused smile, his tone teasing. "You never cease to amaze me."

Ares turns his gaze away from me and starts walking past us. "Come on, we don't have all night." His voice is neutral, reminding me of the first time we spoke.

He passes by without another glance. He really doesn't care. Why does that hurt me so much? Why do I want him to care? Marco gives me one last smile and follows him. I watch them head to Ares's car, which is parked on the street, to pull out some crates of what looks like beer.

Yoshi grabs my hand. "Earth calling Raquel."

I stop looking at Ares and focus on my best friend, the guy I just kissed. *Shit, what a night!*

"I'm sorry, I just … It's nothing."

Yoshi caresses my cheek. "If anyone needs to apologize here, it's me. I'm sorry, I know how you feel about him. I don't expect you to act like you don't care overnight." He adjusts his glasses, and I can't help the smile that springs to my lips. Yoshi is so sweet, and on top of it, he kisses well too.

"We should go inside." I don't want to face Ares again when he comes back with those crates.

Yoshi nods. "Okay, but first I want you to know that this isn't a one-night thing for me. I really care about you, and I want us to try."

"I care about you too, but I don't want to hurt you."

"I know," he says with a smile. "Let's try, and if it doesn't work, we can just be friends, but at least we'll know we tried." He pauses, but I don't say anything. "Just think about it, okay? You don't have to answer now."

I just nod and grab his hand to lead him back into the house. "All right, now let's go, Casanova."

Yoshi laughs, and we go inside together.

>> <<

I tend to underestimate the ability of alcohol to get people drunk in a short amount of time. We're all pretty tipsy, so to speak, but Carlos is past the point of no return. He's unconscious on one of the couches in the house, drooling onto a flowered cushion. Apolo, being the nice guy that he is, checks Carlos's breathing every so often.

I'm having a great time and even manage to completely forget about Ares from time to time. But the more I drink, the more I think about him. I don't know if it's a side effect of the alcohol, but it bothers me. I don't want to think about him, I don't want to scan the room every now and then to see if I can find him, I don't want to wonder what he's doing and who he's with.

I don't care about him, I don't care about him, I keep repeating to myself. Dani gives Apolo a kiss on the cheek, telling him how cute he is, and he just blushes, lowering his head. I shake my head, and then I see him. Ares walks past with a tall, slender brunette with wavy hair. He doesn't even look around; he just continues on his way through the crowd until he reaches the stairs. He walks up them with her, both of them laughing together.

My stomach drops. I know what people go upstairs to do in those rooms. Judging by the look the brunette was giving him, she really wants him. Jealousy gnaws at me, and then I realize that he really doesn't care about me. Just seeing him with that girl makes me feel like my heart is going to explode, and imagining him kissing her turns my stomach. Yet he saw Yoshi kissing me and didn't care; he didn't even look surprised.

That's the big difference between him and me. I feel everything, and he feels nothing. I'm the only one in love. It's always been that way with him. So why am I torturing myself like this? I have to get him out of my mind and out of my heart. I don't want to feel this way anymore. I don't want to feel hurt and disappointed.

I take Yoshi's glass and drink until it's completely empty. Everyone looks at me in surprise. So much alcohol all at once makes me dizzy for a second, but it passes, and I grab Dani's glass and do the same, but she stops me halfway through.

"Hey, calm down, there's no hurry!"

I hand her back her glass, breathing heavily after drinking so much in one gulp. "I'm sorry, I got excited."

She gives me a skeptical look. "Are you all right?"

I force a smile, but the image of Ares with that girl is burned into my mind. "I'm doing great."

My ears get hot, as does my face. Remember the qualities of alcohol? Feeling brave, I take Yoshi's hand and stand up, forcing him to stand with me.

"Hey, what's wrong?" Yoshi says to me in surprise.

"We'll be right back," I tell Dani and Apolo, pulling Yoshi behind me.

Climbing the stairs is harder than it looks, especially if the world is spinning. I hold on tight to the railing, and with the other hand I keep pulling Yoshi, who lets out a confused chuckle.

"Where are we going, Rochi?" he asks. We reach the top of the stairs and find a dark hallway full of doors on either side.

"Let's have fun, like him—like everyone else," I say quickly, but Yoshi is so drunk he doesn't notice.

Inevitably, I imagine Ares behind one of those doors, making out with that brunette, his hands touching her, making her reach a delicious orgasm. My stomach churns, and I gag. I stagger across the hallway with Yoshi following me. I pick a door at random because I know fate won't be so cruel as to make me enter the room Ares is in.

It's a small room with a single bed. I don't bother to turn on the light. The light from the moon is bright enough to see everything. I grab Yoshi by the shirt and throw him on the bed. I close the door, giggling like a fool, playing with the edge of my shirt.

"Yoshi . . ."

Yoshi just mumbles. "What are you doing, Rochi?"

"What do you think?" I try to move seductively toward the bed, but I stagger so much that I have to hold on to the wall.

Yoshi lifts his hand to wag his finger back and forth. "No, Rochi, you're drunk, not like that."

"You're drunk, too, you fool."

I focus on trying to pull my shirt off over my head, but it doesn't go past my neck before I get tangled up, crash into the wall, and fall. I get up as fast as I can, still wobbly. "I'm fine!"

The only response is a loud snore. I give Yoshi a death glare, lowering my shirt back into place.

"Are you serious?" I growl in frustration and pinch his leg. "Yoshi? Come on, wake up! Yoshi!"

Frustrated, I leave the room and lean against the door. I see a light at the end of the hall—no, I'm not dead—and I head toward it. I hear all sorts of sounds as I walk down that hall that I do my best to ignore. I stop in front of a white-framed door with square panels of glass, and I open it because that's where the light is coming from.

It's a balcony, and it's empty.

Or so I think. I close the door behind me, and I can see someone leaning on the balcony railing to my right, cigarette smoke rising above him. I can only see his back, but I know it's him, and my heart knows it too and beats like the masochistic idiot it is.

Ares.

I don't move, my mouth is dry, my tongue feels heavy, but I think that's from the alcohol. He looks over his shoulder at me and doesn't seem surprised to see me. In fact, there's no expression on his face, the same as a few hours ago. I don't know why, after thinking about him all night and looking for him constantly, that now that I have him a few steps away from me, I want to run away.

Ares hasn't looked at me fully, and yet he still manages to make both my heart race and my breathing pick up. The tension on the balcony is too much for me. Like a coward, I turn toward the door again, but, before I can touch its knob, he moves in quick steps and blocks my way.

I always forget how tall he is, how beautiful and perfect every inch of his face is, and the intensity of his eyes. I look down, backing away, but Ares moves with me, forcing me backward until my back hits the balcony railing.

"Running away?" His voice is cold and makes me shiver.

"No." I shake my head, and I get a little dizzy.

I keep my eyes on his chest. Not even the courage that alcohol gives me is enough to face him. The smell of his cologne hits my nose, and I struggle not to close my eyes and inhale exaggeratedly.

I missed his smell, his presence, and his ability to make me feel everything without even touching me.

"Look at me," he orders, but I refuse. "Look at me, Raquel."

Reluctantly, I obey. His eyes sparkle in the moonlight. Unwillingly, my gaze drops to his lips, and I notice that his piercing is missing.

"I-I have to go," I try to step aside to pass him, but he puts both hands on the railing, locking me in.

"What are you doing up here?" he presses me. "Did you come looking for me?"

"Of course not, the world doesn't revolve around you."

He gives me that stupid smirk that I love and hate. "Not the world. But you do."

His arrogant statement annoys me, and I push him, but he doesn't move. "Get out of the way!" I push him again without any success.

"Why? Do I make you nervous?"

I look away, faking disinterest. "Of course not."

"Then why are you shaking?" I don't know what to say, so I just look away. "You're shaking and I haven't even touched you. Don't worry, I won't either."

Why? I almost ask out loud, but I don't say it. He's out of my life. I have to keep my word this time.

Silence stretches between us, and I dare to look up again. His expression is as impassive as ever. How does he manage to feel nothing? How does he manage to hold me so close and not show a single emotion? While I shudder, struggling to keep my feelings in check, he is so normal, so calm. So why won't he let me go if he doesn't care about me? Why is he blocking my way?

And then a tide of emotions sweeps over me. Ares has hurt me a lot, but he doesn't seem to want to leave my life either. I might be a game to him or whatever else, but I'm tired of going around in circles, expecting something from him that he'll never give me. He's not interested in being with me. He hasn't fought me any of the times I told him I wanted him out of my life.

The memory of that day in his playroom comes to my mind. His impatient face, waiting for me to leave. His hand offering me the phone as if in payment for my services.

Squeezing my hands, I push his chest once. "Let me go! Get off!" He moves to the side, and I move away from him. I stagger in the direction of the balcony door, my stomach twisting.

No, not now, don't puke now, Raquel. This is not the time.

I get so dizzy that I grab a metal chair next to the door. And I half fall, half sit on it. Cold sweat runs down my forehead. "I don't feel very well."

Ares appears at my side in a second. "What did you expect? You drank too much."

I don't know how he understands my babbling. "How do you know I drank too much?"

And then I heave.

Yes, ladies and gentlemen, I vomit gloriously in front of the guy I'm in love with. This clearly qualifies as the most disgusting and embarrassing moment of my life.

Ares holds my hair as I vomit all over the wooden floor of the balcony. Tears well up in my eyes from the effort of each gag. When I finish, I feel like I've drunk another whole bottle of alcohol. I can't even hold my body up; I'm like a rag doll. Apparently, vomiting makes me more drunk. I always thought it would be the opposite.

Everything is a blur, and Ares's voice becomes so distant.

TWENTY-SIX
The Story

- ARES -

I grimace as I watch Raquel finish vomiting. I'm holding her head because apparently she can no longer keep her body standing or sitting or upright in any way. I take her face in my hands and blow on it to cool her down. Her eyes are half-closed, and she gives me a goofy smile.

"It smells like cigarettes and mint chewing gum," she says, chuckling. "Like you."

I remove a few locks of hair that have stuck to her face. She tries to slap my hand but fails, her arms are almost completely unresponsive. "You don't have to help me, Greek God, I'm fine."

I raise an eyebrow. "Really? Get up."

"Just leave me here, I'll be fine."

I can't leave her, even though she's not my favorite person after seeing her kissing that nerd.

Don't think about it, Ares.

Letting out a tired sigh, I help her stand up, and then I bend down a little to throw her over my shoulder. She mumbles as I walk through the balcony door. Carrying her across the hallway isn't difficult. She doesn't weigh much, and I'm used to carrying heavier weights during team workouts. I walk into the only room that hasn't been used as a motel today. How do I know that? Because my friends are inside, playing video games and drinking. The first one to see me when I walk in is Marco.

"Let me guess." Marco makes a dramatic thinking pose. "Raquel?"

"Who is she?" the brunette I brought in earlier asks, sitting on Gregory's lap.

Luis raises his hands in ignorance. "Ask Ares, I still haven't figured out what those two are playing at."

I give them all a serious look. "Everyone out, now."

I wait to make sure they leave, and then I take Raquel into the bathroom and drop her into the bathtub. She just sits there, with her head leaning against the side wall.

"You vomited on your clothes," I say, pulling the white flowered T-shirt she's wearing over her head. She protests, but I manage to get it off. Her breasts are exposed, looking as perfect as I remember them, not too big, not too small, just the right size for her body.

This is not the time, Ares.

I pull her skirt down to her heels. My eyes travel down the length of her legs. Her underwear is black, contrasting nicely with her skin. I swallow thickly, focusing on what I'm doing. I turn on the faucet, and she lets out a scream as cold water pours over her head.

"Cold-cold-cold," she stutters, her wet hair sticking to both sides of her face.

Without looking at her, I run the soap over her body, my eyes trained on the wall on one side. I want her more than I care to admit.

After helping her to awkwardly brush her teeth in the bath, I put a towel around her body and carry her over to sit on the bed. "Ares..."

"Huh?"

"I'm cold."

She must be, with all the people in the house, the air-conditioning is on full blast. Raquel seems to have regained a little more strength after the bath. She can at least sit up on her own. I help her dry off and then she throws the wet towel on the floor.

My eyes travel down her naked body, and I need all my self-control not to hug her. I have missed her so much.

She's drunk, Ares, I think, struggling with myself. I unbutton my shirt quickly.

Raquel laughs. "What are you doing?"

I take it off and put it on her, buttoning it up. My shirt fits her so well. "Lie down, you'll get over it if you get some sleep."

"No, I'm not sleepy." She puts her arms across her chest like a spoiled child. "Tell me a story."

"Just lie down."

"No."

She looks determined. I force her to lie down, and I sit next to her, leaning my back against the headboard.

"Tell me a story," she repeats. She sticks to my side, running her hand across my abdomen, hugging me, and I let her because it feels fucking good to have her beside me. I caress her hair, deciding what to say.

She's not going to remember this tomorrow. The freedom of being able to tell her anything motivates me, and I start talking. "Once upon a time there was a boy who believed his parents were the perfect couple, that their home was the best in the world." I smile to myself. "A very naive child."

She gets closer to me, her nose brushing against my ribs. "And what happened to that child?"

"The boy admired his father, he was his pillar, his example to follow. A strong, successful man. Everything was perfect, maybe too perfect. The father traveled a lot for business, leaving his children and wife alone." I close my eyes, taking a deep breath. "One day, the boy came home early from school, after getting an A on a difficult math test. He ran upstairs to show her, he wanted her to be proud of him. When he entered her room . . ."

White sheets, naked bodies.

I push the images out of my mind.

"The boy's mother was with another man who was not his father. After that, everything dissolved into meaningless explanations, pleas, and tears, but for the boy it all sounded so far away. The sense of his home, of the perfect family, vanished in front of his eyes no matter what his mother said."

I stop in the hope that Raquel is already asleep, but she's not. "Go on, I want to know what's next," she says.

"The boy told his older brother, and they waited for their father to get home to tell him. After a lot of arguments and empty threats, the father forgave her. The two children watched their father bow down, forget his pride, and cry inconsolably in the darkness of his study. That strong man looked weak and wounded. Since that day, their father has tirelessly reminded them that falling in love makes them weak. The boy learned not to trust anyone, not to get attached to anyone, not to give anyone the power to weaken him, and so he grew up hoping to be alone forever. The end."

I look at the girl next to me and her eyes are closed, but she still responds. "What a sad ending."

"Life can be sadder than it seems."

"I don't like that ending," she grunts. "I'll imagine that in the end he did meet someone, and they fell in love and lived happily ever after."

I burst out laughing. "Of course you will, Witch."

"I'm sleepy."

"Then sleep."

"Ares?"

"Yes?"

"Do you think love is a weakness?"

Her question doesn't surprise me. "It is."

"Is that why you've never fallen in love?"

"Who said I've never been in love?"

"Have you?"

I sigh and look at her. "I think so."

Her breathing has become light, and her eyes are closed. She's finally asleep. I smile like an idiot, watching her. Seeing her sleep fills me with peace.

What are you doing to me, Witch?

TWENTY-SEVEN
The Second Awakening

- RAQUEL -

Cold.

I wake up, shivering. I open my eyes with a groan. The light stings as it hits my vision, forcing me to squint. Why is it so cold? I don't remember turning on the air-conditioning.

The first thing I see is a shelf full of sports trophies and awards, which confuses me. I don't have that in my room. As the picture clears in front of me, I realize that's because I'm not in my room.

"What?" I sit up with a jolt, and my head throbs in protest. "Ow!"

I hold my forehead, and my stomach growls unsteadily. Where the fuck am I? As if karma wants to answer, something—or rather someone—moves a little next to me.

Terrified, I turn my face to look, and a muffled shriek leaves my lips as I roll backward on the bed with a thud and fall to the floor. "Ow!" I say again.

Shit, shit.

I poke my face just above the bed and confirm it.

It's Ares Hidalgo, in all his glory, lying on his back, with his forearm over his face. The sheets cover him from his waist down, leaving his chest and abdomen exposed, since he's shirtless.

Instinctively, I look down and realize that I have his shirt on.

"Oh! Crap!" I hold my face dramatically.

What the hell happened? I was so determined not to fall this time.

Let's see, think, Raquel. Remember, think.

Everything is scattered in my brain like a jigsaw puzzle with blurry, missing parts. The last thing I remember is being with Dani, Apolo, Carlos, and Yoshi. Then Yoshi and I went upstairs. Were we going to the bathroom?

Argh!

And then Ares. . . on the balcony . . .

And then nothing, emptiness, darkness.

How frustrating!

Surprisingly, falling into his arms again is not what bothers me the most, but rather this very unpleasant feeling of not being able to remember everything. Did we have sex? Honestly, I don't think Ares would have done anything to me if I was that drunk.

I need to get out of here. I stand up and the room spins, so I take a deep breath. Ares is still the same, with his forearm over his eyes, his lips half-open and his chest exposed.

My shoes . . .

My clothes . . .

They must be somewhere.

What time is it?

Dani must be so worried! It was a good decision to tell Mom

that I would stay at Dani's yesterday, otherwise I would be in real trouble. The still sleeping part of my brain reaches for my cell phone, and then my brain wakes up and slaps me.

It was stolen weeks ago, Raquel, wake up.

I walk around, crouched down, without finding any of my clothes, but what—where are my clothes? They should be somewhere around if we undressed here, or did I undress somewhere else and then come in here? Oh my goodness. I notice an open door to my right to what looks like a bathroom, so I walk in. My clothes are on the floor next to the tub.

A feeling of relief runs through my body. I no longer have to go out on the street with only a boy's shirt on. I close the door and pick up my white flowered T-shirt, but the smell of vomit hits my nose and makes me grimace.

Vomit?

Did I vomit? Oh Jesus Christ. What the fuck happened last night?

There's no way I can wear that shirt. The skirt is in no better condition, but I just wash the little bits of vomit off in the sink. I can't leave wearing only Ares's shirt and nothing underneath. The damp skirt doesn't help with the cold, and I shiver again, but I manage to brush my teeth with my fingers.

Yoshi. Oh no. The memory of trying to use him last night pops up in fragmented pieces in my mind. I have to apologize to him.

Walking back into the room, I allow myself to look at Ares again. His naked, white torso contrasts with the blue of the sheets. I stare at him, fighting the urge to throw myself on him and kiss every uncovered part of his body and feel his skin.

Focus, Raquel.

With all the caution in the world, I grab the doorknob quietly, but when I try to turn it, it won't budge. What? I try harder and it won't open. I check the knob and realize that it doesn't have a button to lock it, just a hole where a key goes.

It's locked. Why?

"Are you looking for this?"

His voice makes me jump. I turn, and, to my surprise, he's sitting on the bed with his hand in the air, holding the keys. I hate that I like his face so much that it makes me shake. He has an amused smile on his face.

"Why is it locked?" I ask.

"There was a party here last night, remember?" There's a certain hesitancy in his voice. "I didn't want anyone to come in and bother us."

I try to swallow but my throat is dry. "You and I . . . I mean . . . did we, you know?"

"Have sex?" He's always so direct. "You don't remember anything?"

There's a sadness in his voice, as if he wants me to remember something. Feeling very embarrassed, I shake my head. "No."

His expression turns and he looks disappointed for some reason. "Nothing happened, you vomited, I bathed you and put you to sleep."

I believe him. "Thank you."

He stands up, and I feel small in front of him again.

"Open the door for me," I say. Being alone with him in a room, both of us scantily clad, is too much.

He slips the key into the front pocket of his pants. "No."

I open my mouth to protest, but he walks to the bathroom, closing the door behind him. What the hell? I purse my lips in frustration, waiting for him to come out. What is he trying to accomplish by keeping me locked in here? I hear the shower. Did he go to take a shower? Is he serious?

I'm desperate to get out of here.

Minutes that feel like years pass before he finally comes back out of the bathroom with only a towel around his waist. He drops his clothes in a pile on the bed. Droplets of water slide down his abdomen and his wet hair is slicked back from his face. I guess he's not cold.

I clear my throat. "Open the door, Ares."

"No."

"Why not?"

"Because I don't want to."

I let out a sarcastic laugh. "How mature." He sits on the bed, and his eyes move down from my chest to my legs. I swallow thickly. "I really have to go."

"You can leave after we talk."

"Good. What do you want now?"

"You."

His response surprises me and warms my body, but I try to play it cool. "You really are crazy."

"Why? Because I tell you what I want? I've always been honest with you."

"Yes, too much, I would say," I tell him, remembering the time he made it clear that he didn't want anything serious with me.

"Come here."

Heat rises to my cheeks. "Oh no, I'm not going to fall for your game."

"My game? I thought you were the one playing games."

"What are you talking about?"

"Did you enjoy kissing someone else?"

The anger in his pretty eyes is evident but, still, I lift my chin. "The truth is, yes, I did. He kisses very well. Besides, he—"

"Shut up."

A smile of victory fills my lips. The fact that I can affect him makes me feel powerful. He has always maintained that icy, expressionless demeanor with me, but at this moment I can see the emotions on his face, and it's refreshing. "You asked," I say, shrugging my shoulders.

"I admire your attempt to replace me, but we both know it's me that you want."

He moves closer to me. The smell of shampoo caresses my nose as I feel his body heat pass over me. Looking into his eyes, my heart beats like crazy, but I don't want to give him the satisfaction of knowing he's right. "That's what you think. Yoshi kisses so good that—"

"Stop talking about him. Don't play with fire, Raquel."

"Jealous?"

"Yes."

His answer shocks me, and I stop breathing. Is Ares Hidalgo admitting he's jealous? Did I fall into an unknown dimension?

He runs his hand over his face. "I don't understand you. I dedicate a goal to you, and you go and kiss someone else. What are you playing at?"

"I'm not playing at anything. I'm the one who doesn't understand you."

He smiles and shakes his head. "We don't seem to understand each other." His hand takes my wrists and pulls them up over my head, holding them gently against the door. He uses his free hand to run his finger along the curve of my neck and the edge of my breasts and a shiver of pleasure runs through me.

"But our bodies do."

I'm about to fall, but I remember how cold he was after he took my virginity, and then how he sent his maid to throw me out of his room the second time we were together. I want him with all my soul, but my heart won't be able to take another hit, I know it won't.

I can't. I will no longer fall.

I know he doesn't expect any sudden movements, so I take advantage, and with my body I push him away, using all my strength to free my wrists. Ares looks surprised; his neck is red, and his breathing is agitated.

He tries to approach me again, and I raise my hand. "No."

He frowns. It's the first time I've ever turned him down, and the bewilderment is obvious in his expression. "Why not?"

"I don't want to. I'm not going to fall, not this time."

He runs his hand through his hair. "You think too much. You talk too much. Come here."

He reaches out his hand toward me, but I slap it away before he can touch me. "No, if you think I'm always going to be available to you when you feel like it, you're wrong. I'm not going to be your plaything of the moment."

He looks surprised, as if he is truly hurt by my words. "Why do you always think so badly of me?"

"Because that's all you show me. I've already cut you out of my life, Ares. So, leave me alone."

He gives me his stupid smirk. "Cut me out of your life? That's not something you do in a few weeks, Raquel."

"But I'm starting to do it, and I'll get there."

"I'm not going to let you do it."

I growl in frustration. "This is what I hate about you! You don't take me seriously, but you don't let me go either. Why? Do you enjoy playing with my feelings?"

"Of course not."

"So?"

"I don't understand why you blame me for everything. You

knew what you were getting into; I was clear with you," Ares says.

"Don't change the subject! Yes, I knew what I was getting into, but I don't want any more of this. I want you out of my life, but you won't let me move on." My chest rises and falls with my rapid breathing. "Why, Ares? Why won't you leave me alone?"

"I can't."

"Why?"

I watch him hesitate about what to say, he twists his lips hesitantly.

I let out a sad laugh. "You're not saying anything because you don't have a motive. You just don't want to lose your fun of the month."

"Stop saying that! I don't see you that way!"

"In what way?" I challenge.

Silence again. That doubtful expression.

"You know this conversation is getting us nowhere. Open the door," I say, but he doesn't move. "Open the damn door, Ares!"

He remains still, so I glare toward the window. "Okay, I'll jump out the window."

When I pass by him, his voice is barely a whisper. "I need you."

I stop dead in my tracks with my back to him. Those three words are enough to paralyze me.

Ares takes my hand, turning me toward him. His eyes search mine. "Just listen to me. I'm not good with words, I can't say . . . I can't say it or explain it, but I can show you how I feel about you." He squeezes my hand. "Let me show you. I'm not trying to use you, I swear. I just want to show you." He puts my hand on his chest. His heart is beating as fast as mine.

He brings his face closer to mine slowly, giving me enough time to reject him, but when I don't, his warm lips find mine.

TWENTY-EIGHT
The Change

I am lost.

The second his lips meet mine a current of emotions electrifies my whole body, and I realize that it's hopeless. I am madly in love with Ares Hidalgo.

What started as a crush ended up turning into feelings so strong that I can't handle them. He destabilizes me, he makes me lose control, he awakens sensations in me that I never thought I would feel. And that makes me feel so exposed, what I feel for him makes me vulnerable, easy to hurt . . . and it scares me so much.

His lips move softly over mine. I put my hands around his neck, pulling him closer to me, and his bare chest collides with mine. Even though I have his shirt on, I can feel the heat emanating from his skin. He intensifies the kiss, quickening his mouth on mine, leaving me breathless. God, he kisses so well.

Our movements cause his towel to come untied from his waist, and I don't complain. I feel how hard he is against my bare thigh as he pulls my skirt up. Ares traces his fingers down the back of my thigh, caressing it gently, and when he reaches my waist, he squeezes it with desire.

He breaks away for a second, his eyes fixed on mine.

"I want you so bad, Raquel."

And I love you, I think. But I don't say it, I just caress his face.

He kisses me again and this time the rhythm is wild, rough, relentless, those passionate kisses that I remember so well and that drive me crazy. I walk backward until the back of my knees hit the bed and I fall with him on top of me. My hands go up to his hair and I cling to him as my body begins to burn. He leaves my mouth again to move down to leave kisses and nibbles on my neck. That's my weak spot. I arch against him, letting out a sigh. His hand slips inside my shirt and his fingers move over my breasts, squeezing and caressing them, driving me to madness. Gasping, I let out a moan as his hand explores under my skirt. I have no underwear on—the contact is direct.

Ares stops his attack on my neck and lifts his face to look at me as his finger enters me.

"Oh God!" I close my eyes.

I want him inside me. I can't wait any longer.

Ares grabs my ankles and pulls me to him until my legs are dangling off the bed, but I'm still lying down. Spreading myself open for him, I watch him. He rubs his member against my wetness, and I moan softly, waiting for the sensation that never comes.

"Ares, please."

He gives me a mischievous smile.

"Please what?"

I say nothing. He leans over me to kiss me passionately. He rubs himself against me, tempting, but never filling me like I want him to.

I stop the kiss.

"Please, Ares."

"Do you want me to fuck you?" he whispers in my ear lasciviously. I nod my head again and again, but he does nothing.

Determined, I grab him by the shoulders and push him onto the bed until he falls on his back. I dig into the pockets of his pants for a condom, and, with a seductive smile, I put it on him before climbing on top of him. He looks at me in surprise, but I know he likes this new position. I pull my shirt off over my head, and his hands go to my breasts immediately. His hard member feels deliciously warm against me. I need him now. I need to feel him inside me.

I lift myself up a little and position him at my entrance. I let myself fall on him and feel him fill me completely.

"Ah, shit, Raquel." He moans, and it's the sexiest sound in the world. The sensation is so wonderful that for a few seconds I don't move. "You look so sexy on top of me like that."

He massages my breasts and I start to move. I'm not an expert, but at least I try, and my slight movements make me moan even more. Ares licks his lips, squeezing my hips, guiding me to move faster, penetrating me deeply. I cling to his chest, closing my eyes. Up, down, in and out, the rhythm, the touch of hot, wet skin driving me crazy.

I feel the orgasm coming and I know it's going to be mind-blowing, so I try to hold it in to enjoy this a little longer. I feel powerful on top of him, owning every grunt and moan his lips leave behind. Ares holds my hips and moves with me, giving me deep thrusts that bring me to the brink of orgasm.

"Ah! Ares, yes. Yes! That's it!"

He rises up, his chest presses against mine, and his mouth finds mine. Without stopping his sudden but divine movements, he grabs my hair, forcing me to meet his gaze as he moves inside me. The brightness and ferocity in his eyes make everything feel so much more intense, as if he wants to show me what he feels for me right at this moment, in this look, in this union of our bodies.

I clutch his back, digging my nails into him. The orgasm makes me scream his name and tell him I'm his again and again. Waves and waves of pleasure cross my body, sending shivers to every nerve, every muscle. Ares grunts, and I feel him come.

I rest my head on his shoulder as our accelerated breathing echoes around the room. I don't dare look at him, I don't want to see his expression, I don't want to see him look like he wants to throw me aside because he got what he wanted.

He pushes my shoulders and separates us gently, forcing me to face him. I swallow thickly and look up at him. I'm surprised to see a beautiful smile on his lips and tenderness radiating from his eyes. His hand takes a lock of my hair and tucks it behind my ear.

"You are beautiful."

It's the second time he tells me, but it still takes my heart by surprise, and my pulse races. He opens his lips to say something, but then hesitates and closes them again.

What do you want to tell me, Greek God?

This is the first time I've felt close to him. I know it sounds strange, but the other times we've been together, when we've finished doing it, I felt that he was so far away, so out of my reach. Sharing your body with someone isn't the same as being close with them, I've learned. I raise my hand and caress his cheek, his skin is so soft . . . he closes his eyes, looking vulnerable and beautiful.

I love you . . .

Those words get stuck in my throat, making me lower my hand. He opens his eyes, the question of why I stopped touching him evident in his face.

Because touching you makes me want to say something that would scare you. And I don't want to ruin the moment.

I smile at him and get up to rush to the bathroom. I take a shower, and my stomach growls in protest, the early morning sex has left me exhausted and hungry. Ares knocks on the bathroom door.

"I brought you some shorts and a T-shirt, they're Marco's, but it's better than going out in your vomit clothes."

I cringe at the thought. I open the door a little and pull the clothes out of his hands. They're too big for me, but I'm not complaining. When I look in the mirror, a shriek leaves my lips. A pink and purple mark decorates my neck.

A hickey!

Angrily, I fling open the door. Ares is sitting on the bed with the towel wrapped around his naked hips. Pressing my lips together, I give him a murderous look. He raises an eyebrow and I point to my neck.

"Are you serious? A hickey?"

Ares smiles and is about to say something when someone knocks on the door. Marco's voice sounds on the other side.

"Are you awake?"

"Yes," Ares answers.

"Come down for breakfast, we ordered delivery."

I look at Ares. I don't want to be clingy or bother him, but I don't know if I should stay or leave. Ares stands up and walks toward me.

"We'll be down in five minutes," he tells Marco. He stops in front of me, gives me a short kiss, and heads to the bathroom.

Am I dreaming? Ares is being cute after having sex. Is he on drugs? Did he hit his head on a rock?

When Ares comes back, I use his phone to let Dani know that I'm okay, and I tell her to call Yoshi to make sure he's safe. We head downstairs, and I can't help the nerves that come over me. I know Ares's group of friends, but I'm not yet familiar with them. The only moment we've shared wasn't exactly perfect. I remember clearly how I danced for Marco, Ares's jealous reaction, and Luis and Gregory's laughter.

My hair is in a high ponytail, and I feel a little uncomfortable in Marco's clothes. I hesitate midway down the stairs. Ares seems to notice, and he takes my hand, giving me a look over his shoulder that reassures me that everything will be fine.

As I reach the bottom of the stairs, the first person I see is Luis, sitting on the couch massaging his forehead and eating. Gregory is lying on the large couch, his forearm over his eyes. The brunette I saw last night is sitting next to him, caressing his arm. Marco is standing by the fireplace with his hands on his chest. His eyes meet mine and a crooked smile forms on his lips. The food is on the little table in the middle of the furniture in plastic containers with steam coming out. It must have just arrived.

"I almost left you without any eggs," Luis comments, eating desperately.

Gregory looks up.

"Good morning, sleepyhead." I wave at him.

"Hello."

I'm surprised to see how neat and tidy the room is. Remembering last night's mess, I wonder how it got clean so fast.

After we finish eating, Ares and I walk out of there, saying goodbye to his friends, which relieves me more than I want to admit. I still don't feel comfortable with them, and, to be honest, I don't feel completely comfortable with Ares either. Despite being intimate with him, there are still those awkward silences between us.

Ares guides me to his car to take me home. He gets in and I do the same. It's a beautiful, modern SUV, but it's nothing compared to the driver. Ares puts on his sunglasses and looks like a model ready for a photo shoot. He's wearing jeans and a white shirt that he probably borrowed from Marco. On his right hand, a nice black watch adorns his wrist. He starts the car and turns, catching me staring at him like an idiot.

He puts on some music, and I watch the houses go by through the window.

Tell me a story . . .

I narrow my eyes as the memory of being next to Ares and begging him to tell me a story returns. Did that happen last night? I turn to him and watch him drive. How can he look so sexy doing something as simple as that? The way the muscles in his arm contract when he moves the lever and the confidence with which he turns the wheel make him look irresistible. It makes me want to climb on top of him and kiss him.

Ares stops at a gas station for a few minutes, and I stay in the car, waiting. His cell phone is stuck to the side of the steering wheel with the screen exposed. The announcement of a new message catches my attention and I can see that it's from Samy. I can't see the content, just her name there, which flashes again with three more messages. My stomach churns slightly, but I push it away as Ares gets back into the car. He gives me a smile, and I forget about Samy for a few seconds.

"Ares . . ."

"Huh?"

"I . . . " *I like you, I want you, I always want to be with you like this.* "Uh . . . nothing."

I just stare at him like a fool as he drives the rest of the way. My obsession . . .

My beautiful Greek god.

TWENTY-NINE
The Question

- ARES -

The car ride is more uncomfortable than I expected, and it catches me off guard. I clear my throat before speaking.

"Do you want a ride home or to your friend's house?" I ask, my hands tight on the steering wheel as I take a turn. Raquel is sitting in the passenger seat with her hands in her lap. Is she nervous?

"My friend's." She gives me the address, and silence falls between us. I feel the need to fill it, so I turn on the radio just as "i hate u, i love u" by gnash begins to play. The lyrics steal a smile from Raquel, and I begin to sing it with the intention of lightening the awkwardness between us.

"Wow, Ares Hidalgo sings," she teases. "I should record you and post it; I bet it would get a lot of likes."

I grin openly at her.

"You'd only help my popularity with girls. You want that?"

"Your popularity with girls? *Puh-lease!* You're not even that hot."

"Not even that hot? That's not what you were saying this morning. Should I repeat the things you were asking me to do to you?"

I glance at her, and she turns red. Well, this isn't so bad, she looks much more comfortable now.

"That's not necessary."

I reach out my hand and rest it on her thigh.

"That was a good way to start the day."

"Pervert."

I squeeze her thigh gently.

"But you like this pervert, don't you?"

"Ugh, I can't handle your ego," she says. "It's too big."

"I think that's what you told me this morning."

She slaps my shoulder.

"Ah! Stop having dirty thoughts!"

I laugh, and the relief that everything is flowing more smoothly between us is cut short by my phone ringing. I see Samy's name on the screen and press answer. My cell phone is synced to my car's audio system so I can talk without having to take my hands off the wheel. Samy says, "Hello," and it echoes all around us. It doesn't bother me that Raquel is listening because I have nothing to hide.

"Hello?"

"Hey, what are you doing?" Samy asks, and it sounds like she's eating something.

"I'm on my way home. Why?"

"I thought you were still at Marco's. I left some things there the other day. I was going to ask you to bring them to me."

"I've already left."

Samy sighs on the other end of the line.

"Okay, are we still on for the movie today?" I think I see Raquel tense up next to me, but I attribute it to my imagination.

"Sure, I'll pick you up at seven," I confirm.

"See you later, cutie," she says before hanging up. She's always called me that.

Silence fills the car, and I curse the call for ruining the good vibe we had built.

"Who was it?" Raquel's voice is serious.

"Samy."

"Hmmm, right." Her hands again twisting in her lap. "Are you going out today?"

I nod, stopping at a traffic light.

"Yeah, we're going to the movies with the group."

I take advantage of the traffic light to look at her, but she doesn't look at me. Her eyes are fixed on the window next to her, and she presses her lips together. She's back to being awkward with me, and I don't like it. My thumb taps the steering wheel lightly as I wait for the light to turn green, and when it does, I take one last glance at the girl beside me.

Look at me, Raquel, smile at me, show me that everything is all right.

But she doesn't and that stresses me out. I don't want to screw up again, but apparently that's something that comes naturally to me.

"I have plans too," she says suddenly, in a strange tone. Did it bother her that I'm meeting my friends? She's going out too.

What if it's with that friend of hers?

Raquel looks at me out of the corner of her eye, and I realize that I've been silent for a while, and she's waiting for a reply. But asking her who she's meeting seems worse than keeping quiet. I don't know if telling her that I trust her would make it better or worse.

As we park in front of her friend's house, she barely looks at me as she gets out of the car.

No, this is not right.

Concerned, I get out and follow her.

"Raquel."

She doesn't turn around.

"Raquel." I step in front of her. "Hey, hey, what's wrong?"

"Nothing." But her eyes dodge mine: she's lying.

"I don't understand you. Did I do something wrong?"

"Just forget it, Ares." Her tone is cold now, and it terrifies me.

"Raquel, look at me." She does, crossing her arms over her chest. She's defensive and I have no fucking idea why. I thought that everything was going well and that last night I showed her how much I care. "I'm trying, okay? I'm a mess, but I'm trying."

"What are you trying to do? You drop me off and then say you're going out with your ex." I open my mouth to reply, but she cuts me off. "With your friends, fine, but without me, right? Do you care about me or not? I don't understand anything anymore. And I don't want you to hurt me anymore."

"And I don't want to hurt you," I protest. Obviously, I'm failing.

"So, tell me: What do you feel for me?"

The question catches me off guard. I open my mouth to say something, but nothing comes out, and I close it again. A sad smile crosses her face.

"When you can answer that question, come find me," she says.

And with that, she leaves me standing there with the words choking in my throat, and my heart burning in my chest. I can't answer her question, even though I know the answer.

THIRTY
The Disappointment

- RAQUEL -

Time heals a broken heart.

Whoever said that needed to specify how much time was needed for that to be true. As the days go by, I only feel worse. I distract myself with school, hanging out with Dani, reading, and going for walks with Rocky. Nothing seems to be working. I guess my feelings will eventually fade but not in a few days.

I'm unsure of how I would react if I were to see Ares again, so I look to Dani. "I need you to be my hand brake."

Dani gives me a weird look. "Your what?"

"My hand brake . . . like the one that cars have, so you can stop me when I lose my brakes, which in this case would be my self-control—"

"Stop," Dani interrupts me. "First of all, that's the worst analogy you've ever made and believe me you've made some pretty bad ones."

I open my mouth to protest, but she continues. "Second, you want me to stop you every time you want to open your legs for Ares? Got it. Without so much beating around the bush and meaningless analogies."

"My analogies are the best."

It's after school, and we're in her room. It's Monday, and the beginning of the week has hit me hard. I feel so exhausted. Why do I have to study?

Because you need a future, my mom's grumpy voice lectures in my head. Dani returns with her phone in her hand.

"I already know the whole Ares story, but there's something I don't understand."

"What?"

"Today you were avoiding Yoshi at school as if he had the plague. Why?"

I let myself fall on the bed, hugging a pillow. "I may have skipped telling you that part of the weekend," I answer.

Dani lets herself fall on the bed next to me and turns her face to see me.

"What happened?"

I stare at the ceiling for a moment, saying nothing, and Dani seems to understand everything.

"He finally told you that he likes you?"

I turn my head toward her so fast that my neck hurts. "You knew it?"

"Everyone knew but you."

I hit her with the pillow. "But what . . . ? Why didn't you tell me?"

"It wasn't my secret to tell."

I look at the ceiling again. "Well, that night he told me, and he . . . kissed me."

"Ohhh!" Dani sits up abruptly. "I didn't expect that! How was it? Did you like it? Did you kiss him back? Did he use tongue? What did you feel? Details, Raquel, details!"

I roll my eyes, sitting up as well. "It was . . . good."

Dani raises an eyebrow.

"Well? That's it?"

"What do you want me to tell you? He . . . he's always been there and I had come to feel things for him in a platonic way. I never expected him to like me. Kissing him was nice, but it was . . . unreal. I don't know how to explain it."

"You liked it, but it wasn't as mind-blowing as when you kiss Ares."

"It was different."

"You're lost, Raquel. You are so in love with Ares."

I lower my head, unable to deny it. Dani puts her arm around my shoulders to give me a side hug.

"It's okay. I know it's scary to feel so much for someone, but it's going to be okay."

"I don't know what to say to Yoshi."

"The truth. Tell him that you're not ready to try anything with anyone right now. You have feelings for someone else, and they may not be reciprocated, but that doesn't mean you can suddenly stop feeling. Tell him you don't want to use him."

"I shouldn't have kissed him back."

"And I shouldn't have eaten that hamburger so late, but we all make mistakes."

I burst out laughing, pulling away from her.

"Did you eat a hamburger without me?" I ask. Her phone rings with a message. She excitedly checks it, and a goofy smile fills her lips. "Okay, that smile is suspicious."

She clears her throat. "Of course not."

"Who are you talking to?"

She puts her phone, with the screen facing down, in her lap.

"Just a friend."

I wrestle with her and snatch the cell phone out of her hands. I try to read the messages, but she attacks me, so I run out of the room. Barefoot, I run down the hallway and almost crash into Dean. He's still in his school uniform.

"Raquel, what—"

"Dean! Stop her!" I hear Dani's voice far down the hall. I run even faster toward the stairs. As I reach the top, I stop so abruptly that I almost fall forward.

Ares.

He's just as surprised to see me. Like Dean, he's wearing his black school uniform.

React, Raquel.

I regain my composure and give him a friendly smile.

"Hello."

He smiles back at me, but it's not just friendly, it's that charming smile he has. "Hello, Witch."

And there goes my heart, beating like crazy. His mere presence is wreaking havoc on me.

"Raquel!" Dani appears behind me and freezes when she sees the unexpected visitor. "Oh, hey, Ares."

Ares just smiles at her. Dean returns just in time to save the awkward situation.

"Here are the notes," Dean says, handing Ares a notebook.

"Thank you," Ares says, turning his gaze back to me. "Are you leaving, Raquel?"

"Me?"

"I could give you a ride if you want."

Those beautiful eyes . . .

Those lips . . .

I want to shout no and reject him, but the words don't come out. Dani stands in front of me. "No, she's not leaving yet. We're going to finish some things." I give her a confused look and she whispers, "Hand brake."

Ares gives me one last look before disappearing out the front door.

"Wow, that was interesting," Dean comments, turning to us.

"So much tension," Dani agrees.

"Strong sexual tension, man. I think we all got pregnant," Dean laughs, and I give them both a murderous look.

The cell phone in my hand rings with a message, and I remember what I was doing before the Greek god appeared. I run, with Dani chasing me, and lock myself in the bathroom in her room, which makes me feel stupid because I should have done that in the first place. Checking the messages, my mouth almost drops to the floor. They're all from Apolo. Apparently, they've been talking for some time; they say good morning and good night to each other. I laugh out loud as I exit the bathroom.

"I can explain."

"Apolo? Oh God, I really love karma."

Dani crosses her arms over her chest. "I don't know what you're thinking, but you're wrong."

"You're flirting with him! You like him!"

"Of course not! See, that's why I didn't want to tell you, because I knew you'd get the wrong idea. He's a sophomore and we're seniors."

"So? Oh, come on," I say, grabbing her by the shoulders. She averts her gaze. "You're crazy about him!"

She slaps my hands, removing them from her shoulders. "Stop making things up. I don't like him, end of story."

"One month."

"What?"

"I'll give you a month to come back with your head down and tell me you fell for him. It's not easy to say no to the Hidalgos, believe me."

"I refuse to talk about this anymore."

"Well, don't talk, just listen," I tell her, putting my hands on her waist. "You're only two years older than Apolo. And he's very mature for his age. If you like him, why worry? Haven't you heard that there is no age in love?"

"Yeah. You know who I heard say that? The pedo in the corner."

"Don't exaggerate."

"Let's just . . . forget about it."

"You don't have to lie to me. You know that, don't you? I can see through you."

"I know, I just don't want to say it. I don't want to make it real."

"Oh, my dear hand brake, it's already real."

Dani throws a pillow at me and then seems to remember something. "Oh! Look, I found the old phone I told you about." She hands me a small phone. The screen is green, and you can only see the time. Dani gives a nervous smile. "It's only good for calls and messages, but it's something."

"It's perfect!"

At least I'll be able to communicate, although a part of me still feels sad about my iPhone. I worked so hard, and so many extra hours, to save up and buy it. I remember Ares's words when I went to return the phone to him: *I know you bought it yourself, with your money, with your hard work. I'm sorry I couldn't stop them from taking it away from you, but I can give you another one. Let me give it to you. Don't be proud.*

His gesture was so nice. And then he was such an idiot. I never thought there could be someone who could be both at the same time, but Ares exceeds expectations.

I say good-bye to Dani and walk to the phone store to put my old number on this one. It bores me to do all those tedious tasks, but I have no choice. I want my old number back. Everyone I know has that number.

Ares has that number.

But that doesn't matter to me, does it?

After wasting two hours of my life, I finally get home. It's already getting dark, and my phone hasn't stopped ringing with all the messages I've received. I smile when I see the message from Apolo inviting me to the party at his house almost two weeks ago. How I wish I could have read the message that day.

There are several dramatic messages from Carlos, as usual, and some old messages from Dani and Yoshi, obviously from before they knew I had lost my cell phone. There aren't any from Ares.

And what did you expect? He was the first person who knew that you'd been robbed.

I yawn, closing the front door behind me. "I'm home!"

Silence.

I step into the living room, and I'm surprised to find Yoshi and my mom sitting on the couch. Did he come here straight from school? Why?

"Oh, hi, I didn't expect to see you here," I tell him honestly.

Mom looks extremely serious. "Where were you?"

"At Dani's house, and then I went to the phone compa—" I stop talking because the expressions on their faces scare me. "Is something wrong?"

Yoshi lowers his head. Mom stands up. "Joshua, you can go. I have to talk to my daughter."

Yoshi looks at my worried expression and mutters something as he passes me.

"I'm sorry."

I follow him with my eyes as he disappears through the door. When I look back at her, Mom is standing in front of me.

"Mom, what happ—"

The slap takes me by surprise, echoing throughout our small room. I hold my throbbing cheek, completely stunned. My eyes flood with tears. My mother has never hit me, ever. Her eyes are red, as if she's holding back tears.

"I'm so disappointed. What were you thinking?"

"What are you talking about? What did Yoshi tell you?"

"What I am talking about is that my daughter is out there having sex irresponsibly!"

"Mom . . ."

Her eyes fill with tears, and it breaks my heart. Seeing your mom cry is devastating.

"I gave you so much trust, so much freedom, and this is how you pay me back?"

I don't know what to say, I just lower my head in embarrassment. I hear her take a deep breath.

"You know better than anyone what I went through with your father. You went through it with me! I thought the only good thing we got out of that situation was that you would learn from me, that you would be an intelligent young woman who would know how to value herself." Her voice cracks. "That you wouldn't be like me."

I know what she means. I can still feel her sadness when she remembers Dad and everything he put her through. I really have no way to justify myself. I did everything behind her back when she trusted me.

I look up, and I start to sob. My mom is touching her chest as if trying to ease the pain.

"I'm . . . I'm so sorry, Mom."

She shakes her head, wiping away her tears. "I am so disappointed."

Me, too, Mom, I'm disappointed in myself too.

She sits on the couch. "This hurts me so much, I thought I raised you better, I thought we were a team."

"We are a team, Mommy."

"What did I do wrong?" she asks. "Where did I fail you?" I kneel in front of her and take her face in my hands.

"You didn't do anything wrong, nothing wrong, Mommy. It's my fault." She pulls me to her and hugs me.

"Oh, my child." She kisses my hair and keeps crying, and my heart is so wrinkled and sore that I can only cry with her.

THIRTY-ONE
The Punishment

Gray.

This is how I would describe the next two weeks of my life. Grounded, I can only leave the house for school and for some shifts at work, and then I have to return as soon as the dismissal bell rings or after I'm done with my job.

Even though I promised my mom that Ares was out of my life, she still punished me. I am dutifully serving my sentence because she's right. I didn't do things the right way. Maybe if Ares was my official boyfriend, I could defend myself. But I can't expect her to understand that I agreed to be with a guy who doesn't want a stable relationship.

Yes, the last time I saw him he was nice, but he couldn't even tell me that he likes me. I don't expect him to tell me that he loves me; I just need to hear . . . something… *words* that prove that he does have feelings for me, and it's not just sexual attraction.

I haven't heard anything from Ares for two weeks, and I haven't even looked out of the window to try to see him. What for? What would I gain by doing that? To torture myself more? No thanks, I've had enough.

A part of me feels that the conversation with my mom gave me back my strength and everything I threw aside for Ares. Well, not for him, because he didn't make me—I decided to do it.

The saddest part of this situation? Yoshi.

Surprisingly, it's not my mom's slap that makes my heart hurt. It's Yoshi.

I feel betrayed on so many levels. Yoshi told my mom everything, and it hurts me so much. He's been my best friend since we were little. He's always been there, but the fact that he betrayed me—and in such a big way—leaves me with a wound in my heart. I don't know if he did it because he thought that it was the best thing for me or if it was out of jealousy, but either way it was wrong. You tell someone secrets because you trust them. I trusted him, and he took that trust and destroyed it.

Dani was furious when I told her what he had done. She threatened to hit him along with a couple of other violent things too graphic to describe. I had to calm her down and force her to promise to leave him alone. I don't want any more drama. I just want time to keep passing, for my wounds to start healing, and for these feelings to go away.

Yes, I want a miracle.

Anyone would think that Yoshi would try to apologize, but he hasn't. He just avoids me and ducks his head every time I run into him at school. I've wanted to confront him, yell at him, slap him, see what excuses he uses, but I just don't have the energy for it.

Apolo and I have become a little closer, although every time I hang out with him, I can't help but think about his brother. But I just deal with it. What happened between Ares and me isn't his fault.

I let out a long sigh. It's Saturday, and I'm cleaning the house. I feel like a zombie, moving automatically. I can tell I'm a little depressed. I don't know if it's because of Ares, the situation with my mom, the situation with Yoshi, or maybe a combination of all three.

Rocky is sitting with his muzzle on his front paws, looking at me as if he knows I'm not feeling well. My dog and I have a connection beyond words. I kneel in front of him and rub his head. Rocky licks my fingers.

"You and me against the world, Rocky."

Mom appears in the doorway of my room, wearing her nurse's uniform. "I'm leaving. I have a night shift today."

"Okay."

"You know the rules: don't go out and no visitors unless it's Dani or Yoshi."

"Yes, ma'am."

Her hard expression softens. "I'll call you from time to time on the landline."

That pulls me out of my numb state. "Are you kidding?"

"No, I trusted you, and you used that to party and bring boys to the house."

"Mom, I didn't commit a crime, I just—"

"Quiet. I'm late. I expect you to behave."

A forced smile forms on my lips as I clench my fists at my sides. I can't believe this is happening. My relationship with my mother has fractured, and it's all because of Yoshi.

What gave him the right to tell my secrets to my mother?

Night falls, enveloping my room in darkness. I don't even want to move to turn on the lights. I'm surprised to hear the doorbell ring.

I look through the little peephole in the door and see my former best friend waiting impatiently. He's wearing his favorite sweater and a wool hat. His glasses are slightly fogged up. It must be a bit cold outside. Autumn has already arrived, leaving the hot summer behind.

I think about not opening the door, but I can't leave him out in the cold either.

"I know you're in there, Raquel. Open up."

Reluctantly, I open the door and turn my back on him to head to the stairs. I hear the door close behind me.

"Raquel, wait." I ignore him and keep walking. I climb the first step and he grabs my arm, turning me toward him. "Wait!"

I slap his hand away. "Don't touch me!"

He raises his hands. "Okay, just listen to me. Give me a few minutes."

"I don't want to talk to you."

"It's a lifetime of friendship; I deserve a few minutes." I gave him a cold look. "Give me five minutes, and then I'll leave you alone."

I cross my arms over my chest. "Talk."

"I had to do it, Raquel. You were gawking at that guy. Do you have any idea how much it hurt me to watch him use you repeatedly while you let him? I grew up with you. I care about you." He touches his chest. "Regardless of how I feel about you, you're my best friend. I want the best for you."

"And telling my mom was the solution? Are you fucking kidding me?"

"It was the only thing I *could* do. If I had tried to talk to you, you wouldn't have listened to me."

"Of course, I would have."

"Be honest, Raquel. You wouldn't have. You would have said I was jealous, and you would have ignored me because you're so fucking blind with love that you can't see beyond your nose."

"You have two minutes left."

"Remember what you said to me last Christmas? When you told me it was time to forgive my father?"

I tighten my lips because I do remember. Yoshi's dad had messed up big time with them, and Yoshi was furious. I advised him to at least listen to his dad's side of the story.

"No, I don't remember."

His expression falls. "I was furious with you, I shouted at you: 'How can you take his side? What kind of a friend are you?' And you told me: 'A true friend is one who tells you the truth to your face, even if it hurts.'"

I don't like it when someone uses my own words against me. "That was different. I talked to you. I didn't go gossiping and meddling with your father."

"Yes, you talked to me, and I listened to you. You wouldn't have listened to me, Raquel. I know it, and you know it too."

There is a moment of silence. "Your time is up," I tell him and turn away.

I hear him mutter defeatedly. "Rochi . . ."

"My name is Raquel." My voice comes out colder than I expected. "Thank you for the explanation. Regardless of your reasons, you destroyed years of trust in a flash, and I don't know if it's something that can ever be restored. Good night, Joshua."

I leave him there at the bottom of the steps, and he looks like a gentleman waiting for his lady to come down the staircase. Except that he took it upon himself to destroy any chance with said lady. When I get to my room, I hear him close the front door. I let out a big sigh and walk to my window.

The window that started it all.

"Are you using my Wi-Fi?"

"Yes."

"Without my permission?"

"Yes."

Idiot.

A sad smile crosses my lips. I sit down in front of my computer, and the memory of Ares kneeling in front of me, fixing the router, comes to mind. I glance at the window, and I can almost see him. I shake my head.

What's wrong with me?

Stop seeing him everywhere, it's not healthy.

With nothing to do, I go on Facebook. Well, not my personal Facebook. It's a fake one that I created to check on Ares. I know, I'm a hopeless case. In my defense, I created that account a long time ago and haven't used it since. But now that I've blocked Ares from my personal Facebook, I have to use the fake one again.

It won't hurt me to check his page, will it? There's nothing to lose. His profile has no new posts, only photos where other people have tagged him. The most recent one is from Samy's account, as you might expect. In the photo they're at the movies, and she's laughing with her mouth full of popcorn while his hand is raised as if he was feeding her. In the post she wrote: *Movies with this guy who brightens my days.*

Ouch.

My heart gives a pang, but I keep scrolling down. All I see are posts of people tagging him with pictures of the soccer game two weeks ago and congratulating him, telling him how great he is. I roll my eyes. Keep feeding his ego, as if he's not arrogant enough already.

Taking one last look at the picture with Samy, because obviously I'm a masochist, I close Facebook and go to sleep.

I don't want to think anymore.

>> <<

My cell phone wakes me up. I half open one eye and my eyelid trembles with the effort. It's still dark, what time is it? The phone keeps ringing and I stretch out my hand toward my nightstand, knocking everything over in the process.

I answer without even looking at the screen.

"Hello?"

"Good morning," my mother's voice replies. "Get up."

"Mom, it's Sunday. Did I also lose the right to sleep in?"

"I'm not off shift today until after noon, please finish cleaning the house, and get the laundry started."

"Understood."

Hanging up, I brush my teeth and go downstairs. The doorbell rings, startling me. Is Joshua back? If he thinks coming to see me every day will get him anywhere, he's wrong.

The doorbell rings again and, growling, I shout, "I'm coming!"

I really don't have the energy to deal with Yoshi right now. The doorbell rings again, and I rush to open the door. What hits me first is the chilly air, and then surprise at the person in front of me. It's the last person I expected to see.

Ares Hidalgo.

My heart skips a beat and starts pounding like crazy. Ares is standing in front of me, looking as if he didn't sleep a second last night. His hair is messy, and there are big dark circles under his pretty eyes. He's wearing a white shirt that looks wrinkled and the first few buttons are undone.

A goofy smile forms on his lips.

"Hello, Witch."

THIRTY-TWO
The Unstable Boy

Controlling your emotions is so easy when the person affecting them isn't right in front of you. You feel strong, able to go on with your life. It's as if your self-control and self-esteem are recharged. It takes days, weeks, to get that feeling of strength. But it only takes a second to destroy it. The moment that person appears, your stomach churns, your hands sweat, your breathing quickens, your strength falters, and it's so unfair after you've worked so hard.

"What are you doing here?" I'm surprised by the coldness in my voice, and so is he.

He raises his eyebrows. "You're not going to let me in?"

"Why should I?"

"I-I just. . . . Can I come in, please?"

"What are you doing here, Ares?" I repeat my question, my muscles tensing.

"I needed to see you."

My heart is racing, but I ignore it. "Well, you saw me."

He sets a foot in the door. "Just . . . let me come in for a second."

"No, Ares." I try to close the door, but I'm not fast enough and he enters, forcing me to take two steps back. He closes the door, and in a panic, I blurt out something that I think will scare him away. "Mom is upstairs, I just have to call her to come and get you out."

He laughs, sits down on the couch, and puts his cell phone on the small table in front of him to rest his elbows on his knees.

"Your mother is at work."

I frown. "How do you know?"

He looks up at me, and a mischievous smile forms on his lips. "Do you think you're the only stalker here?"

What?

I decide to ignore his response and focus on trying to get him out of here before Yoshi decides to visit me, or Mom comes back early and World War III breaks out. Maybe if he says what he came to say, he'll go away.

"Okay, you're in. What do you want?"

Ares runs his hand over his face. "I want to talk to you."

"Speak up then."

He opens his mouth, but closes it again, as if unsure about what he wants to say. I'm about to tell him to go away when he says three words that take my breath away, three words I never expected to hear from him, not now, not ever.

"I hate you."

His tone is serious, his expression cold.

The statement takes me by surprise. My heart and my eyes burn, but I act as if I am unaffected.

"Okay, you hate me, got it. Is that all?"

He shakes his head, a sad smile dances on his lips. "My life was so fucking easy before you, so manageable, and now," he points at me, "you've complicated everything, you . . . you've ruined everything."

My stomach tightens, and tears blur my vision.

"You came all the way to my house to tell me that? I think you'd better leave."

He wags his finger at me. "I'm not finished."

"But I think you are, so get out."

"Don't you want to know why?"

"I destroyed your life. I think you've made that clear, now get the hell out of my house."

"No."

"Ares . . ."

"I'm not leaving!" He raises his voice, standing up, and that ignites my anger. "I need this, I need to tell you. I need you to know why I hate you."

"Why do you hate me, Ares?"

"Because you make me feel. You make me feel, and I don't want to." That leaves me speechless, but I don't show it, and he goes on. "I don't want to be weak. I swore not to be like my father and here I am, being weak in front of a woman. You made me like him. You make me weak and I hate it."

My anger dominates my words. "If you hate me so much, what the hell are you doing here? Why don't you leave me alone?"

He raises his voice again. "Do you think I haven't tried?" He lets out a harsh laugh. "I've tried, Raquel, but I can't!"

"Why not?" I challenge, approaching him.

He opens his mouth and closes it, clenching his jaw. His breathing is coming fast, and so is mine. I lose myself in the intensity of his eyes, and he turns his back to me, running his hands through his hair.

"Ares, you have to go."

He turns just enough to face me in profile, with his eyes fixed on the ground.

"I thought this shit would never happen to me. I avoided it, but it still happened to me . . . I don't know if this is what it's supposed to feel like, but I can't deny it anymore." He turns completely toward me, looking defeated. "I'm in love, Raquel."

I stop breathing and my mouth drops open.

He smiles like a fool. "I'm so fucking in love with you."

Did I hear him right? Did Ares Hidalgo just say he was in love with me? He didn't say he wanted me or that he wanted me in his bed. He said he was in love with me. I can't say anything. I can't move. I can only look at him. I can only see those cold walls fade in front of me.

And then I remember the story . . .

His story . . .

What he shared with me that night I was drunk.

The memory is a blur, but his words are clear. He had found his mother in bed with a man who was not his father, and his father had forgiven the infidelity. Ares had lived it all, seen it all. His father had been his pillar, seeing him weak and crying had been a heavy blow to him.

I don't want to be weak. I don't want to be like him. . . .

I understand him now. I know it doesn't justify his actions, but at least it explains them. My mother always told me that who we are depends a lot on the way we were raised and what we experienced in our childhood and early adolescence. Those are the years when we're like sponges, absorbing everything.

And then I see that the guy in front of me isn't the cold, arrogant jerk I first talked to through my window; he's just a guy who had a rough start. A boy who doesn't want to be like the person he used to admire, who doesn't want to be weak. A vulnerable guy, angry because he doesn't want to be vulnerable. And who does? To fall in love with someone is to give them the power to destroy you.

Ares laughs, shaking his head, but the mirth doesn't reach his eyes. "Now you don't say anything."

I don't know what to say. I'm too shocked at the turn this conversation has taken. My emotions are a mess, and my breathing is no better.

"Shit," Ares mutters, turning his back to me. He rests his forehead on the wall.

A laugh escapes my lips. Ares turns to me again, and the confusion is obvious on his face.

"You. Are. Crazy," I say with a chuckle. I don't even know why I'm laughing. "Even your confession had to be ridiculous."

"Stop laughing," he orders, approaching me with a serious expression.

But I can't stop. "You hate me because you love me? Are you listening to yourself?"

He doesn't say anything and just grabs the bridge of his nose. "I don't understand you. I finally have the courage to tell you what I feel. And you laugh?"

I clear my throat. "I'm sorry, really, I'm just . . ."

His expression wavers, and a crooked smile forms on his lips. "You did it."

I furrow my brows. "What?"

"Do you remember what you told me in the cemetery that time I asked you what you want? 'Something very simple,' you said. 'I want you to fall in love with me.'"

I grin. "Yes, and you laughed at me. Who's laughing now,

Greek God?" He tilts his head to the side, watching me.

"You caught me, but you also fell in love along the way."

"Who said I'm in love?"

His approach forces me to step back until my back meets the wall, and, to prevent my escape, he leans over me, caging me in with his hands. He smells of that delicious mixture of expensive cologne and his own scent. I swallow, staring at that perfect face in front of me.

"If you're not in love, then why did you stop breathing?"

I let out the breath I hadn't realized I was holding. I have no answer to his question, and he knows it.

"And why is your heart beating so fast when I haven't even touched you?"

"How do you know my heart is racing?" I ask.

He takes my hand and puts it on his chest. "Because mine is."

Feeling his racing heartbeat under my hand makes my heart flutter.

"This is what I was trying to show you the last time we were together: how I feel about you." He rests his forehead on mine, and I close my eyes, feeling his heartbeat, holding him so close. When he speaks again, his voice is soft. "I'm sorry."

I open my eyes to meet that infinite sea of his eyes. "Why?"

"For taking so long to tell you how I feel." He takes the hand I have on his chest and kisses it. "I'm really sorry."

He moves even closer, and our breaths mingle. I know he's waiting for my approval. When I don't protest, his sweet lips meet mine. The kiss is soft, delicate, but so full of feelings and emotions that I feel the famous butterflies in my stomach. He takes my face with both hands and deepens the kiss, tilting his head to one side. Our lips move in perfect sync. God, I love this boy. I'm so fucked.

He stops but keeps his forehead on mine. I take a breath and speak.

"First time."

He separates his face a little from me to look at me.

"What?"

"It's the first time you've kissed me, and it's not sexual."

He shows me his teeth in that ridiculous smile of his. "Who said it's not sexual?"

I give him a murderous look, and he stops smiling, as a grim expression appears on his face.

"I have no idea what I'm doing, but I just know I want to be with you. Do you want to be with me?" He watches my face, scared of my answer. And that somehow makes me feel powerful. He came here and exposed himself to me. I can make him happy or destroy him. I open my mouth to respond, but the doorbell interrupts me.

I don't know how I know, but I know it's Yoshi. *Shit!*

"Are you expecting someone?" Ares asks.

"Shhh!" I cover his mouth with my hand and force him to back away from the door.

The doorbell rings again, followed by Yoshi's voice. "Raquel!" I *knew* it.

Shit, shit, shit, shit!

"You have to hide," I whisper, releasing his mouth, and dragging him toward the stairs.

"Why? Who is he?" His accusatory tone does not go unnoticed.

"This is no time for jealousy. Come on, walk."

Have you ever tried to move someone taller and stronger than you? It's like pushing a huge rock.

"Ares, please," I beg him. He has to move before Yoshi calls my mom, and she calls me, and the mess starts. "I'll explain later, please go upstairs, and don't make any noise."

"I feel like a lover when the husband arrives," he jokes, but he starts to move and it's a relief. Once he's disappeared up the stairs, I don't know why, but I fix my hair and head to open the door. I pray everything goes well, but Yoshi knows me too well, and he knows when I'm lying or nervous. Too late I realize that Ares's cell phone is on the small table in front of the couch. I cross my fingers that Yoshi doesn't see it.

Virgin of Abdominals, please help me!

THIRTY-THREE
The Testosterone

Things don't have to be perfect.

Perfection can be so subjective. Ares's confession might seem unromantic to others, but to me? It was perfect. To me, he's amazing, moodiness and all.

Maybe I'm blinded by love, maybe I can't see beyond my feelings, but if there's even a slim chance of being happy with him, I want to try. I want to be happy. I deserve to be happy. Who wouldn't like that decision?

Yoshi, that's who. My sweet best friend is shaking with rage. He's holding Ares's cell phone.

"He's here, isn't he?"

I open my mouth to deny it, but no sound comes out. Yoshi presses his lips and diverts his gaze, as if facing me was fueling his anger.

"You just don't learn, Raquel."

I clench my fists at my sides. "And what are you going to do about it? Tell my mother? You've been very good at that lately."

Before he can say anything, I continue. "Tell me, Joshua." He winces hearing me use his full name. "What else can I expect from you? Will you tell her about the first time I got drunk? Or the time I skipped class to sneak out with Dani to go bowling? Tell me, so I can be prepared."

"Raquel, don't do this, don't paint me as the bad guy. Everything I've done has been because—"

"Because you're in love with her, and you're a jealous jerk." Ares's voice startles me, and I turn to see him walk down the stairs, his cold eyes fixed on Yoshi.

Yoshi instantly gets defensive. "This is none of your business."

Ares stands next to me and, with one arm, takes me by the waist and pulls me close. "Yes, it is. Everything that has to do with her, has to do with me."

"Really?" Yoshi lets out a sarcastic laugh. "And when did you earn that right? You've only hurt her, and you'll keep on doing so."

"At least I didn't screw up the relationship she had with her mother in a fit of jealousy." Ares shakes his head. "Do you have any idea how selfish you are? You should learn to play fair."

Wait a second, how did Ares know about Yoshi? I have a feeling that Dani must have told Apolo, and he must have told Ares. Dani and I are going to have a talk. She'll listen to me.

Yoshi makes a face. "I'm not interested in talking to you. I'm here for her, not you. You shouldn't even be here. You should leave."

Ares gives him a cold smile. "Make me." Ares releases me and walks toward him. Yoshi suddenly looks very small. "Come on, try to make me leave. Give me an excuse to beat you up for doing something so shitty to my girl."

My girl . . .

That makes me hold my breath.

Yoshi stands firm. "Typical, you resort to violence when you don't know what to say."

"No, I resort to violence when someone deserves it."

"Then you should beat yourself up," Yoshi replies with a venomous tone. "No one deserves a beating more than you."

I can see Ares's shoulders tense up as he clenches his fists. Immediately, I step between them.

"I think that was enough." I give Yoshi a pleading look. I consider telling him to leave, but I know that's only going to make things worse. The only way to control this is to make them both go. "I think you should both leave."

I glance over my shoulder at Ares, and he doesn't seem surprised. He raises his hands in the air.

"As you wish."

He walks halfway to the door and stops, waiting for Yoshi, who gives me one last sad look before leaving. Part of me fears they'll fight out there, but they're off my property now, and they're both mature enough to make their own decisions.

I let out a long sigh, walk into the living room, and immediately fall on the couch. What a morning! Not only did I have Ares's confession, but I also had to deal with Yoshi. Somehow it's Ares's words about Yoshi that stick in my head: *Because you're in love with her and you're a jealous jerk. At least I didn't screw up the relationship she had with her mother in a fit of jealousy. Do you have any idea how selfish you were?*

Is Ares right? I've tried to believe that Yoshi betrayed me because he wanted what was best for me. With that logic, maybe I could forgive him. However, if he only did it out of jealousy, that makes forgiving him almost impossible.

I hope he doesn't tell my mom that Ares was here. I don't want any more drama.

I'm so fucking in love with you.

My heart races at the memory of those words. I still find it hard to believe. Ares is in love with me. He has *feelings* for me. I'm not just another girl he uses for fun. He's hurt me so many times, but now, for the first time, he's put into words what he feels for me.

The idiot has a heart. I remember his confession, and the intensity in his eyes, and I can't help myself: I let out a childish little squeal. I'm not the only one in love.

With a stupid smile on my face, I go up to my room. Despite everything, I manage to fall asleep again. I know, I have a superhuman ability to sleep under any circumstance.

THIRTY-FOUR
The First Date

Ares has asked me on our first date, and I have nothing to wear.

This is not one of those typical moments when an indecisive person has a lot of clothes to choose from and doesn't know what to pick. I literally have nothing to wear. My mom washed all my clothes, and the only things left are the stuff I don't wear, and obviously I don't wear them for a reason: they don't fit anymore or they're simply too ragged.

Why did Ares have to ask me out today? I still remember his soft voice on the phone when he asked me to please sneak out. How could I say no? I obviously hadn't thought it all through when I said yes. The only one who can save me is Dani.

I call her, and she answers on the third ring. "Funeral Home *Las Flores*, how may I help you?"

"How long are you going to do that, Dani? I told you it's not funny." She lets out a guilty chuckle.

"It's funny to me. What's the matter, grumpy?"

"I need you to pick me up."

"Aren't you grounded?"

"Yes." I lower my voice even more. "But I'm going to sneak out."

"What, what, what, *whaaaaaaaaaaaaaat*?" Dani exaggerates her tone. "Welcome to the dark side, sister."

I let out a long sigh. "Just come and get me, but wait for me at the corner of my street."

"Okay, but you're leaving out the reason why you're going to sneak out. Will you go out partying with me today?"

"No, I have . . . plans."

"With?"

I hang up the call and tuck pillows under the sheets to make it look like someone is in my bed, although I know my mother won't check. She doesn't think I'm capable of sneaking out, and, well, honestly, until a few hours ago I didn't think I was either.

I carefully leave the room. The lights in the house are already off, so I poke my head into my mom's room. I never thought I'd be so happy to hear her snoring. She's sleeping soundly, probably because she had a shift last night and hasn't slept at all until now. A pang of remorse stops me for a second, but then I think of a certain pair of dazzling blue eyes, and that's enough to motivate me to get out of the house.

The cold hits me hard when I step on the street. I'm not wearing a jacket, so I hug myself, rubbing my forearms as I walk. The street is well lit, and there are a few people outside chatting. I wave and continue on my way.

Waiting on the corner, shivering from the cold, I realize that maybe I should have waited in the warmth of my house a little longer. It's barely six minutes later. Dani doesn't live far away, but there are several traffic lights, and I know traffic can get heavy at this hour.

I am freezing to death. Do you see everything I do for you, Greek God?

When I see Dani's car, I'm so relieved that I smile like an idiot. I jump in, and she drives like crazy all the way to her house.

Eighteen outfit attempts later, to say I'm being indecisive is putting it mildly. Dani has given me multiple options and they're all cute, but I want to look perfect for him and nothing seems perfect to me. I know he'll look beautiful in whatever he wears. I feel the need to look my best. This is the first time that I've dressed up in a special way to see someone.

Ares still gets all my first times. How am I going to get over that man if he keeps doing that?

"I vote for the skirt, blouse, and boots," Dani says, chewing Doritos with her mouth open.

"So classy," I say sarcastically.

"They look great on you and adapt to any occasion; we don't know where you're going." She's right, I wonder if we're going to Artemis's bar or some other nightspot. After getting dressed, I start combing my hair when I see Dani stand up and come toward me, pointing her orange Doritos-stained finger at me. "There's something I want to tell you."

I turn around nervously at her serious tone. "Yes?"

"I'm really glad that idiot finally confessed his feelings to you, but . . ." She bites her lower lip. "Remember that he hurt you a lot, and I'm not saying to hold a grudge or anything, I just want you to make him earn your love. You've always served it to him on a silver platter, and he hasn't appreciated it. A few nice words aren't enough, baby. You're worth a lot. Let him realize that, too, and let him fight and earn your affection."

I feel a small pang in my chest at her words, and she must notice the change in my expression because she smiles.

"No, I'm not trying to ruin your first date, it's just my duty as your best friend to tell you the truth, even if it's not pretty. You deserve the world, Raquel. I know it, and that idiot needs to know it too."

I smile back. "Thank you. Sometimes I get carried away by my feelings and lose track of everything I've been through with him."

She squeezes my hand. "I love you, silly."

My smile widens. "I love you, too, silly."

My phone rings. Dani and I share a quick glance.

Incoming call: *Ares <3*

I clear my throat nervously. "Hello?"

"I'm outside."

Those words are enough to make my heart race.

"I'll be right out."

I hang up and let out a squeal. Dani grabs me by the shoulders. "Calm down!"

I say good-bye and head to the door with my heart in my throat. Why am I so nervous?

Okay, calm down, Raquel, you have no reason to be nervous. It's just Ares. You've already seen him naked.

Great, now I'm thinking about Ares naked.

Virgin of Abdominals, why did you endow him so well?

On the street, I see his black car parked in front of the house. Its dark windows don't allow me to see anything inside. I focus on walking. I don't know why it's so hard for me.

Stupid nerves.

As I approach the car, I do the awkward little door dance. I don't know whether to open the passenger door or the back door. He told me he was coming with Marco. Will Marco be in the passenger seat or not?

Ah, how uncomfortable!

I stand there like an idiot, not knowing what to do. Ares notices my indecision and rolls down the window.

"What are you doing?" There's no one in the copilot's seat. I open the door and get in.

"I was just . . ." I glance back and see Marco using his phone. "Hi, Marco."

He looks up and smiles at me. As I straighten in my seat, I look over at Ares, and I realize he is looking at me from head to toe. What he sees brings a crooked smile to those full lips of his.

"And you're not going to say hello to me?" he asks.

I lick my bottom lip. He looks so cute in that white shirt. "Hello."

He raises an eyebrow. "Just that?"

How else? In one swift movement, Ares unbuckles his seat belt, grabs my neck, and stamps his lips against mine. His mouth moves softly, and his lips feel so fucking good on mine. I hold back a moan as he sucks on my bottom lip and bites it lightly.

Marco clears his throat. "I'm still here!"

Ares pulls away and gives me one last short kiss, smiling against my lips. "Hello, Witch."

He goes back to his place, puts on his seat belt, and drives off. While I sit there paralyzed with my legs like jelly. Oh my God, what this guy does to me with just one kiss. Ares puts on some music, and Marco leans over to get in the middle of our seats. "Samy says she's ready."

When he mentions that name, a cold feeling appears in my stomach. Ares turns the wheel, crossing a street. "We'll pick her up. What about Gregory?"

Marco's on his phone. "He's already left with Luis."

"What about the girls?"

"They went with them." My eyes fall on Ares. Which girls? Besides Samy, are there more?

"We're just picking Samy up then."

Ares stops in front of a beautiful two-story house with a lovely garden. Samy is standing next to the mailbox, looking stunning in a short, figure-hugging dress that shows off her long legs, and a nice jacket. She looks incredibly beautiful.

Isn't she cold?

She smiles at Ares, and her adoration is so clear. It's so obvious that she likes him, I wonder if I look like that when I look at Ares. She gets in the back seat, and her smile falters when she sees me.

"Oh, hello, Raquel."

I smile at her. "Hello."

"Aren't you cold?" Marco asks her with a worried expression, and I find it so peculiar how his grim countenance cracks every time Samy appears.

"I'm good," she says.

Ares looks at her in the rearview mirror and smiles. A pang hits my stomach, forcing me to shift a little in my seat. It's so unpleasant to feel jealous. I never felt it in my life until I met Ares. And it doesn't help that they've had sex. They've seen each other naked, for God's sake, that's too much intimacy for a friendship. It also doesn't help that Samy is crazy about him. I don't know if I'm overreacting, but I struggle to stay calm and not show what I'm feeling.

Marco's voice interrupts my thoughts. "Everyone is already there and they're going to order drinks. What do you want?"

Ares shakes his head. "I'm driving, so I'm not drinking."

I'm surprised by the seriousness and maturity of his tone, but I'm pleased too.

Marco snorts. "What a killjoy. We would have come by taxi if driving meant you weren't going to drink."

Ares slows down on a crowded street. It seems to be busy tonight.

"I don't like taxis."

I raise an eyebrow. Oh, the rich guy doesn't like cabs. I can't even afford to take a taxi! The bus is my only solution. I don't even want to imagine what Ares thinks of buses. I'm reminded of the difference between the way we were raised, and how opposite our daily lives are. Our house is one of the last old constructions from the eighties in the neighborhood. The rest of the houses are new customized constructions, Ares's place included. Mom said that when she moved here almost two decades ago, the Hidalgos' house was still being built. She was lucky to get a place before the prices skyrocketed.

Marco interrupts my thoughts again. "What about you, Raquel? What do you want to drink?"

My eyes go to Ares, who is still focused on the road in front of us. I can feel Samy's eyes on me. "Hey, well, I . . . vodka?"

"You don't sound very confident." Marco notices. "Well, vodka, then. I think they ordered a bottle of whiskey and a bottle of wine. I'll tell them to order a bottle of vodka."

A whole bottle? I hope it's for several people, not just me, or tonight could end badly. No, I can't afford to do something stupid today. I have to behave.

When we arrive, I recognize the place. It's an elegant bar that opened recently. I don't think it competes with Artemis's because it is quite far from downtown, while his club is in a particularly strategic location. We pass the entrance, and I'm surprised that the guard doesn't ask for identification.

The first thing that hits me is the high-tech swivel lighting making colorful effects all over the place. We walk past the bar where bartenders are doing tricks with bottles and glasses. Everyone seems to be having a good time. We walk up some stairs decorated with little colored lights until we reach Ares's group of friends.

This is going to be interesting.

>> <<

The awkwardness I felt at breakfast the other day with Ares's friends? Well, I'm feeling something like that now, but much worse. Samy walks past me and heads over to the group to say hi. With my hands in front of me, I interlace my fingers and glance at Ares, who is also greeting everyone.

I hate feeling invisible when people act like I don't exist or pretend I'm not standing in front of them. Especially when it's a group of rich kids who are used to judging you by the clothes you're wearing: Are they branded or not? Are they from this season or not? And no, I'm not generalizing. There are people like Dani or Apolo who have money but don't make a big deal of it, but right now, I can see the way the girls in this group stare at my clothes and make faces. And the guys? They just watch me as if deciding whether I'm pretty enough to bother talking to. Being the only Latina girl among them all makes it even more awkward.

I feel like years pass, when it's only been seconds. I drop my hands to my sides and struggle not to run away. I'd like to say that it's Ares who turns and draws me in, but it's Samy who takes pity on my miserable state and comes back for me.

"Come on, Raquel. Let me introduce you."

I fake a friendly smile while she introduces me to everyone. There are three girls. One with black hair who's called Natalie, a blond next to her called Darla, and the third is the brunette I saw at Ares's team party who had breakfast with us a few weeks ago. Her name is Andrea. There are two more guys sitting beside Gregory, Luis, and Marco. A blond guy who introduces himself as Zahid, and a guy with glasses named Oscar. I know I won't remember all those names, but I don't care.

I glance at Ares. He's sitting next to Natalie on the other side of the table. It's my turn to sit next to Samy, who was the last one to sit down; next to her is Oscar, and they seem to be talking about a music concert. Like a fool, I stare at Ares, who's still talking to Natalie intently.

Is that why you brought me here, Greek God? To push me aside and amuse yourself with past conquests?

Lowering my gaze, I struggle with the bitterness in my chest and the tightness in my stomach. I had so many expectations for my first date with him. I painted so many different scenarios in my head, from romantic dinners to a simple movie outing, or maybe just sitting and talking in his car as he drove around town. But here I am, sitting across the table from him, feeling the same distance between us that was there at the beginning. It's like getting closer to him makes the distance grow.

Everyone around me is talking, laughing, sharing stories, and I'm alone. It's like I'm watching the scene, but I'm not part of it. This is his world, his comfort zone, not mine. And he left me alone in it, without a care in the world. Ares doesn't look at me, not even once. And that's enough for tears to form in my eyes. I stand up quickly, and Samy turns to me. I whisper to her that I'm going to the bathroom.

Passing through a mass of dancing bodies, I let the tears fall down my cheeks. Everyone is too busy having a good time to notice me. The music vibrates throughout the place, but it's quieter in the bathroom. I allow myself to cry quietly in the cubicle. I need to calm down, I don't want to be the dramatic one putting on a show, but this date meant a lot to me, and it's turned out to be a disappointment.

I should go, but this place is way out of town. A taxi would cost a lot, and I don't want to bother Dani again. I know she would come, but I don't want to interrupt her night, and I've already bothered her enough. Maybe I should just hold off until everyone gets tired, and we leave.

Taking a deep breath, I leave the cubicle. To my surprise, Natalie is standing in front of the mirror, arms crossed over her chest, as if waiting for me.

"Are you all right?"

"Yeah."

"I'd like to say that you're the first girl I've ever seen cry because of Ares," she sighs sadly, "but that wouldn't be true."

"I'm fine," I say, washing my face in the sink.

"Whatever you say, little stalker."

My chest tightens. "What did you just call me?"

"Little stalker," she repeats. I freeze. "Oh yes, we all know about your stalker past. Ares used to tell us how his poor neighbor had an impossible obsession with him."

I turn and run away from the bathroom, struggling to control my tears. I want to get out of here. I need fresh, clean air, and something to calm me down. I know Natalie was just looking for a way to get me out of her way, but that doesn't mean her words didn't hurt me. Ares hasn't acknowledged me tonight, and the fact that he told his friends about my crush on him is cruel.

I exit the bar, and the autumn chill hits me. There are some people outside smoking and chatting. With shaking hands, I take out my phone and dial Dani's number. My heart drops to the floor when I realize her phone is off. Hugging myself, I move down the street, still trying to call Dani and hoping she'll answer soon.

- ARES -

Natalie keeps telling me about one of her trips, but my mind is distracted. Raquel has taken a long time in the bathroom, and I wonder if she's okay. Maybe there's a line to get in or something. Although Natalie went a little while ago, and she's back.

I interrupt her story. "Didn't you see Raquel in the bathroom?"

Natalie nods. "She was washing her face, but then I lost sight of her."

I smile at her, looking at the seat where Raquel should be. Something's not right. Maybe I'm paranoid, but I have a strange feeling in my chest. I stand up and walk over to Samy.

"Can you come with me and check on Raquel? She's been in the bathroom for a while now."

"Yeah, let's go. I was thinking the same thing." We go together, and she goes in while I wait outside. Samy emerges with a confused expression on her face. "It's empty."

Something tightens in my chest, and I recognize it as worry. Where is she?

She's gone . . .

The thought crosses my mind, but I reject it. She has no reason to leave. Plus, she had no one to leave with. Samy seems to notice the confusion on my face.

"Maybe she's outside or on the balcony getting some fresh air," she suggests.

Without thinking twice, I leave Samy behind and look for Raquel all over the place.

She's not here.

Despair comes over me as my mind begins to analyze every detail of the night, especially her nervous look, and how she looked for me with her eyes. Now I realize that her disappointment and sadness were so obvious on her face. Well, fuck, talk about realizing things a little too late. Out of breath, I walk out of the bar, my eyes desperately searching for her. I pray she hasn't left, though I wouldn't blame her. I've ruined everything . . . again.

Outside, there are two or three people smoking. I look at both sides of the street, it's empty.

No . . .

She couldn't have left.

I know that if I don't talk to her now, I'll lose her. She's already forgiven me so many times. I know that no matter how big her heart is, it won't be able to forgive me one more time. Running my hand through my hair, I take one last look at my surroundings, searching for her.

Raquel, where are you?

THIRTY-FIVE
The Friend

- RAQUEL -

What a night!

Everything has become so complicated since Ares came into my life. He's been like a little hurricane, destroying everything in his path. He's had his sweet moments, but those are overshadowed by all the times he's screwed up. How can he be sweet one second and then so cold?

I sigh, and my breath is visible coming out of my mouth. It's getting really chilly. Maybe leaving the bar wasn't my brightest idea, but anything was better than standing there holding it all in. I try to call Dani again, but there's no answer. The tree behind me feels hard against my back, so I move away from it. And then I hear him.

"Raquel!"

Startled, I glance up the street and see Ares walking quickly toward me. His concern is evident on his face, but at this point

I don't want to care. I'd like to say I feel nothing when I see him, but I do.

When he reaches me, he wraps me in a tight hug. "I thought I wouldn't find you."

I stand still without raising my arms to return his embrace. He pulls away from me and takes my face in both hands.

"Are you all right?"

I don't say anything, and I just take his hands off my face. He looks hurt, but he lets me. "You're really upset, aren't you?"

"No. I'm disappointed." The coldness in my own voice surprises us both.

"I . . ." He scratches the back of his head, messing up his black hair. "I'm sorry."

"Okay."

He frowns. "Okay? Raquel, talk to me, I know you have a million things to say."

I shrug my shoulders. "Not really."

"You're lying, come on, insult me, shout at me, but don't be silent. Your silence is . . . agonizing."

"What do you want me to say?"

He turns his back to me, holding his head as if he doesn't know what to say. When he turns to me again, his voice is soft. "I'm really sorry."

A sad smile forms on my mouth. "That's not enough."

"I know. I know it isn't. Just . . . give me another chance."

My sadness grows. "That's what this has become, an endless cycle of opportunities. You hurt me, you apologize, and I come back to you like it's nothing."

"Raquel . . ."

"Maybe it's my fault for having high expectations when it comes to you."

A grimace of pain crosses his face. I turn around and start to walk away. I don't know what I'm doing or where I'm going, but I need to get away from him.

"Raquel," he calls me back. "Wait." He grabs my arm, turning me toward him once more. "This is all new to me, and that's not an excuse. I've never . . . tried anything serious with anyone before. I don't know what to do. I know it seems obvious to a lot of people, but it's not to me."

I wiggle out of his grip. "It's common sense, Ares. You have the highest IQ in the county, but you can't figure out that it would be a bad idea to take me to a place where there are two girls you've fucked?"

"Two girls I've fucked?" He looks confused. "Oh, Natalie . . ."

He really didn't remember?

"How do you know . . . ? Ah, shit, I forgot about that. It was a one-night thing, nothing important."

"Of course."

"What else did she tell you?"

I lift my chin. "She also told me that you used to make fun of me with your friends . . . about my crush on you."

He doesn't seem surprised.

"That was long before I talked to you. We hadn't even met."

"And I'm supposed to believe you?"

"Why wouldn't you believe me? I've never lied to you."

"Of course, I forgot that honesty is one of your qualities."

His blue eyes are full of sincerity. "I know that was sarcasm, but I'm really not lying to you. Natalie never meant anything to me."

I cross my arms over my chest. "And what am I to you?"

He looks down. "You know what you are to me."

"After tonight I have no idea."

He looks up, his eyes are shining with a feeling that makes my heart race. "You're . . . my witch. The girl who cast a spell on me. Who makes me want to be different, to try new things that are scary but worth it, because of you."

The tickling in my stomach is unbearable. "Nice words, but they're not enough. I need facts. I need you to show me that you really want to be with me."

"I'm learning. What else do you want me to do?" He looks so vulnerable right now.

"That's on you. You're used to getting everything the easy way, but not this time. If you want to be with me, you'll have to fight for it and earn it. We'll start as friends."

"As friends? Friends don't feel the way you and I feel. They don't desire each other the way we do."

"I know, but you need to earn things after all the times you've ruined everything."

He runs his hand over his face. "Are you telling me I won't be able to kiss you or touch you?" I just nod. "Are you leaving me in the friend zone?"

"No, not really. Well, yes, but with the possibility of getting out if you learn."

An ironic smile fills his lips. "No one has ever left me in the friend zone."

"There's always a first time."

He gets closer to me. "What if I don't agree to be your friend?"

"Well," it takes all my strength to continue, "then, unfortunately, you are out of my life."

"Wow, I really hurt you this time."

A car passes by on the street next to us, the streetlights cast shadows on the side of his face. It's getting colder. "Yes, or no?" I press.

"You know very well that I'll take anything you offer." He runs his hand through his hair. "All right, we'll do it your way, but on one condition."

"What condition?"

"During this period of 'friendship,'" he makes quotation marks with his fingers, "you can't date other guys; you're still my girl."

A couple walks past us, laughing, and continue down the street. I wait and then whisper: "Why are you always so possessive?"

"I just want to make it clear that, although we're starting over as friends, that doesn't mean you're going to be able to date other guys. Got it?"

"Friends don't have those rights."

"Raquel . . ."

"All right, Mr. Jealous, no dating other people, but that applies to you too."

"And it's okay to play dirty."

My eyebrows almost come together. "What do you mean?"

"Just because I'm your 'friend,'" he makes quotation marks with his fingers again, "doesn't mean I can't try to seduce you."

He extends his hand. "Do we have a deal?"

I nod and squeeze his hand. "Yes." He lifts my hand and brings it to his lips, giving it a wet kiss without taking his eyes off mine. I swallow and free my hand. He gives me a crooked smile.

"What do you want to do? Do you want me to take you home or do you want to go back in there?"

I debate the options in my head. I decide to go back in just to test Ares, to see how he's going to deal with this situation now that he's realized he didn't handle it the right way. With a lot more confidence, I go back inside the club with him.

The table is almost empty, with the exception of Natalie and Samy, who are talking. I guess the others have gone dancing. I sit next to Natalie and Ares sits on my other side. She gives me an annoyed look, but I just smile at her.

Volví, perra.

I'm back, bitch, as Dani would say.

"Do you want something to drink?" Ares asks in my ear.

"A margarita," I reply. A short while later, a margarita glass appears in front of me, and Ares sits back down next to me. Electronic music begins to play, and Natalie gets up, moving to the beat. She walks past me and stops in front of Ares.

"Do you want to dance?" She holds out her hand.

I take a sip of my drink, faking a smile.

"No." He doesn't even give her an explanation.

"Oh, don't be boring. Why not?"

Ares shrugs and takes my hand. "Because the only one I want to dance with is Raquel."

I didn't expect that. Natalie goes back to her place. Ares squeezes my hand and forces me to stand up so we can dance. This is going to get interesting.

We push through the crowd until we're in the middle of the mass of bodies moving to the rhythm. I'm nervous; I can't deny it. It's the first time we've danced together. Ares stands in front of me, waiting. He looks so perfectly beautiful under the different colored lights. I bite my lower lip and start to move, and he follows my lead, pressing against me.

I put my hands around his neck, moving my hips gently against him. I can feel his breath on my face, his body against mine. Being so close to him is intoxicating, and I realize that I may be underestimating the effect he has on me with us starting out as friends.

Ares rests his hands on my waist, moving with me. The sexual tension between us is palpable, like an electric current coursing through our bodies. He turns me around and hugs me from behind, wrapping his arms around my waist.

He rests his chin on my shoulder and places a soft kiss on my neck. His lips feel wet and warm against my skin. I don't know how much time passes, but I don't want this moment to end. I want to stay like this with him so that nothing changes, and nothing gets ruined again because I can't bear it.

The music changes and gnash's "i hate u, i love u" plays, and I turn to face him and sing it with him. He looks so cute, singing, looking into my eyes.

Ares takes my hand and makes me do a dramatic move. I burst out laughing, and he keeps singing. The world around us disappears; it's just him and me, singing and dancing like idiots in the middle of the crowd. A sense of peace and joy pervades my heart.

I want to believe in him. I'll give him one last shot to win my love. I'll be cheering for the idiot Greek god who stole my heart.

THIRTY-SIX
The Drunken Girl

Sweat . . .

Margaritas . . .

Laughter . . .

Music . . .

I never thought I could sweat like this, but apparently dancing in a crowd of people has that effect. Everyone is cheerful right now. I'm a little dizzy, so I decide to stop drinking. Marco appears on the dance floor and his eyes meet mine. "Why don't you dance with me, Raquel?"

My eyes travel to Ares, who's talking to his friends but glancing at me frequently. Ares and I are in a very fragile situation right now. Although I'm making him win my heart, I don't want to do anything that could lead to misunderstandings or uncomfortable situations. Marco is waiting for my answer, and I wrinkle my nose.

"Thanks, but maybe another day."

Marco says nothing, just grabs his glass and, without taking his eyes off me, takes a long drink.

Gregory appears out of nowhere and gives me five. "What are you doing for Halloween? Do you have plans?"

I can barely hear him through the loud, pounding music.

"Not really, it's still two weeks away."

"We think we're going to a party in town, I imagine you're coming."

Ares hasn't mentioned it.

"Maybe."

Gregory sighs. "Do you think I should be a vampire or a sexy cop?"

I laugh. Why does he have two such opposite options?

He taps my shoulder gently. "Seriously, I need a girl's opinion."

"Hmmm," I look at him and imagine him in both costumes. "I think you'd make a very sexy vampire."

"I knew it!" He looks proud, and I just smile.

I feel someone looking at me, and I glance around. Andrea is murdering me with her eyes.

"Your girlfriend doesn't look very happy," I tell him, taking a sip of my margarita. Gregory gives her a quick glance.

"She's not my girlfriend." I don't say anything, not wanting to seem nosy, but Gregory keeps talking. "I liked her a lot, but . . . she's just like her friends."

"What do you mean?"

"All the boys at this table are from wealthy families," he says, and my eyes go over each one of them: Ares, Zahid, Oscar, Luis, Marco, and then back to Gregory. "They're the next managers and owners of companies, corporations, businesses . . ."

Gregory points to several guys dressed in black around the bar.

"See those guys? They're bodyguards. We're never alone, even if it looks that way."

But what does that have to do with Andrea? Gregory seems to notice the confusion on my face.

"There are very few people who approach us without an agenda. Andrea . . ." He pauses, and there's a slight sadness in his voice when he continues. "Let's just say that her feelings were not genuine."

I squeeze his shoulder. "I'm sorry."

"I'm fine, I'll be fine. I'll rock Halloween in my vampire costume."

"I'm sure you will."

A lively song plays, and Natalie and Andrea get up and begin to dance for the seated boys. Samy just checks her cell phone. Andrea moves in front of Gregory, and I look away uncomfortably. She better not even think about getting closer to Ares.

Natalie moves in front of Marco, who doesn't bother to hide his disinterest. She moves on to Luis, who applauds her and plays along. I watch her get closer to Oscar and then Zahid. Ares is next, and I stop breathing. I can't make a scene here if she dances for him. What should I do?

Natalie goes to move toward Ares, but he gives her such a cold stare that I feel shivers run through my body. I have forgotten how icy the Greek god can be. She ignores his stare and moves toward him, but before she can reach him, Ares gets up and says he's going to the bathroom, leaving her standing alone.

Natalie purses her lips and returns to her seat. I grab my phone and type a text to Ares.

Me: Good move. I am proud of my friend. :)

His response comes quickly.

Ares <3: You're enjoying this, aren't you?

Me: Nope, not a bit.

Ares <3: You will fall, "friend."

Me: Nah and I am your friend, the quotation marks are not needed.

Ares <3: My "friend" who moans in my ear and asks for more when I fuck her hard.

A shiver runs through me and I feel the heat invade my face.

Me: Very inappropriate, my friend.

Ares <3: Inappropriate are the things I want to do to you; you have no idea.

Phew, it's hot in here all of a sudden. Like the coward I am, I don't answer him, afraid of what he might say to me.

Time is flying by and it's time to go. I can't believe it's three in the morning. In the parking lot, everyone starts to say good-bye. The cold weather isn't sitting well with Samy; Marco is holding her and helps her into the car.

We all get in, and Ares starts the engine. I'm grateful for the heat. Marco blows on Samy's face. "Hey, Samantha."

"I think I'm drunk," Samy says and bursts out laughing. I feel sorry for her.

Ares looks at her in the rearview mirror. "Do you think so?"

Marco sighs, holding her in the back seat. "We can't take her home like this, her mother would kill her."

"I know." Ares starts driving. "She'd better stay at my place."

I turn my head so quickly toward him that my neck hurts, and I give him an incredulous look. Marco rubs the back of his neck.

"Yes, I'll stay at your house too to help carry her."

Calm down, Raquel, they're friends.

Marco will stay, too, it's normal; they're friends staying at their friend's house. But jealousy is eating me up inside. When we get to my house, I hesitate, but I don't want to make a scene, especially in front of Marco. Controlling myself, I fake a smile.

"Have a good night." I open the car door, but Ares takes my hand and brings it to his lips.

"Trust me, Witch."

I take a deep breath. I want to tell him that trust is something you earn, not something you ask for, but I swallow those words and get out.

- ARES -

"Ares, she won't get out of the car." Marco grunts in annoyance.

I close the driver's door and head for the back door. Samy is lying on her side on the seat, her legs dangling out of the car.

"Samy," I call, and she looks at me. "You have to get out now."

"No," she murmurs. "Everything is spinning."

"Come on, Samy," I say and carefully slip my hands under her legs and back to carry her. Marco closes the door behind me. We enter through the back of the house. Marco opens the doors for me. Samy clutches my neck tightly, murmuring.

"My dark prince."

Marco gives me a sad look when he hears her call me that. She's called me that since we were kids because according to her, I've always been there to save her. But she's forgotten that Marco has always been there for her too. He gives her one last look before turning the other way, heading for the kitchen.

"You got this." He mumbles, walking away. "I'm hungry."

I take Samy to the guest room because there's no way I'm going upstairs with her like that. We get into the room, and she staggers but stands with my help. I manage to turn the night-stand lamp on and turn around to face her. "You shouldn't have drunk so much."

She caresses her face awkwardly. "I needed it."

Her black eyes meet mine, and I know I shouldn't ask, but she expects me to. "Why?"

She points a finger at my chest. "You know why."

Silence falls between us, and her expression grows sadder. I glance at the bed, at the fresh sheets. She just needs to sleep it off.

"Ares . . ." she says quietly. "You've been looking at your girl-friend all night, having a good time, you haven't even looked at me."

"Samantha . . ."

"I was watching you; I've missed you so much." The plea in her voice makes me feel ashamed. I care about her, maybe not in the way she expects, but she's still very important to me. "Haven't you missed me even a little bit?"

I consider saying yes because I don't want to hurt her. However, I think of Raquel, her smile, the way she wrinkles her face when she doesn't like something but doesn't want to say it, how I feel when she touches me. It's as if she's touching beyond my skin, as if her hands can reach into my heart and warm it. So, I don't respond, I don't want to give Samy false hope when my heart belongs to Raquel.

Her black eyes fill with tears, and I run my hand through my hair.

"Don't cry."

"You're an idiot. Did you know that?" The anger in her voice is sharp. "Why did you have sex with me? Why did you play with me like all the others? I thought that I was different, that you cared about me."

"Samy, I care about you a lot."

"Bullshit! If you cared about me, you would never have let this go any further. You knew I had feelings for you, and if you didn't reciprocate, you shouldn't have let it go any further."

I approach her and try to reach for her, but she pulls away as if my touch is poisonous.

"Samantha . . ."

Tears fall freely down her cheeks. "Why, Ares? Why did you kiss me that Christmas night? Why did you start something when you knew you felt nothing?"

"Samantha—"

"Tell me the truth for the first time in your life! Why?"

"I was confused! I thought I had feelings for you, but I didn't! I'm sorry." The pain on her face makes my chest tighten. "I'm really sorry."

"You're sorry?" She lets out a tearful laugh. "It's so easy for you to say that! You destroy everything good around you and expect to fix it with *I'm sorry*. That's not how life works, Ares. You can't go around hurting people and just expect to be forgiven."

"I know I'm fucked up, Samantha, but I—"

"You know you're fucked up, but you keep hurting people. You do nothing to change that."

"You don't know what you're talking about, I'm trying to be different."

"For her? You want to change for Raquel, don't you?"

"Yes."

"And . . . couldn't you try that with me? Wasn't I enough for you?"

"It's not about that, Samantha. I just can't control the way I feel. I care about you a lot, but she's . . ." I pause. "She's . . . what she makes me feel is . . . on another level."

Her lips tremble as she whispers: "Do you love her?"

She looks so hurt that I don't dare answer.

"You need to rest."

She nods and staggers to the bed, lying on her side, facing me.

"Would you mind keeping me company until I fall asleep?" I hesitate, but she looks so defeated that I can't bear to hurt her anymore, so I lie down next to her, and our faces are a safe distance apart. She just looks at me, tears rolling down the side of her face.

I caress her cheek. "I'm sorry."

"I love you so much it hurts." Her voice is weak.

It's the first time she tells me she loves me, but her words don't surprise me, maybe I already knew. She understands my silence and gives me a sad smile.

"I need to get away from you for a while. I need to get rid of these feelings. Because, as your best friend, I want to be happy for you, because you finally found someone who motivates you to change, someone who makes you happy, but these stupid feelings ruin everything."

"Take all the time you need. I'll be here when you get back."

She holds my hand. "Do your best, Ares. You have a chance to be happy, don't ruin it. It's okay to open your heart. It doesn't make you weak. Don't be afraid."

"Afraid?" I let out a sarcastic laugh. "I'm terrified."

"I know," she squeezes my hand. "I know it's hard for you to trust people, but Raquel is a good girl."

"I know that, but I can't help feeling so fucking vulnerable," I sigh. "She has the power to destroy me; she could do it so easily if she wanted to."

"But she won't." She closes her eyes. "Good night, Ares."

I lean over and kiss her forehead.

"Good night, Samy."

THIRTY-SEVEN
The Test

- RAQUEL -

Friends...

What was I thinking when I said that?

I'm dying to text him. He hasn't contacted me much, just texts saying that he's dealing with something and he'll talk to me soon. It's been several days now.

How the hell does he plan to win my affection this way? Did something happen with Samy? What if he doesn't want to fight for me anymore? What if he decided to give up? My mind has run through so many options that I'm bordering on insanity. Could that be his plan? To ignore me so I'll give in and take him back like it's nothing. Ha! In your dreams, Greek God.

With a grunt, I close the book in my hands. I put my face on the table. Dani sighs next to me.

"It seems that the punishment you imposed on him is affecting you more than him." Dani turns the page of the book she's reading. "He's never been easy to understand, so I don't know why you're so surprised."

I mess up my hair in frustration.

"I'm supposed to be in control now, but this silence is killing me."

"Maybe that's his plan, don't you think? That you'll miss him so much that when you see him, you'll jump all over him, forgetting about starting out as friends."

"You think so?"

"Shhhhhhh!" The librarian hushes us.

We both gave her a smile. We came here to see if we could finally finish reading the book that the literature teacher assigned us. I like to read, but that particular teacher only assigns outdated, boring books. I'd like to say I appreciate a good classic, but I would be lying.

"The exam is tomorrow; we'll never finish reading it," I murmur quietly so as not to attract the librarian's attention. Dani pats me on the back.

"Have some faith. We're already on page twenty-six."

I cover my face. "Twenty-six of seven hundred, we're lost."

I can't remember the last time I read a book for one of these assignments. How have I survived this class without reading? And then I remember: Joshua. He always helped us with these assignments, and in return, we helped him with any other subjects he had difficulty with.

A wave of sadness sweeps over me as I think about him. The three of us used to come here to read and do our homework. Why did he have to betray me like that? How could he throw away a lasting friendship like that? His sweet smile invades my mind, and I remember the way he adjusted his glasses and wrinkled his nose when he told me how he felt about me.

I like you, Raquel, I really like you.

I can clearly remember the vulnerability on his face when he said that. I can't deny how much I miss Joshua. He's always been a part of my life, and I care about him so much despite everything.

The men in my life are anything but normal.

I am so deep in my thoughts that I don't notice the person standing in front of our table until his hands place four sheets of paper and two coffees in front of us. I look up.

Joshua gives us a smile. "This is the summary of the book. It has key points that only a person who read it would know. I think you'll be fine if you read and study this."

Before I can say anything, he turns and leaves. Dani and I share a surprised look. She picks up the sheets and goes through them.

"He's crazy," she says. "But this? It's perfectly worded and understandable! God, thank you! And coffee." She kisses the coffee. "I must say I don't hate him so much anymore, this—"

Dani stops cold when she looks at me. "Oh, I'm sorry. I got a little excited. We don't have to accept his help if it makes you uncomfortable."

It's not that. His smile, his willingness to help. His expression was so genuine.

Joshua has always been easy to read, the opposite of Ares. Even now when I'm supposed to be in control of the situation, I don't know what Ares is thinking, or what he wants, or how I'm supposed to interpret his silence. I wish I could read Ares the same way I can read Joshua. It's understandable, though, because I've had a lifetime of knowing Joshua, whereas with Ares it's only been a few months.

Time . . .

Is that what I need to understand this man?

"Raquel?" Dani waves her hand in front of my eyes. "Are we going to accept this or not?"

I hesitate for a moment, but there's no point in turning it away. Joshua won't know if we use it or not. "We'll accept it."

We spend the rest of the afternoon reading the summary and studying for the test.

Friday

"We passed!" Dani shouts, checking the grades on the site.

"Ahhh!" I jump up and hug her tightly as we spin around like crazy.

We separate, scream, and hug each other again. We're still at school even though the last class is over. We were waiting to see if the teacher would post the grades from this morning's test.

"What's all the fuss?" Carlos appears at our side.

We separate again, and Dani pinches his cheeks. "Leech! We passed the Lit exam."

"Ow!" Carlos breaks free, stroking his cheeks. "Really? We need to celebrate; it's on me."

"For the first time, you say something intelligent," Dani gives him five, surprising us both. She must be in a very good mood to accept an invitation from Carlos.

Joshua comes out of one of the classrooms and walks in our direction. He's wearing his backpack on one shoulder, and a hooded sweater, with his unruly brown hair escaping from his hat. His honey-colored eyes meet mine, and, for a moment, his steps waver as if he doesn't know what to do, but then he continues walking.

Carlos opens his mouth to say something, but Dani grabs his arm and shakes her head. Joshua passes me on one side, lowering his gaze. I know I should at least say thank you, but the words don't want to come out of my mouth. Will I ever be able to forgive him? Am I being hypocritical for giving Ares so many chances and not being able to give my best friend a second chance? These are questions to which I still don't have an answer. Dani seems to read my mind and turns to him.

"Hey," she calls. Joshua stops and turns to us slightly. "Thank you."

He just smiles at us and continues on his way. However, I can't help but notice the sadness in his eyes, and, for the first time, I put myself in his shoes. Joshua has no other friends other than Dani and me. Socializing has never been his forte. People only approach him for notes or help. He's always been in his world of comics, books, and video games.

He must be so lonely now . . .

Dani appears at my side and takes my hand, squeezing it.

"He made his own decisions," she says. I look at her. How can she read my mind so well? "You're having a hard time because of him. It's okay if you feel bad, but don't feel like you have to forgive him, take your time."

I manage to smile, and, taking one last look down the hallway where he disappeared, I try to focus on the fact that I passed the test.

"I think we should go," I tell them.

Carlos smiles from ear to ear and hugs me sideways. "To celebrate with the owner of my heart!"

Dani grabs him by the ear. "Don't get clingy, or you won't go with us."

"Ouch! Ouch! Got it."

We leave school, teasing Carlos because he didn't pass and yet he's going to celebrate with us. I'm laughing when I cross the corner into the parking lot, and my eyes fall on a black car that I recognize.

I halt in my tracks. Dani and Carlos continue on ahead for a few steps until they realize that I've stopped walking. Dani gives me a confused look.

"What's wrong?"

My poor heart feels him before my eyes can see him, and it begins to beat desperately. I stop breathing, clenching my sweaty hands at my sides. My stomach feels funny. God, I had forgotten the effect that boy has on me.

And then it happens.

Ares gets out of the car, closes the door, and leans his back against it. He puts his hands inside the pockets of the black leather jacket he's wearing. He looks at me and the world around me disappears as those blue eyes meet mine.

I missed you so much . . .

I want to run to him, jump up, and hug him tight until he complains. I want to take his face in my hands and kiss him until I run out of air. I want to feel him against me, with his warmth enveloping me.

Where have you been, you idiot, that you've made me miss you so much?

I focus on the anger and frustration I felt from not hearing from him this week. I try to push away the fantasy of running to him and hugging him, while he spins me around like in the movies. This is reality, and if he doesn't learn now, he'll never learn how to value me.

I have to be strong.

Catching my breath, I calm my heart and walk toward him, passing by Dani and Carlos.

"I'll be right back."

As I walk toward him, I can't help but think about what I'm wearing. My worn-out jeans, old boots, and pink wool sweater aren't the best things in my closet, but how was I supposed to know that

Ares would show up out of nowhere? At least my hair is in a decent ponytail. I stop in front of him, and up close he looks even more handsome. How does he have such long, beautiful eyelashes? I'm so envious!

Focus, Raquel!

Crossing my arms over my chest, I lift my chin.

"His Majesty decided to honor us with his presence," I joke.

Ares smiles, and my control wavers. Without warning, he takes my hand and pulls me to him. I crash into his chest. His scent fills my nose, making me feel safe. He puts his arms around me in a tight embrace and rests his head on mine. He leans in to whisper something in my ear.

"I missed you too, Witch." His voice is as soft and calm as ever.

Like an idiot, I smile against his jacket and close my eyes.

THIRTY-EIGHT
The Man

I allow myself to enjoy Ares's hug for five seconds.

Although I know I can't expect him to change overnight, I think that he should at least try a little harder. It was nice to hear him tell me that he would fight for me, but he followed that up by ignoring me for a whole week. Bad move. It seems like he has trouble using logic, and maybe that's because he's never had to use it with girls. Maybe Ares has never had to try in any way with women. One glance from those beautiful eyes, combined with that sexy smile, is more than enough to get any girl, I know. But I'm trying to break out of that pattern.

Ignoring the protests from my heart and my stupid hormones, I step back, pushing him away from me. When my eyes meet his, I can see the confusion swimming in them. This is so hard.

"What are you doing here?" I ask.

"I came to see you."

"Well, you saw me. I gotta go." I turn on my heel and start walking back to my friends. Ares grabs my arm, turning me toward him again.

"Hey, wait." His eyes inspect my face, as if he were analyzing every detail. "You're mad at me."

"No."

"Yes, you are." He gives me that crooked smile of his. "You look cute when you're angry."

I stop breathing for a second. What am I supposed to say to that?

Be strong, Raquel. Think about that time you decided to give up chocolate because it gave you so much acne; it was hard, but you did it.

Ares is chocolate.

—You don't want acne.

But it's so delicious.

—Acne hurts!

Arguing with myself and not knowing what to say, I just smile.

"I'm sorry, Witch. It was quite a week." His smile fades. "Quite a complicated one."

His playful countenance disappears and is replaced by a sadness that he seems to be struggling to hide. I want to ask him what happened, but I have a feeling he won't tell me.

"It's okay, you don't owe me any explanations. We're just friends after all."

Watching his face, I regret the words the moment they come out of my mouth. He looks hurt and that was not my intent, I just wanted to make a joke to ease the tension. Ares licks his lips, as if trying to overlook what I just said.

"Actually, I came looking for you. I want to go out with you today."

"I already have plans. I'm sorry."

"With them?" Ares glances behind me.

"Yeah, we're going to celebrate passing an exam."

Ares raises an eyebrow. "And you don't usually pass?"

Not with such a high score as today.

"Hey, it's not that, it's just. . . . It's Friday. You know, we make up any reason to celebrate."

"Can't you make up an excuse and come with me?"

"No, you should have asked me in advance."

"Raquel!" Carlos shouts my name. Ares looks him over, from head to toe.

"Who's he?"

"A friend. Really, I have to go." Clinging to my self-control, I give him one last smile and walk away.

I'm about to catch up with my friends when Ares joins me. I give him a strange look. "What are you doing?"

"I'm coming with you," he informs me as if it were a fact. "I'm your 'friend,'" again he makes those quotation marks with his fingers, "so I may as well be part of a friends' celebration."

I narrow my eyes and open my mouth to protest, but Ares steps forward to greet Dani. He introduces himself to Carlos, giving him a firm handshake. Dani gives me a what-the-hell look, and I answer her with a confused shrug.

"Where are we going?" Ares asks, smiling, his charisma on full display. Dani smiles back.

"We thought about going to the café on Main Street."

"You celebrate with coffee?" he asks, giving us a confused look.

Dani arches an eyebrow. "Yes. Any problem with that?"

He raises his hands. "No, none, but I have alcohol at my house."

Ha! Trying to take me to your territory, Greek God? Nice try.

"Really?" Carlos asks, his face lighting up.

Ares nods, finding an ally. "Yes, and very good quality."

Carlos looks at us. "Shall we go?"

Dani and I exchange glances, but she saves the day.

"No, thank you. We prefer coffee."

Carlos pouts. "But . . ." Dani grabs his arm, digging her nails into it. "Ow! Coffee! Yes, coffee is better."

Ares looks disappointed. "Well, I guess I'll have to drink alone with Apolo."

"Apolo?" Dani looks at him suddenly.

"Yes, he must be so lonely at home." He puts his hands in his jacket pockets.

Dani hesitates, and I can see that now she really wants to go to Ares's house. He bought Carlos with alcohol, and Dani with Apolo. I must admit that his moves are good. Dani doesn't say anything, keeping her eyes on the ground. I know she won't say she wants to go, because she'll put our friendship first, as usual. She's leaving the decision in my hands, and that's why I love her so much.

Carlos and Dani want to go, and I'll feel like the bad guy if I say no. Ares knows that. He's very good at manipulation but not at making things right with me. That's where his brain fails him.

"All right, let's go with him." I surrender.

My house is behind the Hidalgos'. I just have to go with them, wait until they're comfortable, and then leave. It sounds like an easy plan, but every time I've gone to Ares's house, we've ended up in bed together. But there's something inside me that tells me this time will be different.

See it as a challenge, Raquel.

On the way to Ares's house, I call my mom to tell her that I'm going to study with Dani at a café. The tension between us has dropped a bit, but I still have to let her know where I am from time to time.

The car smells of him, and, although I try to ignore what his closeness does to me, my body can't control its reactions. Carlos keeps talking about everything he sees, and Dani rearranges her hair when she thinks no one is looking.

A smiling Apolo comes out and waves at us when we arrive, looking so cute with his messy hair. He's wearing a loose unbuttoned plaid shirt, revealing a white T-shirt underneath, and jeans.

"Hey, kid," Carlos greets him. "Do you live here?"

"He's my brother," Ares explains.

Claudia, the red-haired maid, comes down the stairs carrying an empty basket.

"Good evening," she says. We all return the greeting politely.

Ares asks her in a gentle voice, "Claudia, can you make some drinks and take them to the playroom, please?"

Oh no, not the playroom.

Is he doing it on purpose?

I look at him for a second, and his mischievous grin tells me yes.

Dani and Apolo greet each other awkwardly, and I wonder what's been going on between those two. We all go into the playroom, and it's much the same as I remember it: the big TV, the different video game consoles, the couch . . . the couch where I lost my virginity.

The passion, the wildness, the sensations. His lips on mine, his hands all over my body, the friction of our naked bodies. Unconsciously, my fingers touch my lips. I miss him, and it's torture to have him so close while having to keep the distance between us.

"Remembering something?" His voice brings me back to reality, and I lower my hand as fast as I can.

"No." My eyes search for the others, who are turning on the console and setting everything up while laughing at something Carlos said.

"Don't lie." He gets a little closer. "I remember that night when you came in here too."

"I don't know what you're talking about." I feign disinterest and step aside to join the group.

As I pass by him, he takes my arm and stops me.

"Every time I sit on that couch, I remember you: naked, virginal, wet for me."

I swallow thickly, shaking him off.

"Stop saying such things."

"Why? Are you afraid you'll get excited and let me fuck you again?"

I say nothing and walk away from him. Suddenly it's hot in here. *Virgin of Abs, why do you make it so difficult for me?*

"Are you okay, princess?" Carlos asks me when I join the group again. "You're all red."

"Princess?" Ares asks, reaching us. Carlos grins like a fool.

"Yes, she is my princess, the owner of this humble heart."

And that's how the most uncomfortable minute of the day begins, in silence. Ares tenses up, clenching his jaw. Dani and I look at each other, not knowing what to say. Carlos keeps smiling innocently. Finally, Apolo notices the tension.

"That's funny, Carlos."

"Let's get started." Dani changes the subject.

Surprisingly, Ares plays along. "Sure, how about if Carlos and I have the first duel?"

Carlos points to Ares and then to himself. "You and me?"

"Yes, but a duel without a prize is no fun."

"What's the prize?" Carlos asks excitedly.

"If you win, you can take three original games from my collection." Ares looks at me, and I expect the worst.

Carlos's face lights up so quickly. "What if I lose?"

"You call Raquel by her name from now on. No princess or whatever you're used to calling her." The coldness in his voice, in his request, again reminds me how icy Ares can be.

Carlos laughs loudly, surprising us all. No one says anything, I don't think anyone moves. I open my mouth to tell him that he has no right to decide what others call me, but Carlos beats me to it.

"No."

"What?"

"If it's like that, then I won't play."

Ares stretches his hands. "Are you afraid of losing?"

"No, I'm a very funny person, but what I feel for her is no joke to me."

Ares clenches his jaw. "What you feel for her?"

"That's right, and it may not be reciprocated, but at least I have the courage to shout it out to everyone, and I don't go around manipulating and creating stupid games to get what I want."

The knuckles on Ares's clenched fists turn white. Carlos smiles.

"Men fight for what they want openly; children act this way," he says, pointing to Ares.

Ares holds back, and it seems to be so hard for him. Without a word, he turns around and walks out of the playroom, pulling the door shut behind him. I let out a sigh of relief. Carlos smiles at me as always.

Dani sits on the couch next to us and lets out a long breath. "I thought I was going to have a heart attack."

Apolo wears an expression that I can't quite make out. Is he angry? For the first time I can't read his sweet face.

He turns to Carlos. "You were lucky, you shouldn't have provoked him like that."

"I'm not afraid of your brother," Carlos replies, standing up.

Apolo smiles and it's not sweet, it's that cheeky grin the Hidalgos wear when they don't like something.

"You talk a lot about maturity, but you just provoked someone to make yourself look like the mature one and the victim. Who's the one playing stupid games? I'll be right back."

He leaves through the same door as Ares. Regardless of who's right, Apolo will always be on Ares's side. They're brothers after all.

The enigmatic Hidalgo brothers.

THIRTY-NINE
The Feeling

Since I got home from Ares's house, I haven't moved from my bed. It's been a few hours now. Night has fallen, it's cold, and it's starting to rain. A part of me feels guilty, and I don't know why. We did the right thing by leaving. Besides, we didn't want a fight between Carlos and Ares.

The rain always puts me in such a melancholy mood. I sit in the semidarkness, and my small lamp gives everything a yellow hue. My eyes are on the window watching the raindrops fall. Rocky is next to me on the floor with his muzzle on his front paws.

The rain gets heavier, so I get up to close my window. The last thing I need is for my whole room to get wet. Every time I go near those curtains, I remember the first times I interacted with Ares. When I reach the window, my heart stops.

Ares is sitting in that chair where I first saw him. He's leaning forward, his hands holding the back of his head, and his eyes are fixed on the ground.

I blink in case I'm imagining him, but Ares is still sitting there, rain pouring down on him. He's soaking wet, and his white shirt clings to his body like a second skin. What the fuck is he doing? It's fall, for God's sake; he might catch a cold.

"What are you doing?" I shout.

I have to repeat it and raise my voice because the sound of the rain drowns it out. Ares lifts his head to look at me. The sadness in his eyes takes my breath away for a second, then a sweet smile forms on his lips.

"Witch."

"What are you doing there? You're going to get sick."

"Are you worrying about me?"

Why do you seem so surprised that I am?

"Of course," I don't even think to answer. Somehow, I'm offended that he thinks I don't care at all.

He doesn't say anything, just looks away. Is he going to stay there?

"Do you want to come in?" I ask. Regardless of our current situation, I can't just leave him there, looking so sad. I know something's wrong with him.

"I don't want to bother you."

"You're not bothering me, just behave while you're here, and we'll be fine."

"Behave? What do you mean?"

"No seducing me and stuff."

"Okay." He raises his hand. "Word of a Greek god."

He comes upstairs and as soon as he steps in my room, I realize that maybe this wasn't a good idea for two reasons: one, because he looks fucking hot all wet, and, two, because he's dripping all over my carpet.

"You have to take off those clothes." He gives me a surprised look.

"I thought no seduction."

I glance away. "You're soaking wet. Don't get any ideas! Take them off in the bathroom. I'll see what I can find that fits you."

Obviously, I can't find anything that fits Ares, just a bathrobe that my mother was gifted some time ago and never wore. I stand in front of the bathroom door.

"I only found a robe."

Ares opens the door and comes out in his boxers as if it were the most normal thing in the world.

Jesus Christ, he's hot.

I blush and look away, extending my hand with the robe toward him until he grabs it.

"Are you blushing?"

"No," I say, acting casual.

"Yes, you are, although I don't understand why. You've already seen me naked."

Don't remind me!

"I'll be right back," I say.

He takes my hand, clear despair in his voice. "Where are you going?"

"I boiled milk to make hot chocolate."

When I return, he's sitting on the floor in front of the bed, playing with Rocky. Even my dog can't resist him. He looks cuddly in that white bathrobe. I pass him his cup of hot chocolate and sit down next to him. Rocky comes over to lick my arm.

We sit in silence, sipping from our cups, watching the rain hit the window. Even though there's enough space between our bodies for Rocky to pass between us, I still feel those nerves I get when he's around. I look at him, and his eyes are absent, watching the window.

"Are you okay?" He looks down at the cup of chocolate in his hands.

"I don't know."

"What happened?"

"Some things." He runs his finger along the rim of the cup. "I'll be fine, don't worry." I let out a sigh.

"You know you can trust me, right?"

He looks at me and smiles. "I know."

I don't want to pressure him. I know that when he feels ready to tell me what's happening, he will. For now, we sit, watching the rain with a cup of chocolate, and enjoy being together.

- ARES -

This feels good.

I never thought being quiet with someone could be so comforting. With Raquel even silence is different; everything with her has been so fucking different.

From the first time we talked, Raquel has been so unpredictable. I think that was the first thing that got my attention. When I expected a particular reaction from her, she would do something completely different, and that intrigued me. I enjoyed teasing her, making her blush, and seeing that wrinkle in her eyebrows when she gets angry. However, I never planned to feel anything else.

It's just fun, I told myself so many times when I found myself grinning like an idiot thinking about her. *I just smile like that because it's fun, that's all.*

Lying to myself had been so easy, but it didn't last for long.

I knew I was in trouble when I started rejecting girls because I didn't feel anything. It was as if Raquel had monopolized everything I felt, and that terrified me. I have always had control over my life, over what I want, over other people. Giving up that control was impossible; I couldn't give it up to her.

I hurt her again and again. She took each blow, each hurtful word. I wanted to believe that she would give up, and my life would return to normal, but deep down I prayed that she wouldn't, that she would wait a little longer until I sorted out my mess.

She waited, but she also got tired. Now she wants me to start from zero, to fight for her all over again.

Why not?

If anyone deserves my effort, it's her. It's the least I can do after all the pain I caused her. I'm grateful that she gave me a chance to win her back. I'm grateful that she invited me into her room. I needed this. I needed the comfort and peace that she gives me.

Finishing my hot chocolate, I put the cup aside and stretch my legs, placing my hands at my sides. I dare to look at her, and she's still blowing on what's left of her drink. I guess it's warmer for her than it was for me, I was so cold when I drank it.

Taking advantage of her distraction, I slowly observe her. Her pajamas are one of those onesies that have a zipper in the middle and a hood with little ears. She must look adorable with the hood covering her head. Her hair is in a messy bun that looks tousled as if she's tossed and turned a lot.

Couldn't sleep, huh?

Inevitably, my eyes fall on her face, and linger on her lips, which are half-open as she blows her hot chocolate again.

I want to kiss her. To feel her against me.

It feels like it's been forever since I last tasted her lips, and it's only been a week. As if sensing my gaze, Raquel turns to me.

"What?"

I want you so bad. I want to hold your face in my hands and kiss you, to feel your body against mine.

I shake my head slightly. "Nothing."

She looks away, and a blush colors her cheeks. I love the effect I have on her because she has the same effect on me, if not stronger. I can't touch her. She let me in here, and I can't scare her away now.

I sigh, listening to the raindrops hitting the window. I feel so much better now. Just having her by my side makes me feel better.

I am so fucked.

I feel her hand on mine on the carpet, and the warmth of her skin fills me and comforts me. I don't dare to look at her because I know that, if I do, I'll be close to losing control and begging for her kisses.

With my eyes on the wet windowpane, I say it.

"My grandfather is hospitalized."

For a second, she says nothing.

"What happened?"

"He had a stroke and passed out in the bathroom." My eyes follow a raindrop slowly sliding down the window. "It took the nurses at the retirement home two hours to notice, to find him unconscious, so we don't know if he'll wake up or if there will be any aftereffects."

She squeezes my hand. "I'm so sorry, Ares."

"Two hours . . ." I mutter, feeling a lump forming in my throat, but I swallow hard. "We should never have let them take him to that retirement home. We had enough money to pay for a nurse to take care of him at home. He was fine at home. If he had been at home, this shit wouldn't have happened."

"Ares . . ."

"We should have fought the decision. We were fucking cowards. Of course, my uncles wanted him to go. I'm sure they were crossing their fingers that he would die there so they could claim his inheritance. My uncles, my cousins . . ." I make a sweeping gesture with my arm. "They disgust me. You have no idea what money can do to people. My father was the only one who decided not to live off my grandfather's money. He accepted money to start his business and when he became successful, he paid my grandfather back. I think that's why my grandfather was always closer to us. In a way, he respected my father."

Raquel caresses my hand in a soothing way as I continue.

"My grandfather loved us so much, and we let them take him to that place. And now he's . . ." I take a deep breath. "I feel so guilty."

I look down. Raquel moves and sits on my lap. The warmth of her body caresses mine and her hands hold my face, forcing me to look at her.

"It's not your fault, Ares. It wasn't your decision. You can't blame yourself for what other people did."

"I should have fought more, done more."

"I know that if you had found some other option, you would have taken it. You're not going to achieve anything by tormenting yourself this way. Now we just have to wait and have faith that everything will be all right . . . that he'll be all right."

I look her straight in the eye.

"How can you be so sure?"

She gives me a sincere smile. "I just know. You've been through a lot; I think you deserve a break. Your grandfather is going to be fine."

Unable to control myself, I pull her to me and hug her, burying my face in her neck. Her scent calms me. I want to stay like this. She lets me hold her and caresses the back of my head.

It's liberating to tell someone how you feel, letting it out takes some of the weight off your shoulders, like you're sharing the pain. I take a deep breath, burying my face even further into her neck.

I don't know how long we stay like this until she finally pulls away from me, still on my lap. I want to protest, but I don't. Instead, my fingers gently trace her face.

"You're so cute," I say, watching her blush.

The back of her hand caresses my cheek.

"You're cute too."

A pleasant sensation fills my chest. So this is what it's like to be happy. This moment is perfect: the rain beating against the window, her hand on my face, our eyes having a conversation so deep that words could never match it. I never thought that I would have something like this. I thought that love was an excuse to let someone else hurt you. Yet here I am, letting her in, and my fear has diminished, overshadowed by this warm feeling.

I lick my lips, observing every detail of her face. I want to memorize it, so that when she's gone, I can remember her. The sound of the rain mixes with her soft breathing, and my heartbeat echoes in my ears. I open my mouth and say it before I even finish thinking about it.

"I love you."

Her eyes widen in surprise, and her hand stops on my cheek. I know she wasn't expecting it because I wasn't either. The words were out of my mouth before I could control them. She lowers her hand, hesitation and indecision clear on her face.

"It's okay, don't feel pressured to answer me," I assure her, faking a smile. "The last thing I want to do is pressure you."

"Ares . . . I . . ."

I take her face and lean into her, giving her a kiss on the cheek and then moving closer to her ear.

"I said it's okay, Witch." My breath on her skin makes her shiver, and I enjoy it.

When I pull away, she still seems hesitant, squirming against me, and I give her my best smile, squeezing her hips.

"Don't move so much, there's a limit to what I can handle." The blood rushes to her face, and she looks down.

"Pervert."

"Beautiful."

She looks at me again, red as a tomato, and stands up. My thighs feel cold without her closeness. What the hell is wrong with me? It's like I'm desperate for her attention and affection. Who knew that I'd be begging a girl and telling her I love her without getting an answer.

I snort, laughing at myself.

I remember Raquel's words that night at Artemis's bar after she turned me on and left: *Karma is a bitch, Greek God.* Oh yes, it is. Raquel picks up our cups from the floor and sets them on the computer table before she turns and gives me a quizzical look.

"What are you laughing at?"

"At myself," I say openly, standing up.

"It's late," she whispers, crossing her arms over her chest. I feel her becoming defensive, careful even, and I can't blame her. She's afraid I'll hurt her again.

"Do you want me to leave?" I'm surprised by the fear in my voice. She just looks at me without saying anything, so I clear my throat. "It's okay." I walk to the window and see that the rain has stopped, but it's still drizzling.

"Ares. . . . Wait."

I turn to her again, she's leaning on the computer table, her arms still crossed over her chest.

"Huh?"

"You can . . . stay," she says softly. "But no . . ."

"Sex," I finish for her. Raquel opens her mouth to say something, but instead she closes it and just nods.

I can't help the relief that runs through my body. I don't want to leave, and her company is more than enough for me. Although being with her in a bed is a temptation that I may find hard to handle, I'll do my best.

Her dog stretches out in front of the window, while Raquel tosses the pillows on the bed aside, making room for both of us. She lies down, getting under the covers, and I do the same, lying on my side to watch her. Her bed smells of her, and it's so comforting. She lies on her back with her gaze on the ceiling.

We're close enough that I can feel her warmth, and my mind travels to the memory of that night I touched her in this very bed, when I was about to make her mine.

Don't think about that now, Ares.

But how can I not? I want her so badly that I clench my hands so I don't try to reach for her. I turn around until I am on my back because I need to stop looking at her.

I close my eyes, and I'm surprised when I feel her crawl toward me. She slips her arm around my waist and rests her head on my shoulder, hugging me sideways. My heart is racing and I'm embarrassed that now she can hear it.

This is what I need.

"It's going to be okay," she whispers, giving me a kiss on the cheek. "Good night, Greek God."

I smile like an idiot.

"Good night, Witch."

FORTY
The New Awakening

- RAQUEL -

A feeling of warmth and fullness comes over me when I open my eyes to find Ares asleep next to me. Something as simple as him being the first thing I see when I wake up can make me sigh and smile like an idiot.

He's lying on his back, his face slightly turned toward me. His black hair is messy, his long eyelashes caressing his cheekbones. He is so beautiful, but I feel like I've already moved beyond his looks, and I can see the boy behind that perfect physique. The boy who doesn't know how to handle his emotions, who tries not to show weakness to anyone, who is playful when he's not sure what to do, and cold when he thinks he'll get hurt.

Anyone meeting Ares for the first time would say he's the perfect guy. When in reality, for me, he's been like an *onion*.

I know, that's a strange choice of words, and yet it's appropriate.

Ares has layers, just like an onion, and only with time and patience have I peeled them back to reveal the sweet boy who told me he loved me last night.

I couldn't tell Ares that I love him too. The endless struggle to reach his heart has caused me so much pain. With every layer I peeled back, I lost a piece of me. I still have wounds that haven't healed. And there's a part of me that is upset, not with Ares, but with myself for all that I lost for him.

I shouldn't be here. I should have told him to fuck off long ago. However, I can't lie and say that I don't feel anything for him anymore, that I don't feel my stomach tickle, and that I don't stop breathing when he looks at me. I can't say that I don't feel completely happy waking up next to him.

Stupid love.

The dragon tattoo looks so good on his smooth skin. Uneasily, I raise my hand and trace my finger across his tattoo. My eyes travel down his arm, and I can't help but stare at his abs. At some point during the night, Ares took off the bathrobe, and I'm not complaining. The sheet only covers him from the waist down, and I feel like a pervert licking my lips.

My hormones are raging, and if it weren't for the fact that Ares was so depressed last night, I wouldn't have let him stay, because this is too much temptation. I stare at his lips and remember that night he gave me oral sex, how I clutched the sheets, how I moaned, how it felt.

Stop it, Raquel! You're going to end up attacking him.

One . . . Two . . . Three . . .

Come on, self-control, I need you to recharge.

Mentally slapping my hormones, I withdraw my hand and sigh. This is going to be a lot harder than I thought. Ares is too tempting, even in his sleep. I get comfortable, resting my face on my hand to watch him like the stalker I am.

And then he opens his eyes, surprising me. Having him this close, I can see how deep and beautiful the blues of his eyes are. I stay still, waiting for his reaction. Ares hasn't been the best when it comes to us waking up together—he's run away both times—so I prepare myself for the worst.

My mother says that pessimists live a better life because they're always prepared for the worst, and, when the worst doesn't happen, their joy is doubled. I've never agreed with her, but today I might consider her point. I'm so ready to see Ares get up and give me excuses to leave that when he doesn't, my heart races. And then the idiot Greek god does what I least expect.

He smiles.

As if he wasn't beautiful enough just waking up with his hair pointing in different directions, looking vulnerable, the fool offers me a smile so genuine that I feel like I'm dying here.

Double joy.

"Good morning, Witch," he whispers, stretching. I stare like a fool as the muscles in his arms and chest flex.

Virgin of abs, creator of this being, have mercy on me.

Ares pulls off the sheet and stands up; he's only in boxers, so I can see a lot more than I should. He turns to me, tousling his hair.

"Can I use your bathroom?"

You can use me, handsome, I respond in my head.

Raquel, control!

I just nod as my restless eyes wander down to his boxers and notice that he's hard.

"God." I blush, looking away. Ares laughs.

"It's just the morning wood, relax."

My mouth dries up. "Okay."

"Why are you blushing?"

"Are you really asking me that?"

I look at him, careful to keep my eyes on his face. He shrugs.

"Yes, you've seen it before; you've felt it inside you."

I run out of saliva from swallowing so much.

"Ares, don't start with that."

He grins. "Why? Does it turn you on when I talk to you like that?"

Yes.

"Of course not, it's . . . inappropriate." His fingers play with the elastic band of his boxers.

"Inappropriate?" He licks his lower lip. "Inappropriate is what I want to do to you, I miss hearing you moan my name."

"Ares!" He raises his hands in a sign of peace.

"Okay, I'm going to the bathroom."

When he finally walks into the bathroom and closes the door, I can breathe. After using the hall bathroom and trying to sort out the mess my hair became during the night, I return to my room with Ares's dry clothes in my hands to find him sitting on my bed. I hand him his clothes and try not to look at him while he dresses, but when he puts on his pants, I see that ass of his and bite my bottom lip.

"I like making you blush. You look cute," he says, and I blush even more.

"I'm still amazed at how changeable you are."

"Changeable?" he asks.

"Yes."

"And may I ask what I have done today to make you call me that?"

I list them with my fingers: "Last night: romantic. This morning: sexual, tempting. Now: sweet."

He laughs and sits on the bed to put on his shoes.

"I see your point, but it's your fault," he says. "You make me feel too many things at once. So, I react differently every time, you make me this way."

I raise an eyebrow, pointing at myself.

"As usual, blaming me." He finishes with his shoes and gets up.

"Do you have plans today?"

"Let me check my schedule. For real, I'm a very busy girl." More like a not-grounded-anymore girl, but he doesn't need to know that. I glance at the calendar on the wall to confirm that my prison days have come to an end. He walks toward me, and I back away.

"Oh yeah?" he asks.

"Yes." He slips his arm around my back and pulls me into his body, his scent enveloping me.

"I'm not going to take no for an answer. If you say no, I'll seduce you right here, and we'll end up there." He points to the bed.

"You're so arrogant. You trust your seduction skills way too much."

"No, I just know that you want me as much as I want you."

I wet my lips. "Whatever. Let me go, I have no plans."

Satisfied with my answer, he releases me.

"I'll pick you up in the evening." He kisses me on the forehead and turns away.

I let out a big sigh, watching him leave through my window.

>> <<

A date with Ares . . .

Romantic dinner, movies, and a good-bye kiss.

I think it's normal to expect that from a first date. That's how they always are on TV and what Dani, my first dating source, has told me. So I'm surprised when Ares stops his car in the hospital parking lot. I watch him take off his seat belt, and I do the same.

The hospital?

My first date will be in a hospital? How romantic, Greek God.

I sit still, watching as Ares hesitates over what to say. He's wearing a black shirt. I love the way he looks in black, or white, or really any color. He always looks so handsome without even trying. Ares licks his lips before turning his blue gaze on me.

"I . . . had reservations at a nice restaurant, movie tickets, and a delicious ice cream place in mind," he says, pausing for my reply. I say nothing, so he continues. "But when I left the house, I got a call: my grandfather woke up. I didn't want to keep you waiting or cancel the date. I didn't want to screw up again, so I brought you here with me. I know it's not perfect, and it's terribly unromantic, but—"

I place my finger on his lips.

"Shut up." I give him an honest smile. "Nothing has ever been conventional between us, so this is perfect." His eyes soften, charged with emotion.

"Are you sure?" he asks.

"Completely."

I'm not lying, this really is perfect for us, and, to be honest, the typical date wasn't what I expected of him. I expected more from him, I wanted more, and I got it. Ares is letting me in. He's showing me this side of him, and the fact that he wants me with him at this moment means a lot to me.

The walk to the hospital entrance is silent, but not uncomfortable. I can feel the fear and anticipation emanating from Ares. He puts his hands into the pockets of his pants, pulls them out, runs them through his hair, and puts them back in. I can't imagine what he must be feeling. When he takes his hands out again, I take one, and he looks at me.

"Everything will be fine," I say.

Holding hands, we enter the white hospital world. The lighting is so bright that you can see every detail of the walls and floor. Nurses and doctors in white coats pass from one side of the hall to the other. Some carry coffees, while others carry folders. Even though my mom is a nurse, my visits to the hospital have been few because she didn't like to expose me to this place, or that was the reason she always gave me. I glance at my hand intertwined with Ares's and a warm sensation floods through me. After giving his name to some kind of doorman in the elevator, we go up.

The fourth floor is silent, desolate. I only see a few nurses in a stall that we pass as we continue to a long corridor where the lighting is no longer so bright. I find it curious that the intensive care ward doesn't have the vibrant light of the floor below, as if the softer lighting suits the place. I'm sure this floor has witnessed a lot of sadness, good-byes, and grief.

At the end of the corridor there are three people, and as we get closer, I can see who they are: Artemis, Apolo, and Mr. Hidalgo, Ares's father. My nerves jitter as I'm reminded that this is something very intimate for his family. What if I make them uncomfortable with my presence?

Mr. Hidalgo is leaning against the wall, his arms crossed over his chest, and his head down. Artemis is sitting in a metal chair, leaning back in it, his tie undone, and the first buttons of his shirt open. His usual perfectly coiffed hair is in disarray, and I notice he has a bandage around the knuckles of his right hand. Apolo is sitting on the ground, his elbows on his knees, holding his head with both hands. He has a fresh bruise on his left cheek. Did he get into a fight?

When they hear our footsteps, they all look at us. I swallow as I see a question about my presence in their gazes, but when they notice our intertwined hands, something changes, and they seem to relax. Ares rushes to his father, and I let go of his hand.

"How is he?" Ares asks.

"Awake, the neurologist is evaluating him, talking to him, you know, the checkup before doing other tests."

"Will we be able to see him tonight?"

Ares doesn't bother to hide the concern and uncertainty in his voice. I know that he's desperate to know how much the stroke has affected his grandfather.

"I think so," his father replies, relaxing his shoulders. I stand back, not knowing what to say or do. Ares turns toward me, and his father's eyes follow his movement.

"Dad, this is Raquel, my girlfriend."

Girlfriend.

The word leaves his lips naturally, and I notice how he remembers about us starting out as friends, but before he can take it back, I smile at his father.

"Nice to meet you, sir. I hope Grandfather Hidalgo recovers soon," I say. He just smiles back at me.

"Nice to meet you. You're Rosa's daughter, aren't you?"

"Yes, sir."

"Sir? You make me feel old." Although he smiles, the joy doesn't reach his eyes. "Call me Juan."

"Sure." He seems to be a genuinely nice man and that confuses me; I was expecting a bitter, arrogant old man. Although I guess I should have guessed as much when Ares told me about him last night.

My father was the only one who decided not to live off my grandfather's money. He accepted money to start his business and when he became successful, he paid my grandfather back. I think that's why my grandfather was always closer to us. In a way, he respected my father.

Juan has fought and worked hard to get to where he is now, and I think that speaks very well of him. I wonder what happened behind closed doors that caused Ares's mom to be unfaithful to him and careless enough to let her son witness it. I always thought that men were the ones who screwed up homes. I know, it's a terrible generalization, and now I realize that it's not like that; mistakes that ruin lives can be made by both genders.

I nod at Artemis and Apolo, who smiles back. Artemis doesn't look like the type to pick a fight with someone. He always looks so regal, mature, and cool. Or maybe I'm jumping to conclusions.

A tall, older, white-haired doctor comes out of the room, adjusting his glasses. I step back, letting Apolo and Artemis stand next to Ares to hear what the doctor has to say.

"It's good news," he begins, and their sighs of relief echo in the hallway.

The doctor proceeds to explain Grandpa Hidalgo's condition using medical jargon that I don't quite understand. The little I can decipher is that, although there are still some tests to be done, the damage from the stroke is minimal, and Grandpa Hidalgo is going to be fine. The doctor tells them that they can see him now and leaves.

I stand watching as the four men in front of me hesitate; they want to give each other a hug, but their codes of behavior won't allow it, and I find that so sad. Why is it so hard to understand that it's okay to hug each other when you want to cry for joy because your grandfather will be okay? Their emotions cross their faces so clearly: joy, relief, guilt.

I take Ares's arm and turn him toward me, and, before he can say anything, I give him a tight hug. Over his shoulder, I watch as

Apolo hugs his father, and a doubtful Artemis joins them. They get ready to go inside, and I give Ares a few last words of encouragement before watching him disappear through the door.

I sit in the metal chair where Artemis had been. I don't think his grandpa would want to see a stranger after waking up from something like that. I'm waiting, absorbed in my thoughts, when I hear footsteps echo across the floor. When I look up, I see a girl walking toward me, and it takes me a few seconds to recognize her without her uniform: Claudia.

She greets me, and we start to talk. I ask her a question, and she's about to answer when we hear the clear sound of heels heading toward us. Claudia turns, and I follow her gaze.

Sofia Hidalgo walks perfectly in her five-inch red heels, wearing a white skirt that covers her knees and a shirt of the same color with a red print. In her hands she carries a small, discreet purse, also crimson in color. Her face looks flawless with makeup that looks professionally done, and her hair is in a tight ponytail. This lady is in her forties, almost fifty, and she looks thirty. The elegance she conveys is so genuine that anyone would say she was born with it.

She's very beautiful, I think to myself. Then those blue eyes that my Greek god inherited from her fall on me and she raises a perfect eyebrow.

"And who are you?"

FORTY-ONE
The Boyfriend

Silence reigns as Claudia and I stare at Sofia Hidalgo. Out of all the possible reactions I could imagine, Claudia's was not one of them. It reminded me of the sayings: "People are not what they seem" and "Never judge a book by its cover."

When I first saw Claudia, she struck me as submissive: a service girl who was used to lowering her head in front of her bosses, who had witnessed the best and worst moments of the family she worked for but said nothing about it.

Boy, was I abysmally wrong.

Ares's mother waits for my answer, not bothering to hide her contemptuous look. I can't speak. I'm not ashamed to admit that I'm very intimidated by this lady. Sofia crosses her arms over her chest.

"I asked you a question," she says. I clear my throat.

"My name is Ra-Raquel." I extend my hand to her in a friendly manner. She glances at my hand and then back at me.

"Well, Ra-Raquel," she mocks my stutter, "what are you doing here?"

Claudia stands next to me, and with her head held high and a firm voice, she speaks for me: "She came with Ares."

At the mention of Ares, Sofia raises an eyebrow.

"Are you kidding? Why would Ares bring a girl like her?"

"Why don't you ask him yourself? Oh, right, communication with your children is not your forte."

Sofia presses her lips. "Don't start with your little tone, Claudia. The last thing you want to do is provoke me."

"Then stop looking at her like that. You don't know her."

Sofia gives us a tired look. "I don't have time to waste with you. Where is my husband?"

Claudia just points to the door, and Sofia walks through it, leaving us alone. Finally, I feel like I can breathe. I clutch my chest.

"What a scary woman," I say.

Claudia smiles at me. "You have no idea."

"But you don't seem to be intimidated."

"I grew up in that house. I think I developed the ability to deal with intimidating people long ago."

It makes sense, I think, remembering how intimidating Artemis is, and even Ares before I got to know him well, and now this woman? Claudia must be immune to these kinds of strong personalities after growing up surrounded by them.

"I noticed, I just thought that since she's your boss, you . . ."

"Would let her intimidate me and treat me badly?" she finishes for me. "She's not my boss. Juan is, and he's always protected me from that witch, especially after . . ." Claudia stops. "I think I've talked too much about me, tell me about yourself."

I sigh, and we sit down.

"There's not much to tell. I've just fallen under the Hidalgos' spell."

"That's obvious, but I see you've gotten that idiot to admit his feelings."

"How do you know?"

"Because you're here," she replies. "His grandfather is one of the most important people in the world to him, so the fact that you are here says a lot."

"I have heard so much about this gentleman that I'd like to meet him."

"I hope you meet him soon. He's a wonderful person."

We chat for a while, and I realize how much I like Claudia. She's an interesting woman with a strong character. I think we could be incredibly good friends. She gives me a good feeling, and I feel comfortable around her. There are people with whom you just have good chemistry, and we kind of click, even after talking once.

After a while, Ares leaves the room, followed by Artemis and Apolo. Claudia and I stand up. Artemis's eyes meet Claudia's, and he presses his lips together before turning and walking down the hall.

Apolo smiles at us, avoiding Claudia's eyes at all costs.

"Let's go get a coffee. Grandpa asked for you, Claudia. You should go in when my parents leave." And with that the youngest Hidalgo brother follows Artemis.

Ares approaches me, his blue eyes are full of emotion, relief, and peace. I can't imagine how worried he's been the past few days. He takes my hand, and I can't help but notice that he doesn't greet Claudia.

"Come on, Witch." I glance at Claudia, who has her head down, and a murmur escapes her lips.

"I'm sorry," she says. Ares looks at her.

"It wasn't your fault," he says, sounding honest. "His impulsiveness will never be your fault, Claudia." She just nods, and I don't understand shit.

I say good-bye to Claudia and follow Ares. Walking with him hand in hand feels so unreal.

Dad, this is Raquel, my girlfriend.

His girlfriend . . .

The title makes my heart flutter with excitement. I never thought I'd get to be his girlfriend; he's the guy I watched from the shadows, fantasizing about being by his side someday like this, but I never thought it would become a reality.

Ares looks at me, with his cute lips forming a smile, and I swear my heart threatens to pump out of my chest and leave me.

I want to kiss him.

I clench my free hand to control myself so as not to pull him toward me and crash my lips against his. We arrive at the hospital cafeteria, and Ares leaves me at a table after asking me what I want. He goes to order something for both of us. With my hands in my lap, I look around.

I find Artemis and Apolo, sitting at different tables. What's wrong with those two?

Slowly, my head begins to connect the dots: Artemis's bandaged hand, Apolo's black eye, the uncomfortable look and tension between Artemis and Claudia as he left the room. Did they . . . fight over her? They couldn't have. Apolo is interested in Dani, isn't he? And the thought of Artemis being interested in Claudia doesn't sound like him, does it? What the hell is going on?

Ares returns, putting a caramel macchiato in front of me, my favorite.

"Thank you," I say with a smile.

He sits, stretching out his long legs. I know how defined his thigh muscles are under those pants, and I also know what's in between those legs.

Raquel, for God's sake, you're in a hospital.

Shaking my head, I take a sip of the coffee, closing my eyes because it's so delicious. When I open my eyes again, Ares raises one eyebrow. I lick my lips, not wanting to miss a drop of this delight.

"What?" I ask.

"Nothing," he replies. I narrow my eyes.

"What?" I ask again.

"The face you just made reminded me of the face you make when I make you orgasm." My eyes open so wide they hurt, and heat suffuses my cheeks.

"Ares, we are in a hospital."

"You asked."

"You have no shame."

"No, what I have is desire for you."

I clear my throat, taking another sip of my coffee. Ares extends his hand, palm up, offering it to me. I don't hesitate to take it.

"I know I shouldn't have said you were my girlfriend up there; I don't want to pressure you. I know I have to earn things."

"It's okay, really."

His hand separates from mine and I almost pout. He drinks some of his coffee, too, and I'm curious to know what his favorite is.

"What did you order?" I ask. He answers me in a mocking tone.

"A coffee."

"I know that. I mean, what *kind* of coffee did you order?" I clarify. Ares leans over the table, his face getting awfully close to mine.

"Why don't you find out for yourself?" He points to his lips.

This close, I can see how wet they are and how soft they look, but I push him away slightly.

"Good try."

"How long are you going to torture me, Witch?"

"I'm not torturing you."

"Yes, you are, but I deserve it."

We talk for a while, and I notice that his mood has changed drastically. He's relieved, happy even, and I like seeing him like that. This place seems loud after spending so much time in that grim, silent hallway upstairs. My curiosity gets the best of me.

"What's going on with those two?" I point to Artemis and Apolo. Ares takes his time before answering.

"They had a fight."

"Because of Claudia?" I throw my guess out there.

"How do you know that?"

"I connected the dots. What happened?"

"It's not my place to talk about it."

"Ugh, how boring."

Ares crosses his arms over his chest.

"I'm not an old busybody, I'm your boyfriend," he says. It came so naturally to him that he didn't even realize he said it until he noticed my surprised expression. Ares scratches the back of his head.

"You've made a fool of me."

"A fool I really like," I say.

Ares's lips curve into a triumphant smile.

"Do you like me, friend?"

I blush, giggling like a fool.

"Just a little."

After passing by his grandfather's room again, Ares brings me back to my house, parking his car out front. The sexual tension in the air makes it hard for me to breathe. He unbuckles his seat belt and turns his body toward me.

"I know it wasn't the most romantic date in the world, but I had a great time. Thank you for being by my side tonight."

"It was perfect," I tell him honestly, "I'm so glad your grandfather is okay." Ares rests his elbow on the steering wheel and runs his thumb across his lower lip.

"It's time for the important question."

"What question?" I ask. He leans over me, forcing me to bury my back in my seat, and his face is so close to mine that his breath caresses my lips.

"Do you kiss on the first date?"

I haven't thought about that at all. I don't have much knowledge of the dating world, but I remember Dani telling me that she was the type to kiss on the first date. She said she needed to know if there was chemistry or not, so she wouldn't waste her time with future dates.

However, this situation isn't the same. I know there's chemistry, too much I would say, and that he's a great kisser, and that's the problem. I don't know if I can control myself if I kiss him because I know my self-control has a limit. Ares wets his lips.

"Aren't you going to answer me?"

My breathing is already agitated, my heart on the verge of collapse, and I can't speak. Ares lets out a sigh of defeat and returns to his seat.

"I'm sorry. I'm pushing you again."

Unable to help myself, I unbuckle my seat belt and grab him by his shirt collar to pull him to me. His lips find mine, and I moan at the sensation.

Ares growls, grabbing my hair, moving his lips aggressively over mine. The kiss isn't romantic, and I don't want it to be. We've both missed each other too much for it to be romantic. It's a carnal, passionate kiss, full of volatile, strong emotions. Our hot breaths mingle as our wet lips touch, squeeze, suck each other, igniting that uncontrollable fire that flows between us so easily.

His tongue traces my lips, then gets into my mouth, intensifying the feelings. I can't help but moan against his lips. Ares slips his free arm around my waist to pull me closer to him. My body is electrified, every nerve responding to every touch no matter how slight it is.

Ares pounces on me, forcing me back in my seat, without separating his mouth from mine. He uses the lever to push my seat back, and moves from his seat to mine, getting completely on top of me. I'm amazed at his ability to do that so quickly. His legs stay between mine, spreading them apart, and I'm glad I have leggings on under my fall dress, because he pulls it up to my hips, exposing me.

He presses his body against mine and I can feel how hard he is through his pants. His mouth leaves mine to attack my neck. I stare up at the roof of the car as he devours the skin of my neck and moves down to my chest, his clumsy hands pulling down the straps of my dress.

Going against everything I'm feeling right now, I put my hands on his shoulders.

"Ares, no."

He lifts his head, his desire-filled blue eyes meet mine, and my self-control wavers. His chest rises and falls with his accelerated breathing. He gives me a warm smile.

"Okay."

His mouth finds mine again, but this time softly and tenderly. I smile against his lips, and mutter: "vanilla latte."

He pulls away from me.

"What?"

"The coffee you had."

Ares smiles back at me, and he's so fucking gorgeous. He gestures at his pants.

"Do you still think this is not torture?"

"Just a little."

"Sure, it's fine with me, though," he runs the back of his hand across my cheek. "It will only make it much more intense the moment when you give yourself to me again."

"You sound pretty sure that's going to happen."

"I am." His confidence has always been sexy to me. "You think I don't know how wet you are right now?"

"Ares . . ."

"Do you remember how good it feels when I'm inside you? That touch, that friction that drives you crazy and makes you beg me for more."

"God . . ." I put my hands on his chest. "Stop talking like that."

"You're all red." Ares grins and returns to his seat. "I also have the right to torture you."

"Idiot," I mutter, regaining my composure. "I gotta go."

I open the door, and I'm not surprised at how shaky my hand is. I get out.

"Good night," I say and close the door behind me.

Ares lowers the car window.

"Hey, Witch."

I look back at him.

"When you touch yourself tonight, moan my name loudly," I stop breathing, and he winks at me. "I'll do the same, thinking of you."

The car window goes up and he drives away, leaving me with my mouth open.

Stupid, perverted, Greek god!

FORTY-TWO
The Halloween Party

"You look spectacular."

"I feel spectacular," I answer with a big smile on my face as I look at myself in the mirror. I'm the type of person who sometimes feels pretty, sometimes average, and sometimes just awful. It's so strange. It's like I have no exact concept of what I look like, and it doesn't help that beauty can be so subjective.

"I must say, that costume is the best decision you've made in a while," Dani continues, outlining her eyebrows in front of the small mirror in her hands.

We're getting ready to go out tonight for Halloween. Gregory invited me that night at the club, but I still waited for Ares to invite me himself. It wasn't hard to choose my costume. Tonight, I'm a witch. My costume consists of a strapless black dress, tight at the top but loose from the waist down, reaching to the middle of my thighs, a necklace with a red pendant, black gloves, long boots of the same color, and, of course, a big hat.

Dani has taken care of my makeup: dark eyeshadow, perfectly applied black eyeliner, and red lipstick. I feel supersexy. Once I convinced her to go with me, she decided on a wicked kitty costume, ears and all.

"I can't believe I'm going with you," she mutters, getting up.

"Ares told me to bring you." It's true, Ares told me to bring Dani. It was a group outing, and he thought it would be fair to have one of my friends with me. "Besides, Apolo will be there for sure."

"Why does it matter if he's there?" she asks.

I sigh. I know Dani doesn't like to admit her weaknesses, or if she likes someone a lot.

"You don't have to lie to me. I know you're hurt."

"Pfff," she snorts, "please, he and I had nothing."

"But you were just starting something when he suddenly stopped texting you," I reply. "And that's driving you crazy, you're not used to a guy getting away from you."

"I don't know what you're talking about, a lot of guys have gotten away from me."

"Oh yeah? Like who? Name one."

She turns her back to me to touch up her makeup.

"I don't remember a specific name right now, but—"

"But nothing," I interrupt her. "We're going to go. You're going to have fun, and if he talks to you, you ask him directly why he changed, period. That's the Dani I know."

"Okay," she replies reluctantly. "All right, no promises."

I walk up to her and pinch her cheeks.

"Now smile, pretty kitty."

Ares sends me a message telling me he's outside with Marco, and I ask him to give us a few minutes.

I'm really nervous. I don't know how he'll react when he sees me in my costume, and I want to surprise him. The past two weeks have been great for both of us. We've gone out several times, finally having normal dates. However, the sexual tension between us has grown to otherworldly levels. To be honest, I don't know how I have put up with so much.

We get out of the house, and the chilly night air hits me. The first one I see is Marco in a cop costume, and I can't deny that he looks great. Ares comes around the car, and I stop breathing for two reasons: one, he looks ridiculously sexy, and two, his costume is a Greek god. He's wearing some sort of white robe that reveals his defined arms, with a golden ribbon across his chest and a crown over his messy black hair. It's too much for my poor soul.

Virgin of Abdominals, I entrust my being to you tonight.

Ares looks at me, and his eyes travel down my body slowly, each spot burning, smoldering under the intensity of his gaze, as a crooked smile appears on his lips.

"I knew it."

"I knew it too." I point to his costume.

"Come here." He gestures for me to move toward him and I do. Up close, his face looks even more beautiful with that crown on his head. He could easily have been a god; the beauty is there. His hand caresses my arm. "Hello, Witch."

"Hello, Greek God." My hands are restless, so I place them on his chest, lowering them a little to feel that defined abdomen through the thin fabric of his costume. Who could blame me for touching him like that?

"Touching me so early?" he says, as if reading my thoughts. I bite my lip.

"Oops, it's just that the costume suits you so well."

"Oh yeah?" Ares leans toward me. "But I think you'd enjoy touching me without it more."

"Are you proposing something indecent?"

"Very, very indecent, Witch."

I push him away and laugh to ease the tension between us, because if I don't, I'm going to end up under him moaning his name before I even leave the house. I run away from Ares and find Marco talking to Dani.

"Hey, Marco," I call.

"Hi, Raquel. Are we ready?"

"Yes," I answer, feeling Ares's gaze on the back of my head. "Where's Apolo?" Marco shrugs his shoulders.

"He's waiting in the car."

I frown at that. It seems odd that he's not out here greeting us. What's wrong with Apolo lately? He's changed. I haven't even talked to him much at school.

"Let's go," Ares says, opening the driver's door and getting into the car. I do the same. Dani hesitates as Marco opens the door for her to get in. She's going to be in the middle seat, right next to Apolo, who's wearing a sailor costume with a little white hat that makes him look even cuter than usual. I can see the distinct expression of discomfort on Dani's face, and I give her a comforting look.

"The place is packed," Marco comments, checking his cell phone. "I'm so glad we have VIP access."

"What did you expect?" Ares replies. "It's Halloween after all."

"Next year we should dress up as a group." Apolo finally speaks, surprising us. "Something like all of us as *Power Rangers* or *Ninja Turtles*, or characters from a series like *Game of Thrones*, that would be really cool."

"How old are you?" Marco laughs. "Twelve?"

I feel the urge to defend him.

"Hey, there's nothing wrong with dressing up in a group! I like your idea, Apolo."

I give him a smile, and he returns the gesture, but it appears that Marco has no intention of staying quiet.

"You say that when you two didn't even dress up as a couple." He points to Ares and me.

"Of course we did, witch and Greek god," I explain, but Marco snorts. "It's something between us you'd never understand."

Ares laughs. "She's right, Marco. You'd never understand, the longest relationship you've ever had was with the cigarette you just smoked, and now it's over."

We all join in the laughter, and Marco grunts.

"All against me, huh?"

When we get to the bar, I realize that Marco wasn't exaggerating when he said it was packed. There's a line of people outside the place, and a sign over the door indicating that it's already full, and that they can't guarantee entry even if you wait outside for hours. The guard doesn't even blink as he lets us in.

The decor is mind-blowing. Everything is black and orange, with fake skulls and bodies hanging from the ceiling, and spider webs and fake blood on the pillars. The bartenders are dressed as pirates, serving disgusting-looking colored drinks. There are several smoke machines, making it look like the room is full of fog. Everyone is in costume, and my eyes roam all over the place, trying to see them all. The atmosphere is perfect, and it's no wonder so many people want to come in. Artemis knows how to run his business and take advantage of these occasions.

We climb the stairs to the VIP area, where a table awaits us, with Samantha, Gregory, Luis, and Andrea. No Natalie tonight? How lovely.

Gregory's face lights up when he sees me, and I get excited too. He stands up and gives me a hug.

"Raquel, I knew you'd come."

"Of course, I couldn't miss seeing your vampire costume." I give him my thumbs up. "It looks great on you."

Luis also stands up.

"Since when did you two get so close? I feel left out."

"I was wondering the same thing," Ares says as he joins us. He runs his hand around my waist, pulling me to his side.

Gregory shakes his head.

"Easy, baby." He makes sexy eyes at Ares. "I only have eyes for you."

Ares gives him a tired look, and I wiggle out of his grip.

"Relax, vampires aren't my thing."

Luis intervenes. "She likes. . . . What are you supposed to be, Ares? God?"

"A Greek god."

Samantha joins us, greeting everyone with a smile.

"Are you living up to your name?"

Luis finally catches on. "Oh, right, you guys are named after Greek gods. Yours is the one of war or something like that, isn't it?"

"No wonder he's a troublemaker." Gregory sighs, and Ares hits his arm.

"Who you calling a troublemaker?" Ares demands.

Gregory again makes eyes at him.

"Hit me harder, baby."

We all laugh and sit down. Spending time with Ares's group of friends has become more bearable and definitely more comfortable. I think it was a matter of giving myself time to get to know them until I could stop feeling outside the group and be part of it.

Even Andrea can hold a decent conversation without her friend Natalie. However, I haven't forgotten what Gregory told me about her being a gold digger who broke his heart.

Apolo sits as far from Dani as possible, forcing Dani to chat with Luis, who is flirting with her, unaware that my best friend has her heart set on the youngest Hidalgo and can't help glancing at him from time to time.

Feeling more relaxed with this group, I allow myself to have a few drinks. They look disgusting but taste delicious, especially one called Drag Me to Hell, which is a delight. But at this rate, if I keep drinking, I'll end up in hell with a certain Greek god who's hanging around. I can feel my cheeks and ears growing warm. Apparently, alcohol makes me hot, which makes me an easy target for Ares, so I cut back. I decide to walk to the candle room to see the dark side. I don't notice Ares following me until I'm inside, and his voice sounds behind me.

"What are you doing here, Witch?" I turn to him, and his blue eyes are glowing with something dark and dangerous: desire.

I swallow hard for the second time tonight. My eyes notice the small couch to the side, and my heart pounds in desperation. We're alone in the semidarkness.

"We should go back," I say.

Ares approaches me with slow steps.

"Yes, we should."

I lick my lips, watching his body, remembering how he feels naked against me.

"Yes, really, we should go."

He nods, standing so close to me that I'm forced to look up to meet his eyes.

"I know."

"Then why are we still here?" I ask. His nose brushes mine. My lips open in anticipation, my breathing already a mess. He grabs my neck.

"Because tonight," he whispers, "you're going to be mine again, Witch."

And with that said, he presses his lips against mine.

FORTY-THREE
The Lack Of Control

- ARES -

I can't control myself. I don't want to control myself.

I have waited too long, held on too long. My control trembles and cracks with every kiss, every brush of my tongue against hers, every touch of her soft skin against my hands. I slam her against the wall, kissing her desperately, and her witch's hat falls off and gets lost in the darkness.

I try to calm myself and be gentle, to feel every part of her, so even though I want to devour her, to penetrate her, to hear her moan my name in my ear, I take my time. I caress and kiss her until her breathing turns to gasps, and I know she's as turned on as I am. My hands fidget and travel inside that short witch's dress she's wearing, my lips never leaving hers. Moving her underwear aside, I slide my fingers over her wetness. She moans, and I suck on her bottom lip.

"Already wet?"

She doesn't say anything, she just shudders when one of my fingers penetrates her. It feels so hot and wet inside her that I feel like I'm going to explode from how hard I am.

"Ares . . ." she mutters, her voice is full of desire. "We are . . . we shouldn't be here."

I sink my finger even deeper inside her and hear her gasp, clinging to my shoulders. My lips leave hers to lick and nibble the skin of her neck. I know it's her weak spot. She drops her head back, and her hips start swaying to the rhythm of my fingers, driving me crazy. I use my free hand to caress her breasts through her dress.

No more, I can't wait any longer.

Unable to help myself, I pull away from her, removing my hand from her to free my manhood and put on a condom. She protests impatiently.

"Ares, please."

I look into her eyes playfully. She doesn't hesitate to tell me what she wants.

"I want you now, inside me."

"Oh yeah?" I tease her, lifting one of her legs and putting it around my waist. "You perverted little witch."

My hardness brushes against her, and I rest my forehead on hers.

"I'm not going to be gentle," I say.

She bites my lower lip.

"I don't want you to be."

I grab her by the hair, forcing her to look into my eyes, and I move my hips forward, penetrating her completely with a single thrust. We both moan at the sensation.

God, I've forgotten how amazing it feels inside her, wet, tight, hot, smooth . . .

I can't stop looking at her because she looks so fucking sexy and vulnerable like this, her red cheeks, her swollen lips, her eyes shining with desire. She runs her hands around my neck, and I grab her other leg so I can lift her all the way up and start moving, pressing her against the wall with each sharp movement. I kiss her again, drowning out her moans with my mouth.

"Oh God, Ares!" she gasps, losing control.

Soft, wet, and warm. . . . More, I need more. I speed up my movements, pressing her harder against the wall, moving in and out of her wetness. For a second, I think about stopping. I don't want to hurt her, but judging by the way she asks for more, I know she likes it as much as I do.

If this keeps up, I'm going to finish faster than I want to. Carrying her, I move backward until I'm sitting on one of the couches and she's sitting on top of me, with the power to drive me crazier than she already is.

Raquel doesn't hesitate to move on top of me, in circles, back and forth, and I realize this was not a good idea if I don't want to finish quickly. She looks like a goddess, the candlelight giving her slightly sweaty skin a glowing touch. I never thought sex could feel so good. It's not just the physical aspect, but it's also the connection. Our emotions are conveyed in every touch, every look, every kiss.

Shit, she's got me in the palm of her hands. She has the power to destroy me, and the truth is I don't care, being destroyed by her would be a fucking privilege.

She pulls down her dress, exposing her breasts.

Oh yes, a fucking privilege.

I squeeze her waist, guiding her movements.

"Do you like to ride me like this?" I ask. She moans in response.

"Yes, I like it so much."

I spank her and she trembles with pleasure.

"You're all wet." I straighten up a little to lick the skin in the middle of her breasts and then suck on them. "I want you to come on me, just like this."

I feel her tightening around me, I know she's almost there.

"Oh, Ares, it feels so . . . oh!" I move with her, thrusting deep into her. Her moans get out of control, and I know I'm close too.

I hug her, whispering in her ear, but out of the corner of my eye I notice movement to my right. I look over and see a surprised face between a small opening in the curtains that hide us.

Marco.

Instinctively, my hands lift up Raquel's dress and I'm relieved to feel her covered, but she doesn't stop. Marco takes two seconds to react, and I give him a cold look that makes him go away.

I'd like to say that distracted me, but that's not the case. My witch keeps moving on me, on the verge of orgasm, pulling me with her. She kisses me, and the friction of our connected bodies intensifies.

She whimpers against my mouth, her body shudders against me, her wetness is squeezing me, her orgasm driving mine, and I grip her hips as I come.

Suddenly, I can hear the music again, and the sound of our heavy breathing. Raquel hugs me, and I bury my face in her neck. I can feel our hearts racing, and I don't want to move. This feels perfect.

And that's been one of the first big differences with Raquel. Before her, I always wanted to get away from the girl I just had sex with once I was satisfied. But with Raquel I feel this need to stay with her, with her pressed onto me. I still remember how much it scared me, that feeling of wanting to stay by her side. It wasn't something that had ever happened to me before.

I inhale her scent and smile against her skin.

I'm not afraid anymore, Witch.

I don't want to run away anymore.

I give her a kiss and we carefully get up, fixing our costumes. I watch her lower her dress, making it look like nothing happened.

"I guess I'm out of the friend zone," I say. She looks at me with narrowed eyes.

"Don't start."

"I'm not starting anything," I say, playing innocent. "I'm just telling the truth, girlfriend." She tries to hide a smile.

"Girlfriend?"

I just nod.

"Now I'm all yours, and you're all mine, little witch."

"Ha!" She snorts. "Why are you always so possessive?"

I slip an arm around her waist, pulling her to me, and she lets out a giggle. I caress her cheek.

"Because there are people who have their eyes on you."

"Jealous?" She gives me a wide smile. "You look cute when you're jealous."

The first time I ever felt jealousy in my life was with you, I think.

Raquel squirms a little, looking uncomfortable. "I'm going to the bathroom to . . . you know, to clean myself up a little bit."

"I'll wait for you at the table."

She smiles and walks away. I leave the candlelit room and make my way to the table. The first to greet me is Gregory.

"You came back." He gets up to whisper in my ear, "Comb your hair a little, Mr. Obvious."

I run my hands through my hair quickly, and I walk over to Marco.

"Do you have cigarettes?" He nods, pulling a box out of his pocket.

"Do you want one?"

"Yeah. Will you join me for a smoke?"

"Of course." He nods.

We pass through the candlelit room to go to the balcony on that side. I barely set foot out there before I'm remembering the time Raquel left me turned on in this very place. So much has happened since that night.

We light our cigarettes. I take a puff and blow the smoke out into the cool night air. Marco rests his forearms on the balcony railing and focuses on the view. Silence is rare between us; it's awkward, but the conversation that's coming is one we both know we should be having.

"There is no need to beat around the bush between us," he says casually.

"This is not a game to me, Marco," I begin, inhaling again. "Not this time."

"Do you really like her?"

"It's more than that," I answer.

He bursts out laughing.

"Don't fuck with me. Are you in love?"

"Yes."

He grimaces. "I thought she was just the weird girl who stalked you, how things change."

"Marco, I'm serious, she's not a game to me," I repeat. "No games, no bets, no challenges."

He raises both hands in the air.

"Oh, I got it," he says with a mocking tone.

"Say what you have to say."

"Am I supposed to listen to you? Did you care when you screwed things up for me with Samantha?"

"You never told me you really liked her; that it wasn't a game.

How was I supposed to know? By reading your mind?"

"You knew how I felt about her! It shouldn't have been necessary to tell you. I've had feelings for her ever since we were little, and you knew it."

I knew this would come out someday, but I didn't expect to have this conversation today.

"I can't control her feelings. That's not on me."

"But any hope I had with her went to shit when you started fucking her for pleasure, for fun, fooling her."

I put the cigarette out in an ashtray.

"I never wanted to play with her, and you know it."

"But you did," he replies. The anger in his voice is clear. "You screwed us both with your damn selfishness. You never think of others. Only about yourself."

"What do you want? An apology?"

"Nah, I just hope that now that you've found someone you really care about, you'll learn. I just hope you grow up. How would you feel if I took Raquel away from you? Imagine watching me use her for pleasure, knowing that you're there feeling a thousand things for her."

Just thinking about it, I clench my hands at my sides.

"Don't even think about it."

"It feels horrible, doesn't it? I'm glad you can put yourself in my shoes now." He turns his back to me, and sighs. "Relax, I'm not going anywhere near your witch, I just wanted you to understand how I felt."

Swallowing my pride, I speak.

"I'm sorry."

Marco looks at me again, surprise clear on his face, but I continue.

"I'm really sorry, bro. You're right."

"You've never apologized to me."

"I know," I sigh. "But now it's easier to admit my mistakes. I think she makes me a better person."

"I'm glad to hear that."

"And Samy will heal, Marco, and you'll have the chance to win her back."

He bursts out laughing.

"I hope so. For now, I'll settle for her glares."

"So, we're good?" I ask.

"We're good."

With everything clear, we both walk back into the club. When we get to the table, Raquel is laughing out loud with Gregory, and Samantha is standing with Andrea, dancing a little to the music. Apolo and Daniela are on the dance floor, doing some crazy moves.

I move closer to Samantha to whisper in her ear: "I dare you to dance with Marco."

She pouts. "I hate your challenges."

But she does it. We've always done the challenges we set for ourselves. I watch them go to dance, and my eyes fall on my witch. She looks so beautiful laughing. Her cheeks are flushed; I've noticed her face turns red when she's had too much to drink. She notices my presence and her eyes light up, and she raises her hand, beckoning me to her.

Yes, definitely, being destroyed by her is a privilege.

FORTY-FOUR
The Walk Of Shame

- RAQUEL -

"Raquel." Someone is shaking my shoulder. "Raquel!"

Being violently shaken brings me from the world of unconsciousness back to life.

"Raquel!" A demanding whisper reaches my ears, but I don't want to open my eyes. "For God's sake, wake up!"

I open one of my eyes, closing the other as I get used to the light. A figure is leaning over me.

"What—"

A hand covers my mouth and I slowly blink, trying to see who is almost on top of me.

Black hair falling across her face . . .

Dani.

"Shhh! I need you to get up very carefully," she whispers.

I give her a what-the-fuck-is-going-on look, even though she looks desperate.

"I'll explain later, but I need you to get up carefully, and be quiet."

"Wait a second. First of all, where the fuck are we?"

Last night . . .

My mind flashes through a series of images that are too embarrassing to recall in full: margaritas, vodka, dancing on top of the club table, Gregory stripping, Ares and I kissing in front of everyone, and Dani and Apolo giving each other be-careful-or-else-I-will-fuck-you-tonight glances.

Oh, Virgin of Abs, I'm going to hell.

Basically, I committed too many sins in one night. And not only that, we had to take a taxi to Marco's house because his was the only house without adult supervision. More alcohol, more stripper shows, more smoldering looks between Apolo and Dani, and even more kisses between me and Ares.

Dani releases my mouth and I sit up. My stomach churns and my head throbs.

"What's wrong?" My throat burns, dry from so much alcohol.

Dani raises her index finger to her lips and gestures to my side. Ares is sleeping next to me, lying on his stomach, his head facing away from us. The sheet is pulled up to a little above his waist. He's shirtless, his tattoos visible, and his messy black hair points everywhere.

God, waking up next to this man is a privilege. I may be spending all the happiness of my life with this guy, but it's worth it.

Dani brings me back to reality, shaking her hand in front of my face.

Carefully, I stand up. The mattress creaks and we both look at the Greek god, but he is in the afterworld. I get a little dizzy, and Dani holds me up, waiting for me to steady myself.

I won't ever drink again.

I know, I said that last time. Alcohol is like an ex you haven't gotten over. You promise not to fall again, never to try it again, but it seduces you, and you end up back where you started.

I look for the shoes I was wearing last night. They're lying in the corner of the room, and a memory comes to mind:

"Spell me, Witch!" Ares shouts as we awkwardly enter the room. He grabs me by the waist to kiss me lightly. I let out a chuckle.

"You are so drunk."

He looks so cute with his red cheeks and narrowed eyes. Ares points his finger at me.

"You aren't the embodiment of sobriety either."

"Wow. . . . Embodiment. How does your intoxicated brain manage to say words like that?" Ares gives me a big smile, touching his forehead.

"My IQ is . . ."

"The highest in the county," I finish for him. "Smart and handsome. Why are you so perfect?"

He shrugs and caresses my cheek.

"Why are you so perfect?"

And I remember in detail everything we did after that. God.

"Earth calling Raquel!"

With blood rushing to my cheeks, I snap back to reality. Dani gestures with her hand for me to follow her to the door, and I shake my head.

"I can't just walk away and leave him like this."

"You can explain everything later in a text message!" Dani whispers. "I need to get out of here."

"Don't you think he'll feel a little used?"

Dani gives me an are-you-serious look.

"You'll explain later, let's go." When I hesitate, she begs, "Please."

"Okay." Both of us with our shoes in hand leave the room,

closing the door carefully behind us. "Now, can you explain to me what's going on?"

Dani shakes her head. "I'll explain on the way. Be quiet. There are a lot of people sleeping in these rooms."

The hallway is long, with doors on both sides. I want to protest, but Dani starts walking in front of me. My eyes land on the back of her costume top and I see the label. Is it on backward?

Oh, oh, beginner's mistake.

"Dani, did you have sex last night?"

"Shhh!" She covers my mouth and pushes me against the wall.

"Oh my God, you fucked Apolo," I whisper, because this is gold.

"Raquel!"

"Deny it!"

Dani opens her mouth to say something and closes it again. I can't contain my surprise.

"By the Virgin of Abs, you did!"

"First of all, that virgin doesn't exist." Dani furrows her brows. "And secondly, shut your mouth, Raquel. Don't say another word."

"Oh, I didn't expect that," I say, amused.

Dani grabs my arm. "Walk. Don't make this walk of shame any worse than it already is," she says.

"What?"

Dani rolls her eyes.

"The walk of shame. You know, the day after you fuck someone you shouldn't. There's a movie and everything."

I let out a chuckle. "I knew it! I told you I gave you a month to fall for him!"

Dani gives me a murderous look.

"Get moving. It's nine o'clock, and your mom is off her shift today at eleven."

"Oh shit, you should have started there."

We head down the hallway when we hear a door handle turn.

"Oh shit, shit, shit," Dani mumbles, and we walk back and forth without knowing what to do, bumping into each other several times. Finally, we freeze and see Samy coming out of one of the rooms very carefully, with her heels in her hands as well, and her attitude very much the same as ours.

Don't tell me that . . .

Samy sees us and freezes for a second, waving with her free hand. We approach, and Dani takes her by the hand so we can run away together.

"No one judges anyone," Dani says.

When we get downstairs, we find Andrea. Yes, Gregory's I-don't-know-what is carefully opening the door.

"Are you kidding me?" she asks. Dani, Samy, and I share a look and smile.

"This has to be the most popular walk of shame ever," I say.

Samy laughs. We leave the house, stopping in the garden, and Samy checks her phone. It's dead.

"Can anyone call a taxi?"

Andrea smiles at us.

"I brought my car. I can drive all of you."

It's a very nice car, cutesy and small. Samy gets in the passenger seat and Dani and I get in the back. Andrea starts the conversation.

"Don't you find this situation kind of weird?"

Samy nods. "Too much, I would say."

"I'm sorry," I interject, unable to help myself. "But I think we're all curious to know with whom . . ."

Dani agrees.

"No one judges anyone. Let's say the names."

"Gregory," Andrea says with a laugh.

Samy blushes.

"Marco."

"What?" I say, surprised. "I didn't expect that."

Samy sighs in response. "Neither did I."

Andrea narrows her eyes. "Is no one surprised by my revelation? Was it that obvious?"

"Yes," we all say at the same time.

"Ouch," Andrea pouts.

"You're obvious, too, Raquel. Ares, who else?"

I stick out my tongue at her, and she sees me in the rearview mirror and gives me the finger. The fact that we found ourselves in such an embarrassing, vulnerable situation has created a nice atmosphere of trust between us.

Samy turns slightly toward the back seat.

"And you, Dani?"

Dani lowers her head and, with her dignity in tatters, whispers, "Apolo."

"What?" Samy and Andrea's screams make me grimace.

I touch my forehead. "No screaming. Hangover. Remember?"

Andrea stops at a red light.

"I didn't expect that."

"I know, I fucked someone younger than me," Dani says, running her hand over her face. Andrea looks at her like she's crazy.

"No, not because of that, but because I didn't know you knew each other so well."

Samy nods.

"Don't tell me you're feeling bad about your age, Daniela," Samy says. The guilt on Dani's face is obvious. "Apolo is much more mature than a lot of guys our age."

I'm glad that Samy thinks like me.

"That's what I told her," I say. "She's paranoid about it, and what people will say."

Samy gives her a comforting smile and reaches out to squeeze Dani's hand.

"Don't give yourself a hard time, Daniela. Okay?"

Andrea crosses the main avenue.

"I'm sorry to interrupt the romance, but do you mind if I stop by the pharmacy? My head is killing me, I need something for the pain."

"I need a Gatorade to hydrate," Samy whispers.

"Did you lose a lot of fluids last night?" Dani jokes, and we all grimace.

"Dani!"

Andrea parks her car at the pharmacy, and we let out a long sigh. I have a feeling this is the beginning of new friendships. After all, there is no better way to start a bond of trust than by hydrating and dealing with one of the worst hangovers of our lives.

FORTY-FIVE
The Used Ones

- ARES -

Waking up and stretching my arm across an empty bed is not what I expected. With my head spinning, I get up, staggering to the bathroom, and look around. Nothing. I notice Raquel's clothes are nowhere to be found, and I realize she's gone.

Did the witch use me and leave?

I can't believe it. This goes on the long list of first times with Raquel. No girl has ever disappeared the next morning after a night of sex. That's always been my role.

She keeps stealing my thunder.

But why did she leave? I didn't do anything wrong last night, did I? I run my hand over my face, remembering everything we did last night. God, that qualifies as the best sex I've ever had in my life. This woman drives me crazy. I grin like a fool, while assessing the only clothes I have: the Greek god costume. Ah, I don't think so, there's no way I'm going out like this. I look for clothes in the closet of the guest room. Since this is Marco's place and he's used to us staying here from time to time, there are usually extra clothes for the guests.

After changing into shorts and a white sweatshirt, I walk downstairs to the living room, where I am confronted with a scene that looks like something out of *The Hangover.*

Gregory is lying on the couch, with an ice pack on his forehead. Apolo is sitting on the floor with his back against the bottom of the couch and a bucket next to him, looking pale. Marco sits on the couch with an ice pack on his . . .

Marco is the first to notice me.

"Don't even say it."

I can't help but laugh.

"What the fuck?"

"I'm dying." Gregory grunts. My eyes are still on Marco.

"What happened to you?"

Marco rolls his eyes.

"What part of 'don't even say it' didn't you understand? Just forget it."

"It's hard to forget that when you're holding an ice pack over your penis."

Apolo snorts. "Why are you so raw, Ares?"

I sit at the end of the couch, at Gregory's feet, and look at Marco again.

"Did you break it?"

Marco gives me a murderous look.

"No, just . . . I think I have friction burns."

I let out a laugh.

"Shit, bro, and I thought I had a wild night."

Gregory laughs with me.

"Me, too, but no, it seems that Marco was fucked like an old TV."

Gregory and I jump in at the same time: "With no control."

Marco presses his lips together.

"Ha-ha, so funny."

Apolo chuckles.

"That was a good one."

Apolo and I go home and walk straight into the kitchen, still weak and dizzy. We need fluids, food, and a good shower. Apolo collapses at the kitchen table, his cheek resting there. I just grab two energy drinks from the fridge and set them on the table, sitting on the other side. I know Apolo did his thing last night, and I'm curious. He notices me staring at him.

"I don't want to talk about it."

"I said nothing."

"You're thinking about it."

I take a sip of my drink.

"You're imagining things."

Claudia comes into the kitchen and offers to make us some soup. Apolo says he's tired and goes to his room, but I take her up on it. It's my turn to rest my face on the table, while I wait for Claudia to get everything ready. Before I know it, I'm asleep. A kick to my knee wakes me up, and I blink and move quickly, causing a stabbing pain to cross my neck. When I raise my head, I can feel the marks of the wooden table edges on my cheek. I straighten in my chair, and my eyes meet a cold stare.

Artemis is sitting across from me, with a steaming cup of coffee in front of him. He's dressed in his black workout sweatshirt, and his hair is slightly damp with sweat. I still don't understand how he can get up on a Sunday to work out. But, well, there are a lot of things I don't understand about my big brother. He crosses his arms over his chest.

"Rough night?"

"You have no idea," I say.

Claudia sees me and moves around the stove. "Oh, you woke up; the soup is ready."

"Thank you," I say in a relieved tone. "You're saving a life."

She smiles at me.

"Don't get used to it." She pours the soup, and the simple smell emanating from it makes me feel better. Artemis takes a sip of his coffee, and I'm about to take a spoonful of soup when he speaks.

"Don't let Apolo drink too much. It's a bad habit to learn so young."

"I know, it was a one-day thing." I raise my spoon, but Artemis speaks again. "Your high school counselor told me that you haven't applied for business school yet." I put the spoon on the side of the plate.

"We're not even halfway through the school year."

"Better sooner than later. Do you have one in mind?" he asks. I clench my jaw. "It should be easy for you to get into Princeton. Dad and I both graduated there, and you'd be a legacy to get in."

Oh, the Ivy League, the most prestigious, exclusive, and well-known universities in the United States. The selection process is even more rigorous than for other universities. Not only do you have to have excellent grades, but also a lot of money, and then there are the well-known "legacy" admissions: if your parents or close family graduated from one of these universities, you're practically in.

Don't get me wrong, I'm interested in applying to Ivy League schools, but not for the career my brother has in mind. Claudia gives me a sympathetic look and continues cooking. Is my discomfort with this subject so obvious? Artemis doesn't seem to want to shut up.

"Have you thought about which branch you'll choose? Business or legal? It would help me a lot if you go for business. We're thinking of opening another branch office in the south. Construction has just started, and it would be ideal if you could manage it when you graduate."

I do not want to study business.

I want to study medicine.

I want to save lives.

I want to have the knowledge to give the best care to my grandpa and to the people I care about.

I think all those things, but I don't say them, because I know that the moment the words come out of my lips, my brother will lose all respect for me. Abandoning the family legacy feels like a betrayal. What good would a doctor do in a successful transnational corporation?

I've lacked for nothing my entire life, but I haven't had to work for any of it. Legacy has a very sweet side, but people are wrong if they think there's no price to pay. People don't see the pressure of what you're supposed to be, the lonely meals, how hard it is to make a real friend or earn genuine affection. I thought my life would be stuck in that rut until it happened: Raquel saw me.

And I'm not talking about her looking at me. She looked right through me. She came to me with such pure feelings, with such a beautiful, easy-to-read face, that it left me speechless. Raquel has always been so true and transparent in her reactions. I didn't think people like that existed.

She, who doesn't even know how pretty she is, told me so confidently that I was going to fall in love with her. She, who worked hard to buy the things she wanted, has always been lonely because of her dad's absence and her mom's job. She, who has been through so much shit with me . . .

She's still smiling with all her heart.

And it's a smile that disarms me and makes me believe that everything is possible. And that I will be a great doctor someday. Maybe no one in my family supports me or believes in me, but she does.

And that's more than enough.

FORTY-SIX
The Forgiveness

- RAQUEL -

New Year's Eve

Time flies by.

After Halloween, Ares and I hung out several times a week before he went on a Thanksgiving trip with his family. The more time I spent with him, the more I got to know him. I was able to catch those little things, like what a perfectionist he is whenever he does something for school, or how responsible he is with his soccer team, never once missing practice and always giving his best. Ares has amazing discipline, and it's kind of rubbing off on me. Not that I'm undisciplined, but I could definitely work on being on top of things like he is.

And what better example is there than what I'm doing right now: trying to write an essay I should have submitted before Christmas break. My literature teacher gave me extra time to work on it; however, it's not coming along well. Yoshi used to be the one helping me with essays. God, I miss him. The worst part is that from all the topics offered, I chose to write on forgiveness. I'm an idiot. I start typing on the Notes app on my phone:

I'm sorry . . .

Forgive me . . .

I never meant to hurt you.

I don't know what I was thinking.

Asking for forgiveness can be so difficult. It requires maturity and courage. Admitting that you were wrong means facing yourself. It means facing the fact that you are not perfect and never will be, and that you are capable of making mistakes like everyone else.

To make mistakes is part of being human, to admit them is part of being brave.

The worst mistakes are those that you can't erase. No matter if someone apologizes, no matter how much they do, it leaves a scar on your heart. Scars that still hurt when you remember them.

I stop because I'm getting emotional. New Year's Eve has a way of making me feel sensitive, of making me reflect on everything I've done, and what I haven't. I've been through so much this year, and the last six months have been a roller coaster of emotions for me.

"Put the phone away," my mom demands with a sigh.

The clock shows 11:55 p.m. My eyes fill with tears, and it doesn't surprise anyone. I've always cried when midnight approaches on New Year's Eve, whether out of sadness, joy, nostalgia, or a combination of emotions that even I can't figure out.

My mother puts her arm over my shoulder to hug me sideways. We're sitting on the couch at her closest friend's house. Helena has a large family, and we always spend New Year's Eve with them. I guess my mother has never liked the idea of us spending it alone, and neither do I. My mother caresses my arm, resting her chin on my head.

"One more year, baby."

"One more year, Mommy."

Helena appears in front of us, holding her three-year-old grandson in her arms.

"Come on, stand up, it's time for the count."

There are about fifteen people in this small room. The host on the TV screen starts counting backward.

Ten . . .

Dani's laughter . . .

Nine . . .

Carlos's foolishness . . .

Eight . . .

Yoshi's nerdy arguments . . .

Seven . . .

Apolo's innocence . . .

Six . . .

My mother's disappointment . . .

Five . . .

Ares's hurtful words . . .

Four . . .

Ares's sweet words . . .

Three . . .

His beautiful smile when he wakes up . . .

Two . . .

The deep blue of his eyes . . .

One . . .

I love you, Witch.

"Happy New Year!"

Everyone is shouting, hugging, celebrating, and I can't help but smile, even though thick tears are streaming down my cheeks.

I miss Ares a lot. He's spending Christmas and New Year's on an exotic beach in Greece because, apparently, they have family there. I couldn't help teasing him about the Greek gods going to Greece. Ares asked me over and over again if I wanted him to stay, but how could I allow myself to take time with his family away from him? I'm not that selfish.

My mother hugs me, bringing me back to reality.

"Happy New Year, beautiful! I love you so much." I return the hug. Our relationship is still a bit broken, but we're working on it. Of course, I haven't told her yet that Ares and I are dating. I'm taking it one step at a time. Ares called me hours ago to wish me a happy New Year, the time difference taking its toll.

After a few hugs, I sit on the couch. I have nothing to do—the reality of it takes me by surprise. After welcoming the year, Joshua would always come for me, and we would go out and wish happy New Year all over the streets, with everyone awake and celebrating. I glance at my phone at the opened note on forgiveness that I haven't finished.

Joshua has always been by my side, and these last few months have been hard without him because we have so many of our own traditions. We used to go out to play in the first snowfall of the year, welcome the kids in scary costumes on Halloween, have marathons of our favorite series, and buy different books so that when we were done reading them, we could exchange them. We had board game nights and bonfires with horror stories next to my house. We even set the yard on fire once, and Mom almost killed us.

I smile at the memory.

What am I doing?

I may not be able to trust him so easily, but I can forgive him. There's no room in my heart for a grudge.

Without much thought, I grab my coat and follow my heart. I run out of Helena's house and the cold of the newly arrived winter hits me, but I run down the sidewalk, waving and wishing happy New Year to everyone I meet along the way. Christmas lights decorate the street and the trees in the gardens in front of the houses. There are children playing with sparklers and others making snowballs to throw. The view is beautiful, and I realize that sometimes we get so focused on our problems that we don't see the beauty of simple things.

Hugging myself, I start walking faster. I can't run through the snow, I don't want to slip and break any bones; that would be pathetic. My foot gets buried in a pile of snow and I shake it off to continue, but when I look up, I freeze.

Joshua.

With his long black coat, a black cap, and his glasses slightly fogged by the cold. I say nothing and just run to him, forgetting the snow, the problems, the emotional scars, I just want to hug him.

And I do, linking my hands around his neck and pulling him tight against me. I smell the scent of that soft cologne he always wears, and it fills me and soothes me.

"Happy New Year, you idiot," I growl against his neck. He laughs.

"Happy New Year, Rochi."

"I miss you so much," I murmur.

He presses me against his chest.

"I miss you too. You have no idea."

No.

That's not what happened.

No matter how much I wished that had happened, it won't change the reality.

Reality is me running through the snow with tears on my cheeks, with no coat, and clutching my cell phone so tightly in my hand that it might break. My lungs burn from the cold air, but I don't care. My mother runs after me, yelling at me to calm down, to stop, to put on my coat, but I don't care.

I can't breathe properly.

I still remember how quickly my smile faded when I got the call. Joshua's mother sounded inconsolable.

"Joshua . . . attempted . . . suicide."

They didn't know if he was going to survive, his pulse was so weak.

No, no, no. Joshua, no.

Everything begins to flash before my eyes. What did I do wrong? Where did I fail? Why, Joshua? Guilt was the first feeling to fill my heart. It had never, ever crossed my mind that he could do something like this. He didn't look depressed, he didn't . . . I . . .

Arriving at his house, the ambulance speeds past me, and I fall to my knees in the snow. Joshua's neighbors come over and put a coat over me. I clutch my chest, breathing heavily. My mother hugs me from behind.

"It's okay, sweetie. It's okay, he'll be okay."

"Mommy, I. . . . It's my fault. . . . I stopped talking to him. . . . He . . . " I can't breathe, and I can't stop crying.

The taxi ride to the hospital is silent, except for the sound of my sobs. With my head on my mother's lap, I pray. I pray that he survives. This is not supposed to happen. This is a nightmare. My best friend couldn't have done that, my Yoshi . . .

Arriving at the emergency room, I run over to his parents. They look devastated. Their eyes are swollen, and the pain is evident on their faces. As soon as they see me, they burst into tears. I join them, hugging them.

Wiping away my tears, I softly push away.

"What happened?"

His mother shakes her head.

"After seeing in the New Year, he went to his room. We tried calling him, but he didn't answer. I thought he had fallen asleep and went to see." Her voice breaks, the pain clear on her face. "He took so many pills. He was so pale. My baby." Her husband hugs her. "My baby looked dead."

The agony and pain reflected in their faces are so hard to see. I can feel their despair and guilt. Where did we fail? What didn't we see? Maybe everything or maybe nothing. Joshua might have given us signs, or he might have given us nothing, but still this feeling of guilt, of failing him, eats away at us all.

Suicide . . .

An almost taboo word. One that nobody mentions and no one likes to talk about. It's not pleasant, much less comfortable, but the reality is that it does happen, that there are people out there struggling who need help. And I was naive enough to think that it only happened to other people, that it would never happen to someone close to me.

I never suspected that Joshua would do something like this.

Please, Joshua, don't die, I beg, closing my eyes. *I'm here, I'll never leave, I promise. Please don't go, Yoshi.*

Minutes pass, hours, I lose track of time. The doctor comes out, with a face that makes my heart clench in my chest.

Please . . .

The doctor sighs.

"He was very lucky. We pumped his stomach, and he's very weak but stable."

Relief floods through my body. If it wasn't for my mother holding me up, I would collapse to the ground. The doctor talks about referring him to a psychiatrist and a lot of other things, but I just want to see Yoshi and make sure that he's okay and that he's not going anywhere. I need to talk to him and convince him that he can never do anything like that again, and to apologize for pushing him away, and for not trying to make things right between us.

Maybe if I had been . . . he wouldn't have . . .

Maybe.

The doctor tells us that Joshua will be unconscious for the rest of the night, and that we can go rest and come back in the morning, but none of us move. My mother gets us an empty room where we can rest. This is her hospital, and everyone knows and respects her. She's one of the longest-serving nurses in the place.

My mother caresses my hair as I rest my head on her lap.

"I told you he'd be okay, baby. It's going to be all right."

"I feel so guilty."

"It wasn't your fault, Raquel. Blaming yourself won't do you any good, now you just have to be there for him, to help him get through this."

"If I hadn't pushed him away, maybe—"

"Raquel, people with depression don't always show what they feel." My mother interrupts me. "They can appear happy even if they aren't well. It's very difficult to help them if they don't ask for help, and sometimes for them asking for help makes no sense because life has lost meaning."

I don't say anything. I just stare at a window in the distance, watching the snowflakes fall. My mother caresses my cheek.

"Get some sleep. Rest. It's been a hard night."

My eyes burn from crying so much. I close them to try to sleep a little, to forget, to forgive myself.

"You're going to fall!" a little Joshua yells at me from below as I climb a tree. I stick my tongue out.

"You're just upset because you can't catch me," I say. Joshua crosses his arms.

"Of course not. Besides, we said the trees weren't allowed, you cheater."

"Cheater?" I throw a branch at him. He dodges it.

"Hey!" He gives me a murderous look. "Okay, truce, come down, and we'll continue the game later."

Carefully, I climb down the tree. When I'm standing on the ground, Joshua touches me and runs away.

"Got you! It's your turn to catch me."

"Hey, that's cheating."

He ignores me and keeps running, and I have no choice but to chase him.

A squeeze on my shoulders wakes me up, ending that pleasant dream, full of games and innocence. My mother rubs my arm and offers me a coffee with her other hand.

Caramel macchiato, my favorite.

It reminds me of Ares and our first date at the hospital. I haven't dared to call him, to say anything to him, because I know he'll come running, and I don't want to ruin his New Year. I know that's the least of it right now, but I don't want to involve anyone else in this painful situation.

"He's awake; his parents have just been to see him. Do you want to go in?"

My heart clenches, and my chest burns.

"Yes."

"You can do it, Raquel."

My hand shakes on the door handle, but I turn it, and step inside.

My eyes are fixed on the floor as I close the door behind me. When I look up, I cover my mouth to stifle my sobs.

Joshua is lying on white sheets, an IV hooked up to his right arm. He looks so pale and fragile, like he could break at any moment. His honey-colored eyes meet mine and immediately fill with tears. With big steps, I approach him and hug him gently.

"You idiot! I love you very, very much." I bury my face in his neck. "I'm so sorry, please forgive me."

When we separate, Joshua averts his gaze, wiping away his tears.

"I have nothing to forgive you for."

"Joshua, I . . ."

"I don't want your pity. I don't want you to feel obligated to be by my side just because this happened."

"What are you . . . ?"

"It was my decision. It has nothing to do with you or anyone else."

I step back, staring at him, but he doesn't look at me.

"No, you're not going to do this."

"Do what?"

"Push me away," I state. "I'm not here out of obligation. I'm here because I love you, and yes, I'm sorry I didn't talk to you before to try to fix things, but I had already decided to look for you before this happened, I swear."

"I am not asking for anything from you."

"But I want to explain, I want you to know how much I've missed you. How much I care about you."

"So I won't attempt suicide again?"

Where had that bitterness in his voice come from? That disinterest in life? Had it always been there? I remember my mother's words: *asking for help makes no sense because life has lost meaning.* Maybe nothing mattered to him anymore.

I approach him.

"Yoshi." I pause, noticing how he tenses at his nickname. "Look at me."

He shakes his head, and I take his face in my hands. "Look at me!"

His eyes meet mine, and the emotions I see in them break my heart: despair, pain, loneliness, sadness, fear . . . lots of fear. Tears come to my eyes again.

"I know it all seems meaningless now, but you're not alone. There are so many people who love you, and we're here to breathe for you when you need it." Tears roll down my cheeks, falling from my chin. "Please let us help you. I promise you this will pass, and you'll go back to enjoying life just like that cheating kid I played with when I was little."

Joshua's lower lip shakes. There are tears escaping his eyes.

"I was so scared, Raquel."

He hugs me, burying his face in my chest as he cries like a child, and I can only cry with him.

He's going to be fine. I have no idea how to make him fall in love with life again, but I will breathe for him for as long as it takes.

FORTY-SEVEN
The Hidalgos

- ARES -

The blazing Greek sun burns my skin and forces me to hide behind sunglasses. The weather isn't cold like back home, but it's not hot either; it's somewhere in the middle. I've been enjoying it since we arrived.

I'm lying on a chair in front of the resort's crystal-clear heated pool. The view is relaxing. You can see the whole coastline and the beach beyond the pool. For me, Greece has always had an air of antiquity, of history, that gives you a strange feeling but in a good way.

My grandpa is lying next to me, and Claudia is standing next to him, picking up his medicines from a table under an umbrella. She's wearing a red bathing dress that matches her hair and a see-through dress that barely covers her.

"I think I've had enough," Grandpa says, grunting and starting to get up. Claudia and I move to help him, but Grandpa gently loosens my grip on his arm.

"Ares, son, I can still walk alone," he tells me.

I raise my hands in the air.

"I got it." I watch them cross to the glass doors, and the sound of a text notification catches my attention. I grab my phone, but there's nothing. I haven't heard from Raquel in hours. And shit, I'm so out of focus.

I called her to wish her happy New Year when midnight arrived in Greece, but after that I haven't heard from her, not even when midnight arrived in North Carolina. I've sent her messages and I've called her, but there's no answer. Is she still asleep? Even though it's already three o'clock in the afternoon here, it's still early in the morning there.

Another notification sounds, but my cell phone is in my hand, so I know it's not mine. It's Apolo's phone on the chair next to me. He's in the pool swimming, which has always been his thing since he was little. I stare at his phone screen, amazed at the number of notifications he's received from Facebook. He's never been very active on it, but the notifications aren't stopping. I walk to the edge of the pool with a towel and his cell phone, bending down to pass them to Apolo as he emerges from the water, shaking out his hair.

"Your cell phone is going to explode," I say. Apolo gives me a confused look.

"My cell phone?"

"Since when have you been so active on Facebook?"

"I'm not." Apolo sits on the edge of the pool, puts the towel around his shoulders, and shakes the water off his hand before grabbing his phone. I sit next to him because I have nothing better to do now that the witch is ignoring me. Apolo moves his finger over the screen of his phone, and I see his expression of confusion growing.

"Oh shit."

"What's wrong?" I ask. As if my cell phone wanted to respond, the bombardment of notifications starts on mine as well. I'm about to check when Artemis materializes beside us. He doesn't look at all cheerful, hovering over us, and he's holding his cell phone in his hand.

"Apolo." Artemis grunts, and I see my younger brother lower his head. "Why did you upload that picture without permission?"

I stare at both of them. "Which photo?"

"I didn't think this would happen. I only have acquaintances on my Facebook," Apolo explains, but I still don't understand.

"Can someone explain to me what's going on?"

Artemis bends and puts his phone screen in front of my face, showing me the picture we took that morning of the three of us by the pool in shorts and sunglasses, all of us shirtless. That we're related is obvious, and I'm not ashamed to say we look great.

"Someone stole Apolo's Facebook photo and posted it on a Facebook page called 'Hot Guys,'" Artemis explains.

"The photo went viral and has a ton of likes," Apolo says, sounding genuinely surprised. "And the comments are still—"

"In the comments all those women planned to find us," Artemis interjects, giving Apolo a murderous look. "Somehow they did because I have over two thousand friend requests and counting."

Checking my phone, I realize that I have a lot of friend requests and private messages from strangers too.

"Relax, Artemis," I say, trying to calm him down. "It's a nuisance, but look on the bright side, free publicity for the Hidalgo Company."

THROUGH MY WINDOW

Artemis gives us one last glare before going to lie on his chair. He still doesn't look happy, but, well, happy has never been his strong suit either.

"Did you read the comments?" Apolo asks, absorbed by his cell phone. Filled with curiosity, I open the post and start scrolling. I have to stop because the comments are getting dirtier and dirtier. Wow, it's amazing what people can say without even knowing us.

I feel myself being stared at, so I look up and meet a pair of very pretty gray eyes across the pool. A black-haired girl and her blond friend have just stepped into the water on the other side. It's not the first time I've seen them since we arrived at the resort two weeks ago. Apolo follows my gaze.

"The girl who chases you, huh?"

"She doesn't chase me."

"You know it's true, even I've noticed it." Apolo takes a look at her. "She's very exotic, your type."

I run my hand through my hair. My type? Yes, he's right, that used to be my type: girls with dark hair and light eyes. But somehow, I ended up falling in love with a girl who has neither of those things. How ironic is life?

"I don't have a type anymore. There's only her."

Apolo gives me a big smile.

"I'm proud of you."

"And I'm proud of you, my brother who is no longer a virgin," I tease.

"Don't start."

"Ah, come on, it's normal to be curious. *My* first time was a disaster."

"Liar."

"I swear, it took me like five minutes to put on the condom," I say.

347

Apolo grimaces in discomfort.

"Too much information, Ares."

"Always remember to wear protection."

"Ares!"

"What?" I ask innocently.

At that moment my mother walks over. I expect her to say that it's time to eat as a family, but she stands with her mouth open, checking something on her phone.

"We are a trending topic on Twitter," she says.

Artemis throws his head back, grunting. He turns in his chair.

"Don't tell me this is about the photo," he groans. My mother shows us her phone.

"Look, the hashtag Hidalgo is in the top ten."

Social networks will never cease to amaze me.

"Which photo?" Claudia asks, furrowing her brows.

Apolo sits down on his chair, taking a piece of pineapple.

"Remember the picture you took of us this morning?" Claudia nods. Apolo chews for a second and says, "It went viral."

My mother gives him a grimace of disgust.

"Don't chew and talk, Apolo, how rude."

I sit down and check my phone again. I still don't have a message from the witch.

Where are you, Raquel?

Don't you miss me?

Because I'm dying to talk to you.

I open my conversation with her, and I notice she hasn't seen my messages yet. My phone rings in my hands, but my excitement fades when I see it's Samantha. I move away from the table to answer.

"Hello?"

"Oh, happy New Year, Ares."

Her voice sounds self-conscious, something's not right.

"What's wrong?" I ask.

She hesitates on the other end of the line.

"Something happened, Ares."

FORTY-EIGHT
The Gifts

- RAQUEL -

Medication . . .

Therapy sessions . . .

Psychiatric consultations . . .

And a lot of other things related to Joshua's condition are all I heard in the hospital as the day went on. I don't know if it's from tiredness or lack of sleep, but it was hard for me to pay attention, let alone understand what they were talking about.

My mother practically dragged me out of the building when the clock hit midnight again because I had officially spent twenty-four hours there. She said I needed to rest. Dani arrived to keep Joshua company in my place so his parents could rest too. They were devastated. After crying on my best friend's shoulder for a while, I said good-bye to Joshua and left.

This is not how I imagined starting the new year. Apparently, life likes to hit us when we least expect it to see how long we can hold on. I feel like I've been punched in the stomach and left without air, even though I'm breathing. My mind keeps trying to understand, to look for reasons, to point fingers, to blame myself. I still remember my conversation with Joshua before I left:

"I know you want to ask, so just do it."

Joshua smiles at me.

"It's okay," he says.

I rub my arms in an attempt to buy time to choose my words carefully.

"Why? Why did you do it?" I ask.

Joshua looks away, sighing.

"You wouldn't understand," he says.

I sit down on the hospital bed next to him.

"I'll try to understand," I say quietly.

He looks at me again.

"Give me time, I promise to tell you, but right now I . . . can't."

I put my hand on his shoulder and give him a reassuring smile.

"All right, I'll be patient," I tell him.

He places his hand over mine.

"I've missed you so much."

"Me, too, Yoshi. I . . . I'm sorry."

"Shhh." He grabs my cheek gently, forcing me to look at him. "You don't have to apologize, Rochi." His thumb caresses my skin.

"But . . ."

His thumb moves to hover over my lips.

"No, stop."

The touch of his finger against my lips tickles.

"Okay."

"Now go home and rest." He lowers his hand and sits up, giving

me a kiss on my forehead, then lies back down. "Go, I'll be fine with Medusa."

I laugh a little. "Don't call her that or you're going to have a very long night."

Joshua shrugs.

"It's worth it. It's the most appropriate nickname I could think of."

Dani comes in, muttering something about the quality of the hospital's coffee, and finds us grinning like idiots. She raises an eyebrow.

"What? Were you talking about me?"

"Nope," we say at the same time. And I leave them, fighting over nicknames and nonsense as usual.

I arrive home to an empty, silent house. I close the door behind me and rest my back against it, playing with the keys in my hands. I slide down against the door until I find myself sitting on the floor. I pull my knees up to my chest. I know I need to bathe and sleep, but I can't find the energy to do it. I just want to stay here.

I take my cell phone out of my pocket and look at the dark screen. It ran out of battery a few hours after I arrived at the hospital, and I wonder if Ares has sent me any messages. Maybe he's too busy celebrating New Year's with his family to notice my lack of texts, and I can't blame him. I haven't told him what happened with Joshua. My mind has been so focused on trying to understand and believe all of this has really happened, that I forgot to send Ares a message. Then my cell phone died, and I didn't want to tear myself away to go charge it.

With slow steps, I go upstairs and take a hot shower. I can't deny that the water feels good on my skin and eases my tense muscles. Now that I'm a little more relaxed, I let the Greek god invade my thoughts.

I miss him so much.

These weeks have felt like an eternity. It's so disconcerting when you get used to seeing a person almost every day, and suddenly you don't see them anymore. It's still a few days before he comes back, and I know it will be hard, especially now, when I would kill for one of his hugs, and to feel him next to me, giving me security.

In my pajamas, I sit on the bed and plug my cell phone in to charge. I watch it turn on, and message alerts begin to echo throughout the room. Rocky is sleeping peacefully in the corner; the sounds of notifications don't seem to bother him at all.

Quickly, I open Ares's conversation. I have a lot of messages from him and I didn't expect to.

12:15 a.m.

I was calling to wish you a happy new year, and you didn't answer.

12:37 a.m.

Witch?

1:45 a.m.

Why don't you answer the phone?

2:20 a.m.

Did you fall asleep?

9:05 a.m.

Raquel, I'm starting to get worried. Are you okay?

10:46 a.m.

Shit, Raquel, I'm really worried now.

That was his last message.

I bite my lower lip as I begin to type a response; however, I don't even finish typing the first word when my phone rings in my hand.

Incoming call: *Ares <3*

My heart speeds up, threatening to burst out of my chest. I take a deep breath.

"Hello?"

There's a second of silence, as if he didn't expect me to answer, as if he was used to me not answering.

"Where are you?" he asks, and the seriousness in his voice surprises me.

"At my house," I reply.

"Look out the window." And he hangs up. I stare at the phone in confusion before my gaze falls on the window. It's snowing again, so the window is closed. I get up and walk over to it, moving the curtains aside.

Ares is standing on his patio. He's wearing jeans and a black jacket over a white shirt, and he looks a little tanned. His black hair is in that messy style that suits him perfectly, just him. I'd like to say that I'm getting used to seeing him, that I'm getting used to the depth of those blue eyes, the confidence of his posture, and how beautiful he is, but I'd be lying. I don't think I'll ever get used to it, and especially now that I've gone two weeks without seeing him.

My body reacts to him as usual, my heart pounding desperately, my stomach turning, and my hands sweating a little. However, it's not the physical reactions that always take me by surprise but the sensations, what he makes me feel, the excitement that fills my chest, how he makes me forget that there is a world around me.

Snowflakes fall on him, landing on his jacket and in his hair. I can't believe he's really here. I fumble to open the window. He gives me that smile that would take anyone's breath away.

"Hello, Witch."

I don't know what to say. I'm speechless, and he seems to know it, because he quietly hops the fence that divides our yards and climbs up the ladder to reach my room. I step back, facing him. His eyes look right through me. I want to speak and tell him what happened, but from the way he looks at me, I know he already knows.

Without warning, he pulls me forward until I crash onto his chest. He holds me tight, making me feel safe. And at that moment, I don't know why, but tears well up in my eyes, and I find myself crying inconsolably. Ares just comforts me, caressing the back of my head.

"He ... almost died ..." I struggle to say the words. "I don't know what I would have done if he ... I feel so guilty."

He just lets me cry and mumble all the things I want to say, pressing me tight against his chest. God, I've missed him so much. We break away, and he takes my face in both hands, his thumbs wiping away my tears, and then he presses his lips lightly to mine, giving me a soft, gentle kiss.

He rests his forehead on mine.

"Why didn't you tell me?" he asks. I step back, putting distance between us. I can't concentrate with him so close to me.

"I ... I don't know, it all happened so fast. Besides, you were so far away; I didn't want to bother you."

"Bother me? Raquel, you are one of—if not the—most important person in my life. You will never bother me; your problems are my problems. I thought the whole point of being a couple was to be able to count on each other. It upsets me that you feel you can't count on me."

"I'm sorry."

"Don't apologize, that's not what I want, I just want you to tell me if you're ever in a difficult situation. Don't keep quiet because you don't want to bother me, okay?" I give him an honest smile.

"Okay."

"Do you want to talk about what happened?" he asks. I take a deep breath.

"No," I reply.

"Okay." Ares picks up a dark backpack that I hadn't noticed on the floor and puts it on the computer table. From it, he pulls out a beautiful gift bag.

"Merry Christmas, Witch," he says, extending his hand with the gift. I stare at him, surprised.

"You didn't have to give me anything," I say. He strokes his chin as if in thought.

"I think you told me you only accept gifts on special occasions, so I have to take advantage of this moment."

"Do you remember everything I tell you?" I ask.

"Yup. Everything I care about stays here." He touches his forehead. "Come on, take it. You don't have any excuse to refuse."

Sighing, I grab the bag. Ares looks at me impatiently. He seems more excited than I am, and his excitement spreads to me a little. I put it on the bed and open it. The first thing I pull out is a golden box with chocolates that not only look expensive but foreign.

"Chocolates?"

"I know, I know, I'm a cliché," he says, raising his hands. "There's more."

"Hey, I thought it was one gift," I accuse him.

"As I said, I have to take advantage of this opportunity."

The next thing I pull out is a small square box that I remember very well: the iPhone. I give him an are-you-kidding-me look.

"It's a new one! It's not the one from that time, I swear," he says quickly. "I know you like iPhones and you haven't been able to buy another one, and that phone Dani lent you is one phone call away from self-destructing."

"You are . . ."

"Please?" He has those begging eyes that remind me of the cat from Shrek.

"You just want a phone so I can take sexy photos to send you."

Ares acts surprised.

"How did you know?" he demands. I roll my eyes, smiling, and pull out a small, elongated box. When I open it, my heart melts; it's a gold necklace with a pendant with my name on it, but the *R* in Raquel is crossed with Ares's name. It looks like a little cross of our names. No one has ever given me something so detailed and cute. I don't know why I feel like crying again.

He helps me put it on and gives me a short kiss on the back of my neck before stepping back and leaning against the computer table, crossing his arms over his chest.

"Thank you so much, Greek God, that was really nice of you," I tell him honestly. "I never thought you'd be this sweet."

"I have my moments."

"I bought you something too," I say. His eyes widen. He wasn't expecting it. "It's not much, and it's not wrapped because I didn't expect you to get back so soon."

Nervously, I reach under my bed and pull out the plastic bag containing the two little things I bought and give it to him.

"I feel terrible for giving you your gift like this after you gave me something so nice," I say quickly. Ares gives me a tired look.

"Could you stop saying things like that? Let's see. . . . Let's see . . ."

The first thing he takes out is a book and reads the title aloud: "*Medicine for Beginners.*"

His smile fades, but his face fills with so many different emotions that my heart expands against my chest. He stares at me silently for a few seconds. "Thank you."

"Keep going, there's more." I watch as he carefully takes out a stethoscope. "I wanted to give you your first doctor's instrument, so you can always take me with you when you're a doctor."

I wish I could describe how he looks right now, with the emotions crossing his face, but I'd be at a loss for words. His blue eyes are watering as he slowly licks his lips.

"You really think I can make it," he says quietly. I give him a confident smile.

"I don't think so, I know you can make it," I say, giving him the thumbs up. "Dr. Hidalgo."

Ares puts the stethoscope on the table and rushes over to me.

"Shit, I love you so much." His lips are on mine before I can tell him that I love him, too, and that even if no one else supports him in his dreams, I always will no matter what.

FORTY-NINE
The Support

Three Months Later

Senior year has been no joke.

I can count on my fingers the days I've had time for some fun or to go out with my friends or Ares. We've all been consumed by the excellent-grades-required monster in order to have a remote shot at a good college when we graduate. It's been crazy, and we're all drained. Now, after a week of testing, I can finally relax a little and enjoy my boyfriend, who's lying on his side next to me.

The eyes are the mirror of the soul. . . .

Where have I heard that phrase before? It doesn't matter, I just know that it's true. I never imagined I could see so much by looking into someone's eyes, like I'm reading their biography.

Ares doesn't say anything, he just stares at me, and his eyes look so bright with the morning sun reflected in them. I don't know how long it's been since we woke up. His hand rests on the side of my face, his thumb caressing my cheek. I wish I could stop time so we can stay like this forever, without having to face the world or worry about anything else. I realize that happiness is not a perpetual state, it's just perfect little moments.

Ares closes his eyes and kisses me on the forehead. When he pulls away, the emotions in his eyes are as clear as water: love and passion. It makes me remember the beginning when I couldn't decipher him at all. And then fear settles in the pit of my stomach. When something is so perfect, the fear that something could ruin it can be overwhelming.

The alarm on his cell phone interrupts our moment.

"We have to go," he says.

"Argh!" I shout. I guess my little break from school is over. "Remind me why I have to study."

Ares stands up and stretches.

"Because you want to be a psychologist and help people, and for that you need to finish high school," he states, making me smile like a fool.

"Good motivation." I get out of bed with just his shirt on. "I'll let you be my first patient if you promise I'll be yours."

The good mood vanishes into thin air. Ares looks away without responding and starts walking toward his bathroom. I frown but say nothing; the subject of his university studies has been a sensitive one for the past month. He needs to talk to his parents and make a decision about which colleges to apply for soon, as the application deadlines for many schools are passing.

After watching him disappear behind the bathroom door and hearing him run the shower, I look for my backpack, which I find sitting next to a small library of books from school. I take advantage of the evenings when Mom is on night shifts to come and stay with him, and I bring my school bag with clothes so I won't be late in the morning. At first, it was awkward and embarrassing to be with Ares's parents and siblings, but as time went on, I realized that this house spends more time empty than occupied. Even when they're home, they tend to be locked in their own worlds or, in this case, rooms.

The one person I've interacted with quite a bit has been Claudia. She and I simply have chemistry, we get along well, and, although at first glance she may seem cold, she's actually very sweet.

These past three months have been wonderful. Ares has behaved like a prince. We've hung out, spent time with my friends and his friends, enjoyed wonderful sex. . . . We haven't had any fights, and I thank Our Virgin of Abdominals for that. I deserve this period of peace after all I went through in the beginning.

I'm taking my clothes out of my backpack and putting them on the table with Ares's laptop when several envelopes next to the computer catch my eye. One has a stamp that I recognize: The University of North Carolina.

I press my lips together. That's where I applied, but Ares has never been interested in going there. He always told me he wanted to study at one of the Ivies. Curiously, I pull out the letter inside, and my heart stops as I read it.

Thank you for your interest in our Business Management program for the semester. We will be reviewing your information and qualifications and will notify you of our decision.

What the fuck . . . ?

Business management? University of North Carolina?

At that moment Ares comes out of the bathroom with a towel around his waist, while drying his hair with another one.

"You can go in now, I . . ." He stops when he sees me with the paper in my hand.

"UNC? Business management?" I show him the paper.

"I was going to tell you . . ."

"You applied to UNC? For business management? What did I miss?"

"Raquel . . ."

"What happened to medicine? Princeton? Yale? Harvard? What happened?" I don't give him time to answer. I don't know why I'm so upset. Ares looks away.

"I have to be realistic, Raquel."

"Realistic?" I ask in disbelief. He throws the towel aside and runs his hand over his face.

"Management or law, that's what my family needs." I can't believe I'm hearing him say this.

"What about what you need?" I ask. He ignores my question.

"It's the same college you applied to. Aren't you glad to know we'll be together?"

"Don't try to make this about me," I retort. "This is about you and what you want for your life."

"This is what I want for my life. To be useful to my family, and to be by your side, that's all I want."

"No," I shake my head. Ares raises an eyebrow.

"No?" he asks.

"You're just taking the easy path. You're giving up without even trying and taking refuge in the thought that at least we'll be together."

"At least?" he repeats. "I didn't know being together was so unimportant to you."

"Again, don't try to make this about me or about us."

"How can it not be about us? If I apply to those other colleges, do you know how far apart we'll be? I'm going to have to move to another state, Raquel."

I know . . .

I've thought about it so many times . . .

But I can't be selfish . . .

"I know, but you'll be studying what you want to study and following your dream. That's enough for me."

"Don't give me that shit." He moves closer to me. "You want us to split up?"

"I just want you to do what you want to do."

"This is what I want to do. This is what I'll do. This is my decision."

I run my hands through my hair.

"It's not. Why are you so stubborn?" I demand. I see him hesitate.

"Because I love you," he says, and I stop breathing. "And just imagining being away from you tears me apart."

"I know. I feel that too." I move closer to him and take his face in my hands before I continue. "I love you, too, and because I love you, I want you to be happy and achieve everything you want in this life."

He puts his forehead on mine.

"I can't be happy without you."

"I'm not going anywhere. We'll find a way, long-distance relationship or whatever." I pause. "I'd rather do that than see you every day in a place that has never interested you, studying something you hate. I don't want to see you suffer that way."

"My family won't support me."

"Have you talked to them? At least try." I give him a short kiss. "Please?"

"Okay." His lips meet mine in a soft kiss that's filled with so many emotions that my heart races. I reciprocate, running my hands around his neck, kissing him deeply. Feeling his wet torso against me, my hormones rage, and it doesn't help that he's only wearing a towel. Our mouths move harder against each other, brushing and licking, and I press my breasts against him with desire.

Ares lifts me up, setting me on the computer table, and reaches between my legs. I interrupt the kiss breathlessly.

"We're going to be late."

"A quickie." He kisses me again, lifting the shirt I'm wearing, and underneath I'm naked. The towel falls to the floor and Ares pulls me tighter against him, forcing me to spread my legs wide for him. I'm on the pill now, so we don't use condoms anymore.

Before I can say anything, he penetrates me, and a moan of surprise escapes me but is stifled by his lips. His movements are rough and deep, but they feel fucking good. I hold tight to his neck as he thrusts into me, the table crashing against the wall with each thrust.

Our kisses become uncontrolled and wet, and it's not long before we both reach orgasm. Breathing fast, we hug each other. Having so much sex has its advantages, we know each other intimately, and we know where to touch, lick, and how to move to make each other come.

Apolo walks in without warning.

"Ares, let's—Oh shit." Apolo turns his back to us quickly. Ares picks up the towel and covers himself, stepping in front of me to cover me. Apolo continues to stare into the distance.

"We're going to be late. I'll wait for you downstairs."

As soon as he leaves, I burst out laughing, tapping Ares's shoulder.

"I told you to close that door."

I know, we've become cheeky and shameless. Ares gives me a short kiss and carries me toward the bathroom.

"Come on, we'll save time by showering together." I let out a laugh and bury my face in his neck.

- ARES -

"Well?" my father begins, holding a glass of whiskey in his hand. We're in the study on the small couches to one side of my father's large desk. Artemis is sitting beside him, checking a chart on his tablet, and my mother is on his other side, looking at me curiously. Apolo is sitting next to me on the opposite couch, giving me the occasional worried glance. I called this family meeting. I'm not going to lie, my hands are sweaty, and my throat is so dry it hurts.

"Ares?" my mother calls. Everyone is waiting for me. I can't give up without a fight, and the thought of Raquel's disappointed face motivates me.

"As you know, it's time to apply to colleges," I begin. Artemis puts down his tablet.

"Do you need help with that? I can make some calls."

"No, I . . ." Shit, I didn't think this would be so hard. The moment I say the words, I'll expose myself, and I don't want to get hurt.

"Ares, son," my father encourages me. "Say what you have to say."

Summoning my courage, I take a deep breath.

"I want to study medicine."

Sepulchral silence. I feel like I've been exposed, thrown naked in front of everyone, begging not to be hurt. Artemis begins to laugh.

"Are you kidding me?" he asks. I want to chicken out and say yes, but I can't do that, not when I've come this far.

"No, I'm not kidding," I say.

My father sets his glass aside.

"Medicine?—"

"I thought we'd been clear about what the family needs, Ares," my mother cuts in. "Your father needs another manager or head of legal in his companies," she says.

My father immediately backs her up.

"I told you we're opening another branch office in a few years. We're expanding, and I need my children to be part of it. It's our family legacy."

"I know," I say. "Believe me it hasn't been easy for me to tell you this. I don't want to be ungrateful. You've given me everything, but . . ." I speak with my heart in my mouth. "I really want to be a doctor."

My mother clicks her tongue.

"Does this have to do with that idea you had as a child of wanting to save your grandpa? Son, he's always had the best doctors; you don't have to become one for him."

Artemis puts his hands on his knees. "Just apply to a legal or business program."

"No," I say, shaking my head. "This isn't a whim or just because of Grandpa. I really want to be a doctor. I don't want to study management, let alone law."

"And you're just going to put aside your family's needs? Don't be ungrateful," my mother says, crossing her arms.

"I just want to be happy," I mutter. "I want to study what I want."

Artemis gives me an incredulous look.

"Even if that means turning your back on your family?"

"I'm not . . ."

"No." My father interjects. "We've all made sacrifices for this family, Ares. Do you think Artemis wanted to study management? No, but he did it for us. We have what we have because we've all put aside individual wants for what we need as a family."

"Really? How happy are you, Artemis?" My older brother gives me a cold look, and I look at my father. "Or are you, Dad? What good is so much money if we can't do what we want?"

My mother reprimands me. "Don't be impertinent! Your father has already given you an answer."

"I'm not going to study management," I repeat. I can see my father clench his jaw.

"Then you won't study anything." His coldness surprises me. "Nothing will come out of my pocket for your schooling if you don't study what we need. I will not support a son who does not support the good of his family."

Apolo speaks for the first time.

"Dad . . ."

A lump forms in my throat, but I don't let tears fall from my eyes. I don't want to look weaker than I already have.

"Dad, I want to be happy," I say, not caring that everyone is watching me. "Without your support I can't make it. Without financial support there is nothing I can do. Medical schools are expensive. Please support me."

My father's expression does not waver.

"The answer is no, Ares."

My mind travels to an old memory when Dad was different, before he turned out like this.

"Dad, you know you are my hero . . ." The little boy runs around his father and hugs him. My father smiles at the child—at me.

"I always will be, I will keep you safe."

My mother's betrayal has changed him so much. Controlling the pain in my heart, I get up and walk out the door. I can hear Apolo talking to my father in the background, pleading with him, but I just keep walking.

When I get to my room, Raquel rises from the bed, looking at me cautiously. I thank the world for having someone who supports me unconditionally, who won't turn her back on me, who I can break down in front of without embarrassment.

I'm trembling, and my vision is blurred by tears. She was right. I want to study medicine with all my heart, and now that dream has shattered. Raquel walks toward me slowly, as if she is worried that any sudden movement will push me away. Her mouth opens, but she says nothing. When she reaches me, she hugs me, and I bury my face in her neck, crying. I'm not ashamed, not with her. She knows every side of me. She has believed in me far more than my own father.

"Shhh," she whispers, stroking my hair. "You'll be all right, it's going to be all right."

I hear the door open and immediately pull away from Raquel,

wiping away my tears defensively. Apolo comes in, and his eyes are red.

"You can count on me," he says with determination. "I want you to know that not everyone in this family is turning their back on you. Count on me."

He smiles at me, but the sadness in his eyes is obvious.

"We'll look for scholarships. We'll both work part time. We'll figure it out . . ." His voice breaks. "You deserve to be happy, and you're not alone. Do you understand?"

This idiot . . . I smile and nod.

"I understand."

"Good." He gives me a thumbs up. Raquel grabs both our hands, smiling at us.

"We'll figure it out," she says.

I know it's not going to be easy and the odds are against it, but for some reason I believe them, so I smile.

"We'll figure it out."

FIFTY
The Job

- RAQUEL -

Apolo, Ares, and I are doing our best working the evening shift at Dream Burgers after school.

However, I'm hating my boyfriend right now. I know, how could I when I can hardly believe he's really my boyfriend? But why does he have to be so attractive? Why does everything have to look good on him? The Dream Burgers uniform is the most antisensual clothing in the world, and yet Ares looks great in it.

I grunt, noticing a group of three girls smiling at him and sharing glances while he's taking orders behind the register. I understand them, I really do, but this Dream Burgers has turned into a fucking circus since Ares started working here a week ago. I swear we've seen an increase in our female clientele because of him. The manager is just as fascinated with Ares, and I have to watch half the town come in here every day to see my boyfriend.

I sigh dramatically, preparing a coffee for one of the orders. Gabo laughs beside me.

"Oh," he teases. "You seem a little upset."

"Of course not," I practically snort in response. "I'm perfectly fine."

"I have been dethroned," he says in a dramatic tone, putting his hand on his heart. "Before, I was the king of this Dream Burgers."

I burst out laughing and tap him on the shoulder.

"Idiot."

"Oh look." Gabo points behind me to the group of girls still ordering. "Today they were brave enough to give him their numbers." We watch the girls give Ares scraps of paper between giggles. Ares takes them kindly, but he doesn't smile. His expression remains disinterested.

Sorry, but they have a lot of work to do to get to where I am now.

"I don't know why they keep coming," Gabo says. He puts some fries in a to-go bag, completing an order. "He doesn't even smile at them. Can you imagine if he smiled at them? We'd have a fucking ovary explosion in here."

"Or a flood," Apolo chimes in, walking out of the kitchen. He looks cute with the transparent beanie over his hair.

"You're not helping," I say as I prepare orders for the drive-thru. Apolo gives me that innocent smile he has.

"Calm down, your break is coming up."

It hasn't been easy to ignore all the attention Ares receives, but I've tried to manage it as best I can. Even though we don't earn much working half shifts at Dream Burgers after school, it's something. Apolo decided to work to support his brother as well. Ares and I have both applied for several scholarships and are waiting for the responses.

I wait until Ares has finished attending to the group of girls and they leave before I pass behind him and whisper slyly: "I'm watching you."

Ares turns, with that crooked smile I love so much forming on his lips, and I feel like the queen of the world because he smiles for me so easily.

"Watching me has always been your hobby, hasn't it?" he asks, crossing his arms over his chest.

"I don't know what you're talking about," I reply, but of course, I know exactly what he's referring to—my stalker days.

"No? Wasn't *AresAndMeForever* your Wi-Fi password?"

"You're not the only Ares in the world," I tell him.

"I am the only Ares in your world," he counters. I raise an eyebrow.

"Why so sure?"

Apolo appears beside us.

"Stop flirting, we have customers." He points to two girls waiting for Ares to take their order. "My God, where do all these girls come from?"

I let out a sigh of annoyance and stand in front of the register.

"Welcome, may I take your order?" I ask. The girls don't hide their disappointment.

"Hey." They share a look between them before the bolder of the two responds. "We don't know what we want yet, so we'll think about it." They take a few steps back and start to walk away. Really? Ares puts his hand on my waist, pushing me slightly away from the register.

"Trust me, Witch." As soon as Ares takes charge, the two girls return, smiling like there's no tomorrow.

Breathe, Raquel.

"It's time for your fifteen-minute break. Go," my boss tells me, and I don't hesitate to get out of there. The fresh spring air hits me as I leave. I sit on the sidewalk beside the store, relaxing my legs. I need to get away from girls chasing my boyfriend for a while.

I hear the door open, and a twenty-something girl who always orders a Dream Burgers coffee and sits down to write at one of the tables comes out, carrying her backpack. She's a regular customer, but I still don't understand why she's always here. There's nothing special about this place. We make eye contact, and she smiles kindly at me.

"Are you all right?" she asks.

"Yeah, I think so," I reply.

She seems to hesitate for a second, before sitting down next to me.

"I don't want to sound weird, but I've seen it all."

"What do you mean?" I frown at her.

"Is the new guy your boyfriend?"

"How do you know?" I ask.

She laughs, and her blue eyes light up.

"I'm very observant, the advantages of being a writer, and, besides, I've been there." I give her a look of disbelief, and she looks away. "Oh, believe me, being the hot guy's girlfriend is not as great as it sounds. I can't tell you how many times I found myself wondering if I was enough for him, or what the heck he saw in me when he had so many other options."

Exactly.

"It's really easy to put yourself down in a situation like this." She turns to me. "But the reality is that love isn't something that's born and grows based on appearances. It needs substance to be real. Physical attraction can be the beginning of feelings, but it'll never be enough. It'll always need that something more, that connection that you can't get with just anyone."

I don't know what to say, so she continues.

"For him, you're that something more, that connection. Sure, there are people prettier than you, smarter than you, more talented than you, but no one is better or worse than you, and no one is you." Silence falls between us, but it's not uncomfortable. I nod and smile at her.

"Thank you. I feel much better."

"I'm glad."

"I'm curious," I begin. "Are you still the girlfriend of that handsome guy?"

"No." She shakes her head and raises her hand, showing me her ring. "I'm his wife now."

"Oh wow." The joy she exudes when she says it is contagious. "You look so happy."

"I am, but it wasn't easy at first."

"I wish I was more mature and didn't get jealous, but sometimes I can't help it," I say. She laughs at my honesty.

"Jealousy is completely normal when you're in love, but how you act about it is what will tell you if it's harmful or natural."

"You sound too wise to be so young." I snort.

"I told you, I've been through a lot, and I think it helped me."

A car passes by and parks in front of us at a safe distance. The young woman stands and brushes off her pants.

"My ride's here," she says.

"Your husband?" I ask, raising an eyebrow. She nods and we stand up.

"I hope I helped." She smiles again.

"You have, really."

I catch a movement out of the corner of my eye, and see a man getting out of the car. *Virgin of Abdominals!*

He's tall, with dark eyes and messy black hair around his face.

He's wearing a dark blue suit, but the tie is half-loose as if he's just tucked his fingers behind it, and he has a mysterious, half-hidden tattoo on his neck. The young woman lets out a giggle next to me.

"He's hot, isn't he?"

I blush. It wasn't my intention to look at her husband that way. He walks over to us and looks at her with pure adoration on his face.

"Hello, strawberry," he says, giving her a quick, short kiss.

She turns her gaze to me.

"Evan, this is Raquel, she works here." Evan smiles kindly at me, and I see dimples forming on his cheeks.

"I hope my wife didn't bother you too much," he says.

"No, not at all." I shake my head. "She just gave me some very good advice."

He runs his hand around her shoulders.

"Yeah, she's good at it."

She laughs, and her whole face lights up.

"We should go. It was a pleasure, Raquel." They start walking, when she suddenly turns around.

"Oh, by the way, my name is Jules. I'll see you around." I watch them tease and push each other and then hug again as they walk to the car.

What a cute couple, I think. I decide to get back to work.

FIFTY-ONE
The Birthday

I love you . . .

It's so easy to say, yet so difficult to express through actions.

We tend to be selfish by nature, some more than others. We want what is best for us and what benefits us. We've been taught to put ourselves before others, and told that if we don't love ourselves, we can't love someone else. And in that respect, it can become true: how much you love yourself can be reflected in your ability to love others. However, there are times when we have to put aside what we want for ourselves for the welfare of the other person. To me *that* is true love.

I know what Ares needs and what he really wants for his future, and I'm supporting him 100 percent. But I can't deny that I'm terrified at the idea of separating, of losing him. Just imagining it makes my chest tighten and my stomach feel funny, but I love him, and because I love him, I have to put aside what I feel for him, for his happiness.

How fucked up is love?

I stare at the letter in my hands. I've been accepted to the University of North Carolina on a partial scholarship to study psychology.

I'm really happy. I can't deny it. This is what I've always wanted, and there shouldn't be anything to overshadow it. The only problem is that I want to share my happiness with Ares. I know he'll be proud of me, but I also know that this only makes it more real that we'll be going our separate ways when this school year is over. It's a bittersweet feeling, but I guess that's life.

"That's not the reaction I expected," Dani comments, stretching out on my bed. "They accepted you, you idiot!"

"I don't know. I still can't believe it."

She sits down, snatching the letter from my hand, and reads it.

"And with a partial scholarship? This is a miracle, because you don't have any talent." I give her a murderous look.

"I told you that winning interstate chess tournaments would do some good."

Dani sighs. "I still don't know how you're so good at chess, your IQ . . ." I raise an eyebrow at her. "Is apparently good enough to get a scholarship," she finishes. "Yay!"

I put the letter on the nightstand and get up. The sun streaming through the window falls on Rocky, who's asleep on his back with his paws in the air and his tongue out. He's definitely my doggy incarnation. Dani glances at him, concerned.

"Is he all right?" she asks. "He looks like he's dead."

"He's fine. He has weird sleeping poses," I answer. Dani bursts out laughing.

"Like his owner."

Dani spent the night with me, because today is . . .

"Happy birthday to you!" my mother comes in with a tray of breakfast, smiling broadly at us. "Go back to bed, Raquel, or else breakfast in bed becomes meaningless."

I smile at her.

"Yes, ma'am."

I return to Dani's side. Her black hair is a bit greasy, and her makeup is smudged. Last night we drank a little at our prebirthday sleepover, which ended with both of us crying over the Hidalgos. Me, because I got the acceptance letter and would be moving away from Ares, and her because . . . well, I don't know what the fuck is wrong between her and Apolo. She loves him, then she doesn't, then she wants to get over him, but she can't. I think everyone has had a friend who has no fucking idea what she wants from a guy.

Mom puts the tray on my lap. There's plenty of food for both of us, and a small muffin that has a lit candle on it. I blow out the candle, and they clap their hands like seals that have just eaten. I can't help the smile that spreads over my face.

"Happy birthday, beautiful." Mom leans over and gives me a kiss on the forehead.

"Thank you, Mom." I start eating and offer a piece of pancake to Dani, who grimaces, and gives Mom an apologetic look.

"No offense, Rosa, but I really don't have an appetite."

Mom scoffs. "Too much to drink last night?"

Dani looks surprised. "How did you know?"

"This room smells like a mixture of beer and vodka." Mom sighs. "With a touch of wine for good measure."

Dani's eyes widen.

"How did you know what we drank?"

Mom just shrugs, and I roll my eyes, answering her.

"Who do you think bought the alcohol, silly?"

Mom heads for the door.

"Eat and get up. Your aunts and cousins are about to arrive, and we have a lot to do before tonight's party."

The birthday party . . .

Although we're not very close with the rest of the family, my mom's sisters always come on my birthdays and bring my cousins. I get along with some of them, but there are others I can't stand.

"Ah," I shriek as my mother leaves the room. "I hope Aunt Carmen's daughters don't come. They're unbearable." Dani nods in agreement.

"Yeah, they're always DM-ing me on Instagram, asking what they need for an audition for Mom's modeling agency. They're superannoying."

"Come on. We better get ready." Dani lies back down, pulling the sheet over her head. "Come on, Morticia," I take the sheet off.

"Morticia?"

"Look in a mirror and you'll understand."

"Very funny." She gets up and reluctantly walks with me to the bathroom. You haven't passed the boundaries of trust in a friendship until you've been brushing your teeth in the sink while your best friend pees right next to you.

"And . . . you invited him?" she asks. I knew this question would come sooner or later.

"Of course, he's my friend," I answer after rinsing my mouth.

"I know, I just wanted to . . ."

"Psychologically prepare yourself to see him?"

"No, just . . ." She doesn't finish her sentence, and I turn to look at her, still sitting on the toilet.

"We've had this conversation a thousand times, and I don't understand what's going on in your head. If you like him so much, why aren't you with him?"

"It's complicated."

"No, it's not, Dani. It's very simple: you like each other very much, and you're happy together. Why can't you be together?"

She runs her hands over her face. "I'm scared, Raquel."

"Scared?" That takes me by surprise.

"What I feel for him scares me so much; I've never felt so vulnerable."

Oh. My. God. Dani is the fucking female version of Ares. How did I not realize this? And what have I done to surround myself with people like this?

"Are you serious, Dani?" I cross my arms over my chest. "Are you listening to yourself? Scared? Fuck fear. You're never going to live life to the fullest if you're living in fear of getting hurt."

"I'm not like you," she admits, licking her lower lip. "You're so strong. You rise up when something bad happens, and you smile as if life hasn't hit you so many times. I'm not like that, Raquel. I'm a weak person hiding behind a strong facade, and you know it. I don't get up easily. I find it hard to smile at life when something bad happens to me, that's the kind of person I am."

"You aren't strong? Who beat up Rafa in second grade when he called me all sorts of names? Who stood by their mother and helped her build a prestigious modeling agency? Who juggles schoolwork and helping her mother with her business?" I shake my head. "Don't give me that shit about you not being strong, you're one of the strongest people I know. It's okay to be afraid, it's normal, but don't let fear control your life."

Her face lights up.

"I'd hug you, but . . ." She points to her pants over her ankles.

"Imaginary hug," I say, slapping her forehead and leaving the bathroom. "Come on, Morti, we have work to do."

"Stop calling me that," she says, and I hear her flush the toilet.

"Look in the mirror."

I laugh as I hear her squeal.

"By the nails of Christ and the flip-flops of Moses!"

I take the tray with the leftovers downstairs and find Mom in the kitchen, checking the cake in the oven. It's the perfect moment to talk, and this conversation we're about to have has to happen sooner or later. Especially since I've invited the Hidalgos to tonight's party. Mom glances at me over her shoulder as she pours some coffee in her cup.

"Mom, I need to tell you something." I clear my throat, sitting on the kitchen table. "Can you sit down for a second?"

She frowns but sits across the table from me.

"You're scaring me," she says. I let out a long breath.

"I know I've told you I've been hanging out with Ares as friends these past couple of months," I start, and she sips her coffee. "Ares and I . . ."

"You're dating," she finishes with a calm expression.

"You knew?"

"Sweetie, I'm your mother, and this is a small town. I've heard it all from different people. How you guys are all working together at Dream Burgers, how happy you seem." I hesitate because her expression isn't angry, but it's not happy either.

"Why didn't you say anything?" I ask.

"I wanted you to tell me. I've been waiting for a while," she replies. The trust and communication between us fractured when the thing with Yoshi happened, and yet she was giving me time to tell her, to trust her. She was closing the chapter and opening a new one. It makes me feel like she should have found out from me.

"I'm sorry, Mom, I should have said something sooner. I—"

"Raquel," she interrupts.

"No, let me say this. I haven't handled this the right way, and I'm really sorry about that. You've been a great mom, and I just . . . I keep messing up." For some reason, I'm getting emotional, and tears blur my vision. Mom sighs and extends her hand to hold mine on the table.

"Sweetie, no tears. There's no need for those. It's your birthday. We're okay, Raquel. You're not a kid; you're nineteen now." She squeezes my hand. "My only questions for you would be: Is he treating you well? Are you happy?"

"Yes."

"Then that's all I need to know." She pauses for a second. "Oh, are you being . . . you know, careful?" I know what she means.

"Mom!"

"Hey, I'm not ready to be a grandma, and you're not ready to have a kid." I laugh a little and she gets up to walk around the table. She leans in for a hug. "We're a team, no secrets, okay?"

"Okay, Mom." I wrap my arms around her waist.

"Now, let's get ready for the party."

>> <<

"Then I said, 'Of course not, silly, you're too ugly to go out with me,' and he was kind of shocked, so I just gave him a dirty look and left. The whole school talked about it for months."

Dani and I share a look while listening to Cecilia, my least favorite cousin, and I think with her little speech about rejecting a boy you can imagine why. I used to like her before my uncle started making good money, which made her, her sister Camila, and my aunt Carmen unbearably arrogant. Now they think they're better than all of us since they're the only wealthy ones in our family. My uncle is the only one who's still the same.

The party preparations are ready. Mom has decorated the back-yard with white Christmas lights and balloons that match the floral dress I'm wearing. Everything looks nicer than I expected.

Cecilia is about to continue talking when I see Joshua walk in.

"Yoshi!" I cry, walking away from my chatty cousin. He gives me one of his big smiles.

"Rochi, happy birthday." He hugs me tightly, and when we break apart, he hands me a small gift box.

"Thank you." I turn to greet Joana, the girl he's been dating for the past month, who he met in his therapy group. "Hello, welcome to the madhouse."

"Joshua said you would say that as a welcome." She giggles.

I shake my head. "He knows me too well."

Joshua glances behind me at the group of cousins.

"Oh, I see they all came. This'll be interesting."

The place fills up quickly and, truth be told, it's not that diffi-cult given the size of the backyard. A few friends from school, some neighbors, and my aunts and cousins are enough to fill it.

I glance at my phone and there's no message from Ares, but I'm not worried. I saw him last night for a few minutes before Dani arrived for the sleepover. He told me that he'd let me have the day to share with my family, but that after the party I'd be his. He's coming to the party with Apolo. I also sent invitations to Artemis and Claudia as a courtesy, but I don't think they'll come.

I'm about to answer a question one of my cousins asked me when everyone's gaze moves toward the entrance to the backyard. I slowly turn around.

You know those slow-motion moments in movies? That's what I'm experiencing right now, and I'm not the only one. The whole party seems to have come to a standstill as the Hidalgo brothers walk toward us. Artemis is wearing a black suit without a tie and the first buttons of his shirt are unbuttoned, his hair is combed back perfectly, and he has a slight beard adorning his manly face. Apolo smiles broadly, his pretty face lighting up, his damp hair caressing his ears and forehead. He's wearing a dark blue shirt with jeans. And Ares . . .

Ares is in the middle, walking as if the world belongs to him, like the fucking Greek god he is. The sleeves of his black shirt are rolled up to his elbows, revealing a beautiful black watch, and he keeps running his fingers through his messy hair. That dazzling face gives me a crooked smile, and his blue eyes sparkle, taking my breath away.

Virgin of Abdominals . . .

"Holy Mother of God." I hear Cecilia exclaim behind me. My aunt's mouth is literally hanging open. "Where did those guys come from?"

Everyone watches them in absolute silence as they approach me. Artemis is the first to speak.

"Good evening."

Ares gives me a mischievous smile, and leans into me, giving me a short kiss.

"Happy birthday, Witch."

>> <<

How to leave a party in absolute silence?

Just invite three Greek gods, it works perfectly. Even the music has stopped, but don't think it's some magic trick or something. No, it's just that my aunt Helena is in charge of the music, and she's dazzled by the three guys in front of me.

The truth is, I understand what my relatives are feeling. It takes time to get used to the Hidalgos. I feel the need to break the silence.

"Thanks for coming, guys," I tell them from the bottom of my heart. I can't deny that I'm surprised to see Artemis here. I never imagined he would come. Apolo gives me a sweet smile, and I hear Camila sigh behind me.

"You don't have to thank us for anything," Apolo says. "Thanks to you for inviting us."

My aunt Carmen, of course, cannot keep quiet.

"Raquel, baby, where are your manners?"

And so begins that awkward moment when you have to introduce your beautiful boyfriend and his siblings to your family.

"Apolo, Ares, and Artemis, these are my aunts Carmen and Maria, and my cousins: Cecilia, Camila, Yenny, Vanessa, Lilia, and Esther."

After all the protocol, and my cousins half fainting, the Hidalgos cross over to a group where Dean and other guys are talking.

My cousin lets out a shriek.

"Oh my God, Raquel!" Camila exclaims. "Your boyfriend is . . . I can't explain it." Cecilia is mute. My aunt Carmen says nothing either. My aunts wander off to talk, leaving me to the large group of girls alone.

"Apolo. . . . Even his name is pretty." Camila sighs, grabbing my shoulders. "Does he have a girlfriend?"

My eyes meet Dani's. She seems pretty annoyed at Camila's interest.

"Oh, I think he does have a girlfriend," Dani interjects.

"Oh no." Camilla pouts, "Of course he has a girlfriend. How could that cute, beautiful thing not have a girlfriend?" she asks, staring at Apolo.

Yenny takes a sip of the lightly spiked fruit drink we prepared.

"Fuck relationships, I'd give anything to fuck the oldest brother."

"Yenny!" Cecilia spits out her drink. I can't help but smile. Vanessa gives Yenny a high five.

"You read my mind. One night is all I ask of any of those guys," says Vanessa. I raise an eyebrow, and she laughs. "Take it easy, not yours, the other two."

"Apolo also has a girlfriend," Dani intervenes. "Remember?"

"So?" Vanessa looks at her, and Dani can't hide her annoyance.

"So? Would you mess with a guy who has a girlfriend?"

Vanessa snorts.

"I don't want to marry him. One night, a few hours will be enough." They all whistle and fuss, reacting to how direct my cousin is. I admit it reminds me of how direct Ares is. Apparently, there's someone like that in every family.

Dani gives her an incredulous look.

"He's younger than you," Dani says, as if it's the last word on the subject. Yenny and Vanessa shrug their shoulders. "Don't you care what people will say about you?"

Vanessa shakes her head, smiling.

"You need a refresher, babe, or do you still believe in that macho bullshit that it's okay for men to date younger girls, but it's wrong if women do it."

"Exactly." Yenni nods in agreement. "He's a teenager aware of what he wants. If both parties like each other, and there's consent, what's the problem?"

Camila rolls her eyes. "Both of you shut up, Apolo is mine."

My eyes meet Ares's glance. He's holding a red plastic cup in his hands and takes a drink. There's a mischievous smile dancing on his lips as he puts down the cup.

"I'll be right back," I tell my cousins, approaching Ares. I can't look away. As always, I feel trapped in the blue of his eyes. Every step I take quickens my heart. One by one, the people around me disappear, until it's just me and him. The Greek god and the witch.

The moody one and the stalker. I stop in front of him, grinning like an idiot.

"How did it feel to be mentally fucked by all my cousins?" I ask. He strokes his chin, as if thinking.

"I feel a little used," he says and I chuckle.

"Sure, like you're not used to getting those reactions."

Ares raises an eyebrow. "Are you jealous?"

"Pffff, please." I roll my eyes. Ares grins, running his thumb across my cheek.

"You look sexy when you're jealous." His thumb comes down and caresses the edge of my lips, and I stop breathing. "Seeing you in that dress is killing me."

I swallow hard. He removes his hand from my face.

"You know why?"

My aunt Carmen walks by before I can answer. "Raquel, your mother is calling you. She's in the kitchen."

"I have to go help." I turn around, but Ares grabs my arm and turns me back to him. He gets close enough to me that I can smell his delicious cologne, and then leans in to whisper in my ear.

"Your family thinks you're such an innocent girl. If they only knew how you moan and beg me to give you more when I fuck you."

I gape at him.

"Ares!"

"Or how wet you get when I give you a simple kiss."

Holy Virgin of Abdominals, pray for us, amen.

Ares releases me. I put my hand on my chest, keeping my cool for a moment, and then I run away from there as fast as I can. How can he turn me on with just words? Ares definitely has a gift. Taking a calming breath, I walk into the house. Mom is waiting for me in the kitchen with some trays.

"I didn't mean to bother you tonight, but I just need help handing these out and I promise not to bother you again."

"Calm down, Mom, I don't mind helping. They're my guests after all." I grab the tray and turn to leave when Mom clears her throat.

"You two seem really happy," she says, looking in my eyes.

"Really?" I ask, pleased.

She just walks past me with a smile on her face, and I walk out with the tray and a matching smile on mine. I meet Claudia at the entrance.

"Hey, you came," I say. She looks very pretty in a purple dress with her hair loose and shiny.

"That's right, happy birthday." She attempts to give me the gift in her hand, but then she sees that mine are full.

"You can put it on that table over there, the boys are in the back," I tell her.

She hesitates.

"All three?" she asks, and I nod.

"Yeah, come on in," I encourage her. "I'm going to hand this out and I'll meet you there, okay?"

I'm just about to reach the group where Dean, Apolo, and Artemis are standing when Camilla intercepts me.

"I'll take these to them," she says, taking the tray from me and heading toward the guys before I even have time to process everything. I watch her smile cheekily at Apolo after offering them the tray, and then she just stands there talking to him. I must admit, she's brave.

"How dare she?" Dani's voice makes me jump because I didn't notice her at my side. Her expression is somber.

"I'm going to kill her."

"She's just talking to him. I don't think he likes her," I say, trying to calm her insecurities. Yenny and Vanessa take advantage of Camila's boldness and join her, using her to subtly insert themselves into the conversation.

"Who are those people?" Claudia's voice rings on my other side, making me jump slightly again. Why do people keep appearing next to me out of nowhere?

"They're my cousins," I explain, letting out a long sigh.

Claudia presses her lips together.

"I need a drink."

"Me too." Dani agrees. "Come on, I know where the vodka is."

"Hey, go and enjoy." I give them the thumbs up, but they both grab me by an arm and drag me with them.

This is going to be fun.

FIFTY-TWO
The Observer

- ARES -

I've never been one for birthday parties.

The Hidalgo house hasn't had birthday parties for a long time. Now it's just birthday dinners that end in silences and awkward smiles. My home hasn't been the same after everything that happened; the vibe isn't the same. With my friends, we always go out to a club to celebrate, so they're not really birthday parties either.

Still, I find myself enjoying this party. It's not set around a long table with too much silverware or at a noisy club. It's normal, and the atmosphere is familiar and relaxed. People are chatting comfortably around me. Dean and Apolo are talking about something from school.

But to be honest, the reason I like this birthday party is not the environment but her: Raquel. My eyes fall on the girl with tousled hair and expressive eyes who has infiltrated my soul completely. She smiles openly at something Daniela says and her whole face lights up. She looks gorgeous. If a birthday party makes her smile like that, I'll attend them all. I'll even gladly organize them.

I never thought she would be the one to make me feel all this. As a kid, I remember seeing her several times through the fence between our homes, but it wasn't until over a year ago that I actually saw her. I still remember that day I noticed her looking at me from her window. Of course, I played it like I was oblivious. Yet her curiosity about me piqued mine about her, and I began to want to know more about her: what she liked, what she did, and where she went to school.

And then one day our paths crossed, and, although she didn't realize it, I still remember it clearly.

"Let's get out of here." Dean yawns as we walk through all the temporary exhibits and tents at his sister's school fair. "I still don't understand why she stopped attending our school to come to this one."

Daniela's classmates had organized a fundraiser for their extra-curricular activities and personal projects. Dean dragged me with him to support his sister, but Daniela had already sold everything she brought and left, so we didn't need to stick around anymore.

As we pass through the crowd, I can see several tables in the distance with items still for sale. One table in particular catches my attention.

Raquel, that girl who watches me from her window all the time, stands at the side of her table, offering handmade jewelry to everyone who passes by, but no one pays any attention to her. Her table is full of neatly arranged and untouched bracelets. I doubt she's sold anything. A Funds to pay for my chess lessons *sign is behind her table.*

Chess, eh?

I stop because for some reason I don't want her to see me. Dean stops and looks at me.

"What's wrong?"

"You go on without me to the parking lot, I'll catch up with you."

He gives me a quizzical look but continues on his way. As he passes in front of Raquel's table, he greets her, and she smiles at him.

She has a very nice smile.

I use the people walking by as a shield to watch her. Her face is so expressive, it's as if I can tell exactly what she's thinking just by looking at her.

What are you doing, Ares?

My conscience reproaches me, but I'm just curious.

She sighs and sits behind the table, defeated. She grimaces in frustration, and finally her face fills with sadness, and I don't like it. It makes me uncomfortable to see her sad. I haven't even spoken to her, and it already affects me this way.

You haven't sold anything, curious eyes?

I look around for someone I know, and I find a boy who sometimes goes to our soccer field to practice with us. I give him money to buy all the bracelets she has on the table. I stand and watch from a distance as Raquel's expression changes from pure sadness to disbelief to happiness and excitement. She thanks the guy a bunch of times and passes him a bag with the bracelets.

The boy brings me the bracelets and leaves while I stand there, bag in one hand, staring at the curious girl whose smile I enjoy watching.

"Ares?"

I return to the moment. Apolo furrows his brows, waiting for a response to something I didn't hear. His eyes go from me to Raquel, and everything seems to click in his mind.

"She's really got you bad."

I don't bother to deny it, and Dean shakes his head as he puts his hand on Apolo's shoulder.

"We've lost him."

"I know, and you still have me to thank. It's all thanks to me."

"Shhh!" I silence him because I don't want him to tell Dean about the beginning of it all. My mind travels easily to another memory:

"You want to me to do what?" Apolo furrows his brows in confusion. I sigh uncomfortably.

"I've already explained."

"But I don't understand why you need me to do that."

"Just do it."

"And you think she's going to believe me? Ares, she knows we're wealthy. How can she believe that we don't have internet, and that we're stealing hers?"

"She'll believe you."

"If you want to talk to her, why don't you just do it?"

"I don't want to talk to her," I say. Apolo raises an eyebrow.

"Really? Why don't you go up to her and tell her you're stealing her Wi-Fi?"

"Because I want to prolong this as long as possible, make her suffer a little, she deserves it for stalking me."

Claudia walks in with a basket of freshly laundered clothes.

"Oh, sibling plotting," she says, giving us a look. "This is new."

Apolo doesn't hesitate to bring her into the conversation even though I gesture at him to shut up.

"Ares wants to use me to talk to the girl next door," he tells her. Claudia laughs a little.

"Oh really? Do you need new victims, Hidalgo?" she teases. I give them both a murderous look.

"It's not about that," I say defensively.

"So, what's it all about?" she asks, putting the basket on the bed. I ignore her, looking at Apolo.

"Are you going to help me or not?"

Apolo stands up. "Okay, I'll do it tonight." And he leaves the room before I can say anything to him.

Claudia arranges my clothes on my shelves in silence, a smile dancing on her lips.

"What?" I ask. "Say it."

"I have nothing to say." She keeps smiling.

"Say what you want to say," I sigh.

She finishes her chore and turns to me, holding the empty basket against her hip.

"I'm glad you finally decided to talk to her."

"I don't know what you're talking about."

Claudia licks her lips, smiling. I don't understand what she finds so amusing.

"We both know you do. It's been so much fun seeing you two mutually watching each other. I always thought she'd be the one to talk to you first, but, apparently, you couldn't take it anymore."

"You're talking nonsense. Mutually watching each other? As if I needed that."

Claudia nods. Her face wears an expression of mockery that annoys me a little.

"Whatever you say, Hidalgo, but asking Apolo for help shows how interested you are."

"You're crazy, Claudia. It's not what you think. I just want to teach her a lesson."

"Since when do you invest your time and energy into teaching a girl a lesson? Why plan it so carefully?"

"I'm not going to have this conversation with you."

Claudia bows in mockery.

"As you say, sir."

And she leaves, still smiling.

I smile at that memory as my eyes land on Raquel again. Maybe it took me so long to talk to her, to confront her, because I knew she would be the one to make me feel this way, the one to hold my heart in her hands. Maybe I knew it from the beginning and that's why I fought against it so hard. Even while keeping my distance, the bag with her handmade bracelets was always under my bed as a physical reminder that the girl who saw me through her window had smiled because of me, and that smile would be etched in my memory forever.

FIFTY-THREE
The Dance

- RAQUEL -

Ares returns as they're getting ready to sing my birthday song. It was getting late, so we all moved inside the house, and we're scattered around the living room. I stand in front of the cake, and he stands on the other side of the table. Everyone starts singing while I awkwardly stare at the candles, not knowing where to look. Finally, I focus on those blue eyes, and the voices fade around me. He looks so beautiful in the dark, with the lights from the candles on my cake illuminating his face.

I love you . . .

I want to say it, but I know there are too many eyes on me.

I blow out the candles, and everyone applauds and congratulates me. Ares takes a step back, disappearing into the crowd. I receive hugs, kisses, and congratulations, while my eyes search for the Greek god without success. Where has he gone? Most of my aunts suffer from cake sickness, which means that when the song is sung and they've had a piece of cake, it's their cue to go to sleep. The party is over for them.

My cousins take advantage of this to put on different music once we're alone. Whistling and cheering, they start dancing. Camila turns off the rest of the lights, leaving us in almost total darkness, which makes it harder to find Ares.

After checking one side of the "dance floor" without finding him, I pass through the crowd, brushing shoulders and backs. The vibe in this group feels electric, almost sexual. In the middle of them I stop, remembering that night at the club, when Ares watched me from the VIP area like a predator. I remember how I looked for him after that.

I've always chased him. I've always sought him out. Maybe now it's his turn to seek me out.

I start dancing, feeling the rhythm, which is soft but so sensual. The lyrics are full of sexual overtures. I don't normally listen to this kind of music, but it's fucking catchy and good to dance to.

I feel him before I see him.

His body heat brushes against my back as I keep moving, my hands taking the end of my dress and lifting it up a little, slowly jiggling. The distinctive scent of his cologne reaches me. Even though I know Ares is there behind me, I don't turn around, I just keep teasing him. His breath caresses the back of my neck, making me bite my lower lip.

His hands fall over mine, pulling my dress up slightly to pull it down again, caressing my thighs in the process, and the brush of his fingers against my skin makes my breathing quicken.

He presses me against him, and I can feel his whole body against mine. He's the one who always tortures me, and it's time to give him some of that back. I push my ass against him, rubbing, tempting, up and down, and I'm not surprised at how hard he is. Ares presses his hands over mine, growling into the side of my neck.

He bites my ear gently.

"You're playing with fire, Witch."

Well, yes, and I want to burn.

One of his hands leaves my thigh to move up my body, caressing my abdomen. I stop breathing when he reaches my breasts, but he doesn't touch them, and I'm dying for him to do so. He knows it.

His breathing is heavy in my ear, sending a current of arousal throughout my body. The hand still on my thigh moves up inside my dress, his fingers brush me over my underwear, and I let out a moan.

"Ares . . ."

The rubbing of our bodies has become rougher and more sexual, and I'm thankful for the noise and the darkness that camouflages us. With his hand hidden inside my dress, Ares moves my underwear aside, and I stop breathing in anticipation. His finger probes, slipping into my wetness. I hear him moan in my ear.

"God, you're killing me."

His finger penetrates me, and I feel my legs swoon.

This is too much.

He licks my neck, his fingers driving me to madness. I moan when he pulls his hand away, but he grabs my hair, pulling my head back so he can kiss me.

"We need to get out of here," he murmurs against my lips. "Or I swear I'm going to fuck you right here in front of everyone."

He takes me by the hand and drags me through the crowd of people. We walk through the darkness of my house quietly, as most of the adults are asleep, and I thank the heavens that Camila and Cecilia haven't gone to sleep yet because they would be in my room.

When we get inside, I barely manage to lock the door before Ares pushes me against it, kissing me desperately.

His hands travel to my breasts and he fondles them, his thumb brushing my nipples through my dress. I stifle a moan of pleasure and tilt my head back. His lips leave mine to kiss my neck, my breasts. His hands slip inside my dress to pull down my underwear. I step out of it and, my vision blurred with desire, watch Ares kneel in front of me, lifting my dress.

"Ares. . . . What . . . ? Ah . . ." his mouth finds me and my head falls back against the door. Ares lifts one of my legs over his shoulder, continuing his attack, sucking, licking, and I cover my mouth to try to control my moans.

I can't hold out much longer.

"Ares!" I moan on the verge of orgasm, and he continues relentlessly, taking me to the edge of the abyss, and I fall. Streams of pleasure move through my body, making me tremble, closing my eyes, and drowning my moans in the back of my hand. The waves of orgasm leave me with my heart racing and my body sensitive.

Ares stands up, and, before I can say anything to him, he takes me by the hand to the window, and turns me toward it with him behind me.

"Take off your dress." I obey him; I like it when he gets bossy. "Lean forward."

I rest my hands on the thick glass of the closed window. I bite my lip, leaning forward, exposing myself for him, which excites me even more.

I hear him unzipping his pants and the anticipation is driving me crazy.

"This window is where it all started, huh?" I hear him say, and my eyes travel to that plastic chair in the yard of his house. "From here, you argued with me that night and look at you now." His hand caresses my ass. "Exposed, wet, eagerly waiting for me to fuck you." He gives me a little spank that makes me jump because I wasn't expecting it. His hand grips my hair, lifting my face, and I see my reflection in the window glass, naked, vulnerable.

I can see him behind me, naked from the waist down, his shirt barely covering him. I can see *all* of him and I lick my lips. Ares leans over me to murmur in my ear.

"Beg me to fuck you."

I'm so turned on that I'm not ashamed to beg.

"Please fuck me, Ares, I want . . ."

He doesn't let me finish and penetrates me with a single thrust, stealing a small scream from me.

My hands slip a little on the glass as he grabs my hips to get as deep as he can.

"Oh God, Ares."

It feels so good I can barely stand up. With one hand on my hip, he uses the other to caress my breasts, intensifying the sensations all over my body. Being able to see my reflection, and seeing him there behind me fucking me, is the sexiest thing I've ever seen in my life, in, out, in, out. The feeling of skin on skin, of his hot manhood inside my wetness is wonderful.

His fingers dig into my hips, and his movements become more desperate and clumsier. I know he's close to coming, which pushes me toward my second orgasm.

I watch him close his eyes, feel him get even harder inside me, and we come together, moaning and shuddering. That's where it all started, my breathing out of control, my eyes looking through the window.

FIFTY-FOUR
The Grandpa

- ARES -

Watching her sleep relaxes me.

It gives me a sense of peace and security that I never thought anyone could provide. I run the back of my fingers across her cheek gently, not wanting to wake her, though I know it would take much more than a simple touch for that. Raquel is exhausted. I left her exhausted. A cocky smile forms on my lips, and I wish she could see it so she could joke or tease me about it.

I know she would say something like, *arrogant Greek god.*

She looks so vulnerable and beautiful in her sleep. Her transparency, the ease with which I can read her, is one of the things that drew me to her. I didn't have to worry about ulterior motives, lies, or false feelings. She is for real, so clear, and obvious with everything she feels. That's exactly what I've always needed: clarity and honesty. It's why I can expose myself in this way and allow myself to follow my feelings, release them, and open my heart to her.

I lean over and kiss her forehead.

"I love you," I whisper. She stirs a little but stays asleep. Watching her sleep makes me feel a little stalker-ish, reminding me of our beginnings.

My little stalker witch.

The one who thought I didn't know she was stalking me. All those times I acted like I didn't know she was watching . . .

A knock on the door brings me back to reality. I cover Raquel completely with the sheet and get up, dressing quickly, but I can't find my shirt, so I open the door without it. Two girls, whom I recognize as Raquel's cousins, but whose names I can't remember, look petrified when they see me standing there. Their eyes run up and down my naked torso shamelessly. One of them blushes, sharing a glance with the other.

"My goodness, you're so hot," she exclaims.

"Cecilia!" The other girl scolds her. Cecilia bites her lip.

"I'm just telling the truth, Camila. He knows he's hot, so why deny that we're dazzled?" she asks. I ignore her compliment.

"I imagine you're the cousins who are sleeping in Raquel's room," I say drily. Camila nods.

"Yeah, we're sorry to interrupt," she says. I give her a polite nod in return.

"Don't worry, come in," I offer, and Cecilia follows me into the room. "I was just leaving. I need to find my shirt."

"What's the point?" she asks. "You look perfect without it."

Camila grabs her arm.

"Cecilia!" She gives me an apologetic look. "I'm sorry, Ceci has had too much to drink."

"Don't worry," I mutter. I pick up my shirt from the floor and lean over to give Raquel a short kiss on the cheek before putting it back on. "Don't wake her up. She's exhausted, and it's been a long day for her."

"Okay," Camila agrees.

"Good night," I say. I walk out into the hallway and head for the stairs.

"Ares," I hear one of them shout from behind me. I stop and turn to see who's calling me. Cecilia walks toward me slowly, smiling.

"I . . ."

"What?" I demand. My voice takes on its usual icy, defensive tone.

"I don't understand," Cecilia says. "You and her, it doesn't make sense."

This girl has no idea how cold and brutally honest I can be. She's only seen my sweet side; the one that only comes out with Raquel and no one else.

"You don't have to understand. It has nothing to do with you."

"I know . . ." She takes another step toward me. "But you're just so perfect . . . and she's so . . ."

"Stop." I warn her. "Be very careful about what you say about her."

"I wasn't going to say anything bad." She pouts.

"The truth is, I'm not the least bit interested in what you have to say," I cut her off and leave. "Good night."

>> <<

"Why didn't you tell me?" Raquel has her hands on her hips. She looks upset. "Ares?"

"I don't know," I reply.

It's a few days after her birthday party, and we're finally alone again in her room. The bad news had come in various forms: e-mails and rejection letters. The main reason they gave was that the deadline for scholarships had passed, and that the spots were already taken by people who had applied on time.

Raquel had found out from Apolo because I hadn't told her when I started getting responses. I didn't know how to tell her. I had given up hope, but she hadn't. I didn't want to take that away from her.

I can't lie, the rejection makes me sad, but my consolation is knowing that at least I'll be able to attend the same university as her. I'll be miserable studying business, but at least I'll be miserable next to her.

"Are you mad at me?" I ask. Raquel sighs and puts her hands around my neck.

"No," she says, giving me a short kiss. "I'm so sorry it didn't work out, but we'll figure something out."

"Raquel . . ." I shake my head at her.

Her eyes meet mine. "No, don't even think about giving up."

"Do you think I want to give up? But we can't cling to nonexistent hopes either."

"Did you try talking to your grandfather?"

"What for? He already told me he won't get between me and my father."

"Go back and talk to him," she pleads. I shake my head. "Ares, he's your last resort. Please try again."

"I don't want to be rejected again," I admit, lowering my head. Raquel holds my face, forcing me to look at her.

"One last try. Please?" she asks again. I kiss her softly, my fingers tracing her cheeks slowly. When I step back, I smile at her.

"One last try."

>> <<

Grandpa Hidalgo doesn't seem surprised to see me. He's sitting in my father's study. Claudia is sitting next to him, laughing at something.

"Hello," I say a little nervously. "How are you, Grandpa?" He smiles at me.

"Some days are better than others, that's how old age works," he replies. I take a seat in the chair on the other side of the table. "Claudia, my dear. Can you ask my son and Artemis to come in here for a moment?"

He's calling my father and Artemis? What for? This is not going to end well. Claudia exits, closing the door behind her.

"Grandpa, I . . ." I pause, thinking of how to begin. He raises his hand.

"I know why you're here."

I open my mouth to speak, but my father walks in, followed by Artemis.

"What's up, Dad? We're busy. We have a video conference in ten minutes." My father gives me a quick glance but doesn't say anything. Artemis looks confused.

"Cancel it," Grandpa orders, smiling. My father protests.

"Dad, it's important, we're . . ."

"Cancel it!" My grandpa raises his voice, surprising us. Artemis and my father share a glance, and Dad nods, so Artemis makes the call to cancel. They both sit off to the side, a little distance away from Grandpa and me.

"What happens now?" my father asks with a sigh. Grandpa takes a moment to regain his composure.

"Do you know why Ares is here?" he asks, his voice back to his normal tone. My father gives me a cold look.

"I guess to ask for your help again," he says. Grandpa nods, prompting Artemis to speak up.

"Which I imagine has annoyed you because you've already told him no," he interjects.

"There's no need for this, Grandpa," I say, standing up. "I get it."

"Sit down." I don't dare challenge him, so I sit back down. My grandpa turns slightly toward my father and brother. "This conversation is far more important than whatever stupid business you are conducting. Family is more important than any business, and you seem to have forgotten that."

Nobody says anything, so Grandpa continues.

"But don't worry, I'm here to remind you. Ares has always had it all. He's never had to fight for anything. He's never worked in his life. He came to me for help, and I turned him down to see if he would give up the first time, but he exceeded my expectations. This kid has been working day and night, begging for scholarships and applications for months, fighting for what he wants."

Artemis and my father look at me with identical expressions of surprise.

"Ares has not only earned my support; he has earned my respect." Grandpa looks me straight in the eye, and my chest feels tight. "I'm so proud of you, Ares. I'm proud that you bear my name and carry my blood."

I don't know what to say.

Grandpa's smile fades as his gaze falls on my father.

"I am very disappointed in you, Juan. Family legacy? May death come for me if I ever thought that family legacy was something material. Family legacy is loyalty, support, caring, passing on all those positive characteristics for all generations to come. Family legacy is *not* a damn company." The silence that follows is agonizing, but my grandpa has no problem filling it. "The fact that you have become a workaholic to avoid dealing with your wife's infidelities does not give you the right to make your children as unhappy as you are."

My father clenches his fists.

"Dad."

Grandpa shakes his head. "What a shame, Juan, that your son begged you for support, and you turned your back on him. I never thought I would be so disappointed in you." Grandpa turns his gaze and gestures toward Artemis. "You made him study something he hated. You've done everything you could to make him like you, and look at him. Do you think he's happy?"

Artemis opens his mouth, but Grandpa raises his hand.

"Shut up, son, even though you're just the product of your father's bad parenting, I'm also upset with you for turning your back on your brother, for not standing up and supporting him. I feel sorry for both of you, and these are not the moments I want anyone to associate with our family name." Artemis and my father lower their heads. My grandpa's acceptance is something extremely important to them. "I hope you can learn something from this and improve. I have faith in you."

I am struck by the sadness in my father's and Artemis's expressions.

Grandpa looks at me again. "I started your enrollment process for medical school at the University you told Apolo about." Grandpa hands me a white envelope. "It's a bank account in your name, with enough funds to pay for your degree, college expenses, and inside are keys to the apartment I bought near campus for you. You have my full support. I'm only sorry you had to see your own father turn his back on you. The good thing about all of this is that you experienced not having it all and having to work for what you want. You'll make a great doctor, Ares."

I can't move. I'm speechless. Of all the scenarios I'd imagined, this one had never crossed my mind.

Grandpa shakes his hands and slowly stands up.

"Well, that's it. I'll go get some rest," he concludes and leaves the room. With his head down, my father walks out behind him. I'm still sitting there with the envelope in my hand, processing everything, when Artemis stands up and faces me.

"I'm sorry," he says, looking me in the eyes. My older brother has rarely said those words to me. He runs his hand over his face. "I'm really sorry, and I'm glad that you can follow your dream. You deserve it, Ares." A sad smile crosses his face. "You have a strength that I didn't. Grandpa is right to admire you."

"It's never too late to change your life, Artemis."

He shakes his head.

"It's too late for me. Good luck, brother." And with that he walks away, leaving me alone.

I don't know how to feel. My emotions are so jumbled, but I recognize the main one as pure happiness.

I made it.

I'm going to be a doctor.

I'll study what I want and I'll save lives.

The only thing that dulls my happiness is the thought of the girl waiting for my call to tell her what happened. The girl I love, and the one who will be miles away from me once the semester starts.

Grandpa is wrong about only one thing, I've never had it all, and this time seems to be no exception.

FIFTY-FIVE
The Prom

- RAQUEL -

Bittersweet . . .

That's how the news feels when Ares tells me what happened with his grandpa. I'm happy for him, even though the selfish part of me is kind of sad.

Now it's real: we're going to be separated. Just imagining being away from him makes my chest feel tight, cutting off my breath. Yet I know it's his dream. I know it's what he wants, and I would never do anything to stop him.

But boy, does it hurt.

"Raquel? Are you listening to me?"

Dani's voice sounds far away even though she's right next to me.

"Ah, sorry, my mind is elsewhere."

"It's our prom day, try to be present." She touches her forehead to emphasize that my mind needs to stop spinning and enjoy this day. Part of me can't believe that my senior year of high school is coming to an end, and that summer is here again, heralding almost a year since I first spoke to Ares.

"My love!" I hear from behind me, and I don't have to turn around to know who it is. Dani rolls her eyes.

"Here comes your intense prince," she teases as strong arms grab me from behind.

"My Juliet, my beautiful, my everything," Carlos whispers dramatically. I pull his arms off me and face him.

"Carlos, what have I told you about hugging me all the time?"

If Ares knew . . .

Carlos pouts. "But hugging is a normal thing between future spouses."

"Future spouses. . . . You get crazier every day." Dani rolls her eyes and grabs him by the ear as usual.

"Ow!" Carlos groans in pain but still manages to make eyes at her. "Crazier with love, you mean." Dani squeezes his ear again. "Ow! Ow!"

"You're so cheesy." Dani lets him go, falsely retching. Carlos rubs his ear.

"How are you spending prom day?" I ask, leaning my back against my locker.

"It feels like any other day," he replies.

Dani sighs and gives me a sad look. Carlos takes our hands.

"Don't worry. It'll be great," he reassures us, making me smile. Carlos is such a sweet and contagiously cheerful person. I really will miss him.

Nostalgia hits me by surprise. In a few weeks, there'll be no more of these hallways, no more of my lifelong classmates, no more of Carlos's craziness, and no more conversations in class before the teacher arrives. It's really coming to an end. Not only will I be leaving high school, but I'll be leaving this town to live in the residence halls on a college campus. I'm leaving all of this behind, and a part of me is terrified. Luckily, Dani and Yoshi are going to the same school as me. I won't be separated from them. I'll just have to separate from him.

My Greek god . . .

I push those thoughts away. They're too painful.

Carlos clears his throat.

"I know it's a silly question, but will you go to prom with me?" he asks. I give him a friendly smile.

"Carlos . . ."

Dani slips an arm around my shoulder, hugging me sideways.

"I'm sorry, Casanova, she's already coming with me."

Dani and I decided to be each other's date when we realized we didn't have one. Ares has to attend his own high school prom, not ours.

Carlos grunts.

"Ah, don't tell me you're going to do that best friend thing, how boring," he complains. Dani smiles mischievously at him.

"Well, yes, neither of us has a partner to go with, so it's done."

Carlos makes eyes at me. I give Dani a kiss on the cheek and look at him.

"I'm sorry. I'm her bitch tonight."

"I knew you guys had a hidden relationship," he says.

At that moment, Joshua joins us, adjusting his glasses.

"Joshua!" Carlos grabs him by the shoulders dramatically. "They're going to prom together. Tell them not to. Tell Raquel to go with me."

Yoshi sighs, placing his hands over Carlos's.

"Carlos, I don't know if you remember that she has a boyfriend.

Tall guy? Captain of a soccer team? And I'm pretty sure he'll kick your ass if you go with her."

"I'm not afraid of him," Carlos says, letting go of Yoshi. "Love makes me bold."

Yoshi pats him on the shoulder.

"You'll be pretty beaten up if you go with her."

Dani moves away from the wall where she was leaning.

"Class is finally over. It's time to go, we have to get ready for tonight."

"For what?" Carlos pouts. "You don't have a boy to impress."

"We don't need one," she says with determination. "We don't have to get ourselves pretty just to impress a guy; we enjoy looking in the mirror and admiring our own beauty."

"Oh, someone went deep," Carlos says. Yoshi nods in agreement.

We say good-bye to the boys and walk down the hallway toward the exit. It's time to get ready for prom.

>> <<

"Ohhhhhh!" Dani and I sing at the top of our lungs in the middle of the dance floor. That red cocktail definitely has alcohol in it. I don't know how they managed to sneak it in, but I'm not complaining.

It's our fucking prom.

Dani sings to me and offers me her red plastic cup for a toast. My best friend looks wonderful in a low-cut black dress that matches her dark hair, and great makeup. I've always admired her cheekbones and her facial structure; her face is so compelling. It's no wonder she's had a couple of modeling jobs with her mom's agency. Dani was born for it.

For my part, I'm wearing a red dress that's tight in the waist and fits my hips nicely, but it's loose from there on down.

We grab the edges of our dresses to jiggle better. We're crazy, but we're having a great time. Dani picks up her phone and records a Snapchat or Instagram story of us dancing, showing off our glasses with a bunch of hashtags, among those #WeDontNeedBoys, #AlcoholAtProm, and #OoopsWeDidItAgain. I laugh as I watch her put her cell phone down to send it; however, her expression changes as she looks at her phone, her eyebrows almost knitting together. Her eyes meet mine, and I give her the what's-up look.

She clicks on someone's Instagram story and hands me her phone. The first thing I see is Ares's face. He looks perfect in the suit he's wearing, with a dark colored tie that you can't quite see in the photo because it's dark where he is. In other circumstances, I would have enjoyed a chance to look at him, but now it has the opposite effect, and I feel my good mood evaporate.

He's not alone.

Natalie is next to him, and they look too close to each other for my taste, their cheeks almost touching in order to appear in the selfie. Her hashtags only make the situation worse: #WithTheHidalgo, #FutureDoctor, #HotterThanEver, and #WhatHappensHereStaysHere. I feel heat wash over my face, and my stomach clenches with what I recognize as jealousy. Dani reaches over to scream in my ear over the music.

"I'm sure she did it on purpose."

Oh, I know she did, but I'm still seething. Jealousy is so nasty. It fuels my imagination and different images of the two of them kissing, touching, and dancing together cross my mind. I shake my head because I'm sure that won't happen, and I trust him. However, I can't deny the discomfort I feel because I know they have a history together.

We leave the dance floor, and I grab my phone.

Don't act immature, Raquel, I think as I compose a text to Ares.

Me: How are you doing?

He doesn't reply immediately and that bothers me even more. He must be having such a good time that he's not responding to me. God, I have to stop thinking like that.

My phone vibrates with a response:

Ares <3: Cool, I only need you here to make everything perfect.

Me: Who are you with?

Ares <3: With the entire school . . . ?

His sarcasm doesn't make me laugh, but I don't know how to ask him exactly who he's with without sounding intense. I don't answer him, and he texts me again:

Ares <3: We're almost out of here to go to the after-party.

The after-party will be at Ares's house, of course. I don't answer him because I know I have to trust him, and I think he'll notice my discomfort if I talk to him right now. I decide to push the image of them together away from my mind and focus on having a good time with my friends. We start dancing as a group, taking turns to move to the middle and show off our dancing skills, which are not very good, but with the disco lights on us we look like experts.

I must say that whoever is adding alcohol into what is supposed to be the fruit cocktail is going a little overboard; it's getting stronger and stronger. I'm afraid that one of the chaperons will try it, and we'll get in trouble. However, that worry disappears with the fourth glass.

After a while, my phone vibrates in my hand.

Incoming call: *Ares <3*

I turn away from the music and walk out of the gym into a quiet hallway. Seeing his name on the screen reminds me of that picture with Natalie again. Swallowing with difficulty, I answer.

"Hello?"

"Hey, everything okay?"

"Meh, yes." My voice sounds strained.

"You've never been good at lying, Witch."

"I'm fine."

"You know how you tend to twist your lips to the side when something bothers you?" That makes me frown. "You're doing it right now," he says, and I look up to see him walking toward me down the dimly lit hallway. If he's beautiful in plain clothes, in a suit and tie he looks out of this world.

Ares takes the cell phone from his ear and gives me a smile. It's not loaded with mischief or arrogance. It's a genuine smile, and it disarms me. He looks so happy to see me that I forget about Natalie or any of my doubts.

He loves me. It's written all over his face, in his eyes, in his smile. And I feel foolish for doubting that for a second, and all because of a single photo. What he and I feel is so genuine and pure. He reaches his hand to my face and gives me a short kiss to whisper against my lips: "You look beautiful."

"You're not bad yourself," I admit.

"What happened?" His thumb strokes my cheek. "What upset you?"

Honestly, nothing bothers me anymore; I only care about him and this moment. So, I stand on my tiptoes, grab his tie, and kiss him, taking him by surprise. It's not a gentle kiss. It's a kiss where I let out all my feelings, all this love that consumes me. It doesn't take him long to keep up with me, our mouths moving together, our breath quickening.

When we separate, I take him by the hand to an empty class-room on one side of the hallway and close the door behind me. Ares watches me, amused and hungry for my kisses, for me. Biting my lower lip, I face him with the teacher's desk right behind me. Ares doesn't dissimulate; I know this is turning him on as much as me. His eyes scan me in an unabashed way.

"Almost the last day of high school," he says, grabbing my hips. "And you've never fucked in this place." He lifts me up, so that I'm sitting on the desk, and moves between my legs, his thumb caressing my mouth. "That's about to change, Witch."

His lips fall on mine in a possessive but overwhelming and delicious kiss.

FIFTY-SIX
The Last Party

- ARES -

"Spread your legs," I growl against her lips. It's not a request but a command. Between kisses, she has managed to close them, keeping me slightly away, pressed against her knees. She thinks it can stop me. I grab her hair, my eyes meeting hers. I can see the amusement in her gaze, she's challenging me.

"Spread your legs, Witch," I repeat, pressing my hand into her hair. She smiles at me.

"No."

I kiss her again, my mouth relentlessly on hers, claiming her, leaving her panting. She likes to tease me, to challenge me, and she likes it when I lose control and give it to her rough. So I slip my free hand between her legs as she struggles to try and close them, squeezing my hand, but I reach her panties and my finger brushes over them, stealing a moan from her.

I leave her lips to move down to her breasts, sucking and biting them through her dress. I use my finger to pull her panties aside and touch her there directly with my thumb.

"Oh, Ares." She bends her head back.

"Do you think you can resist me?" I ask her, even though I know she can't. Her wetness is all the answer I need.

"Yes, I can," she whispers between gasps. I raise an eyebrow, while freeing her hair and using both hands to remove her underwear.

"No, Ares," she teases, but she doesn't put up any resistance at all. She likes to play this game, the attempt at resistance, only to be fucked hard. Abruptly, I force her legs open, and she shudders. I grab the back of her knees and pull her until she is on the edge of the table, open and exposed to me.

The scent of her arousal is delicious and almost makes me fuck her right there, but I hold back. I want her to beg. I kneel in front of her, and she cries out when my mouth makes contact with her. I devour her unceremoniously without stopping. Her moans echo throughout the dark room, exciting me even more. Her moans are my favorite sound after her voice. Her legs shake on my shoulders.

Moan, shudder, and beg for me, Witch.

Your pleasure fills me in inexplicable ways.

You are everything to me.

I can feel her shaking and I know her orgasm is near, so I stop and stand up, leaving her hanging. Our eyes meet, and hers are pleading. Her brown hair looks black in this darkness. I run my thumb across my lower lip, wiping it clean.

She doesn't move, doesn't close her legs, she just stares at me. I take my time unbuttoning my shirt and she watches as each button comes off, exposing me. As I take it off, her hands run over my chest, down to my abs.

"You're so sexy, Ares Hidalgo," she murmurs, surrendering. I grab her hand and push it down to my pants so she can feel how hard I am. She squeezes me lightly and makes me grunt. Oh no, she's not going to have power over me, not tonight. I slip between her legs, bringing our faces closer.

"Beg me to fuck you, Witch." She gives me a mischievous smile.

"What if I don't?"

"You'll go back to that party wet and unsatisfied," I tell her. She bites my lower lip.

"You'll suffer too."

I step back from her and unbutton my pants.

"No."

"Are you giving up?" she asks, raising an eyebrow. I shake my head, letting my pants fall to the floor along with my boxers, and begin to touch myself. Her hungry eyes look at me with desire. I brush against her wet entrance but don't penetrate her, and I step back.

She opens her mouth to protest but then closes it again, fighting with all her being. She doesn't want to lose. I'll make it harder for her then. I begin to play between her legs, her wetness slipping from my fingers, and she closes her eyes, moaning.

"Beg me, Witch." She shakes her head.

"I . . . Oh, Ares."

"I know you want to beg me," I murmur, moving my fingers faster. "I know you want to feel me inside you, fucking you, hard, over and over again."

I know she likes it when I talk to her like this. It turns her on, and I'm crazy about her reaction to my words. I kiss her again, using my tongue inside her mouth to let her know how much I want her. A single plea from her will be enough for me to bury myself in her and end this torture. When we separate to breathe, she removes my hand from her wetness and with wide eyes says it.

"Please fuck me, Ares." Her words send a current of desire coursing down my body to my manhood.

"Say it again," I demand. She puts her hands around my neck and whispers in my ear.

"Please fuck me hard, Ares."

She doesn't have to ask again. I grab her waist and pull her to me, her legs around my hips. I thrust into her with a single move, and a choked cry leaves her lips. She's so hot and wet that the sensation leaves me motionless for a moment.

I recover and attack her neck, beginning to move quickly in and out of her. Raquel leans back, supporting herself with her arms behind her.

"Oh God, yes, Ares, I love it, more, please."

I hold on to her hips to speed up the rhythm. I can see everything and that turns me on. I'm a visual man, so I love positions where I can see everything.

Raquel moans uncontrollably.

"That's the way you like it, huh? Hard?" She keeps moaning. "You're mine, Raquel," I tell her, "and I'm fucking yours."

"Yes!" She grabs my neck again, and her hands move down my back until I feel her nails digging into my skin. "Faster!" she pleads, and I growl with desire, obeying.

Nibbling on her neck, I keep moving, feeling her completely. I bury myself and lose myself in her. I squeeze her hips so hard that she winces, though I know she loves to make me lose control.

My rhythm grows relentless and fast, and I can feel her getting even wetter. Her orgasm is getting closer and that only brings me closer to mine. Her moans become even louder. Her words bolder and more sexual, and that's all I need to come inside her, with her. Our orgasms rage, leaving us breathless and in absolute pleasure.

I rest my forehead on hers. Her eyes are closed.

"Raquel." She opens her eyes and looks at me and then it

happens, that big difference, that connection that burns between the two of us. "I love you so much." The words leave my mouth, she always makes me so cheesy.

"I love you, too, Greek God," she says breathlessly.

We get dressed and walk out into the lonely hallway back to the gym, where prom is still in full swing. Raquel walks awkwardly and uncomfortably, and a smirk dances on my lips. She notices and furrows her brows.

"Enjoy it, you idiot."

I play innocent. "What's wrong? Can't you walk?"

"Don't start," she threatens, giving me a light punch on the arm. I grab her hand.

"You deserved it for provoking me," I say. She snorts. Running my thumb across her cheek, I reach up and kiss her softly, enjoying every little brush of our lips. When I pull away, I kiss her nose.

"Come on, Witch, time to get back to the dance, and let everyone know that your boyfriend just gave you the fuck of your life." I wink at her, and she taps me on the shoulder.

"You're still an idiot, Greek God."

"An idiot you beg to fuck you."

"Shut up!"

Smiling, we enter the gym.

- RAQUEL -

Ouch.

It hurts to walk. I never believed it when guys said, "*I'll fuck you until you can't walk properly,*" but now, thanks to Ares, I know the truth. He's walking around with an arrogant expression.

I give him a killer look, to which he responds with a wink as he continues talking to Joshua. Ares and Joshua have been getting along great lately, and I'm happy about it. There's nothing better than your boyfriend and your best friend getting along.

Dani, on the other hand, is giving me a look that I know all too well.

"What?"

"You got fucked hard, didn't you?" she asks.

"Dani!" I protest, averting my gaze. She raises her glass and clinks it with mine.

"Cheers, you bitch. I love it."

Anyone would be offended, but Dani means it affectionately. I know, it's weird, but what can I say? My best friend is weird.

Ares approaches us.

"We'll go to the after-party at my house, right?" He asks us.

"Yes." Dani nods. "Dean sent me a text, apparently they're already there."

We all leave the dance and head to Ares's car. It's barely nine o'clock. I can't believe so much has happened in such a short time.

>> <<

As soon as I walk into Ares's house, I hear someone call my name.

"Raquel!" Gregory shouts, stretching out his arms, and I hug him tightly. "Congratulations!"

I like Gregory a lot, and I get along really well with him, way better than with Marco. Marco is so . . . I don't know how to explain it. His personality is very closed, so similar to Ares when I met him, and maybe that's why they're best friends.

"Enough," Ari says, pushing Gregory away from me.

Gregory looks around. "Okay, Mr. Boring."

I glance around the beautifully decorated room. There are a few people already there, including some guys from Ares's school. There are also a few adults, and I guess that they're the parents of his friends. My eyes spot Claudia in a very nice black dress with two other girls dressed like her, and then I notice them passing champagne and snacks around. Oh, they're servers.

I look for Ares's parents, but I don't see them, and my eyes fall on an older man sitting on the sofa in a very elegant suit. Grandpa? Yes, that's him. Ares has shown me pictures of him, and there are more hanging around the house.

Grandpa Hidalgo has an incredible air of confidence. I don't know how to explain it, but it's as if wisdom emanates from him. When Ares told me about the way his grandpa spoke to his father and Artemis, he earned all my respect. A big part of me wants to go hug him and thank him, but I know I'm a stranger.

Artemis is next to him, wearing a suit as well. I don't think I've ever seen him in casual clothes. Elegance definitely runs in this family.

I leave Ares talking to his friends and turn to Claudia, who smiles at me when she sees me.

"Hello, congratulations."

"Thank you," I say. "It was a very . . . interesting year."

"I know," she agrees. "But you made it, I'm happy for you."

"Me too. How are you?"

She shrugs. "Surviving, you know."

"I'm glad to see you."

"Do you want some?" She offers me a glass of champagne, and I take it.

"Thank you. I should let you get on with it."

I walk away to sit on a sofa on one side of the room. They must have moved it to make room for people. I swirl the glass in my hands, watching the liquid inside it, my mind distracted, thinking a thousand things at once. The couch sinks slightly as someone sits quietly beside me. I recognize the smell of that sophisticated, expensive cologne.

"To what do I owe the honor?" I joke, turning to look at him. Artemis smiles at me.

"Curiosity. Your mind doesn't seem to be here."

"It's that obvious, huh?"

"I admire your ability to celebrate despite what this means for your relationship."

"It's not easy."

"I didn't say it was." He loosens the knot of his tie a little. "That's why I admire you."

"My mother said the same thing, something about being mature for my age."

"Ares is lucky," he says. I raise an eyebrow.

"Is that an indirect compliment?" I ask. He says nothing, taking a sip from his glass, so I tease him some more. "Artemis Hidalgo, the iceberg, just gave me a compliment. Am I dreaming?"

"Don't act so surprised." His countenance has an air of sadness and melancholy. "I can tell the difference between good and bad people." He points at me with his glass. "You are one of the good ones, and that's why you have my respect."

I don't know what to say.

His eyes fall on Ares, who is openly laughing at something Gregory just said.

"I never thought he'd have the ability to overcome what happened to us, to believe in someone in this way, and change for the better. Not just because he was able to fall in love. Ares isn't the same capricious boy he was a year ago who didn't value anything or anyone. Somehow that gives me hope. Maybe all isn't lost for me." He drinks the rest of his champagne in one gulp. "Thank you, Raquel."

He gives me an honest smile, and I realize it's the first time I've seen him smile. He gets up and walks away, leaving me speechless.

FIFTY-SEVEN
The Trip

Run . . .

Shit. Shit.

I still hear barking behind us.

Oh shit.

I should have exercised. Why am I so out of shape?

Because you don't exercise, you idiot, you just said so.

In the distance I can see Ares's silhouette. Marco passes me by, like The Flash. Once again, I hate soccer players.

My heart is about to burst out of my chest as Dani also catches up with me.

"Run, Raquel, run!"

"I'm not . . ." I run out of air. "Forrest Gump!"

Dani laughs. "I know, but I always wanted to say that. Seriously, run!" She flies by, and I give her the finger.

"What the fuck do you think I've been doing?" I mumble.

Samy, Apolo, and Joshua also pass me. Oh no, them too? I'm officially the last one. I'm about to panic when I see Ares come back for me. He grabs my hand to literally pull me after him. The dogs are barking loudly behind me, and I don't even dare look.

How did we end up being chased by four dogs? Let's just say alcohol and bad decisions played a part—with emphasis on bad decisions.

I had the bright idea to continue the celebration after the party at Ares's house was over. My idea was to drink at my house and listen to music, but, of course, that wasn't enough. Dani, my so-called best friend, came up with the wonderful idea to show us a lake she found last week while jogging or whatever. So, obviously, all of us with alcohol on the brain bravely let her bring us there. But what Dani didn't know is that the lake isn't open to the public because it's not for the public. It's private property, part of a ranch guarded by dogs.

And that's how we ended up running for our lives.

With Ares's help, I jump the fence—the fence that should have warned us initially that it wasn't public land—and we leave the dogs on the other side. I fall to my knees dramatically, my heart pounding in my ears, in my head, everywhere.

"I'm . . ." I can only breathe heavily for a moment. "I'm going to die."

Ares, Marco, and Apolo look like they haven't just run for their lives. They're not even sweating. To my relief, Dani and Samy are a few steps away from me, grunting and breathing just as heavily as I am. And Joshua, well, let's just say Joshua is not in his right mind.

Samy can barely speak when she says: "I'm going to kill you, Daniela."

"I . . ." Dani raises her hand in lieu of speech.

"That was . . . unbelievable!" Joshua says. We all give him a what-the-fuck look. He runs his hand over his face. "It was like a video game, live play, the adrenaline, wow."

Okay, there's a chance that some of us are still very drunk. Dani laughs out of nowhere. Scratch that possibility; we're all still drunk. Joshua's sweet brown eyes fall on me.

"And I have to say, if this were a video game, you'd be so dead, Raquel. I would never choose your character to play."

For the second time that night I give the finger to someone. Alcohol is making me rude. I raise my eyes to the sky, surprised at how clear it's getting.

"Oh shit. Is that the sun?" I ask. Dani laughs again, and Joshua joins in. Apolo follows my gaze.

"Oh, it's dawn."

At what point did the night pass us by? Alcohol made us lose track of time.

Marco watches Samy, and the adoration is obvious in his eyes: he's so in love. He and Samy are dating now, and I'm glad. Samy deserves to be happy, and he's a good person. My eyes fall on Apolo, who's looking at Daniela discreetly. I wonder if there's hope for them or not.

The delicious new summer weather settles against my skin, warming it. It's so nice to be outside like this with no coats or jackets. I missed this.

"It's a perfect day to go to the beach," Dani says.

"You're right, I wish we could go." Samy pouts. Joshua paces back and forth. He gets very hyper when he drinks.

"Why don't we go?" he asks. We all turn our heads toward him, and he continues. "Ares and Marco are sober, and we can all fit in their cars."

"Don't go around making decisions for others," Dani says, hitting him with her elbow, but Ares smiles.

"No, I think it's an excellent idea," he says to Joshua, and Apolo nods in support. "Yeah, this is probably the last time we'll all be together like this."

While Dani, Joshua, and I will be attending the same college, I can't say the same for the others, including Ares. It hurts so much every time I think about it that I've pushed it to the back of my head. It's as if refusing to think about it makes it less real.

Joshua raises his hands in the air.

"To the beach, everybody!"

I can't help but smile. His enthusiasm is contagious, and I'm so happy to see him happy, especially after everything that happened to him. I was thrilled when I found out that he was going to attend UNC with me. I want to be close to him, not only because I want to take care of him, but because I want to be there if at some point he relapses or feels lonely. Depression isn't something that can be cured overnight. It takes time, and there may be situations that could lead to a relapse, and if that happens, I want to be there for him.

Samy narrows her eyes, looking behind me.

"Is that Gregory?"

I turn around. Sure enough, Gregory is walking toward us with a bottle of what looks like Jack Daniel's in his hand. But what . . . ?

"Finally, I've found you guys!" he shouts, approaching us. He told us he would catch up with us, but that was about an hour ago, and when he didn't show up, we assumed he wasn't coming.

"How the fuck did you get here?" Marco asks, laughing. Gregory shakes his phone.

"Uber."

Marco pats him on the back. "You're like a damn cockroach. It's so hard to get rid of you."

Gregory acts offended. "A cockroach? Really?"

"Haven't you heard that cockroaches would survive radiation

from a nuclear blast?" Samy intervenes. "It's a compliment to your endurance."

Marco smiles at her, looking pleased, but says nothing. I have noticed that, although he is not very expressive and affectionate with her, his look says it all. I find it sweet when a cold boy falls in love.

"I don't care," Gregory shrugs. "At least I got here, and I think I heard someone say *beach*. Count me in."

Joshua looks at Ares, Apolo, Gregory, and Marco, and mutters: "Wow, you guys are incredibly handsome."

We all laugh, and Gregory winks.

"Single at your command."

Joshua gives him a tired look. "No, I mean you guys are the first male friends I've ever had, and you're too good-looking; this isn't going to work."

"You're breaking up with me," Gregory says, pretending to run out of air. "And we haven't even started?"

Joshua ignores him. "I mean, if I go out with you, I won't get girls."

I turn my gaze to him and grab his cheeks.

"You're handsome, too, Yoshi."

I can feel Ares's heavy gaze on me, and I slowly lower my hands.

Marco grimaces. "Yoshi? Like the turtle in Mario Kart?"

Apolo laughs a little, but I give them a stern look.

"It's not a turtle. It's a dinosaur."

Gregory grabs the bridge of his nose. "Can we focus on going to the beach?"

Samy nods. "The cockroach is right, it's a two-hour drive, so let's go."

Dani worries about the logistics of the affair, and I admire her for thinking about it when we have been dawn-drinking.

"We don't have bathing suits or food," she notes.

Gregory clears his throat. "As my grandpa would say, 'no matter what you lack, you will find it somewhere along the way.'"

"Didn't your grandpa leave your grandmother for a woman he met on the road?" Marco asks, raising an eyebrow.

"Exactly, he lacked love and found it along the way. Hey, stop ruining my cool moments."

With Marco and Gregory arguing, we started walking to where we left the cars.

Time to travel.

>> <<

Ares is driving with the window on his side open. One arm rests on it and his other hand is on the steering wheel. He's shirtless, wearing only a backward cap and sunglasses. The sun streams through the window and slides over his skin, highlighting the definition of every muscle in his torso.

Virgin of Abdominals, why did you bless him this much? Why do you bring such a being into this world? So that poor mortals like me must suffer every time we see him?

Gregory's head appears in the middle of our seats.

"I feel like the son back here," he says. "Mom, I want booby."

I tap him on the forehead with my fingers.

"Very funny."

"Child abuse," he says, moving to the other seat. He grabs Ares's shoulder and shakes him. "Dad, aren't you going to do anything?"

Ares sighs.

"Relax, son, I'll punish her later." He gives me his crooked smile.

"Uuuuuugh!" Gregory scrunches up his face dramatically.

Ares laughs. "How do you think you came into the world, son?"

"I give up! Now!" Gregory returns to his post with his arms folded across his chest as if in a tantrum. Apolo, who is on his right side, grimaces, and Dani, who is on his left side, ignores us, looking out the window. Joshua left with the others in Marco's car.

We stop at a store to buy what we need for our impromptu adventure. I walk by where the bathing suits are hanging, trying to pick out a simple one. Ares appears in front of me, with a one-piece in his hands.

"How about this one?" he asks. I cross my arms over my chest.

"I like two-piece swimsuits."

"But this one would look great on you, and you can wear it with these shorts," he shows me one in his other hand, smiling. "A good combination."

Ha! Nice try, Greek God!

"No thanks, focus on picking something for yourself."

"Please?" Ares pouts. God, he has such nice lips, so kissable.

"Nice try," I say, turning my back to him.

Ares wraps his arms around me from behind to whisper in my ear. "Well, but if I get jealous, you know what happens." I swallow hard. "So, when you end up fucked in the sand on the beach, don't complain."

"No matter what I wear, you're still going to fuck me," I say, turning in his arms for a short kiss. He smiles at my lips.

"You know me so well."

"So, I'll choose what I want." He opens his mouth to protest. "And, if you protest," I run my hand down his abdomen to his pants, squeezing lightly, "you're not getting any sex tonight."

Ares bites his lower lip, raising his hands in the air in defeat.

"Choose what you want."

"Thank you." I wave him away, and he obeys. Who has the power now, Greek God?

I choose a simple red swimsuit, some sunglasses, and a beach hat. Dani joins me with what she has selected, and we leave ready to go to the beach.

"Beach! Here we come!" Gregory exclaims with his fists in the air.

I think this trip is going to be very interesting.

FIFTY-EIGHT
The Campfire

Ares...

I can't take my eyes off him. He's laughing at a story that Gregory is dramatizing with his hands in the air. They are both shirtless, sitting in the sand with the beach in the background. The sea breeze moves my hair back. I'm sitting on a log close by, enjoying the view.

The sunset is here, and I don't know how we spent the whole day on the road when the beach was only two hours away. Well, actually, I do know. At every stop, we were joking and talking nonsense for a long time.

Apolo, Marco, and Yoshi are playing with a ball we bought along the way, running around in the sand like kids. Dani is walking along the shore, enjoying a moment of solitude and tranquility, I guess. Samy is sitting next to me on the log.

"Beautiful view, isn't it?" she asks.

"Yeah, it was worth the trip."

She offers me a metal cup.

"Would you like a drink?"

I take the cup and sip. The strong whiskey flavor burns my throat.

"Whiskey?" I give it back to her and watch her drink without even wrinkling her face.

"I guess hanging out with the guys has affected me. I picked up a lot of their likes and dislikes."

I swipe the back of my hand across my mouth, as if that will take the taste away.

"Do you have any other friends?"

"No, it's always been them." Her eyes travel to Gregory and Ares, and then to Marco and Apolo. "But I'm fine. They've been great to me."

"It must be nice knowing them since they were little," I comment, hoping she'll say more.

Samy laughs to her herself. "Oh, believe me, I know so many embarrassing stories! Although Claudia beats me, she knows way more than I do." I give her a look full of questions, and she seems to read my mind because she raises her hand in a sign of peace. "No, I don't know what's going on between her, Artemis, and Apolo either."

"Apolo?" I frown.

She opens her eyes wide, her expression indicating that she said something she shouldn't have.

"Hey." She tucks her hair behind her ear. "I mean. . . . Not that there's anything wrong, I just assumed. . . . Just forget it."

My mind travels back to that time in the hospital when I realized that Artemis had hit Apolo, and it all makes sense. My gaze falls on Dani, and my need to protect her wins out over everything.

"Does Apolo have something with Claudia?" She doesn't say

THROUGH MY WINDOW

anything, so I push her. "Samy, I don't like to pressure people, but Dani is my best friend, and I would do anything for her. I need to know if I should tell her to forget about Apolo."

"If I knew what was going on, I'd tell you. Really, Raquel. But I have no idea. Artemis is an indecipherable block of ice. Apolo is so honorable that he would never talk about a girl. And Ares, well, he's honest about everything except his brothers' stuff. They have an incredible sense of loyalty."

I believe her.

The few times I've tried to get information out of Ares about that situation have been a failure, including once when I tried to use sex as a weapon for informative extraction, and only ended up fucked and just as curious.

Ares joins the other guys to play ball as Gregory walks over to us.

"Tropical beauties!"

That brings a smile to my face. Gregory is so energetic and cheerful that he reminds me of Carlos. Samy offers him a drink.

"How come you always have so much energy?"

Gregory drinks and exhales noticeably. "It's the strength of youth," he says, sitting on the sand in front of us. "What were you talking about? You had serious expressions."

"Nonsense," I say, rubbing his head as if he were a puppy. "Who's a good boy?"

Gregory barks and sticks out his tongue.

Samy rolls her eyes. "It's because of you that he doesn't grow up," she says.

Gregory gives her a hurt puppy dog look.

"I'm not going to rub your head." Gregory continues with his eyes, and I can only watch with a smile on my face. Samy sighs. "Good, boy," she says and rubs his head.

435

Gregory sticks out his tongue and licks her hand. "Ah!"

"The sun's about to set," Sami points.

"We should build a campfire before we lose the sunlight," I suggest. Why do I always come up with ideas like this?

Eight walks in search of firewood later . . .

In the movies, lighting a campfire isn't that complicated; it looks easy. Well, welcome to reality. It's fucking hard. We're all sweaty and darkness is already upon us, but finally the campfire is lit. We sit around it with the reflection of the fire on our faces.

I sit next to Ares, leaning my head on his shoulder and watching the flames, which have blue sparkles. It calms me and gives me a sense of peace. The wind on the beach, the sound of the waves, the boy next to me, the friends around me, it's a perfect moment, and I pay attention to every detail to keep this memory in a special place in my heart.

"I'm going to miss you," Gregory breaks the silence, and I think he's saying what we're all thinking.

Apolo throws a piece of wood into the fire.

"At least you're going to college, too, Gregory. I've got to stay in high school by myself."

Dani stares at him. Her feelings are obvious. I wonder if mine are this obvious when I look at Ares.

Of course they are, I mentally growl at myself.

Marco returns from his car search with bags of marshmallows in his hands. The food has arrived. Samy helps him with the bags.

"Yes! I want to eat something sweet so badly."

Gregory coughs. "Marco can give you something sweet, you know, to suck on."

Samy grimaces. "You're the worst."

Dani gets the wonderful idea to talk.

"Besides, that's not sweet."

"Ohhhhhhhhh!"

I can only cover my face. Dani blushes as she realizes she just made a serious mistake. That's what I like to call *verbal suicide*. They'll make fun of her forever and ever with that.

While they tease Dani, Ares whispers to me: "Want to walk along the beach?" God, I love his voice. I straighten up and look at him.

"Only if you promise to behave."

He smiles openly at me.

"I won't make promises I can't keep."

"Ares."

"Well, I promise not to do anything you don't want me to do." He takes my hand, a mischievous smile dancing on his lips. I narrow my eyes.

"Nice try. You already used that strategy once. I won't fall for it." He pouts in mock frustration.

"I didn't think you would remember."

I tap him on the forehead. "I remember everything, Greek God."

"That's obvious," he says, rubbing his forehead. "Who would forget the wonderful fuck I gave you that morning? You moaned so much and—"

I cover his mouth.

"Okay, let's walk." I stand up abruptly. "We'll be back," I say quickly to the group.

Ares follows me silently, but I can feel his stupid smile even though I don't see him. We reach the shore, and I take off my shoes, holding them in my hand, and letting the waves wash over my feet every time they lap the shore. Ares does the same. We walk together, our free hands intertwining, and the silence feels so good. We both know we have a short time left together, but we don't talk about it. What's the point of talking about it? I'd rather enjoy every second without having conversations that will only cause us pain.

As my mom would say, *Don't suffer before it's time. When the time comes to cross that bridge, you will.*

However, from Ares's expression, I can see that he wants to say something about it, so I decide to talk about something else before he opens his mouth. I remember my conversation with Samy.

"Can I ask you something?" I ask. He brings my hand up entwined with his and kisses it.

"Of course."

"Claudia and Apolo, do they have something going on?"

"I've already told you . . ."

"Okay, okay, just tell me one thing," I consider my words. "Dani is crazy in love with him, and I don't want her to suffer, Ares. You don't have to tell me what's going on exactly, just tell me if I should tell my best friend to forget about him or to keep her hopes up, please."

Ares looks at me, twisting his lips. I see him hesitate. Finally, he speaks.

"Tell her to forget about him."

Oh.

That hurt me, and I'm not even Daniela. I guess that's the thing with best friends, you feel for them, with them, sharing not only stories but emotions too. Ares doesn't say anything else, and I know I won't get anything more from him, so I drop the subject. I just watch him walk beside me and I remember so many things that my heart gets tight.

You think I don't know about your little childish obsession with me? Yes, I want you, Witch.

I'm at your service, always, Witch.

You are beautiful.

Please stay with me.

I can be your Christian Grey anytime you want, you perverted little witch.

I'm in love, Raquel.

I can only see the outline of his pretty face as my mind makes me relive it all over again.

"Ah, I'm a masochist," I say in a whisper. Ares looks at me.

"Sexually? Because I've noticed that you like to be spanked and . . ."

"Shut up!" I tell him immediately. "No, I mean emotionally. You were such a jerk to me at first."

"Define jerk.'"

I let go of his hand and give him the finger.

"It's just, how could you consider giving me a cell phone right after we had sex for the first time? Common sense, Ares, common sense."

His happy expression fades.

"I'm sorry, I won't ever be able to apologize for all that, I have no excuse. Thank you for not giving up. I've changed for the better because of you."

I don't take his hand, playing hard to get. Ares jumps and points at the sand near my feet. "Crab!"

"Ah! Where?" I instinctively hug him. He hugs me back sideways.

"Come, I will protect you."

"Ah." I push him as I catch on to his lie.

Ares steps forward and kneels in front of me, offering me his back.

"Come on, up." The memory of him doing that the night I was robbed comes to me. I think about how he had made me feel safe, and how nice he was to me that night.

I won't leave. Not this time.

I think about breakfast the next day, when he had taken my hand to gently let me know that I was safe, and that he wouldn't let anything happen to me. It was the first time I saw the tender side of Ares.

I climb on his back and he stands up, letting me wrap my legs over his hips, and I put my hands around his neck to hold me. Ares carries me along the shore, and I realize that this day is full of special moments. I rest my face on his shoulder. The sound of the waves fills my ears and the warmth of Ares's body mingles with mine. How will I survive without you, Greek God? I push that question out of my head.

"Ares."

"Huh?"

I lift my head from his shoulder to lean closer to the side of his face.

"I love you."

He's quiet for a moment and it makes me narrow my eyes until he speaks.

"I'll stay."

"What?"

"You know, if you ask me to, I'll stay. Right?"

"I know."

"But you're not going to ask me to."

"No."

He sighs and doesn't say anything else for a while. I could never ask him to stay or to give up his dream for me. I can't be so selfish. I can't take that away from him. It wouldn't be fair that, while I fulfilled my dream, he would have to do something he'd hate.

I always thought that when people said, "love is not selfish," they were fooling themselves. But now I'm guided by the principle that it's okay to put aside what you feel for the welfare of another—for someone else's happiness—as long as you don't compromise yourself. Now I think there is no greater proof of love than that.

I rest my head on his shoulder again. I hear him whisper so low I can barely hear him.

"I love you too, Witch."

With those words, I let him carry me along the shore, savoring every second of this moment.

FIFTY-NINE
The Farewell

The day has come . . .

The day he has to leave. He'll go from being a few meters away from me to being hundreds of miles away. Silence reigns between us. It's not uncomfortable but painful because we both know what the other is thinking: this is the inevitable reality. The sky is beautiful and the stars are shining in their maximum splendor, perhaps in an attempt to lessen this heartbreaking sadness.

There is a certain inexplicable pain in the inevitable. It's much easier to walk away from someone when they've broken your heart or when they've hurt you. It feels impossible to do so when there's nothing wrong between you, when the love is still there, alive, beating like the heart of a newborn, full of life, exhaling promise for the future.

My eyes fall on him, my Ares.

My Greek god.

There he is, with his hair tousled and his eyes red from the long night, and yet he looks beautiful.

"Ares . . ."

He doesn't look at me.

"Ares, you have to . . ."

He shakes his head.

"No."

Oh, my beautiful boy.

I struggle with the tears filling my eyes, and my lips shake. My love for him consumes me, suffocates me, gives me life, and takes it away. His flight leaves in half an hour. He has to enter the area where he'll wait to board the plane, where I can't go. We're in the waiting area of the airport, and we can see the sky through the huge windows.

His hand brushes mine gently before he takes it firmly in his. He still doesn't look at me, his blue eyes focusing instead on the sky. I can't stop looking at him. I want to remember every detail of him when he's gone. I want to remember what it feels like to be by his side, to feel his warmth, his smell, his love. Maybe I sound cloying, but the love of my life is about to get on a plane, so I have the right to be cheesy.

"Ares?" Apolo's voice comes from behind us. It has that same sense of urgency and sadness that my voice had when I reminded him it was time to go. Ares takes his eyes off the stars and lowers his head. When he turns to face me, I strain to smile through the tears forming in my eyes, but I fall short. He licks his lips but says nothing, and I know he can't speak. I know the moment he speaks he will cry, and he wants to be strong for me. I know him so well. He squeezes my hand tightly, and tears escape my eyes.

"I know," I say simply. He wipes away my tears, holding my face as if it will disappear at any moment.

"Don't cry."

I laugh falsely.

"Ask me for something a little easier."

He gives me a short kiss, but it's filled with so much emotion that I cry silently again. The saltiness of my tears blends with our kiss.

"Don't give up on me, love me, chase me, but don't forget me, please," he begs.

"As if I could forget you." I smile against his lips.

"Promise me that this is not the end. That we'll try until we can't anymore, until all resources and means are exhausted, until we can say we have tried everything and still try a little further."

"I promise."

I wrap my arms around his neck and hug him. He kisses the side of my head.

"I love you so much, Witch." His voice cracks slightly, and it breaks my soul.

"I love you, too, Greek God."

When we part, he wipes away his tears quickly, and takes a deep breath.

"I've got to go."

I just nod, tears sliding down my cheeks and falling from my chin.

"You're going to be a great doctor."

"And you're going to be a wonderful psychologist."

I can feel my face contort as I stifle my sobs. Ares says good-bye to Apolo, Artemis, and his parents. I walk with him toward the security gate. When we reach it, I stop and wipe away my tears.

"Let me know when you get there, okay?"

He nods and lets go of my hand. He joins one of the security lines, then he stops and walks quickly back to hug me one more time.

"I love you, I love you, I love you, I love you. You are the love of my life, Raquel, I love you."

The sobs escape me, so I wrap my hands around his waist.

"I love you too," my voice breaks. "I love you."

"Please, let's fight for this, I know it won't be easy, I know there will be hard times, but . . . please don't stop loving me."

"You won't . . . you won't be able to . . . get rid of me so easily," I tell him with a broken voice. When we separate, I see how red his face is, and the tears on his cheeks. "I promise you, I will always be your stalker."

He runs his thumb across my cheek.

"And I'll always be yours."

I give him a confused look.

"I was stalking you, too, you silly witch."

"What?"

"We never ran out of internet. I asked Apolo to pretend with me. It was my excuse to talk to you. You've always had my attention, Witch."

I don't know what to say, idiot Greek god, why did he choose this moment to tell me? Ares takes some bracelets out of his pocket, and I gasp when I recognize them. I made them a long time ago for a school fair, but I couldn't manage to sell any until a boy bought them all. Had Ares sent that boy? Had he done that for me even when we weren't speaking to each other? Ares puts a pair of the bracelets in the palm of my hand and closes it.

"You've always had my attention," he repeats with feeling, and that only makes me cry even more.

"Ares . . ."

"I have to go." He kisses my forehead. "I'll let you know when I land. I love you." He gives me a short kiss and disappears through the security door before I can regret not begging him to stay.

With my hand on the transparent windows of the airport, I watch his plane take off and disappear into the sky. I feel like a hole has opened in my heart and it will never close. Maybe it will heal, but the scar will always be there.

Part of me imagines him coming back like in the movies, telling me that he loves me and won't leave me, but it's not like that. Real life is crueler than romance movies. I close my hand into a fist over the window.

Good-bye, Greek God.

Ares's parents and Artemis are already gone, but Apolo remains by my side, weeping openly. The journey back to the house becomes the saddest hour of my life. Apolo and I share a taxi but neither of us speaks. Both of us are absorbed in our own sadness. Trees, houses, people, and cars pass by the window, but I don't see anything.

I don't even say good-bye to Apolo when I get out of the car. I walk into my house like a zombie. My room welcomes me with silence. My eyes slip to the window and pain squeezes my chest tightly. My mind teases me, imagining Ares coming through the window smiling, his pretty blue eyes lighting up at the sight of me.

I look at the front of my bed and remember that night I made him hot chocolate and he told me about his grandpa. Ares has grown so much as a person. From an idiot who didn't value anything to a man who values everything, who finds it easier to express his feelings, who understands that it's okay to be weak or even cry. I don't want to take credit for that because no one changes if they really don't want to change. I was just the push he needed to get started. I sit on my bed without looking at a specific point.

Dani opens the door with a bang. Her gaze meets mine, and that's all it takes for me to lose control.

"Dani, he's gone," I say quietly. She gives me a sad look, moving closer to me. "Really, he's gone." I start to cry inconsolably, letting it all out. I feel like a part of me has gone with him, and maybe it has. Dani rushes over, throws her purse on the floor, and hugs me.

"He's gone," I keep repeating over and over.

In my best friend's arms, I cry all night until I fall asleep. I wake up slightly to a text telling me that he has arrived, but after reading it, I just cry myself to sleep again.

Three Months Later

"And then I told him he was an idiot," I say with the phone in front of me, talking about Joshua. "How could he even think of putting an egg in the microwave?"

Ares laughs, his face encapsulated in my phone screen. We're Skyping while I'm cooking in the college dorms.

"And that wasn't the worst of it," I continue. "He put a pink shirt in the wash with his whites. Guess who only wears pink now?"

"And I thought I'd be the one making the most mistakes with this living alone thing."

I squint at him. "You burned all the pots in your apartment."

"I was learning."

"You don't even know how to make coffee."

"You haven't tried it."

"Thank God," I mumble.

Ares scoffs. "Yesterday I made pasta, it was a little sticky but edible."

"Look who's here," I show him a stuffed witch he gave me when we met at Thanksgiving break a few weeks ago. "She's my roommate."

"Speaking of roommates. Where's Dani?"

"At a frat party."

"And Joshua?"

"At the same party."

"Your roommates are at a party, and you're here talking to your boyfriend, so loyal."

"Parties have never been my thing." I sigh. I lick my finger to taste the soup I'm preparing. "Mmm, it's delicious."

"I wish I was that finger."

"Ares!"

"What? I miss you, Witch. I'm going to die from a lack of love and sex."

I roll my eyes. "Only you can be romantic and sexual at the same time."

"I need the Christmas break to come." He runs his hand over his face. "You know what we should try?"

"We're not having phone sex, forget it."

"I had to try."

"But if you behave yourself, I might send you a sexy photo," I tell him. He gives me that cheeky grin I like so much.

"Oh, well, fair enough."

"Christmas is a week away. I'll stick to you like bubblegum. You know that, don't you?"

"I love bubblegum then."

"Are you flirting with me?"

He bites his lower lip. "Is it working?"

"It might be."

We keep talking and I laugh at his silly attempts at flirting. So far, we've been fine, missing each other a lot, but we're seeing each other at least once a month. I'm not saying it's easy, but it's tolerable, and it makes me think we can survive this.

>> <<

When Christmas break comes, I make two steaming mugs of hot chocolate as soon as I get home. My mom is in the kitchen, and I tell her how I'm doing in the first few months of college. Afterward,

I bring the mugs upstairs and carefully set them down next to me beside the bed.

It doesn't take long until I see Ares at the window. I run to him, jump on him, and give him a desperate kiss that leaves me breathless. Those lips I love so much greet me with the same desperation. The kiss is passionate and tastes like the words *I missed you.* Our mouths move together in that perfect synchrony.

When we break the kiss, our breath is ragged. His beautiful blue eyes are lost in mine, and I run my fingers over his face to tangle them in his hair and kiss him again. After a while, we sit in front of the bed, each with a cup of hot chocolate in our hands. It's starting to snow, and there are little snowflakes floating outside the window.

We clink our mugs together in a toast, and I realize it will take a lot more than distance to break what we have. He and I are in a time of change in our lives, but that won't stop us from being together and getting through it. And I know that, when hardship comes, we will both give 100 percent to the fight. Maybe it will defeat us or maybe we will prevail, only time will tell. Even if it ends at some point, I will be able to say that I fought until the last second, until I couldn't fight anymore, because I know he will too.

We are the witch and the Greek god after all.

The one who felt everything, and the one who felt nothing. Now we both feel more than enough.

And there, in the silence of my room, with a cup of hot chocolate in one hand and the other intertwined with his, I watch the snow fall through my window.

The End

Acknowledgments

I want to start by thanking my husband, Enmanuel. His love and dedication contributed immensely to me being able to finish *Through My Window* on time. He cooked, prepared delicious coffee, and provided valuable input on some parts. Thank you, love. We are a team, and I love you.

A big thanks to my mom, Glady, for her everlasting love and for always reminding me to breathe and take care of myself when I get too consumed in writing. Love you, Mami Bella.

To my friends: Mariana, Darlis, Alex. Thank you for being there in the moments when things got difficult, and when I needed a push, advice, or some love and feedback. You girls are my pillars. *Chamas, ustedes son las maltas de mis empanadas, lo saben.*

Of course, to the Wattpad publishing team: Deanna, Fiona, Delaney, Casey, and everyone else involved. You made the editing process so comfortable for me and helped me shape this book into its best form. I'm forever thankful. And of course, to Caitlin, who's been there since day one. It's literally been years, girl. Thank you for everything.

And finally, to my Wattpad readers, you have been a fundamental part of my life for the past ten years. You have always been there for me. You have always believed in me, even when I didn't believe in myself, and for that, I am forever grateful. We did this together as a family. I love you, bolitxs.

And to you, the reader, who picked up this book and gave it a chance. Thank you.

About The Author

Ariana Godoy is the author of the best-selling novel *A Través De Mi Ventana*, which is being adapted into a film by Netflix Spain. A Wattpad star, Ariana has over one million followers on the platform, and her stories have accumulated over two hundred million reads. She is also very active on social media and is a successful YouTuber. Ariana enjoys K-dramas, coffee, and writing from her little apartment in North Carolina.